Praise for Kim van Alkemade

On *Counting Lost Stars*

"Powerful and haunting, *Counting Lost Stars* is historical fiction at its finest. Brilliantly connecting two time lines, Van Alkemade explores a little-known aspect of Nazi depravity in using technology to further its murderous aims, a technology that computer programmer Rita Klein years later will ultimately turn to redemptive and life-changing use. *Counting Lost Stars* offers moments of connection and reconnection that will leave the reader breathless, and a much-needed portrayal of humanity at its finest, and most selfless, to inspire us all."

—Natalie Jenner, internationally bestselling author of *The Jane Austen Society* and *Bloomsbury Girls*

"I loved this book."

—Armando Lucas Correa, author of *The Night Travelers*

"A page-turner that kept me staying up late and rising early to find out what happens next, this is a cautionary tale of the dangers of data collection in the hands of a despotic government that thrives on hate and divisiveness. The novel is a call to us to reconsider the scope and implication of our running headlong into every technological advance, as the narrative subtly reminds us of the possible repercussions of these new capabilities. Kim van Alkemade is a masterful storyteller in the best sense of the word."

—Dahlma Llanos-Figueroa, author of *A Woman of Endurance* and *Daughters of the Stone*

On *Orphan #8*

"*Orphan #8* peers unflinchingly into a little-known chapter of America's history, at an orphanage where innocent children are experimented upon in the name of science. With rare honesty and emotional courage, Kim van Alkemade tackles some of the largest ethical questions of our time. Yet the sense of moral outrage that permeates this novel is tempered by an understanding that all our paths are a complicated series of missteps. *Orphan #8* will leave you breathless, eager to turn each page, until you reach its dramatic and utterly beautiful ending."

—Dolen Perkins-Valdez, author of *Balm*

"Kim van Alkemade has moxie. In her provocative novel, family is saturated with betrayal, care is interrupted by ambition and desire, and the past is intimately explored, invoking the abandoned child in all of us. *Orphan #8* brims with complicated passions and pitch-perfect historical details. A riveting, memorable debut."

—Catherine Zobal Dent, author of *Unfinished Stories of Girls*

COUNTING
LOST STARS

COUNTING
LOST STARS

A Novel

Kim van Alkemade

WILLIAM MORROW
An Imprint of HarperCollins*Publishers*

COUNTING LOST STARS. Copyright © 2023 by Kim van Alkemade. All rights reserved. Printed in the United States of America. No part of this book may be used or reproduced in any manner whatsoever without written permission except in the case of brief quotations embodied in critical articles and reviews. For information, address HarperCollins Publishers, 195 Broadway, New York, NY 10007.

HarperCollins books may be purchased for educational, business, or sales promotional use. For information, please email the Special Markets Department at SPsales@harpercollins.com.

FIRST EDITION

Designed by Diahann Sturge
Art throughout © Claudio Divizia / Shutterstock

Library of Congress Cataloging-in-Publication Data has been applied for.

ISBN 978-0-06-328991-8

23 24 25 26 27 LBC 5 4 3 2 1

Dedicated to the memory of my father
Gerard Pieter Jacobus van Alkemade III
1934–1987

Chapter One
Rita Klein

New York State
May 1960

I first suspected they were lying to me when my skirt didn't fit. No matter how I tugged at the zipper or sucked in my stomach, I couldn't make the waistband bridge that gap of flesh between the hook and its eye. So there I stood, feet flat on the floor of the hospital room, flummoxed. They'd all promised—the doctor, the social worker, even my own mother—that I'd be back to normal once it was over. My blouse had buttoned up okay. Why not the skirt? Maybe it was stupid of me to think a garment I hadn't worn in months would fit again so soon, but what did I know? They were the ones who told me what to expect. All I did was believe them.

I tried the zipper again, refusing to credit the evidence of my own body. At every meal for the past five months, whenever we'd complained about the meager portions of poached eggs or skinless chicken or lettuce with only a squeeze of lemon for dressing, the house matron had assured us the restrictive menu was designed to get us back in our old clothes as quickly as possible. We'd all followed the same diet. If my clothes didn't fit, it was likely no one else's did, either. But if they'd lied to us about the food, was the rest of it a lie, too?

I shook the thought from my head. It was ridiculous to think all those professional people were involved in some elaborate deception. I reminded myself it only happened three days ago. Today I was going home. Starting tomorrow, I'd put all this behind me and get on with my life.

At least the food had given us girls something to talk about. We were all too ashamed to share the circumstances that had gotten us in trouble. We weren't even supposed to reveal our real names, let alone exchange telephone numbers for staying in touch or addresses for visiting. Whenever I tried bringing up a topic from the day's headlines, the conversation fell flat. Current events, like that U-2 spy plane shot down over the Soviet Union, felt too remote to matter while we were sequestered in that isolated mansion. When Mossad agents brazenly captured Adolf Eichmann in Argentina, even the other Jewish girls weren't interested in the prospect of that murderous Nazi going on trial in Israel. No one seemed to care whether or not John F. Kennedy got the Democratic nomination, which I guess made sense. Most of the girls were too young to vote, and anyway, whichever man ended up in the White House wouldn't change a thing for those of us biding our time at the Hudson Home for Unwed Mothers.

I twisted the skirt around in frustration, fruitlessly attempting to zip it from the front. Back when I was getting ready for the trip upstate, I hadn't packed much into the pink Samsonite my parents had given me as a high school graduation present. It was winter then, and my wardrobe was down to a couple of shapeless dresses, a few loose blouses, a stretched-out sweater, and a cuffed pair of my brother's blue jeans. On top of this sad pile of fabric I carefully placed the skirt I'd bought back in August for my night out with Leonard. It was the most sophisticated article of clothing I'd ever purchased, the black linen modestly lined in silk yet snug enough to hint at the garter clips holding up my stockings. The salesgirl at Macy's assured me it would be perfect for a date with a businessman from out of town. That she thought the man in question was a matrimonial prospect went without saying. In New York City in 1959, it was a pretty safe bet that any girl in her twenties who wasn't already hitched was on the hunt for a husband. I'd have sworn I was immune, but after I met Leonard, I couldn't resist walking past the jewelry stores on Forty-Seventh Street, window-shopping diamond rings.

I was disappointed when the summer computing course we took together at the Watson Laboratory ended and Leonard went back to his sales job at IBM's headquarters in Endicott. I resigned myself to never seeing him again, so it caught me by surprise when he called to say he was coming to the city for the weekend and asked if I would join him for dinner at the Rainbow Room. Once I said yes, I couldn't help fantasizing about a proposal by dessert. I told myself to stop being silly. It would be our first official date, and besides, I wasn't planning to marry until after college. Some of the girls at Barnard were more interested in making a curriculum of the men at Columbia than studying for their own exams, but I'd gone there for a bachelor of arts, not an MRS degree. Not that married women couldn't graduate. Plenty of girls disappeared from campus while on their honeymoons, returning a few weeks later adorned with gold rings, new names, and satisfied smiles. Well, the joke's on me, I thought. I'd been away for an entire semester with nothing to show for it. Less than nothing.

As if it never happened. That's what everyone promised, and I was determined to take them at their word. But if the nine months between that summer night with Leonard and this spring morning were no more than missing pages torn from the calendar of my life, then why wasn't I able to get my skirt back on? I gave it one last try, but there was no fitting the unforgiving linen over the loose pudding of my abdomen. I shoved it down to my ankles and tossed it in the suitcase. Instead, I pulled out that pair of jeans. Never mind, I told myself, tucking in my blouse and stepping into penny loafers. I never wanted to wear that skirt again, anyway.

I went over to the sink to splash my face with cold water. Looking in the mirror, I saw my cheeks were still puffy, but other than that my reflection was the same as it had been before: brown eyes, long nose, thin lips, round chin. In high school, when my rich friends were getting nose jobs for their sweet sixteen, Mom said there was nothing wrong with the way I looked, which wasn't the same as saying I was beautiful. I wouldn't win any contests, but I guessed I was pretty enough.

I was wrestling a comb through my curly hair when a perfunctory knock followed by a waft of perfume announced the entrance of Miss Murphy. I sneezed, thinking what a mistake it was for a social worker to douse herself in Shalimar. I'd learned in psychology class about the power of scent to trigger the brain. How was I supposed to wipe away the memory of these months, I wondered, if any time I smelled bergamot and vanilla I'd be reminded of this exact moment?

"Hello, Rita. I'm glad to see you dressed and ready to go." Miss Murphy was an efficient and professional woman whose heavy perfume was at odds with her pleated skirts and schoolmarmish cardigans. A few girls at the Hudson Home figured she must be a lesbian, like that teacher in Lillian Hellman's play, as if that were the only reason for a woman to still be single in her thirties. "I never knew what a darling figure you have. Turn around and let me take a look at you."

My outfit hardly deserved a fashion show, but I did as I was told. Miss Murphy put down her briefcase and came closer. "This will go away in no time," she said, placing the palm of her hand on the bulge of my belly without so much as a please. "Has the bleeding stopped yet?"

I sat on the edge of the hospital bed as she pulled up the visitor's chair. "It's tapered off, and I've been walking up and down the corridor like you suggested."

She gave an approving nod. "The doctor tells me everything went well."

"Really? I wouldn't know, I guess." The truth was I didn't remember the birth at all. When my water broke—three days ago, at dawn—the house matron had packed up my suitcase and put me in a taxi for the short ride to the local hospital. I labored by myself, the private room a lonely luxury. It wasn't long before I was crying for my mother. I couldn't understand why she wasn't with me when I needed her most. She'd been there when I had my tonsils out and the time I got stitches after falling off my bike. She'd never left my side that summer I was so sick the doctor tested me for polio. Sure, I'd made a mistake, but wasn't I still her daughter?

I was a blubbering mess by the time the obstetric nurse came to prepare me. Without a word of explanation, she administered an enema, shaved my pubic hair, and swabbed my vulva with Mercurochrome. She was followed by a ham-handed doctor who pronounced me sufficiently dilated to be taken to the delivery room. The last thing I remembered was the anesthesiologist telling me to count backward from ten. I think I got to seven. When I opened my eyes, I was in my bed again, stiff and sore and soft around the middle. It was night. The room was quiet. It was over.

"I wish all the girls were as sensible as you, Rita." Miss Murphy lifted her briefcase onto her lap and unlatched it. "There are social workers who think it does a girl good to hold the baby for a while to say goodbye, but as far as I'm concerned it just complicates matters. Aren't you glad you took my advice?"

I was, yes. The way some of the girls blathered on about seeing their babies made no sense to me. What difference would it make to count its toes or find out what color eyes it had? There was no point trying to memorize a face we weren't even allowed to photograph. I understood all too well the babies weren't ours to keep. Their real parents, as Miss Murphy reminded us during the group sessions she conducted at the home, were married couples with secure careers and comfortable houses who were eager to adopt. She warned us, too, about the terrible things that would happen if we selfishly changed our minds. Scolding us with a wagging finger, she'd say, "A single mother could never provide a baby with everything it needs. And just imagine how that innocent child will be tormented on the playground for not having a father! Then there are your own futures to consider. You girls may still be young and attractive, but you'll never marry well if you're saddled with a baby." When one of us expressed her hope that she'd meet a nice guy someday who'd be willing to become her kid's dad, Miss Murphy shook her head. "Believe me, no respectable man wants to take on someone else's bastard." Her words were harsh, but I appreciated her directness. Managing the girls was part of her job, sure, but we weren't her real clients. Miss Murphy worked for the babies, not their mothers.

"You certainly make my life easier, Rita, as calm and collected as you are," Miss Murphy said. "You remember Linda, who left the home last month? She made quite a fuss about signing the surrender papers, even after I reminded her the agency only covers expenses when an adoption occurs. I had to present her with an actual bill for the doctor and the hospital and her stay at the home. 'That's what you'll owe us,' I said, 'if you keep this baby.'" She raised an eyebrow in warning. "After all, we're not in the business of subsidizing a girl's promiscuity, are we?"

"I guess not," I said, understanding very well the price of these last few months. Despite the skimpy portions, I was lucky to have gotten a bed at the venerable Hudson Home for Unwed Mothers. The old mansion along the river was no longer elegant, exactly, but it was comfortable and well equipped, with expansive grounds where we could take our walks hidden from judgmental eyes. The house matron claimed only girls from good families were accepted into the home, though I suspected what made them "good" was having enough money to supplement the adoption agency's paltry housing allowance. I was certain my mother would've sent me to some shabby Catskills boardinghouse if it hadn't been for the hefty check Leonard wrote on my behalf. "So, did Linda sign?"

"Yes, she did, though I'm not looking forward to that follow-up visit, I can tell you. Hopefully, six weeks will be enough time for her to realize she did the right thing. You, on the other hand, I'll be glad to see again. What are your plans, dear?"

"My father just wrote that he got me an interview for a summer job." I'd never heard of Antiquated Business Machines before Dad's letter, but one of his customers owned the company. When Dad told him I'd completed the Watson Laboratory's summer course on computing, the man insisted I come see him.

"Good for you, dear," Miss Murphy said. "It's important to keep busy. Before you know it, you'll be back in college, finishing your degree."

I shrugged. Her talk of college and degrees depressed me. It was right after Thanksgiving when I'd gone to see the Barnard College physician for my required yearly exam. I was grateful that, as a senior, this would be the last time I'd have to expose myself to Dr. Marjory Nelson's scrutiny. Oh, she was nice enough, and if I had to put my feet in those stirrups, I'd rather have had a woman staring at my crotch than a man. My only concern, as I scooted to the edge of her table that day, was that she'd see I wasn't a virgin anymore. I wasn't even thinking about my menstrual cycle until she asked if it had become more regular. I told her it was still unpredictable. The last time I remembered having my period was during the computing course—I'd had to excuse myself from class to go change my pad—but I hadn't been tracking it since.

Missing a few months now and again wasn't unusual for me. My freshman-year exam with Dr. Nelson was the first time anyone explained to me why my periods were so irregular. "It's a mother's responsibility to present the physical facts of menstrual health to her daughter in a positive way in order to establish a normal cycle," she'd said, clucking her tongue in disapproval when I told her my mother never taught me anything about it. In this modern day and age, Dr. Nelson believed, a mother was to blame if she allowed her superstitions to warp her daughter's life. I didn't exactly think my life was warped by having irregular periods, but it was comforting to know whose fault it was.

As Dr. Nelson began her examination that November day, all I feared was the cold pinch of her speculum. I had no idea my whole world was about to change. The prospect of getting kicked out of Barnard hit me harder, at first, than the shock of Dr. Nelson telling me I was pregnant. While she left me alone to get dressed, I recalled rumors of students who'd had their problems solved before their futures were ruined. One girl took a sudden trip to the Caribbean and came back a week later, good as new. One convinced a psychiatrist her pregnancy would drive her to suicide; she got her abortion at a hospital under the law that allowed the procedure to save the life of the mother. One floor counselor was known to recommend a reputable Park Avenue doctor whose fee was more than a semester's tuition. One girl, I'd heard, barely survived a baseball-bat job from a so-called practitioner in a back alley. I couldn't imagine myself in any of those scenarios. As it turned out, I'd never need to.

"I've spoken to your mother," Dr. Nelson said, coming back into the room. When I protested her betrayal, she told me it was standard procedure to notify parents when the girl in question was a minor. I was about to turn twenty-one in December. If my appointment had been a few weeks later, my parents would never have known. "I explained to Mrs. Klein that you'll have to withdraw immediately. I'll certify it's for health reasons to allow you an honorable discharge, but you won't be permitted to sit for exams." When I asked what that would do to my grades, Dr. Nelson said I wouldn't be earning any. For a moment, I harbored the hope of returning the following year to finish my degree, but that was quickly quashed. Even if the registrar had allowed it, my family couldn't afford Barnard without my scholarship. "The Mary Gertrude Aldrich Fund," Dr. Nelson reminded me, "was established to assist a student who shows in her college life the moral qualities which go to the making of fine womanhood. I can't very well say you still qualify, can I?"

So when Miss Murphy brought up the topic of college, it wasn't a happy subject for me. "I'll probably transfer to Fairleigh Dickinson," I told her. "It's nothing like Barnard, but at least I can commute." My parents, who'd spent less on my brother's entire degree from Montclair State than they'd wasted on me, had made it clear they wouldn't be throwing good money after bad on my education. Letting me live at home would be the extent of their support from now on.

"I suppose a diploma from Columbia would have been nice," Miss Murphy said, "but it doesn't really matter where you get your degree, does it?" I thought that was a rotten thing for a woman who boasted about her master's in social work from Smith to say. "At any rate, I made a note in the baby's file that its parents are both highly intelligent. That sort of thing helps make the best placement."

Her words jolted me. How did Miss Murphy know anything about Leonard? On the birth certificate I'd been given to sign, the word "unknown" had already been written on the line labeled "Father," as if I didn't even know who'd gotten me pregnant. It shamed me, but that was Leonard's condition for making the financial contribution I needed to secure a place at the Hudson Home and pay for the private hospital room. When I'd hesitated to accept his terms, my mother argued it was a smart bargain. His name wouldn't do me any good, she said. It was his money I needed, and he was getting off cheap, if you asked her, compared to what a divorce would have cost him, what with alimony and child support.

Miss Murphy put a piece of paper on her briefcase, which was propped on her knees like a lap desk. "Sign this document, dear, and you'll be free to go."

I was as eager as she was to get this over with, but as I reached for the pen, strange things started to happen. My heart rate shot up. My throat got tight. My hand shook as if the paper were generating an impregnable magnetic field.

"Go ahead, Rita." Her voice was sharp. "Right on this line."

As if it never happened, I reminded myself. I was a signature away from putting my worst mistake behind me and getting on with my life. It was probably the lingering effects of the anesthesia that were making me feel so weird. I swallowed hard and gripped the pen. It was awkward leaning over like that with no place to balance my elbow. Miss Murphy tried to help by steadying the briefcase with her forearms, but that only obscured the document. My signature looked oddly loopy but she appeared satisfied.

"Is that it?"

"That's it." Miss Murphy tucked the paper back in the briefcase, latched it shut, and got to her feet. "In six weeks, I'll drive down to check on you, and then you'll never have to see me again. I can't tell you how excited the adoptive couple is." She lowered her voice to a conspiratorial whisper. "I really shouldn't be saying this, but he's a successful doctor, and his wife's a trained nurse. They'll be perfect parents. Speaking of parents, yours are coming to pick you up today, isn't that nice? You won't have to take the train home."

"My father, too? Are you sure?" I was certain Miss Murphy had made a mistake. I doubted Dad would shutter Klein's Shoes on the Saturday of Memorial Day weekend. He couldn't afford to, for one. I'd been helping him balance his books since I was a teenager and I knew how slim the store's margins were. But there was something else, too. On the rare occasions he did lock up during business hours, he always posted a sign explaining why. GONE TO MY SON'S WEDDING. ATTENDING A FRIEND'S FUNERAL. It kept the people who shopped with him loyal, he said. If he simply closed for no reason, what was to stop his customers from going across town to Bamberger's instead? I couldn't imagine what explanation Dad had come up with for locking his doors today.

"Yes, I'm sure. I spoke to Mr. Klein myself this morning. They'll be here in half an hour. I have one other girl to visit, then I'll come back to get you. I told your father to meet us by the service entrance. I'll be taking you down the back stairs." With that, Miss Murphy swept out, the scent of Shalimar swirling in her wake.

I folded my coat over the suitcase, then went to gaze out the window while I waited. All I could see from the hospital room was a few sparrows hopping from branch to branch in a tree outside, but I watched those birds with the intensity of a naturalist. I'd gotten in the habit, at the home, of staring out the window for hours. There, I'd been rewarded with a sweeping view of the Hudson River: flat and gray when I arrived in January, choppy with ice come February, fast with flotsam by March, golden in the setting sun of April, bustling with fledgling herons in May. I'd been looking forward to seeing the gangly chicks fly from their rookeries along the shore, but there was no going back to the home now. The girls who left for the hospital never returned to say goodbye. They simply went away, clutching their bellies and crying for their mothers. It was part of the process, Miss Murphy explained. Always move forward. Never look back.

I pictured Dad driving up the Albany Post Road, his hands precisely at ten and two on the steering wheel of his new Rambler. I hadn't seen my parents since the winter day when Mom bundled me up in an old coat to camouflage the swell of my belly. Living in the apartment above the store meant every customer was witness to our comings and goings, and I could tell Mom was worried she'd waited too long to send me away. As she tugged the frog closures into place, she asked, "Are you ready for this, Rita?"

How could I be ready for something I barely understood? All I knew was that she was being nice to me for the first time since Dr. Nelson broke the news. "I'm ready, Mom," I lied, unwilling to mar the moment.

I'd followed her downstairs and out the door next to the shop entrance. The neon sign that spelled KLEIN'S SHOES in flickering script cast a rosy glow on the display window filled with fashionable footwear. Mom tapped on the glass to get Dad's attention. He had no customers at the moment, so he grabbed his coat and joined us on the sidewalk, flipping the OPEN sign to BACK IN FIVE MINUTES. We walked to the bus stop on Teaneck Road three abreast, arms linked. They'd been spreading the story that I'd withdrawn from college to go stay with my widowed great-aunt Ida, who was recovering from a broken hip, they said. Ida was our only relative that I knew of—Mom and Dad had met as kids in the Orphaned Hebrews Home, so no grandparents on either side—and if she'd really been hurt, I'd have been happy to help her, so that much rang true. In reality, though, Aunt Ida was a perfectly healthy woman who conveniently lived in an obscure village west of Schenectady.

At the Hudson Home for Unwed Mothers, I'd heard whispered stories of parents who hid their daughters under blankets in the backs of cars that whisked them away at midnight. My dad didn't have that option. For Irving Klein, the lives of his children were a professional asset, small talk about our accomplishments forming the foundation of relationships with customers who'd known us all our lives. If I mysteriously disappeared, it'd be all anyone could talk about. When Mom had proposed the Aunt Ida story, Dad stewed in silence awhile before saying, "If we want people to believe that bullshit, we'll really have to sell it."

So we shivered together at the bus stop that January day, our show of familial solidarity intended for public consumption. When the Short Line to Manhattan pulled up, my parents kissed my cheeks and handed up my suitcase with loud instructions to give their love to Ida. By the time I waved goodbye from a window seat, their backs were already turned. In the city, I'd walked alone from the Port Authority to Grand Central to catch the Hudson Line up to Garrison. A discreet taxi driver met me at the station and drove me, without conversation, to the home that would hide me for the duration of my shame. I'd assumed the entire journey would play out in reverse, but apparently my parents had decided it would look better to come get me themselves.

"Mrs. Klein?"

I turned to see who'd opened the door. It was one of those teenagers who volunteered at the hospital. Candy stripers, they were called, and she did look a little like a candy cane, tall and skinny in her red-and-white smock. She must not have read my chart carefully, I thought, or she'd have known better than to address me as Mrs. anything. The nurses called us girls from the home by our first names, as if we were no longer worthy of the family names our fathers had bestowed on us at birth. Our names didn't matter much in the end, anyway. The original birth certificates listing us as mothers would soon be secreted away in the agency's files. New ones would be issued naming the adoptive couple as parents. It was all part of the plan for our babies to grow up never knowing we existed.

Assuming the candy striper was there to ask when she could get the room ready for its next occupant, I answered, "Yes, I'm Rita Klein."

"I brought your baby for a visit." The door swung wider. As if delivering room service in a hotel, the girl wheeled in a bassinet. Through its plastic sides, I saw a bundle of blanket. "I'll just leave this here, all right? If you need anything, you can press the call button." She stepped out, shutting the door behind her.

I stood frozen by the window. I wasn't supposed to see the baby. I didn't even know if it was a boy or a girl—until I suddenly remembered asking that very question of the recovery nurse who checked on me as I emerged from the anesthesia. "A healthy baby boy. He'll make some wonderful couple very happy," she'd said, patting my hand. "From your misfortune has come a mitzvah."

The misfortune stirred in his bassinet. I shuffled across the floor, hypnotized. He could be anyone's baby, I thought. They all looked pretty much the same, didn't they? I'd never seen this one before. The candy striper had made a mistake bringing him to my room. Maybe she'd mistaken which baby she'd brought.

I checked the label on the bassinet. Above the date of birth were the words BABY KLEIN, as if no one had bothered to name him. But that wasn't right. I remembered, now, the nurse asking me for a name. "We need it for the birth certificate," she said. "His real parents will change it later, so just say the first thing that comes to mind." I thought of David, who wrote the Psalms that were my favorite passages in the Torah. David, who soothed King Saul with his harp and defeated Goliath with his slingshot. David, who fell in love with Bathsheba even though she was married to another man.

I leaned in. I didn't realize, at first, that the drops splattering the baby's crown were my own tears. When had I started crying? There was nothing to cry about. All I had to do was press the call button. The candy striper would come and take him away. The baby would be adopted by his perfect parents. My mother and father would drive me home. I'd go on with my life as if it never happened.

Except I couldn't stop looking at David long enough to go push that button. I saw his face through a gauzy haze, as if my baby were a starlet in a Hollywood movie. The rush of warmth and love almost overwhelmed me until I reminded myself those were the side effects of oxytocin. In one of Dr. Nelson's lectures, she'd explained how the hormone had recently been synthesized and was being used in obstetrics to induce labor and stimulate lactation. As if on cue, two wet circles appeared on my blouse. How strange, I thought. I hadn't felt a thing.

I didn't decide to pick David up. It simply happened. I watched my arms reach out, saw my hands slip beneath his neck and his body, felt my muscles contract to counterbalance his weight as I lifted him from the bassinet. What was it the recovery nurse told me? Seven pounds, nine ounces. Such a precise measurement for such a fleeting moment in a person's life, as if the mass of our cells at the time of birth foretold something profound about our future.

I'd never know what David's future held. The doctor and the nurse who were destined to raise him probably wouldn't even tell him he was adopted. When I'd asked, at one of our group sessions, if that meant our babies would be brought up living a lie, Miss Murphy told us studies had shown it would be more damaging for a child to believe he wasn't wanted by his mother.

My eyebrows pulled together in a knot so tight it ached my head. Something wasn't making sense. How could he be unwanted? No one had ever asked me whether or not I wanted my baby. It was as if a girl gave up her right to want anything once she got pregnant out of wedlock. The social workers told us the only thing that mattered was what was best for the baby, and according to them, an unwed mother was no good to anyone, least of all her own child. The circular logic of the argument made me dizzy. Somehow, we had proven our unworthiness to be mothers by becoming mothers in the first place.

I thought of a course I'd taken at Barnard—Theory of Functions of Complex Variables. Professor Elliott had drilled into us that no equation could be considered solved unless every step in its calculation was proven correct. She'd used as an example the calculations that go into the engineering of a bridge. The smallest mistake, she said, could lead to a catastrophic collapse. It was a variation on the old adage "show your work" that we'd learned doing long division in elementary school. Miss Murphy had laid out her arguments with the utmost conviction, but what if she'd skipped a crucial step in her eagerness to arrive at a predetermined answer?

David was getting heavy in my arms. I sat on the windowsill and rested my elbows on my knees, his skull cradled in my palm. If I were to raise him, I thought, I'd bring him up the Hudson to show him the herons hatching along the shore. I'd teach him everything I loved about numbers and their magic. I'd take him to all the museums, and the planetarium, too. I saw it as clearly as a film reel spooling through a projector. I couldn't remember, in that moment, any of the reasons why those scenes could never be real.

He yawned, his toothless mouth a perfect circle, then blinked his lids open. My brain was sending out mayday signals like a sinking ship—he's not yours, he doesn't belong to you, you've already signed him away—but the ocean in my ears drowned them out as we locked eyes, my baby and me.

Stupid, stupid girl, I thought, for the hundredth time—except now, I wasn't berating myself for going to that hotel room with

Leonard. This time, I was angry with myself for never questioning Miss Murphy, or Dr. Nelson, or even my own mother. For a single woman to raise her own child was inconceivable to them, but it wasn't outside the realm of possibility, was it? I'd just seen a glimpse of it. It might not be the answer I arrived at in the end, but I was desperate, now, to think it through. All I needed was a little more time.

The door banged open. David startled, limbs flung wide. The way his fingers opened and closed at the ends of his pudgy arms reminded me of the sea anemones in the aquarium at Coney Island. I touched the tip of my finger to his palm. He grabbed it with his miniature fist, the strength of his grip a shock.

"You weren't supposed to bring it in here," Miss Murphy said, the frantic teenager hard on her heels. She rushed over and grabbed David out of my arms. I was too surprised to put up a fight, but his little fist held fast, his infant nail slicing through the ridges of my fingerprint as she pulled him away.

He began crying then, a quavering sound that stiffened my nipples. I got to my feet, but Miss Murphy was already handing him off to the candy striper. "Take this baby back to the nursery right away."

"Yes, ma'am, I'm sorry." The stripe-smocked girl put him in the bassinet. Its rubber wheels squealed as she rolled it across the linoleum floor.

I started to go after him. Miss Murphy snaked an arm around my waist, pinning me to the spot. "I'm sorry you had to go through that, Rita. You'll be all right, just take a breath."

I did, gagging on the scent of Shalimar. Every cell in my body yearned to follow the fading sound of my baby's cry. I'd seen his fingers, all ten of them, but I hadn't even looked at his toes. Or his feet, the soles of his tiny feet. I tried to take a step. Miss Murphy held me back.

"No, please, you don't understand." The vibration of my voice in my throat started me sobbing. "It's still not adding up. I haven't figured it out yet. I need to hold him a while longer."

"It's too late for that, Rita. Remember, you already signed the paper." Keeping one arm tight around my waist, Miss Murphy led me to my suitcase. "You better put your coat on, dear. Your blouse is a bit of a mess. Now, let's go find your parents."

Chapter Two
Cornelia Vogel

The Hague, Netherlands
May 1941

Cornelia Vogel turns to the next form, places a fresh Hollerith card on the plate of her punch machine, and checks the clock. Only three more minutes until their supervisor, Mevrouw Plank, blows her whistle to signal lunch break. Trained operators are expected to complete a card every two minutes, so there's plenty of time, in theory, for her to finish. Instead, Cornelia's fingers hover above the keys of the punch machine. For her, three minutes—closer to two and a half, now—won't be enough.

Cornelia glances down the aisle between desks to be sure that Mevrouw Plank's attention is elsewhere. Just two minutes left. Definitely not enough time to start a new card, she decides, letting her hands rest in her lap. If only there were an open casement to let in a glimpse of the sky or the salt smell of the sea. Huize Kleykamp, the villa that houses the Ministry of Information, isn't far from the beach at Scheveningen. If the punch-card room weren't located in its windowless basement, she might be able to hear the waves crashing beyond the dunes. Instead, her ears are irritated by the discordant din of dozens of girls tapping away at their machines, each to a slightly different rhythm.

Mevrouw Plank blows her whistle. "Half an hour, girls," she calls out. Cornelia gets up and takes her place in line, but instead of joining her coworkers for lunch in the villa's cafeteria, she impulsively climbs Huize Kleykamp's sweeping central staircase to the uppermost floor, where the man who directs the Ministry of Information has his office.

She's glad to see that Mevrouw Kwakkelstein, the secretary who sits in the anteroom to the director's office, is not at her desk. Cornelia doesn't want to explain herself. She approaches the door labeled GERARD VOGEL, DIRECTOR and makes a fist, but she can't bring herself to knock. Not yet. She takes a breath to gather her courage. She'd rather be anywhere else in the world at this moment—well, almost anywhere. As much as she dreads the conversation she's about to have with her father, it's better than returning to a job she hates.

She hopes he won't blame her for wanting to quit. If anyone's to blame for the situation Cornelia finds herself in, she thinks, it's Hitler. She'd only been at Leiden University for a few months, eagerly pursuing her linguistics degree, when the Nazis introduced their odious anti-Semitic laws. The college's rector, Professor Cleveringa, gave an impassioned speech in which he called on their German occupiers to respect the Dutch constitution, which did not distinguish among citizens by creed or race. Inspired by his words, Cornelia joined hundreds of students in walking out of their classes, determined to show the Germans they wouldn't stand idly by while Jewish professors were unjustly ousted.

Cornelia shakes her head, thinking how naïve they were to imagine Nazis could be influenced by law or logic. The very next day, the Germans arrested the rector who'd spurred the students to action and shuttered the university in retaliation. Now all the professors, not just the Jewish ones, are out of a job, and all of the students, even the meek ones who never took a stand, are locked out of their classes. Cornelia hopes to transfer to the University of Amsterdam next year, but until then, she's stuck living back home in The Hague. When her father offered to get her a job as a punch-card operator at the Ministry of Information, Cornelia accepted, even though she had no idea what the work entailed. At least it couldn't possibly be more tiresome than helping her mother with housework, she figured.

She was wrong. Like all the other punch-card operators, Cornelia's days consist of reading answers written on a form, matching them to codes she has memorized, then punching holes through the corresponding digits on a Hollerith card—a process she's meant to repeat every two minutes for hours at a time. Since she started the job, she's placed thousands of rectangular manila cards on the plate of her punch machine. Every day, she stares at the precise rows of 0 through 9 printed on each card, the minuscule digits stacked in eighty columns narrow as strands of spaghetti, until her vision is swimming.

It was a mistake for her to take this job in the first place. No, she corrects herself—it was a mistake for her father to have suggested it. Cornelia Vogel was never meant to do clerical work. She's been educated to be a scholar since age thirteen, when she started learning Latin and Greek at Gymnasium Haganum. She's only stuck with card punching for this long for fear of disappointing her father. This isn't the first time she's come to his office, determined to quit, only to end up inventing some other excuse for her visit. Today will be different, she tells herself. With a deep inhalation, Cornelia straightens her spine and knocks.

"Who is there?"

Anyone unfamiliar with Gerard Vogel's voice—abrupt, sharp, insistent—would assume he's been interrupted in the middle of some critical task, but to Cornelia's ear her father sounds the same as when he asked her to pass the sugar bowl at breakfast. She eases the door ajar and speaks through the narrow gap. "It's me, Father."

"Ah, Cornelia, come in."

Gerard Vogel steps out from behind his desk, his high forehead looming over horn-rimmed glasses that magnify his close-set gray eyes. From a distance his stature is unremarkable, but his single-minded intensity adds volume to his presence so that, standing before him, Cornelia feels diminished. She reached her father's height by the time she was fifteen—with a hat on her head, she is the taller of the two—but she's never outgrown the feeling of being a little girl hungry for the scant crumbs of his esteem.

Gerard gives Cornelia a quick kiss, his lips barely touching her cheek. She has her mother's moody green eyes, but her brown hair, high forehead, and boyish hands all come from him. She wonders what it's like for a man to see himself reflected so exactly in a woman.

Gesturing her to the chair across from his desk, he sits back down behind it. "So, to what do I owe this visit?"

Cornelia opens her mouth to speak, but the words stick in her throat. She presses her hands to her nervous stomach and grimaces.

"What's the matter, Cornelia? Are you ill?"

"I want to quit, Father." There, she's said it. Flapping her hands to dispel her nerves, she barrels ahead. "I'm sorry, but I can't spend one more minute in that basement punching tiny holes in Hollerith cards. It's driving me mad."

"But you found it interesting at the beginning." He leans back in his chair, peering at her over the rim of his glasses. "What has changed?"

It's true that learning the computer codes felt, at first, like learning a new language. Cornelia was good at that part. When it came to translating theory into action, however, the other girls in her training class swiftly adapted their secretarial skills to this new task while Cornelia struggled to develop the necessary dexterity. Even at her best, she's the slowest card puncher in the group, as her supervisor, Mevrouw Plank, never fails to point out. At worst, Cornelia's mind wanders from the task at hand until minutes pass without her punching any cards at all.

"I enjoyed memorizing the codes, but they haven't changed in weeks. You know how hard it is for me to concentrate when I'm bored, Father. I do the same thing over and over, hundreds of times a day, until my brain is so numb I can't think straight. Have you ever spent even one hour punching cards? It's impossible."

"Don't be so dramatic, Cornelia. It's not impossible. Every one of those girls is capable of punching cards quickly and perfectly, day after day, without complaint."

Cornelia knows it's no use trying to explain it to him. Her father's job entails collecting and analyzing massive amounts of statistical information. She doubts he spares a thought for the tedium of rendering that information into codes the computer can process. If it were truly mindless work, at least Cornelia could contemplate other things. She's accustomed to conjugating Latin verbs in her head while she waits for the tram or reciting Homeric passages in Greek while she washes dishes. But matching written answers to memorized codes requires just enough focus to crowd out other ideas, while Mevrouw Plank's constant hovering puts Cornelia on edge. Not an hour goes by without her supervisor interrupting her to check that each card is perfectly punched, its smooth surface free from any crease or tear. The Hollerith computer is so finicky, the cards are ushered around the ministry with the care of a chef whisking a soufflé from oven to table. Which reminds Cornelia of a question she's been meaning to ask.

"Father, I know the punch cards come from America, but America is boycotting Germany, and Germany is occupying Holland, so how do they get to The Hague?"

"Through Switzerland, I suppose, like everything else. Is that the kind of idle thought that prevents you from concentrating on your job?"

"Among others." She leans forward in her chair. "Here's something else I've wondered about. The Ministry of Information deals with population statistics. Why are you using computers to conduct an animal census? It isn't even about people." Ever since the Germans ordered an enumeration of every agricultural animal in the Netherlands, farmers across the nation, under threat of arrest, have grudgingly trudged into their local police stations and town halls to fill out forms designed for this very purpose. For weeks now, Cornelia has been coding the information on Hollerith cards, punching holes to represent the number of cows, calves, bulls, chickens, goats, swine, piglets, horses, and foals on every farm in the country. Her only act of resistance has been coding fewer animals than some farmers reported, effectively hiding them from the Germans by making them invisible to the computer. It's a puny form of protest, but it's all she can do from inside the ministry. "What's the point of it all, Father?"

"The point?" He tents his hands, fingertips pressed firmly together. "Suppose a thousand horses are needed for transport to Germany. Generalkommissar Wimmer asks me to provide a list of farmers from whom those horses can be requisitioned. Now, we wouldn't want anyone to lose his livelihood, so we want to identify farmers who have more than, say, three horses, so that giving up one animal won't drive them to ruin. Perhaps we also want to specify farms with a few swine, so the pork can make up for the lost horse meat. We have in our possession forms filled out by every farmer in the country listing all the animals they possess, but how are we going to find only those with three or more horses and some swine? Can you imagine how long it would take to compile such a list by hand?"

"Weeks?" she ventures.

"At least. Punching cards may be a tiresome task, but the result is tremendous efficiency. Once we have the information coded onto punch cards, the Hollerith can print a list of exactly those farms as fast as the cards can be fed through the hopper."

"But doesn't that make it awfully easy for the Nazis to steal our horses, Father?"

Gerard Vogel startles Cornelia by slapping his palm on the desktop. "I'm just doing my job, the same as every employee at the ministry. Queen Wilhelmina herself has commanded the Dutch civil service to continue operating as normal under occupation. Besides, Holland is a special case. We didn't declare war against Germany. We would have stayed neutral if Hitler hadn't invaded. As long as we do as we're told and stay out of trouble, we'll all get through this war safely."

"Only if you can claim to be Aryan," she says, thinking of all the Jewish civil servants and teachers who have been fired from their jobs.

"You know I don't agree with those anti-Semitic rules, but what would you have me do? Speak out and end up in Buchenwald, like Professor Cleveringa?"

Cornelia, intimidated, slides her eyes from his gaze, looking instead at the chalkboards that dominate the walls of his office. Covered in flowcharts and diagrams, they make the room feel even smaller than it is. When the Nazis relocated the Ministry of Information from their cramped government offices to the spacious Huize Kleykamp, it was assumed Gerard Vogel would choose the villa's former library, with its marble mantel and mahogany shelves, as the director's office. Instead, he installed himself in a small room on the uppermost floor, barely big enough to fit a desk and his chalkboards. The room's main asset is its view of the courtyard, where he has been able to observe the construction of an underground bunker commissioned by the Germans to house the Hollerith machines. Built of concrete a meter thick, the bunker ensures that even an act of sabotage or an Allied bombing won't interrupt the processing of punch cards. Recently completed, it's camouflaged now beneath paving bricks and parked bicycles.

Gerard Vogel reaches across the desk, takes his daughter's hand, and lowers his voice to a whisper. "One day this war will end and Holland will be free again, but until then we must face the truth. Rotterdam was bombarded. General Winkelman capitulated. The royal family fled to London. People who resist are being arrested. In dangerous times like these, we must find safe harbor where we can. Do you understand?"

"Yes, Father." Cornelia wants to take comfort in his touch, but his fingers have closed around hers with a pressure that makes her knuckles ache.

"Fortunately, the work I do is vital to the Germans." He lets go of her hand as his voice rises to its normal level. "They certainly appreciate me more than the Dutch bureaucracy ever did. I developed a superior design for identity cards years ago, but I could never convince the government to approve it for use. Yet Generalkommissar Wimmer took one look at my prototype and pronounced it the best he'd ever seen. Today, everyone in Holland carries a card I designed, with a duplicate registration filed here at the ministry so no one can pass off a forgery." He gestures to one of the chalkboards. "Now I've figured out a method for conducting a population census entirely without enumerators. Wimmer has acquired an alphabetizing Hollerith tabulator for my exclusive use in completing the project. He wouldn't do that if he didn't need me, and as long as he needs me, I am safe. I thought if you worked here, you'd be safe, too."

Cornelia knows his intention is to reassure her, but his talk of safety feels more like a threat than a promise. "I'm sorry, but I simply can't stand punching cards. I'm sure the only reason Mevrouw Plank hasn't fired me is because you're my father."

As if his daughter were a candidate being interviewed for a job, he sits back in his chair and asks, "So, what do you propose to do?"

She forces herself to meet his eye. "If I complete my degree, maybe I could work as a translator?"

"You are a brilliant girl, Cornelia. If Leiden University hadn't been closed, you'd be there right now, dazzling your professors, I'm sure. It is closed, however, and I can't imagine the Germans allowing it to reopen. That is the reality, and we must accept it."

"But Leiden isn't the only university with a linguistics department."

"Is this about Amsterdam again?" He shakes his head in frustration. "As long as this war lasts, your mother and I want you close to home. Besides, Amsterdam is no place for a young woman on her own."

"Well, if you won't support my going to university, can't you at least find a different job for me?"

"There's not much call at the ministry for someone with your skills, Cornelia. We deal with statistical information here, not foreign languages."

A telephone call interrupts their conversation. "He has? Yes, I'll come right away, thank you." Gerard Vogel jumps to his feet and peers out the window. Coming to look over his shoulder, Cornelia sees men unloading boxes from a truck in the courtyard. He backs up, stepping on his daughter's toe.

"Ouch!"

"I'm sorry, Cornelia, but I must go." He buttons his suit jacket with precise snaps of his fingers. "Willem Nooteboom, the engineer from the Watson Business Machine Company, is here to deliver the alphabetizing Hollerith."

She follows her father out of his office, where they find Mevrouw

Kwakkelstein back at her desk. She is a dignified woman who owes her rosy complexion to bicycling ten kilometers every day—five early each morning, rain or shine, light or dark, to reach work before her boss, and five back each evening, never leaving before Gerard Vogel has gone home for the night.

"Oh, hello, Cornelia. I didn't realize you were visiting your father."

"It was my lunch break," Cornelia explains.

"And now lunch is over and you're on your way back to work, isn't that right?" Gerard says.

Mevrouw Kwakkelstein looks back and forth as father and daughter engage in a silent standoff. Grasping at any excuse to avoid returning to the punch-card room, Cornelia picks up a pad of paper and a pencil from the secretary's desk. "Shall I come with you, Father? Perhaps I can help by taking notes."

He sighs, too impatient to argue. "Very well. Come along, Cornelia."

She trails her father back down Huize Kleykamp's regal staircases. Before the Ministry of Information took over the elegant villa, its galleries hosted fashionable parties and art exhibitions. Now they're crammed with filing cabinets and typing tables and desks at which sit hundreds of Dutch civil servants who, by virtue of simply doing their jobs, serve their German occupiers. In the chandeliered dining room, which has become the ministry's cafeteria, the gathered clerks and secretaries hastily put down their coffee cups and sandwiches to wish Director Vogel good day. He accepts their deference as his due, nodding in acknowledgment without slowing his stride. In the basement, they hustle past the punch-card room, where the girls, back from lunch, are tapping away at their machines, Cornelia's desk conspicuously unoccupied. At the end of the corridor, they turn a corner and come to a sudden stop at a makeshift door that reminds Cornelia of the entrance to an abandoned mine shaft.

"Generalkommissar Wimmer won't like to see this unfinished," Gerard Vogel mutters. "He specified the bunker was to be secure at all times. We need to get the carpenter and the locksmith here immediately. Make a note of that, Cornelia."

Following her father down a concrete ramp, Cornelia feels as if she's descending into an Egyptian tomb. Inside the bunker, stale air seeps through vents in the low ceiling. A conduit affixed to the walls carries power from a generator, its distant thrum muffled by the thick walls. A cramped passageway leads to a warren of rooms that house the ministry's various Hollerith machines. "I reserved this one for the alphabetizer," Gerard says, ushering Cornelia through the nearest doorway.

Crates packed with straw are arrayed around the perimeter of the room. The machine's components huddle on a canvas cloth spread out on the floor as if a family of oddly shaped parts has come together for a picnic. Cornelia sees what looks like the carriage of an enormous typewriter. There is a chute the exact size and shape of a punch card, tall enough for a stack of hundreds. Large pieces of black-enameled metal suggest typing tables and filing cabinets—the cover plates, Cornelia guesses, that will hide the inner workings of the machine. There are piles of braided wire bundled together like hair gathered into a ponytail. There are panels the size of tea trays, the surface of each puckered with tiny plugs. There are dozens of smaller parts, too—switches and spools and dials and gears—peeking out from the cotton batting in which they were swaddled for the journey. Standing in the midst of it all, waving and pointing as if he were the conductor of a mechanical orchestra, is the man Cornelia assumes is Willem Nooteboom.

"Be careful with that!" He dashes out to the passageway, where a workman is in danger of losing his grip on a handcart. Willem rescues a crate from the cart and places it on the floor with the gentleness of a mother putting a baby down for a nap. "You have no idea how far this machine has come. I won't have it ruined now." Though his words are clipped, his voice is quiet, as if a shout might rouse the sleeping pieces of machinery. He pries the lid off the crate and lifts out what looks to Cornelia like a bread box. With a sigh of relief, he pronounces the part undamaged.

"That's the last of it, *meneer,*" the workman says.

"Secure that door at the top of the ramp as best you can on your way out, won't you?" Willem turns a slow circle, counting off the parts and boxes, until his gaze falls on Gerard Vogel. "Ah, Meneer Vogel. What do you think?"

"I think we have a lot of work to do."

"Yes, we do, starting with replacing that door." Willem gestures toward the ramp. "I recommend steel, preferably with a vault lock. Perhaps Generalkommissar Wimmer can requisition one from a bank?"

"A bank vault?" Cornelia says. "Are the Holleriths really so precious?"

Willem startles as if she has appeared out of thin air. "They are, yes, Mevrouw Kwakkelstein."

"Excuse me, Meneer Nooteboom, this isn't my secretary. This is my daughter, Cornelia," Gerard says.

"My apologies, Mejuffrouw Vogel. I've only spoken with Meneer Vogel's secretary on the telephone. And yes, the Hollerith machines are all valuable, but this one is especially so. There are only twelve alphabetizers in all of Europe."

"No one has been able to get a new one," her father adds, "since the American company stopped doing business with Germany."

"That's true," Willem says, as if Gerard Vogel's words could be doubted. "At Dehomag, they're producing other models of Hollerith machines as fast as possible, but the German subsidiary doesn't have the technology to manufacture an alphabetizing tabulator.

Their engineers have been able to fashion some replacement parts, but most still have to come directly from New York. These fuses, for example."

Willem takes a step closer as he extracts a tin box the size of a pack of cigarettes from his pocket. Affixed to the lid is the American company's label. Designed to look like a globe, its northern hemisphere consists of the word "Business." The word "Machines" forms its southern half, while "International" spans the globe's equator. Cornelia isn't sure if the name of the company is Business Machines International or International Business Machines. Either way, the English words tell the story of a transatlantic journey.

"How did you get those?" There is awe in Gerard Vogel's voice.

"Through Geneva, naturally," Willem says. "Reichsführer Himmler himself helped Dehomag acquire a dozen boxes of fuses, one for each of the alphabetizers. Your census must be very important, Meneer Vogel."

"It is important to Generalkommissar Wimmer that I conduct a complete census of the Dutch population, but as you know, he does not trust our countrymen to be reliable enumerators of their neighbors. To assemble an alphabetical census from existing records in time for it to be useful requires the Hollerith. The machine requires fuses. Therefore, fuses must be found."

Cornelia stops herself from pointing out that something so important to the Nazi high command couldn't possibly be good for the Dutch people. She doubts her father is distracted by such thoughts. His work has always been the most important thing to him.

Willem returns the box of fuses to his pocket. "Have you finished the census forms?"

"Yes, the forms are designed. Tomorrow they go to the printer."

"Good. Then I can start on the wiring diagrams for the control panels. I was recently in Berlin for specialized training at Dehomag's headquarters. What an operation they have! It seems like everything in Germany runs on Hollerith. The problem with the alphabetizer," Willem continues, "is that, because it was imported directly from America, all of the original documentation is in English." He retrieves a printed booklet from his briefcase and shows it to them. "I'll have to train the technicians who'll be helping me, but there are no instructions in Dutch. I need a translation as soon as possible, but I don't know who can be trusted to do it."

Cornelia sees her chance to escape the punch-card room and seizes it. "I can do it."

Her father shoots her a cold look for preempting his authority. "My daughter is impetuous, Meneer Nooteboom, but she does know how to operate the punch-card machine, and her English is excellent."

Willem gives her a distracted smile. "How perfect. Could you begin immediately?"

Cornelia silently pleads with her father. He relents. "She is currently unoccupied, yes."

"Very well then." Willem hands Cornelia the booklet. "Don't be intimidated by the technical terminology. There are bound to be words you don't understand. Engineering is very different from literature. You may know the language but not the vocabulary."

As she thumbs through the instruction manual, her father pulls her aside to whisper in her ear. "This is extremely important to me, Cornelia. You must make no mistakes. Promise me."

Cornelia tamps down the anxiety his words induce. "I'll do my best, Father, I promise. And you'll tell Mevrouw Plank?"

"That she no longer has to coddle her worst worker for my sake? Yes, I will."

Cornelia supposes she deserves the sting of his words. "My dictionaries are in my room. Shall I go home to get started?"

Gerard Vogel dismisses her with a nod of his chin. Cornelia ascends the ramp from the Hollerith bunker, relieved to be back aboveground. In the courtyard of Huize Kleykamp, she finds her bicycle among the hundred or so parked there, amused to imagine her father somewhere beneath her feet. She walks her bike to the checkpoint and opens her satchel for the German soldier on duty, ready to explain why she's taking home an English-language instruction manual. He doesn't ask. After checking her identification, he waves her on.

The satchel bounces against her back as Cornelia hops on her bike and crosses the moat surrounding the villa. She is starting down the street when her progress comes to an abrupt halt. Pedaling backward to stop, she stands on tiptoes to see what's causing people to pile up in front of the Vredespaleis, the Peace Palace. There is a changing of the guards at the palace gates. Traffic is stopped all around Carnegieplein. Pedestrians, cyclists, automobiles, and trams are backed up into Scheveningseweg and Burgemeester Patijnlaan. How infuriating, Cornelia thinks, that the whole city must come to a standstill while half a dozen German soldiers exchange places in those ridiculous goose steps, straight legs lifted high as a cabaret dancer's.

At last the guards are changed, a whistle blows, and the street bursts back to life. Exertion pinkens Cornelia's cheeks as she rides across Carnegieplein and along Laan van Meerdervoort, every push on the pedals fueled by her determination to prove herself to her father. Sure, she hates that her job will somehow help the Nazis, but she reassures herself she'll only be translating words from one language to another. It's not as if she will be responsible for what they say.

Chapter Three
Rita Klein

Teaneck, New Jersey
May 1960

I was hysterical by the time Miss Murphy handed me over to my frightened parents in the parking lot behind the hospital.

"Rita's experiencing a normal hormonal reaction—nothing to worry about," Miss Murphy reassured them. Patting my arm, she said, "Believe me, you'll be right as rain after a good night's sleep. When I see you in six weeks, you'll hardly remember who I am."

I lifted my tear-streaked face from Mom's shoulder to see if she could possibly be serious, but Miss Murphy simply smoothed her skirt, adjusted her cardigan, and disappeared back into the hospital. She'd already gotten my baby, which was all she really wanted from me. Any extra minute spent with his mother was apparently a waste of her time.

Mom steered me toward the Rambler, where I dropped into the backseat like a sack of laundry. "Turn on the radio, Adele, why don't you?" Dad said after starting the engine. He probably thought the music would drown out my sobbing, but all it did when Mom tuned into a station was ruin the theme from *A Summer Place* for all of us. I was crying so hard, I couldn't see out the car window. I only knew we'd missed the approach for the Bear Mountain Bridge when Dad started cursing about having to battle traffic across the Tappan Zee.

I was still whimpering when we crossed into New Jersey. In Teaneck, Dad parked behind the store so we could go in through the delivery door, out of sight of the Saturday pedestrians on Cedar Lane. You'd have thought I was an escaped convict or something, the way Dad held me back in the stockroom while Mom crouched behind the cash register, eyeing the sidewalk like a spy. When the coast was clear, they hustled me out the store's entrance, beneath the banner announcing MEMORIAL DAY SALE STARTS TUESDAY. Mom swooped me through the adjacent door to our apartment so fast I barely caught a glimpse of the sign Dad had taped to the display window: CLOSED TO VISIT A SICK RELATIVE.

If I hadn't gone away, we'd have been celebrating my graduation about now. When my brother, Charlie, got his degree, Dad set up a party in the store with dozens of cupcakes and gallons of punch. Customers old and new, members of our synagogue, women from Mom's mah-jongg league, and Dad's friends from the chamber of commerce all stopped by to wish Charlie well, crisp five-dollar bills tucked into their congratulation cards.

There were no cakes or cards to welcome me home after five months away, just empty rooms and the stale smell of Dad's favorite dinner, liver and onions. Our apartment above the store had always been a drab place. Mom didn't believe in buying new what we already had, so nothing was ever replaced, not even when horsehair poked through the upholstery or the braided rugs began to unravel. The new car they drove, the nice clothes we wore, the stylish shoes on our feet—these expenses, Dad insisted, were necessary to make a good impression on his customers. If it had been up to Mom, all of our clothes would have been picked from the rag pile. As it was, her bras and slips were held together with safety pins.

My own room was a hodgepodge of mismatched furniture. A

bulletin board salvaged from some school renovation dominated the wall above my desk. There was a patchwork quilt on the bed and curtains made from an old bedspread on the window. The lamp on my nightstand was a ceramic cat whose lifted paw held a bare bulb. It was depressing, sure, but the familiarity of my room after the months away hit me like an anesthetic. I collapsed into bed, craving sleep.

Sleep wouldn't come. Instead of those floating squiggles you see when your eyes are closed, the image of David's tiny face swam across my vision. My brain kept telling me I was doing the best thing for my baby, but my guts were tied up in knots like a kid caught cheating on a test. I sucked my fingertip until the cut from David's nail started bleeding again, unable to shake the sick feeling that I'd made a terrible mistake. I hunkered in bed, head under the covers, through the whole holiday weekend, as if my room were a third-class cabin on a storm-tossed ship.

When the Memorial Day parade came marching down Cedar Lane, my parents stood outside the store handing out little flags, courtesy of Klein's Shoes. When we were kids, Charlie and I always helped, the four of us like an advertisement for the American family. After the parade, my brother and I would go around picking up the flags accidentally dropped on the sidewalk. We told anyone who asked we were collecting them out of patriotism. In reality, Mom wiped off the dirt, ironed the flaps of fabric, then put them away to hand out again next year.

After the parade, Mom and Dad drove to Westchester to meet up with Charlie and his wife, Debbie, at her parents' house for a backyard barbecue. I was invited, too, but I was in no shape to go anywhere. Home alone, I wandered through the kitchen opening every cabinet and drawer. Despite all those months complaining about the food at the Hudson Home, my appetite was limited to crackers smeared with Velveeta and mugs of canned chicken soup.

I didn't leave the apartment for a week. If I wasn't in bed, I was on the lumpy couch watching television in my pajamas. It didn't matter what was on. When Dad tuned in to Mike Wallace's interview with the boxer Joe Louis, I watched that. When the Jack Paar show came on after my parents went to bed, I watched that, too, even though Joey Bishop was guest hosting that week. I watched whatever old movie followed the eleven o'clock news, whether it was *Ghost of Frankenstein* or *Son of Dracula*. Some nights, I stared at the test pattern on the television set after the last station went off the air at two in the morning.

By Sunday, Mom had had enough. She shook me awake from a nap, then sat on the edge of my bed. "I know that social worker said you'd need some sleep, but you've been lollygagging around for a week now. It's about time you pulled yourself together, Rita. I told Dad to go ahead and set up that interview for you in the city tomorrow."

I couldn't picture myself going outside, much less into Manhattan. "I'm sorry, Mom, but I still don't feel right."

"Listen, Rita, you made a mistake, and you paid for it. We've all paid for it. When I think about the tuition we wasted . . ." She sighed heavily. "Never mind all that now. It's over and done with. First thing tomorrow morning, you're going to take a shower, get dressed, and go to that interview."

"Look at me, Mom. Do you really think I'm ready to start a new job?"

"I don't care if you get the job. I just want to see you put in the effort."

Remember when you thought I had polio? I wanted to say. Remember how you held me for hours, so patient and kind? I swallowed the sob in my throat. "I'll try."

"Good." She got up and smoothed my blanket. "Whatever sleep you need, you get it tonight. Tomorrow's a new day, okay?"

"Okay." Maybe it was all in my head, I thought. Maybe by tomorrow, I'd stop feeling like I was lost at sea.

"That's my girl." Mom turned back before closing my bedroom door. "Too bad you weren't this sleepy when you were a baby."

Her words hit me like a slap across the face. At every one of my birthdays, Mom used to trot out the same old story of how she had to put me in the carriage when I was an infant and walk up and down Cedar Lane in the middle of the night to get me to sleep. All my life, I'd been apologizing for being such a bad baby, but at that moment all I could think about was my own baby's cry. What if David was colicky like I was? Mom used to make a joke of how she was so exhausted one night, she wanted to put me in a box and mail me to Alaska. The punch line was that I hadn't come with a return address, but David had been delivered to his new parents by an agency. Did they have a return policy for the babies who failed to meet expectations?

Somehow, I got myself up and showered Monday morning. I felt like I was dressing a doll as I tugged on a girdle, clipped on stockings, hooked my bra, and dropped a dress over my head. In the kitchen, Mom poured me a cup of coffee, which did perk me up, but I told her I still didn't think I could manage an interview.

"There's nothing wrong with your brain, is there?" she asked. I was trying to find the words to describe the tangle of steel wool that was short-circuiting my synapses when Mom started talking again. "You're such a smart girl, Rita. How many other women in New York have ever heard of that Watson computing course, let alone completed it?" Hardly any, I thought, if my class was any indication. "All you have to do is answer some questions. That shouldn't be too hard, now, should it?" She looked so hopeful, I made myself nod. Pleased with herself, she said, "Come on, then. Dad wants you to stop by the store before you catch the bus. And grab a sweater, it's cool out."

The latest summer styles were arrayed enticingly in the display window: two-toned kidskin mules, pig slingbacks with a Louis heel, wedge sandals with slender straps. When we walked in, Dad was kneeling in front of Mom's friend Mrs. Katz, easing her stockinged foot into a pink patent leather pump with a tapered toe and a spike heel. There weren't many women from our synagogue who would have chosen that look. Most of Dad's customers, who counted on their shoes to last, opted for comfort over fashion, but Mrs. Katz could afford it. Her husband was a successful dentist— our dentist, in fact, who'd filled my molars with silver amalgam and wired my brother's mouth for braces. Mrs. Katz was talking about her son's upcoming bar mitzvah, which would be followed by a catered reception with a hired band. Her dress was trimmed in pink lace, she said, which made these shoes perfect for her outfit. The only problem, which became painfully apparent when she stood up to walk around the store, was her bunion.

"Rita, darling, is that you?" Mrs. Katz came tottering toward me, arms wide. There was no avoiding her smothering hug. "How is your aunt? I saw the sign on the shop window last Saturday. Is she better?"

"Our visit did her a world of good," Mom said before I could open my mouth. "Ida swears she'd never have recovered without Rita's help these past months."

"You're an angel for taking care of her like that." Mrs. Katz stepped back, squinting at my face. "You seem awfully pale, Rita. I hope you didn't wear yourself out."

"I—I'm fine," I stammered, irrationally afraid she'd guess I'd so recently given birth. "It was a long time to be away is all."

"Make sure you get some sun this summer. Now, what do you think of these?" She turned out her ankle to show off the shoes. "You know I value a young person's opinion."

What I thought was that she'd be crippled by the time her

boy declared himself a man. "They're very stylish, Mrs. Katz." I glanced down at my boring beige stacked-heels. "You make me jealous."

"They are pretty, aren't they? I'll take them."

"Wonderful," Dad said, smiling. "Adele will ring you up, if you'll excuse me for a moment?"

Dad beckoned me toward the back of the store, where discounted winter shoes left over from the Memorial Day sale were piled on a table. It had been months since we'd stood so close, and though he was as well-groomed as ever, there were purple bags under his eyes and blackheads in the greasy creases around his nostrils. I was about to ask if everything was okay when I realized if there was something wrong with him, I was probably the cause of it.

"This is where you're going today." Dad handed me a card embossed with the name ANTIQUATED BUSINESS MACHINES, along with the company's address in the Empire State Building. "Mr. Pettibone is expecting you at eleven. I don't know what the interview will be like, but he told me that Watson Laboratory course you took would be good preparation for whatever job he's got in mind. We're in the chamber of commerce together, and he's an important customer of mine, too." His eyes rested briefly on my face before sliding away. "I'm counting on you not to embarrass me, Rita."

The bell over the door rang as Mrs. Katz went out and three young mothers came in. They parked their baby carriages by the window and gathered around the sale table, their backs turned on their older kids, who started running around the store. I could tell from the look Dad exchanged with Mom that he wanted her to stay and help.

"Okay then," I said, waving a general goodbye. "I'll see you later."

"Rita." Mom spoke over the head of the toddler she was picking up from the floor. "We're going out to China Lane for dinner, so be home by six, okay?"

"Sure." I doubted I'd have much of an appetite, but it wasn't as if I had anywhere else to be.

Walking up Cedar Lane to the bus stop, I passed Bischoff's ice cream parlor, where every milestone of my childhood had been celebrated. I couldn't help feeling nostalgic for those uncomplicated days. Back then, Dad was only a salesman, scrimping and saving so he could buy the store for himself. Those times were from hunger, as Mom used to say, but they managed somehow. Maybe I could have managed, too, if my parents had been willing to help me. But what respectable woman would patronize Klein's Shoes knowing the owner's unwed daughter was raising a bastard in the upstairs apartment?

Forty minutes later, I stepped out of the Port Authority bus terminal onto bustling Eighth Avenue. All my life, coming into the city had been something special. Visits to the Museum of Natural History, picnics at the Central Park Zoo, ice skating at Rockefeller Plaza—Manhattan was so glamorous compared to the sleepy suburb of Teaneck. Getting that scholarship to Barnard had made me feel like my real life as a city girl had finally begun. When Leonard took me to the Rainbow Room, it was as perfect as a scene in a movie. But getting pregnant was not in the script. Like it never happened, I reminded myself, spotting my destination.

The silver spire of the Empire State Building pointed to the sky like a beacon as I zigzagged the blocks to Fifth Avenue and Thirty-Fourth Street. The lettering above the entrance glowed golden as I pushed through the revolving doors, the lobby in daylight as spectacular as I remembered. I avoided the tourists heading up the escalator to buy tickets for the observation deck and followed a scrum of suited businessmen into one of the office elevators, shouting from the back of the crowded car for the operator to take me up to the fifty-seventh floor.

The Art Deco romance of the building's lobby didn't carry over to the office corridors, where the terrazzo floors were dulled from thirty years of shuffling feet and the brass knobs tarnished by a generation of sweaty palms. I walked past a dozen identical oak doors until I found the one labeled ANTIQUATED BUSINESS MACHINES. I entered with all the enthusiasm of a student called to the principal's office.

"May I help you?" The middle-aged receptionist was seated behind a desk equipped with an intercom, a telephone, and an avocado-green electric typewriter. With her silver hair teased into a towering beehive, she seemed as confident and poised as my professors at Barnard, but her purple ensemble was much more flamboyant. She wore a lavender jacket over a dress boldly printed with Dutch irises, as if she were a walking Van Gogh canvas. The stones dangling from her ears were amethysts, as were the beads around her neck. Even her eye shadow and lipstick were shades of mauve, which looked a bit garish against her beige foundation.

"I'm Rita Klein. I have an interview with Mr. Pettibone at eleven?"

Her eyebrows rose as she gave me the once-over, my tan dress and navy sweater dull compared to her glorious colors. "I'll let him know you're here, Miss Klein." Instead of using the intercom, she exited through a door behind her desk. I glanced at her feet, thinking the color matching must surely end at her shoes, but no, even her pumps were violet. Left alone, I looked around at the banal photographs of New York City that decorated the walls. The window was open, but the room felt hushed. From this height, the sounds of traffic on Fifth Avenue were softened to a distant music.

I thought back to my summer at the Watson Laboratory course on computing. Though affiliated with Columbia University, the course wasn't primarily for college students. Professors took it, too, to learn how computers could help in their research, as well as high school physics teachers eager to understand this new technology. There were a couple of military men who attended every class in uniform and a pair of graduate students who worshipped our teacher, Mr. Hankam, despite his lack of academic accolades. Then there was Leonard, a salesman down from IBM's headquarters in Endicott, New York. He'd claimed the seat beside mine on the first day of class, his cologne tickling my nose.

I was nervous being the only woman in this intimidating crowd, but Leonard put me at ease right away. He talked to me as an intellectual equal while treating me like a lady—opening doors, offering his arm, picking up my tab when we'd all gather for drinks after class. He took me to lunch at Tom's so often my heart learned to flutter at the sight of those red neon letters. But at the end of the course, after we'd all applauded Mr. Hankam, Leonard shook my hand with the formality of a final farewell. I figured it was over, whatever it was. A flirtation, apparently, nothing more. It wasn't as if I'd fallen in love with him, I told myself—until he telephoned a few weeks later and I swooned.

"Stop it, Rita," I said out loud, grateful the receptionist wasn't back yet. Banishing memories of Leonard, I forced myself to think about what I'd learned during the course. The *Barnard College Bulletin* for April 1959 was the first in which the field of computing machines was listed as an allied subject for students majoring in mathematics. My adviser, Professor Joanne Elliott, told me that all the computing classes were taught at Columbia and admission was competitive. She recommended I take the Watson Laboratory summer course to see if I was interested before vying for a seat in one of the classes come fall.

From the outside, the town house on West 116th Street looked like it belonged in the pages of an Edith Wharton novel. Inside, though, the Watson Laboratory was a vision of modernism. Electrical conduits had been retrofit along every wall to power the computing machines. Tabulators clattered as punch cards were fed through their hoppers. Sorters chugged and whooshed, shooting the processed cards into pockets. Typebars printed reports with the rat-a-tat-tat of warfare. Entering a classroom to encounter blackboards covered with control panel diagrams made me feel like I was embarking on a voyage of scientific discovery. That I was the only woman in the room reminded me what a pioneer I was.

Well, I wasn't a pioneer anymore. Instead, I was a cliché character right out of that Rona Jaffe novel: ambitious young woman goes to the big city to find success, gets seduced by a married man, and ruins her prospects by ending up pregnant.

The purple lady reappeared, beckoning. "Mr. Pettibone will see you now, Miss Klein, if you're ready."

Was I ready? I didn't even know what I was doing here. I followed her through an empty conference room feeling like a pawn on someone else's chessboard.

"Come on in, Miss Klein." Mr. Pettibone held his office door open in such a way that I had no choice but to duck under his outstretched arm. I fit easily—he was a big guy, and tall, too—but I resented being made to feel so childish. It was a corner office, with another door on the adjacent wall and two huge open windows. Glancing out, I could see clear across Manhattan to the Hudson River.

"Great view, isn't it? My kids love to sit on the radiators and look down at the people. Makes my wife so nervous I've got to lock the windows before she'll even let them in here. Did you know if you dropped a penny from this height it could kill someone? Go ahead and take a seat."

The leather armchair Mr. Pettibone pointed to wheezed as I sank into it. I expected him to walk around behind his desk, but instead he dropped into the chair beside mine and crossed his legs. No wonder my father valued his business, I thought, noticing his expensive shoes. Dad was usually a traditionalist when it came to business attire. He hardly ever recommended strapped shoes, let alone triple-monk cap-toes, but the buckles gave the illusion of width and Mr. Pettibone, despite his height and girth, had strangely slender feet.

"So, I understand you completed the Watson Laboratory course last summer, and you were taking a class on computing machines at Columbia before you withdrew, is that right?" I'd barely nodded before he barreled on. "That's very impressive, Rita. You don't mind if I call you Rita, do you? I feel like I know you, your father's told me so much about you. Let me say, it was selfless of you to leave school to care for your aunt. I'd have thought Barnard would want to encourage that kind of altruism instead of punish you for it by taking away your scholarship. Not that you need a degree from some highfalutin college to be a success. Take me, for example. I used what I'd learned about computing machines at Quartermaster School in the army to land a job with IBM after the war. Started out in sales, working on commission. Now I've got my very own business in the most famous building in the world."

The more Mr. Pettibone filled the office with his talk, the more I relaxed. Maybe I'd get lucky and not have to say anything at all. He was explaining how IBM had always retained ownership of its technology by only leasing their machines, until the late 1950s, when they were forced to sell some older models to satisfy a Justice Department anti-monopoly consent decree. "By then, I had plenty of clients who were set in their ways. They didn't want to switch their operations to some new system. All they wanted was to keep managing their inventory and processing payroll and printing out reports the same way they always had. So, I partnered up with my army buddy Frank McKay, and together we raised the money to buy up a bunch of old computing machines. Now we've got a few hundred clients. Some of them send us their ledgers and we punch the cards for them here. Others send us their cards already punched to be processed. And for some clients, we develop entirely new programs. That's the kind of job we're trying to fill."

The cushion of his chair sighed in relief as Mr. Pettibone got up to use the intercom. "Gladys, send Frank in here, would you?" He chuckled to himself. "I can't wait to see the look on his face when he sees you, Rita. I didn't tell him we were interviewing a girl."

The door swung open and the man I assumed was Mr. McKay entered the office. Where Mr. Pettibone was physically bulky and ostentatious in his dress, Mr. McKay was slender and simply attired in a gray suit with a white shirt that seemed even whiter against his brown skin.

"Frank!" Mr. Pettibone brought him over to me. "Take a look at this little girl here. What do you think about interviewing her for the Olympia job?"

Frank McKay stared at me like a scientist attempting to identify an obscure species. "I thought you ran the ad under 'Help Wanted: Male'?"

"She didn't see it in the paper. Her father sells me my shoes. This here is Irving Klein's daughter, Rita. She took a course last summer at the Watson Laboratory, and a class on computing machines at Columbia, too. I thought we should at least give her a shot."

I was beginning to feel like a prank Mr. Pettibone was playing on his partner. To recover my dignity, I got to my feet. "Pleased to meet you, Mr. McKay."

The puzzled expression didn't leave his face, but he took my offered hand in a firm grip. It occurred to me that I'd never seen a Black man or woman at the Watson Laboratory. It made me wonder if IBM intentionally discriminated against them. The thought flashed through my mind to ask Leonard, but of course that would never happen. In the letter that had accompanied his check, he'd made it crystal clear I was never to contact him again so long as I lived.

Mr. Pettibone pushed aside the intercom to lean on his desk, but Mr. McKay remained standing, his back straight as a soldier's. "Thank you for coming in, Miss Klein. Please, have a seat."

I had no choice but to sink back into that wheezy cushion. Mr. McKay reached behind Mr. Pettibone's desk and got a poster that he brought over and rested on the arms of the chair, trapping my hands uselessly beneath it. "Can you tell me what this means?"

Apparently, the interview had begun. I examined the poster. It was printed with the template of a control panel. Drawn over it in a tangle of curved lines were the wiring connections that would instruct the computer to execute a specific program. At the Watson course, Mr. Hankam used to talk us through each connection, explaining the various calculations the machine could do depending on how the panel was wired. The more I stared at the poster, the more my vision blurred. It was too close for me to take it all in.

I pushed the poster toward Mr. McKay. "Would you hold that up for me?" I asked, getting up and taking a few steps back. I hadn't contemplated anything this intricate in months and my brain was slow to find the right context. Eventually, though, it was like those days last summer when everything in the classroom slipped away as I lost myself in the meaning of the connections. I didn't so much figure out the answer as allow it to emerge.

"It's wired for crossfooting." I glanced at Mr. Pettibone. He didn't seem to understand me. "It's used to build tables by differencing." Mr. McKay enigmatically raised an eyebrow. "It tells the computer to total the rows and columns in a book of accounts."

"Any of that make sense to you, Frank?" Mr. Pettibone asked.

Mr. McKay brought his eyebrows back in line and relaxed his face. "It sure does. I don't mind telling you, Miss Klein, I've shown this to half a dozen men who claimed to be experienced IBM operators. Not one of them could explain what it meant."

"I'm not surprised." This interview might not lead to anything in the end, but it reminded me how much I enjoyed thinking about computing machines. "Plenty of people can wire a control panel by following the diagram, but that doesn't mean they understand the theory behind it. As it happens, this program was one of the first I learned for the IBM 602 calculating machine. If you'd used a template from any other computer model, I might have been stumped, too."

"I appreciate your honesty, Miss Klein." Mr. McKay looked at Mr. Pettibone. "Do we have any other interviews scheduled?"

"One more, this afternoon."

"Well." Mr. McKay considered me. "You passed the first test, Miss Klein, but there's more to the job than understanding a wiring diagram. How about you and I talk some more?"

"Good idea." Mr. Pettibone patted me on the back with one of his huge hands. I had to stiffen my legs to stay upright. "I'll admit, I mostly offered to interview you for your father's sake, and to see the expression on Frank's face." He chuckled again. "But you're the first one he hasn't dismissed out of hand. Good luck, Rita."

I smiled and thanked him, even though I was angry at being

treated like some kind of circus trick. What was that Samuel Johnson quote? That a woman preaching was like a dog walking on its hind legs—not done well, but surprising to see done at all. Mr. Pettibone obviously thought of me as a clever joke. I wasn't sure yet about Mr. McKay.

Chapter Four
Cornelia Vogel

The Hague, Netherlands
May 1941

Rain is gathering in the bellies of purple clouds, but it holds off until Cornelia arrives in the Koningsplein neighborhood, where the Vogels have lived for as long as she can remember. The redbrick row houses that line her street all have the same pattern of windows—two on the ground floor, three on the first, three more above that, and one in the dormer under the tiled roof. Each house has a pair of identical doors—one for the lower flat, the other for the upper—whose paint colors have been chosen from a limited palette of rust, cobalt, and hunter. The only difference between one home and the next is what can be seen through the front windows: lace curtains framing a vase of peonies, a lazy cat stretched along the sill, a glimpse of art on the walls within. Cornelia relishes these hints of personality. Once night falls, every window will be obscured by blackout fabric, rendering the street as lifeless as a graveyard.

Cornelia veers into an arched passageway between two row houses and pedals down a narrow alley that bisects the block. Behind her house, she hops off her bike and unlocks the gate into her backyard. Although the space is small, Cornelia's mother has used her green thumb to make the most of it. Wisteria covers the fence between their yard and the next. Hollyhocks stand tall alongside the garden house. The flower bed is bursting with bulbs, daffodils and hyacinths in March yielding to tulips and irises in April. It's May now, bumblebees hovering above globes of allium and finches chirping in the forsythia branches.

Cornelia's brother, Dirk, is in the garden, his mop of blond hair hanging in his eyes as he rolls the mower over their postage-stamp patch of grass. He must have just gotten home, she thinks, noticing he hasn't yet changed out of his school clothes. Dirk is twelve years old now, the innocence of childhood cut short by the war. Though she still sees traces of the sweet boy he was, these days he acts more like the headstrong adolescent he's becoming.

"Hold the door open, will you, Nellie?" Dirk runs over to the garden house, the mower's blades whirring as they turn. Cornelia has spent her whole life insisting everyone call her by her proper name—not Cora or Nels or Corien. Dirk, who couldn't pronounce her name when he started talking, is the only person in the world she lets call her Nellie.

Rain starts pouring down as Cornelia follows Dirk into the garden house. She guides her bike around the potting bench, cluttered with seedlings and soil, to park it alongside those of her mother and brother. There's a washing machine in the opposite corner, an electric model from Miele bought before all things German began to leave a bad taste in one's mouth. Cornelia reaches up to touch the laundry hanging on lines strung from the ceiling; when it's dry, it will be her chore to collect it. Along the wall, sturdy shelves hold sacks of grain and crates of produce, last year's onions and potatoes beginning to sprout. Dirk grabs two wrinkled apples, tossing one to his sister before taking a bite.

The siblings linger, munching on their apples, while the downpour wears itself out. To pass the time, Cornelia asks Dirk how it's going at school. He tells her about a boy in his class who was stupid enough to show up that morning wearing the uniform of the Nationale Jeugdstorm, the youth wing of the Dutch Nazi Party. The teacher made a point of leaving the room for some errand. In her absence, the other kids taunted the miserable boy. Dirk himself ripped off the *stormvogel* badge pinned to his hat and threw it to the floor.

"What did your teacher do when she returned?" Cornelia asks.

"Pretended not to see him crying." Dirk finishes his apple, core and all, then brushes the hair from his eyes to look up at the sky. "This rain's not stopping anytime soon. Let's make a run for it, Nellie."

As they dash across the garden, Cornelia glances up at their neighbor's flat. She's always been glad her family lives downstairs, where the Vogels enjoy not only the garden and patio, but also a cheerful sunroom where philodendrons flourish. The upstairs neighbors have no sunroom or patio, only a covered balcony off the kitchen, where Professor Blom is stretched out on a wicker lounge with a newspaper in one hand and a sandwich in the other. He keeps his eyes on his paper. Cornelia doesn't call out a greeting. This is as it should be. Like a horse fitted with blinders to block the sight of traffic, the Dutch understand that a certain level of aloofness is necessary to live in such close proximity to one another.

Though they've been under the same roof for years, Cornelia knows only the most basic facts about her upstairs neighbors. He's a history professor; his wife is American; their daughter, Leah, is a year or two older than she is; and they are Jewish. The most important fact, as far as Cornelia is concerned, is that they are nicer than the nasty widower who used to live there. He'd spend hours on the balcony, fouling the air with pipe smoke and threatening to climb down the fire ladder to thrash Cornelia and Dirk if they didn't quiet down. When the man died, Cornelia knew she ought to be sad, but she couldn't stop herself from turning cartwheels on the grass.

Cornelia and Dirk come into the narrow kitchen to find their mother tying an apron around her waist. Helena Vogel's twist of blond hair and moody green eyes give her the look of an actress playing the role of housewife. She stops them in the doorway. "Take off those wet shoes, I just swept the floors." Her children do as they're told, but while Cornelia sets her shoes on news-paper to dry, Dirk edges through the kitchen carrying his by the laces. Helena catches his sleeve. "Where are you off to, young man?"

"I'm meeting up with my friends to study, don't you remember?" He pulls away and stomps down the hallway, but before he opens the door to the vestibule he comes back and gives his mother a boyish hug. "I'll be home before the evening meal, Mama," he says, his voice soft now. "Don't worry."

"Don't tell me not to worry." She kisses the top of his head, then lets him go. "And don't antagonize any NSBers out there." Now that The Hague's police force is bloated with members of the Nationaal-Socialistische Beweging, the Dutch Nazi Party, any rebellious behavior runs the risk of arrest.

"When are we eating?" Cornelia asks. "I missed lunch today."

"I haven't started the rabbit stew yet. Why are you home so early?"

"I have a new job to do." Cornelia explains about the technical translation she'll be working on. While she talks, her stomach growls.

"Go on and get started," Helena says, measuring a spoonful of tea leaves into the pot. "I'll bring you something."

Cornelia climbs the steep staircase from the ground floor to the first, the treads so narrow only the ball of her foot finds purchase. Off the hallway, five doors lead to five rooms. The bathroom is windowless and utilitarian; Cornelia stops there first to use the toilet and wash up. Her parents' bedroom is at the back of the house, with a bay window that follows the outline of the sunroom below and the neighbor's balcony above. Of the two children's bedrooms, Dirk's is a bit bigger, but all he can see from his window is the roof of the garden house. Cornelia prefers her room, next to her father's study at the front of the house, where she enjoys a view of the street.

She drops her satchel on the bed and scans her bookcase until she finds Bruggencate and Broers's *Engels-Nederlands Woordenboek*. She places the English-Dutch dictionary beside the instruction manual on her desk, which is tucked into the triangular space under the Bloms' staircase, the clomp of their footfalls a frequent distraction as she works. The slanted ceiling is decorated with pages torn from magazines, but instead of actors and movie stars, Cornelia has chosen images of places where she can imagine conversing in all the languages she knows. Her favorites are the Cathedral of Notre-Dame in Paris and the Empire State Building in New York City. She has pictures of the Acropolis and the Colosseum, too, even though the Greek and Latin she's learned in school are far removed from the living languages spoken in Athens and Rome. She ripped down her picture of Neuschwanstein Castle the day Hitler's paratroopers descended on The Hague. Though her German is excellent, she is determined, now, never to visit the country.

Cornelia is about to begin when her mother comes in with a cup of tea and a cheese sandwich. "How goes it?" Helena asks.

"I don't know yet, I've just started."

"Well, you'll have plenty of time to work. Your father telephoned to say he won't be home until after seven." Helena shakes her head. "These deadlines he's under seem unreasonable to me. I'm afraid Generalkommissar Wimmer is driving him too hard."

"No harder than he drives himself." Cornelia takes a bite of the sandwich. The buttered bread is fresh and the cheese fragrant. "Everyone at Huize Kleykamp treats him like royalty. If anything, he may be too proud of his work."

"Your father has always been a proud man."

"That's true." Cornelia sips her tea. "The census worries me, though. What good can come of the Nazis knowing everything about the population of Holland?"

Helena tuts impatiently on her way out. "All that information is already in the population registers, Cornelia. It's not as if putting it on those punch cards will tell the Germans anything they couldn't already find out. Let your father do his job, and you do yours."

Cornelia thinks her mother is being naïve. If using the Hollerith doesn't really change anything, why are the Germans willing to provide her father with such a rare and expensive machine? The answer is right there in the introduction to the manual:

> *Management must be reliably informed with up-to-date information about material, inventory, and production in the form of lists and reports that become the basis of administrative action. Many computations must be made, checked, and summarized before data can be presented in report form. When the information is contained in punch cards, management reports can be prepared with efficiency, accuracy, and speed.*

Cornelia shudders, not only because in this case, "management" is the Nazi regime that occupies her country. That string of words— "efficiency," "accuracy," "speed"—reminds her of the Luftwaffe's blitzkrieg attack on Rotterdam. Don't overreact, she tells herself. The computer is not a weapon. Reports don't kill people. Lists aren't deadly. Cornelia rolls back her shoulders and settles to her task.

An hour later, she drops her pencil and drags her fingers through her hair in frustration. She wanted to have a few pages finished before her father came home, but the translation is not going well. It isn't that the words in the manual are obscure or complex. Many of them are common and simple. The sentences, too, are declarative, the syntax direct. The problems begin when she gets past the introductory text and into the specifics of machine parts, where some of the vocabulary is so technical there are no corresponding entries in her dictionary.

Take the word "typebar," for instance. It isn't in the dictionary, but its components are simple enough. The problem is how to combine them. Is the meaning of "type" more akin to *letter* or *schrijf*? For "bar" should she pick *reep* or *staaf*? If Cornelia were a student tasked with translating poetic turns of phrase, she'd know how to weigh the relative merits of one word over another. Translating the Hollerith manual, however, is not some esoteric assignment. Willem Nooteboom needs it so his technicians can maintain the computer. Her father is counting on it to produce the census Generalkommissar Wimmer has ordered. Her whole family depends on her father's job to keep them all safe. Cornelia imagines him looking over her shoulder at the papers scattered across her desk, his impatience palpable. *Don't worry about what the computer can do for the Germans,* she imagines him saying, *just get back to work.* She turns again to the entry for "type," but the choices still confound her. She glances with envy at the next entry down in the dictionary, "typhoid." There's one Dutch equivalent, *tyfeus.* Simple and clear. If only translation were always so easy.

But if it were that easy, Cornelia thinks, there'd be no reason to study linguistics. A language is more than a system of symbols. Languages are living things that embody the history of a nation and shape the perception of the people who speak it. The computer, on the other hand, is designed to eliminate the nuances of human language. Instead of a dictionary, there's a codebook. Rather than a detailed etymology for every word, each code represents a single fact that can be tabulated and collated, added and subtracted, sorted and listed. Cornelia realizes the language of the punch cards may be transnational and ahistorical, but the computer reflects the priorities of the people who built it. Only a society that values efficiency over poetry, she thinks, would invent a machine like the Hollerith.

Needing a break, Cornelia goes to look out her window. The rain has stopped, leaving the wet pavement shimmering in the evening light. Men in hats and jackets are returning from work, their bicycles pedaled purposefully. A young couple bikes close together, the boy's arm around the girl's shoulders. A mother rides by with her daughter sitting on the rear rack, the girl maintaining an effortless balance. Women with shopping bags hanging from their elbows hurry up the street, late already to prepare the evening meal. It's all so normal, so reassuring—so Dutch.

A bike veers from the lane and stops below Cornelia's window. It's Mevrouw Blom, her scarf flying loose and her coat flapping open in that casual American way of hers. She sets the bike on its kickstand while she fishes a key from her purse. Strapped to the rack is a box of groceries; in the basket between the handlebars, a bunch of orange gladioli.

Of course, Cornelia thinks, how did it not occur to her until now? English is Lillian Blom's native language. Since the Jewish professors were dismissed from their jobs, Philip Blom has been tutoring students at home. Cornelia hears them on the stairs, coming and going at all hours. Perhaps his wife would likewise consider taking on a pupil—if only Cornelia can figure out how to approach the woman who is practically a stranger to her.

When Cornelia sees her neighbor drop her keys on the sidewalk, she rushes downstairs and bursts out the front door. Lillian Blom is holding on to the bike for balance as she bends over. Cornelia grabs its handlebars just as it risks falling. "Allow me to help you, *mevrouw*."

Lillian stands up, keys in hand. "*Dank je wel*." Her accent delights Cornelia, the way *dank* sounds more like the English "lank" than "honk."

"Perhaps I could carry your groceries upstairs for you?"

The woman blinks slowly, as if translating Cornelia's offer. "That would be helpful, yes. If you take the box, I'll manage the bike."

Toting the groceries, Cornelia edges past the two bikes already jammed in the Bloms' vestibule. The flight of stairs turns sharply at the top and soon Cornelia is above her own desk, her feet making the sounds she knows so well. She carries the box into the kitchen and sets it by the sink. It's exactly the same as the kitchen downstairs, except for the disarray. Crumbs are scattered across the counter, unwashed dishes soak in the sink, and a dirty pot sits on the stove. She wonders if this careless housekeeping is an American trait or a Jewish one. Such untidiness certainly isn't Dutch.

Looking out to the balcony, Cornelia sees Professor Blom is still there, the open newspaper resting on his knees. When he doesn't respond to her greeting, she notices that his eyes are closed. She also notices a stain on his shirt and a bit of bread crust lodged in his mustache. Embarrassed, Cornelia steps out of the kitchen. In the living room, a bright splash of red above the mantel catches her attention. She can't stop herself from getting a better look. It's a painting of red poppies in a white vase, some in full crimson bloom, others drooping pink buds. Cornelia comes closer. The blue background is painted in thick strokes, slashes of violet and lavender mixed with indigo. Stepping back, Cornelia is amazed that such haphazard dashes of color can coalesce into such beauty.

"Do you like it?"

Cornelia jumps at the sound of Lillian Blom's voice. "Pardon me, *mevrouw,* I didn't mean to intrude."

"Don't be silly," Lillian says. "You Dutch are always so worried about giving offense. I suppose it's easier to say nothing than the wrong thing, but it makes people here so unfriendly."

Cornelia has never thought of it this way. Allowing their neighbors privacy has always seemed to her a virtue, but what if their averted eyes and brusque greetings struck a foreigner as cold? "I'm sorry, *mevrouw.*"

"Oh, it's nothing to do with you. Philip explained how it is here." She faces the painting. "So what do you think?"

Cornelia wants to say *hypnotisch* but decides to try an English word instead. "It's mesmerizing."

Lillian Blom breaks into a smile. "Mesmerizing, exactly. I didn't know you spoke English, Cornelia. Tell me, do you know it well enough to speak it with me?"

"*Ja, natuurlijk.*" Cornelia switches to English. "It would be a pleasure to speak English with you, Mrs. Blom."

"That's music to my ears. And please, call me Lillian." They both turn back to the painting. "Do you recognize it?"

Cornelia has never seen this image before, and though the painting is not signed, the swirling blue background is familiar. "It reminds me of Vincent van Gogh."

"You have a good eye. It's not in every catalog, but I can tell you for certain it's authentic." She touches a crest of paint on the canvas. "It's the most valuable thing we have, better than a bank account. My father bought it for me as a birthday present at the 1913 Armory Show in New York City."

"Is that where you grew up?"

Lillian nods. "My parents have an apartment in the Dakota. That's in Manhattan. As a girl, I had all of Central Park for my front yard. If I hadn't met Philip, I'd be there now." A troubled expression passes over her face, but she forces a smile as she faces Cornelia. "We don't really know anything about each other, do we? Perhaps you'll have a cup of tea and visit with me awhile."

"Yes, thank you very much." Cornelia follows her into the kitchen, pleased that their interaction is going so well.

Lillian lifts the kettle from the stove, then catches sight of the orange flowers, which she's left lying on the counter beside the box of groceries. The smile drops from her face. "I really shouldn't have bought those. Philip says we need to be careful with every guilder, but it gets so bleak here lately. I wanted a little color in the house." Tears suddenly run down her cheeks. The kettle clatters into the sink as Lillian covers her face with her hands. "I don't know why I keep trying, Cornelia. No matter what I do, it doesn't change the situation. Next week, next month, next year—no one knows when the blow will come, but you can be damned sure it's coming. We dragged our feet and missed our chance. Now we're stuck with nowhere to go."

"What's happening?" Professor Blom has come in from the balcony. Lillian throws herself into her husband's arms, her shoulders heaving.

Cornelia is mortified. "I don't know, *meneer,* we were talking . . ."

He glares at her as if accusing her of causing his wife's hysterics. "Who are you, anyway?"

"That's our downstairs neighbor, Cornelia. Or are you called Nellie?"

Cornelia whirls around to see who has spoken. A young man stands behind her, illuminated by the afternoon light coming in from the balcony as if he's stepped out of a Vermeer painting. He's wearing an artist's smock over trousers so loose they might be pajamas. His face is remarkably smooth, with a smudge of what Cornelia thinks must be drawing charcoal on his cheek. His dark hair, long for a boy, is tucked behind one ear. His eyebrows and lashes are black as ink against his olive skin. Cornelia catches her breath. She's never seen a young man so handsome. No, she corrects herself—so beautiful.

Cornelia blinks. Her vision adjusts. It isn't a young man at all, but a woman dressed like a boy. At that moment, she realizes who it must be. Leah, she says to herself, her mouth shaping the name on a silent breath. Leah Blom.

"So, are you?"

It's as though Cornelia's watching a film that has skipped a frame. "Am I what?"

"Called Nellie?"

She's about to answer as she always does—no, I'm not, I prefer Cornelia—but Leah is smiling as if the name tastes sweet on her tongue. Suddenly, Cornelia doesn't care about being serious and grown-up. All she cares about is Leah's smile. "Nellie, sure, you can call me that."

"Okay, then." Leah steps past Cornelia to place her hand on her mother's back. "You should rest now, Mommy."

"Yes, Lillian." Professor Blom's voice is tired but patient. "Let's go upstairs and find you some aspirin."

Cornelia steps back apologetically as they brush past her. Leah watches her parents disappear upstairs, then turns, her brown eyes looking directly into Cornelia's green ones. "So, what are you doing here, Nellie?"

"I saw your mother outside. She was struggling with her bike and I thought—" With Leah staring at her like this, Cornelia forgets all about her idea of asking for help with the translation. "I thought I'd lend a hand."

"Got more than you bargained for, didn't you? Here, let me

make it up to you." Leah retrieves the dropped kettle, fills it, and sets it on the stove. Striking a match to light the gas, she says, "Did I hear you speaking English?"

"Yes, was that wrong? Is that what upset your mother?"

"Oh, no, this isn't your fault." Leah shakes the tin of tea leaves, which sounds woefully empty, and dumps what's left into the pot. "She's been like this off and on since the start of the war. The attack on the synagogue last week made it worse."

Cornelia heard about it, of course—another provocation by the NSB, arson in honor of Hitler's birthday. "Is that where you worship?"

"My parents do." Leah leans back against the counter. "I'm not religious myself, but that makes no difference anymore. As far as the Germans are concerned, it's our blood that makes us Jewish, not our faith."

"Your blood?" Cornelia is reminded of something she learned during a history lesson on the Crusades. "But isn't that a medieval superstition?"

"Not blood libel—though they've revived that, too. I mean blood as in race. The Nazis have made a science of it, based on an American theory called eugenics. There's actually a course taught on it at Columbia University. That's in New York." The kettle whistles, steam sputtering from its spout. While the tea steeps, Leah puts away the groceries, then prepares a tray with cups, saucers, a sugar bowl, and two tiny spoons. "Let's sit out on the balcony. Grab that box of biscuits, will you?"

Leah sets the tea tray down on a stool beside the lounge, sweeping aside her father's newspaper to stretch out on it herself. Cornelia sits on a wicker chair. Looking down at her garden, she's taken aback by the perfect view the Bloms have from their balcony. When the Vogels are outside, they're able to maintain the illusion of privacy by not looking up, but for the Bloms, there's no pretending they have the house to themselves. Cornelia can even see through the window into the garden house, where she guiltily glimpses her mother taking dry laundry off the lines.

"The first time I ever saw you was right down there." Leah pours the tea and hands Cornelia a cup.

"Really?" Cornelia has no memory of their initial meeting.

"It was when we came to see the house. That old man left it in such a mess, Mommy wanted to leave before we even looked around. Then we came out here and there you were, turning cartwheels on the grass. I thought it must be a good place to live, if such a pretty girl could be so happy here."

Cornelia blushes as she imagines how childish her cartwheels must have looked. Then she thinks of Leah calling her pretty and blushes more deeply.

"Do you take sugar?"

"Yes, please." Cornelia reaches into the bowl Leah holds out and extracts a square of brown sugar.

"I used to ask Mommy why you never invited me downstairs. She always made some excuse. After a while, I gave up asking."

Cornelia's impulse is to try to explain it all away, but there's no denying that her family has merely tolerated the Bloms. When they bought the flat upstairs, Cornelia overheard her parents complaining about Jews encroaching on Koningsplein instead of staying in their own neighborhood by the synagogue on the Voldersgracht. Her father and Professor Blom occasionally confer about some repair to the property that needs to be done, but their mothers hardly ever interact. Like most Dutch families, the Vogels have few close friends of different faiths. Helena chats pleasantly enough with the Protestant baker who supplies her daily loaf of bread and the Catholic florist whose blossoms fill the vases in her home, and Gerard listens to the political debates tradesmen carry over from their union meetings when he stops by the local pub for a pilsner after work, but the families they visit, the schools they attend, and the groups they belong to are all rooted in the Calvinist church—just as the Protestants and the Catholics and the trade unionists have their own groups. Their separate social, political, and cultural spheres form the pillars on which Dutch society depends for its peace and prosperity. Every schoolchild learns that Jews have lived in Holland since the sixteenth century, but because they don't belong to any of the pillars, many Netherlanders don't consider them truly Dutch.

Cornelia dips her head in shame. "I'm sorry we haven't been better neighbors."

Leah shrugs. "I know how it goes. It might have been different if we went to school together, but I started attending the Nederlandsch Lyceum soon after we moved in. You went to Gymnasium Haganum, didn't you?" Cornelia nods. "It is strange, though, that we've hardly ever met in all these years. I almost didn't recognize you."

"I didn't recognize you at first, either," Cornelia says, thinking of how she mistook Leah for a boy. Leah's got one knee pulled up, exposing her ankle. The sleeve of her artist's smock falls back to her elbow as she lifts her teacup to her mouth, revealing a gold bangle around her slender wrist. She wears a ring, too, a bulky signet that emphasizes the delicacy of her fingers. A lock of Leah's hair has escaped from behind her ear to fall prettily across her cheek. Cornelia can't believe she ever thought the stylish bob was a man's haircut.

"Well, we're in the same boat now, aren't we, Nellie?" Cornelia isn't sure what boat they share until Leah explains that her college, Technische Hogeschool Delft, was also closed by the Germans. "At Leiden it was lofty speeches and protests, but in Delft some of the faculty were actively recruiting students into the Resistance. One of my teachers had to go into hiding to avoid arrest."

Cornelia thinks of Professor Cleveringa in Buchenwald and shudders. Below, Helena comes out of the garden house and crosses the lawn, a basket of folded clothes in her arms. She looks up and stops in her tracks, surprised to see her daughter on their neighbor's balcony. Cornelia pats the air with her hand as if to say: Go on, I'll explain later.

Leah drains her cup and sets it down, then swings her legs over so that she's sitting on the edge of the lounge, facing Cornelia. "Tell me, Nellie, why are you really here?"

The question catches Cornelia off guard. She's almost forgotten she had an ulterior motive for assisting Lillian Blom with her groceries. "Well, to be honest, I was hoping your mother would help me with something, but I realize now I shouldn't impose on her."

"Help with what?"

"A translation. You see, my father got me a job at the Ministry of Information, punching cards for the Hollerith computer."

"What do you mean, punching cards?" Leah curls her hands into fists and pantomimes fighting. "Like a boxer?"

Cornelia laughs at the joke. While Leah munches on a biscuit, she explains all about her training. "It turns out I'm a really terrible punch-card operator, so instead, I'm translating the instruction manual for the Hollerith alphabetizer from English into Dutch. I'm having trouble with some of the vocabulary and I thought, because your mother is American, she might be able to help me." Cornelia pauses. It's against every social convention to ask a personal question, but she can't help herself. "What did she mean when she said you missed your chance?"

Leah sighs, resting her chin on folded hands. "My grandparents have been begging us to move to New York ever since Hitler came to power, but Daddy kept assuring them Holland would stay neutral, like in the last war. Once the Germans invaded, it was too late. We were stuck here. If Mommy still had her American passport, she might have gotten permission to book passage, but she had to give up her nationality when she married my father. Besides, she'd never leave the two of us behind. Now it's a waiting game."

"Waiting for what?"

"To see what the Nazis have planned for us Jews." Leah sighs again. "Let's change the subject. About your translation—"

"Oh, never mind about that now."

"I'll do it," Leah says. It isn't an offer or even a question but a statement of fact. "My English is perfect, and my training as a technical illustrator might help, too."

"Are you sure?"

Leah nods decisively. "I can't afford to do it as a favor, though. You'd have to pay me, like my father's students pay him."

"Yes, of course. You'd be my tutor."

"All right then." Leah picks up the tea tray. "I should go see how my mother is doing."

Cornelia brushes crumbs from her lap and stands. "When shall I come back?"

"How about tonight, after the evening meal? I'll organize things in my room so we have a place to work."

Leah drops the tea tray off in the kitchen, then leads Cornelia downstairs. The vestibule is barely passable, crammed now with three bicycles. In the space left clear to allow for the swing of the front door, Leah draws Cornelia close to kiss her cheek.

"There, we're friends now, aren't we?"

Cornelia is embarrassed to feel her face get warm where Leah's lips have touched her. "Friends, yes. How much should I—?"

"Oh, whatever you think is fair. See you later, Nellie. And remember, when you come back, no more speaking Dutch! If I'm going to be your tutor, I'll make sure you practice your English, *goed*?"

"*Ja, goed.*" Cornelia decides to start now with a saying she heard in an American film. "See you later, alligator."

Leah tosses her head back and laughs. Cornelia thinks the line of her throat is the loveliest thing she's ever seen. "After a while, crocodile."

Outside, Cornelia stands for a moment on their shared stoop. Though it's only a matter of inches between Leah's front door and her own, she can't shake the feeling she's returning from a journey to a foreign land.

Chapter Five
Rita Klein

New York City
June 1960

The cha-chunk cha-chunk and rat-a-tat-tat of business machines filled my ears as I followed Mr. McKay into an open work space large as a lecture hall. Looking around, I counted five different computer installations. The newest was the one I'd used at the Watson course, the IBM 602. "We were lucky to get hold of this machine," Mr. McKay said, fondly patting the squat box as we walked past it. "It's only from 1948, so not really antiquated, but these were never reliable in the field. IBM's been selling them off since they replaced their old 602s with an improved model. She's temperamental, but I've managed to tame her."

Beyond the 602, the machines became progressively older in what looked like a timeline of computing technology. The oldest really was an antique, with curved legs and black-enameled cover plates.

"Is that a Hollerith?" I asked. At the Watson Laboratory, we'd learned all about how Herman Hollerith's tabulating machine company, which got its start processing the 1890 census, eventually became part of Thomas Watson's IBM.

"Yes, an alphabetizer from the 1930s. You continue to surprise me, Miss Klein."

Looking around the office, I saw a couple dozen women but

no other men. The prevalence of females reminded me of being at Barnard and I began to feel more at ease. Some typed up paperwork or rifled through filing cabinets. Others stood at the various machines, inputting punch cards or monitoring sorters or tearing printed reports from typebars. Most were seated in front of electronic key punchers, coding information onto cards for the computers to process. I was pleased to see that Anti-quated Business Machines embraced integration throughout the company—in fact, more of the women were Black than white.

At the back of the room, a number of large chalkboards on wooden stands created an alcove that served, apparently, as Mr. McKay's office. I took the seat beside his desk while he tilted his banker's chair so far back I was afraid he'd fall.

"My apologies for my partner's sense of humor, Miss Klein. As you see, we've got nothing against hiring women, and we don't usu-ally ask for experience. As long as a girl's got a quick mind and an aptitude for logic, I actually prefer to train her myself, but for this particular job we've got to move quickly. I assumed anyone who was already familiar with control panel programming for the 602 would be a man. Now, why don't you tell me more about that summer course? I've heard great things about the Watson Laboratory."

I felt more comfortable here than I had in Mr. Pettibone's plush office. Planting my feet firmly on the floor, I explained that the course was designed to introduce computing machines to non-specialists. Mr. Hankam's lessons emphasized how computers could be programmed to solve real-world problems. I recalled a time at the Watson course when he was up at the chalkboard, explaining a program he'd created for an astronomy professor at Columbia. I felt like I was seeing beyond the stars in the sky to the calculations that governed their movement.

Access to the IBM machines was the whole point of the labo-ratory, and we all got to practice what we were learning. I told

Mr. McKay how thrilled I was when a program I'd diagrammed and wired for the 602 worked on the first run. Some of the men in my class were itching to get their hands on the massive 650 magnetic processing machine, which looked like something out of an *Outer Space* comic book, but Mr. Hankam insisted we master the basics of control panel programming before letting anyone attempt to code in FORTRAN.

"So you've been in the same room as the 650?" Mr. McKay crossed his legs, tipping his chair even farther back. "I'd love to work with that machine, but we could never afford it here. The console unit alone leases for three thousand a month. Tell me, did you ever get to try your hand at FORTRAN?"

"I wrote one short program toward the end of the Watson course," I said, "but it was back to control panel programming for the class I took at Columbia." I'd walked into Schermerhorn Hall that September feeling confident and well prepared, but the professor was more focused on machine engineering than computing applications. I was the only girl in that class, too, and the guys left me out of their late-night study groups. When they found out I could diagram control panels, though, they were eager to get me to do their grunt work. As far as they were concerned, building computers took a man's brain; programming them required the tedious attention to detail they figured women were good at.

"Control panel programming is exactly what this job calls for," Mr. McKay said. "I'm looking for someone who can understand the accounting specifications of a government contract, then program the IBM 602 to produce the required reports. Do you think you can do that?"

I understood the basics of accounting from helping Dad balance his books, and my math skills were exceptional. A government contract sounded intimidating, though. "I'm not sure. I suppose it depends on the contract."

"I find your lack of bluster refreshing, Miss Klein. How about I give you some background on the job we're looking to fill?" Mr. McKay pulled open his desk drawer and extracted a pack of cigarettes. He lit one for himself, then, as an afterthought, tilted the pack toward me. I shook my head, knowing it wasn't a good look for a young lady. "Olympia Metal is a Brooklyn manufacturer of steel and aluminum cookware. They've been a family business since the Civil War and they're one of our oldest clients. Mr. Plunkett, the father of the current owners, had the vision to start using punch cards to control inventory during the Depression, but they've never modernized since. The older son, Joseph, had plans to bring their computer system up-to-date, but when he was killed in a car accident, his share of the company went to his widow, Francie. The other half is owned by the younger brother, James. Those two can't agree on anything, so nothing's changed. We still run their reports on the Hollerith alphabetizer."

"But I don't know anything about that old machine," I objected.

"You don't have to. You see, Olympia recently won a navy contract to supply galley trays and cutlery for the USS *Constellation*. You've heard of it, haven't you?"

"Sure." It was in all the papers when the Brooklyn Navy Yard was picked to build the new aircraft carrier. I hadn't given much thought, before, to all the supplies a ship that size would need.

"The Hollerith can't do multiple sorts in a single operation, let alone perform functions like crossfooting. For this job, we're going to have to use the 602, which is why I showed you that diagram. Are you following me?"

"So far."

"We need someone who can design programs for the 602 using Olympia's existing codes for inventory and supplies and costs, as well as create new codes to track the items being manufactured for the contract. Like I said, I don't mind training someone who's smart and willing to learn, but there's not enough time to start from scratch. *Constellation* is set to launch in October. I need a programmer who can hit the ground running and keep up the pace for the rest of summer. Is that something you'd be interested in, Miss Klein?"

A wave of exhaustion suddenly washed over me. "I'm not sure what to tell you, Mr. McKay."

"Tell him it's lunchtime and you're hungry." Gladys, the receptionist, was standing behind my chair in all her purple glory. "Most of the girls bring sandwiches from home that they eat in the break room, if you'd like to join us, Miss Klein."

"Thank you, but I didn't bring anything."

"Well, there's a Chock Full o' Nuts nearby, if you don't mind fighting your way up to the counter."

"Let me treat you." Mr. McKay righted his chair, got out his wallet, and handed me a dollar. "Take your time, and when you come back—if you decide to come back, I should say—I'll have you read over the contract so we can have a more informed discussion."

With that, Mr. McKay took out a packed lunch in a brown paper bag. His parsimony surprised me; Mr. Pettibone certainly struck me as a three-martini man.

As I walked with Gladys toward the reception area, I asked where I could find the ladies' room.

"It's through there," she said, pointing. "I hope you do come back and try for the job, Miss Klein. Mr. Pettibone budgeted the salary on the assumption they'd be hiring a man. It would set a good precedent around here for a woman to earn a hundred dollars a week."

I sat in the bathroom stall for a while, gathering my thoughts. The job sounded out of my league, but I was a quick learner.

At least, I used to be. I hoped pregnancy hadn't permanently muddled my brain. In the restroom mirror, I tried not to see the stupid girl who'd made the worst mistake of her life, but an educated woman who was qualified for an important job. Why, then, did my reflection stare back at me with the frightened eyes of an imposter?

Down in the lobby, I realized I didn't have the appetite for lunch. Instead, I rode up the escalator and used Mr. McKay's dollar to buy myself a ticket for the observation deck. I was supposed to be looking toward the future, not dwelling on the past. What better place to decide my next step, I thought, than on top of the Eighth Wonder of the World?

My ears popped as the elevator rocketed up eighty-six stories in only one minute. The day had gotten warm, but there was a nice breeze up here and the view was perfect. The Williamsburg and Queensboro bridges bracketed the East River like parentheses around a watery clause. The long rectangle of Central Park was a green Sarouk carpeting the blocks north of Columbus Circle. To the west, the glass roof over Penn Station reflected what light it could from its sooty panes. Looking south, I caught the amber glint of Lady Liberty's torch in the distance. Out in New York Bay, an ocean liner bisected the crisscrossed wakes of ferries and barges. What shore was it steaming toward? I wondered.

It boggled my mind to think how much had changed since I'd come up here last October with my roommate from Barnard. Victoria Clarke was a wealthy debutant from Pittsburgh with a passion for art, while I was a scholarship case majoring in mathematics, but we both loved exploring the city. That day, we'd ditched our books to check out the spiraling galleries of the new Guggenheim Museum. Afterward, she suggested we watch the sunset from the observation deck. We stayed until dark, stars rising above the skyline like embers from a fire.

I had no idea, that night, I was already pregnant. Vicki was the only girl at Barnard I told after Dr. Nelson dropped the bomb on me. She couldn't have been nicer or more sympathetic, but as we talked, the gap between her future and mine got wider by the minute. She was cramming for finals, picking out spring semester classes, making plans for after graduation—living the life I thought I'd have. Now, because of one mistake, my name would be omitted from the 1960 edition of *The Mortarboard* as if I'd never gone to Barnard at all. Vicki wrote to me a few times after I left school, cards and letters that my parents forwarded to the unwed mothers' home. I remembered, now, leaving those letters in the drawer of my nightstand when I went to the hospital. The house matron must have thrown them away. I thought of Vicki's kind words in the trash and wished I could get them back.

I wished I could get a lot of things back. But I couldn't go back to Barnard. I couldn't go back in time to my date with Leonard. I couldn't go back to Macy's and put that tight skirt back on the rack. All I could do now was go forward.

I'd been thinking of the summer course at the Watson Laboratory as the beginning of my downfall, but maybe it could be the foundation for building myself back up again. If I got the job at Antiquated Business Machines, I'd earn enough by September to cover my tuition. At Fairleigh Dickinson, though, there were no courses in computing machines. I might as well switch to education, I thought, gazing out over the city. Children needed good math teachers, especially the girls. Thanks to the teacher's union, New York City schools offered great benefits and a pension. I'd be set for life.

I stepped up to one of the binoculars, dug a quarter out of my pocketbook, and dropped it in. Settling my forehead against the eyepiece, I saw my life unfolding before me as clearly as the view.

A year from now, I could be renting a studio apartment in Manhattan, teaching in a nearby public school, going to museums and movies on the weekends. Liking what I saw, I pushed the vision further, trying to picture myself two, five, ten, fifteen years from now. Instead, the images that hijacked my mind were of my son at each of those ages.

I saw David as a toddler, walking unsteadily with outstretched arms. I saw him reluctant to go to kindergarten, clinging to his mother's skirt. I saw him at ten years old, hair in a crew cut and knees scraped from playing baseball at the park. I saw him on a high school trip to the Empire State Building, eagerly looking through this same pair of binoculars.

But what if David never came here? His new parents could live someplace far away, like Albuquerque or Seattle. I might wander the earth for the rest of my life and never cross his path. Even worse was the thought that, one day in the future, I might walk right past a gangly teenager never knowing he was my son.

A physical pain doubled me over. Why hadn't I grabbed my baby out of the bassinet and made a run for it? Probably because I had no idea what step I'd have taken after bursting through the hospital doors. With an infant in tow, I'd have had nowhere to go and no way to make a living. What kind of life would that be for my son? Instead of a bastard born to an unwed mother, David would grow up the cherished child of a doctor and a nurse. He'd have a perfect life with perfect parents. Who was I to deny him that?

All I'd asked for was a little more time. Why couldn't Miss Murphy have left David in my arms long enough for me to tell my baby that I loved him? He never heard me say those words. What if he spent his whole perfect life never knowing he was loved by his mother?

"Do you need another quarter, miss?"

It was only when I heard the man's voice that I realized the binoculars I was hanging on to like a life raft had run through their time long ago.

"No, thank you." I stepped back, wiping tears from my cheeks. I expected the man to walk away, but he stayed put, considering me. He was older than I was—around thirty, I guessed—though skinny as a boy after a growth spurt. His dark hair swooped dramatically from a side part. His hazel eyes were small for his face, which was all sharp cheekbones and angled chin, but they rested on me attentively. I wondered if he thought he was intervening in a suicide, but he needn't have worried. Upset as I was, I was no Evelyn McHale.

"Perhaps you were lost in thought? That often happens to me up here. I look out at the view and before I know it"—he snapped his fingers—"an hour has gone by and it's time for another tour."

I couldn't place his accent, though it reminded me, oddly, of Greta Garbo. "How many tours have you taken?"

He laughed, his Adam's apple sticking out like a swallowed almond. "No, I give tours." He lowered his chin and held out his hand. "Jacob Nassy."

The way Jacob folded his fingers around mine made me realize how cold my own hands had become. I held on a little longer than was strictly polite for the warmth. "Rita Klein."

"Little Rita," he said, dropping my hand.

I was confused. Was he teasing me or being overly familiar? Then I realized. "Oh, because *klein* means 'little' in German. Is that where you're from?"

"No." He smiled, as if enjoying a game. "Guess again."

Aunt Ida had called me *kleyn bubbeleh sheyne* often enough for me to know my last name meant "little" in Yiddish, too, but that wasn't a country. I tried the nearest thing. "Israel?"

"Alas, no, I have never been home to Zion." He kept looking at me with that same half-smile.

I thought again of Greta Garbo. "Sweden?"

He shook his head. "No, but that is closer." He raised an eye-brow to offer me another guess, but I was getting annoyed with this game. How had it even started? He seemed to sense my impatience. "I grew up in Rotterdam, in Holland."

"So *klein* means 'little' in Dutch, too, the same as German?"

He nodded. "Dutch has many words in common with German, as with English, also."

The sharp edge of my grief was softening the longer we talked. "What are some English words that are similar to Dutch?"

Jacob tilted his head. "Water. Warm. Sun. Summer." He pronounced the words with a strong Dutch accent: *vah-ter, vahrm, zone, zoh-mer.*

"Are you being serious?" I asked.

"Indeed. Some of the spellings are slightly different, but at heart they are the same. And many of the places here in the city have Dutch names, from the time when New York was still New Amsterdam."

Every schoolkid in the region learned about Peter Minuit's purchase of Manhattan from the Lenape for a handful of glass beads. The name Stuyvesant persisted, too, but I was curious what other places harkened back to the days of the Dutch West India Company. I was about to ask Jacob to tell me more when he checked his watch. "Pardon me, but my next tour is starting in a few moments. Am I to understand that you speak German, Rita?"

"I can muddle through a Rilke poem, but I only started studying it in college. French has been my language since high school."

"Well then, you are lucky. I give my tours in German, French, Dutch, or English, depending on what language the tourists ask for. Would you like to join the group?"

"I didn't buy a tour ticket." The idea was tempting, though. At least it would be a distraction.

"A ticket doesn't matter to me. I work for the tips, but for friends my tours are free." When I hesitated, he added, "Do you know what souvenir the Queen Mother brought back to Britain for her grandchildren when she visited the Empire State Building?"

I couldn't help but smile. "No, I don't."

"You must join my tour and then you will learn." He began walking toward the gift shop. I fell into step beside him. "There will be an examination at the end," he said, winking, "so pay attention."

The group waiting for him included a family from Bavaria, a couple of businessmen from Geneva, and some United Nations delegates from Haiti. Between my minimal German and bookish French, I managed to follow along as Jacob Nassy led the group around the deck, describing the sights and filling them in on the history of the building. He tossed out numbers like crumbs for pigeons—that the Empire State Building had been erected in less than fourteen months, that it had seventy-three elevators, that the twenty-two-story transmission tower beamed out all seven television stations. These didn't stick with me the way his stories did, though. He became so dramatic describing the foggy day in 1945 when a B-25 bomber plane crashed into the building's seventy-ninth floor I felt like I was watching a newsreel. I hadn't known the gleaming spire King Kong clung to was originally intended as a mooring dock for zeppelins. When he finally answered the trivia question about the Queen Mother's souvenirs, I made sure to note it.

Members of the group pressed folded dollar bills into Jacob's hand as they thanked him at the conclusion of the tour. When everyone else had wandered off, I said, "Pennant pencils. The Queen Mother got one for each of her grandchildren."

"Excellent! You were able to understand me, then?"

"The French more than the German. Thanks for inviting me, Jacob. It was fun. I didn't expect to have fun today."

"I never expect to have fun. When it happens, it's always a surprise. Today was a surprise for me, also. It was a pleasure to meet you, Little Rita."

"You, too, Jacob. Goodbye."

I'd given his hand a proper shake, but he still held on to mine. "But I don't want to say goodbye. I want to see you again. Tell me, Rita, for how long are you visiting the city?"

"Oh, I'm not a tourist. I'm interviewing for a job in the building."

His face lit up. "You work here?"

"Like I said, it's just an interview. I haven't gotten the job yet."

"In that case, I propose we leave our next meeting to fate. If you get the job, you'll come back to see me. Promise?"

Jacob Nassy seemed like a nice guy, I thought. The kind of nice guy who never would have flirted with a young mother holding a baby in her arms. "Maybe," I said, yanking back my hand. "I've got to go."

I fled toward the exit, suddenly desperate to get out of the clouds and down to earth. As the elevator plummeted toward the lobby, I thought about fate. For months now, mine had rested in other people's hands. Getting pregnant, leaving Barnard, going to the Hudson Home—I hadn't chosen any of it. Even this interview wasn't my idea. But if I was going to take back the reins of my destiny, pursuing the job at Antiquated seemed like a logical first step. I returned to the office, determined to try my best.

"I'm glad you came back, Miss Klein," Gladys said, her mauve lips lifting into a smile. "Mr. McKay appreciates gumption."

I was sitting at one of the office workers' desks, reading over Olympia's navy contract, when the other applicant came in for his afternoon interview. I guess he'd understood the wiring diagram because there he was, a white man with blond hair in a cheap blue suit sitting across from Mr. McKay. He exuded more confidence than I ever could, bragging loudly that he'd learned everything there was to know about the IBM 602 at his last job, for an insurance company. In that open office, I couldn't help overhearing. Glancing over, I saw him light a cigarette for himself without offering one to Mr. McKay in turn. Looking closer, I noticed his shoes were scuffed and unpolished, the laces frayed. I wondered how long he'd been out of work.

The whole time Mr. McKay was telling him about the Olympia contract, the guy kept looking over his shoulder. "Shouldn't Mr. Pettibone be explaining all this?" he finally asked. "I mean, I'm sure you know a lot about servicing the machine, Frank, but I assumed I'd be interviewed by my superior."

There was a hiss like a punctured tire as every woman in the office sucked in a breath and held it.

"You're absolutely right." Mr. McKay stood up so fast the insurance guy was forced to crane his neck up at him. "Unfortunately, Mr. Pettibone has gone out on a sales call for the rest of the afternoon. Gladys?"

"Yes, Mr. McKay?" She appeared instantly at his side, her purple outfit enhancing her regal bearing.

"Please show this gentleman out." He strode across the work space into Mr. Pettibone's office, slamming the door behind him. Everyone exhaled in a whoosh. The insurance guy scrambled to catch up with Gladys, whose violet pumps clicked swiftly across the floor.

I wasn't sure if his failure would result in my success, but I turned my attention back to the navy contract with renewed determination. I soon saw for myself what Mr. McKay had already suggested. If Olympia's existing inventory system was anything like what Dad used in his store, it would never keep up with what the navy demanded. For one thing, the reports for this contract had to track every coil of steel back to the supplier, with the weight of Olympia's finished products compared to the weight of the raw material to document the amount of waste. The navy wanted everything cross-checked and collated before they'd approve an invoice for payment, and there were provisions in the contract for penalties if the items didn't pass quality control, or were delivered late, or failed to meet specifications.

After my first read-through, I realized doing this job would require more than programming control panels. I didn't know anything about metal manufacturing, but I knew what data needed to go into the computer. For the 602 to process information at this level of detail, some of the reporting requirements would have to be integrated into the manufacturing process itself—which is what I told Mr. McKay an hour later, when he called me over to his desk.

"And how would you do that, Miss Klein?"

"I have no idea." I expected my stupidity to frustrate him. Instead, he smiled.

"Of course you don't. How could you? But you're on the right track with your way of thinking. How about we spend the next few days familiarizing you with Olympia's current accounting systems and computer codes."

"Does this mean I'm hired?"

"Like I said, I prefer to train someone myself, and you've got a solid foundation to build on." He tilted his chair as far back as it could go. "How about we call this week a trial period? I'll pay you an hourly wage while you're learning. If you catch on fast enough, I'll send you to the factory in Brooklyn on Friday to meet the Plunketts. If they approve, I'll have Gladys put you on salary starting next Monday."

"Really?"

He nodded. "James Plunkett is focused on sales—he's the one who went after the navy contract. His sister-in-law, Francie, deals with inventory and accounting. It'll be important for you to see firsthand the entire manufacturing process, from the raw materials to the finished product. We have a lot to do before I send you to Brooklyn, though. I'll expect you back here at nine o'clock tomorrow morning, Miss Klein."

My parents were thrilled to hear how well I'd done at the interview. At dinner that night, they bragged about it to all the family friends who stopped by our table at China Lane to welcome me home. Everyone repeated the same story—selfless Rita sacrificing her scholarship to care for her sick aunt Ida—until I started to feel like Dorothy at the end of *The Wizard of Oz* movie. Even though she knows her journey down the yellow brick road was real, everyone back in Kansas conspires to convince her it never happened, that it was all the fault of a bump on her head. I went to bed that night wondering how long it took until Dorothy believed them.

Chapter Six
Cornelia Vogel

The Hague, Netherlands
September 1941

A waft of subterranean air tickles Cornelia's nostrils as she pulls open the bank vault door to the Hollerith bunker. Her sneeze echoes eerily down the concrete ramp. She descends as reluctantly as Persephone into the underworld, dismayed all over again that this is the job she's ended up with. When she presented Willem Nooteboom with the completed instruction manual back in May, Cornelia hoped her English skills would lead to other translation assignments. Instead, Willem requested Cornelia be assigned to work with the Hollerith alphabetizer. Gerard Vogel, eager to settle his daughter in a job he thought she'd stick with, agreed without so much as asking her.

With a sigh, Cornelia enters the claustrophobic room that houses the alphabetizer. Incandescent lights cast a harsh glare on the various machines of the Hollerith installation, each of which is familiar to her now. There's the sorter, with its row of slanted pockets like the stretched pleats of an accordion. There's the collator, the summary punch, and the statistical machine, squat black boxes similar as triplets. A punch machine sits by itself on a small desk for when a damaged card needs to be duplicated. Off to the side, wired control panels are stacked on a rack like cafeteria trays piled with spaghetti. In the center of the installation is the alphabetizing tabulator. Assembled, it's the size of a steamer trunk, its legs splayed as if struggling under its own weight while its tray juts forward like a pugnacious jaw. Atop the contraption is the typebar that rattles off names and numbers at the rate of one hundred lines per minute. Behind the Hollerith's cover plates are the bundles of wire connecting hundreds of sockets that enable the machine to process the millions of bits of data fed into it by the punch cards. Whenever Cornelia sees the alphabetizer with its cover plates open, she can't help but think of Rembrandt's depiction of an anatomy lesson, the corpse's skin peeled back to reveal the nerves and muscles beneath the surface.

Cornelia spies Willem Nooteboom crouched behind the machine, sliding a control panel into place. His face is pale from having spent so much time in the Hollerith bunker. If there's anyone at the Ministry of Information working harder than her father, Cornelia figures it's him.

"Good morning, Willem, how goes it with you?" She folds her coat over the back of a chair, setting her hat and satchel on the seat.

His body rises joint by joint like a crane over a construction site. "Ah, Cornelia, there you are. I've been waiting."

She hands him the thermos of coffee she filled in Huize Kleykamp's cafeteria. He unscrews the lid, savoring the steam rising from it. She checks her watch to confirm that she's not late. In fact, she's a little early. Does he sleep here? she wonders.

"I'm going to be very busy today, Cornelia. You'll have to manage this order on your own." He gulps coffee as he points to a cart holding a dozen boxes of punch cards, each labeled with the same batch number. "It's a somewhat complicated series of steps, but you've done each of them before. As long as you follow the processing order carefully, you shouldn't have any problems."

It'll take hours to process all those boxes, Cornelia thinks. It was tedious enough dealing with one card at a time when she was a punch operator, but at least she could safeguard the occasional farm animal. Now Cornelia handles thousands of punch cards every day, but they arrive without the codes that would tell her what the holes represent. Without knowing the codes, it's as if she's fumbling blindly in the dark. At least the job has one perk: Willem usually sends Cornelia home once she's processed the day's batch of cards, which she's learned to do as quickly as possible. Even so, she isn't sure how much longer she can stand spending her days belowground when the only place she wants to be is in Leah Blom's attic.

Back in May, on the first night Cornelia went to the Bloms' for help with the translation, Leah opened the door so quickly it was obvious she'd been waiting in the vestibule. Upstairs, Cornelia exchanged brief greetings with Leah's parents, who were sharing the light of a single lamp in the living room, Philip with his nose in a book, Lillian hunched over her sewing. As soon as they were out of earshot, Leah said, "Honestly, Nellie, it's like sitting shiva the way they mope around every night. Come on up, I've got everything ready."

At the top of the stairs, there were only three doors, not five. Passing Leah's parents' room, Cornelia caught a glimpse of an unmade bed. "There's the bathroom if you need it," Leah said, then pointed to a curtain of bamboo beads in the third doorway. "And that's me."

Sweeping the beads aside with a musical clatter, Cornelia felt like the explorer Gertrude Bell entering a Bedouin tent. In Leah's room, candles in jars cast their flickering light on the Persian rugs and Indonesian silks that covered every surface. Even the air itself was different here, warm and dusty and scented with beeswax. A Chopin nocturne played in the background, as if they were in a motion picture scene set to music.

"*Ik vind jouw kamertje heel mooi,* Leah."

"Didn't we agree to speak only English? Now, try that again, Nellie."

Abashed, Cornelia switched languages. "I think your room is very pretty."

"Thanks." Leah looked around as if noticing it with fresh eyes. "I like exotic things. Maybe it's because my mother's American, but I've always felt like I belonged somewhere else, do you know what I mean?"

Cornelia thought of the pictures above her desk and nodded. "I'm always dreaming about places I want to visit someday."

Leah's smile lit up her face. "I knew you'd understand me." She went to the turntable, flipped the record, and set the needle down. Piano notes shimmered in the air like fireflies set to music. "Jews aren't allowed to have radios anymore, but thankfully there's no rule against phonographs. Come sit, Nellie."

Settling themselves on an upholstered bench under the window, Cornelia realized the dormer itself was a kind of gallery, sketches and watercolors tacked to every available inch of wall. "Did you do these?"

Leah nodded. "My training is in technical illustration, but I like to draw for my own amusement."

Cornelia leaned closer to one of the drawings. An older man and woman smiled at her as if in greeting, their faces so lifelike she actually smiled back.

"Those are my grandparents." Leah pointed to a charcoal sketch of a castle rising above a broad lawn. "That's their apartment building in New York City. They live right across the street from Central Park."

Cornelia glanced at Leah. "You've been to America?"

"Sure, loads of times. Grandma won't do the crossing herself— she's been afraid of the ocean ever since a friend of hers went down on the *Titanic*—so Grandpa books us passage to visit them every few years. My earliest memory is of him taking me ice skating on the frozen lake in Central Park. I'll show you." Leah got a sketchbook from her drawing table. Sitting beside Cornelia, she rifled through the pages. "There we are. Mommy says the ice was crowded with other skaters, but the way I remember it, it was only the two of us."

The sketch was stark, the lines spare, but the image of a man stooping to hold the upstretched hand of a small child was vibrant. "This is beautiful, Leah. Can I see some more?"

Scenes spilled out like a silent movie as Leah flipped through her sketchbook. Her grandmother's hands drawn in tender detail. Little sketches of pigeons and squirrels and ducks. Complicated scenes of trains elevated above the road, of sidewalks crammed with people of every shade and shape. Leah had done the Atlantic crossing five times, a record of international adventure that made Cornelia feel ridiculously provincial. Gerard Vogel was always too busy to take his family on a proper holiday. Other than bicycle trips in the countryside with friends, the farthest Cornelia had ever traveled was to visit her mother's relatives in Vlissingen.

She pointed to a page where Leah's grandparents seemed to have suddenly aged. Their figures were drawn as if from above, but the sketch lacked any detail to place the scene. "When did you do this one?"

"The last time we left New York. I drew it from the railing of the ship." Leah touched the faces of her grandparents, smudging the charcoal. "The news had just come out about the violence in Germany on Kristallnacht. Grandma was crying. Grandpa begged us to stay, but Papa assured them Hitler would never target Holland." Leah closed the sketchbook. "Hey, we have work to do, don't we, Nellie? Let's sit over there, I brought up a chair for you."

Leah's drawing table was where she spent her days, she explained, doing technical illustrations for clients who paid her in cash and claimed her work as their own. To prepare for their tutoring session, she'd adjusted the desktop from slanted to flat, shoved aside a pyramid of rolled papers tied with string, and gathered up her colored pencils in a jar like a bouquet. She switched on the work light, illuminating the Hollerith instruction manual Cornelia placed on the desktop. "Now, let's see what you've got here."

They sat side by side, their chairs so close Cornelia could smell the clove on Leah's breath. She noticed how Leah's lips pursed when she puzzled over a word and the way her lashes fluttered when she looked down at a page. Cornelia, self-conscious about her English, occasionally fell back into speaking Dutch, but Leah held her to their agreement and soon the language began to feel more natural in her mouth. Leah's insight into the instruction manual's vocabulary enabled them to make rapid progress. It was with a twinge of regret that Cornelia realized they'd finish the translation within a week.

They worked without regard for the clock, the passing of time marked only by the intervals when Leah got up to change the record on the phonograph. The buzz of the doorbell finally broke the spell. Lillian shouted upstairs that Dirk was asking for his sister. Cornelia looked at her watch, dazed. "I didn't know it was so late."

Leah yawned. "Neither did I. Your mother must want you home before curfew."

When Cornelia tried to pay her, Leah pointed to a jewelry box. "That's my bank. You can make your deposits there." Cornelia did, the zinc coins dropping quietly onto a velvet lining. The transaction shifted the mood for a moment, but with a shrug of her shoulders Leah recovered her nonchalance. "Come on, I'll walk you down."

"No, don't." The words jumped out of her mouth, surprising

Cornelia. Afraid she sounded silly or impolite, she tried to explain. "I want to picture you here, in this room, until I come again."

Leah gave her a quizzical smile, then kissed her cheek. "Until tomorrow, then, Nellie. I'll be here waiting for you."

Summer has come and gone since that moment. Every hour she's not in Leah's room feels to Cornelia like being in exile, especially here in the Hollerith bunker.

"Willem, please, could you review what I need to do before you leave?"

"Of course." He takes the clipboard from the cart and shows it to Cornelia. Her forehead knots in concentration as he goes through each step in the processing order. Following his finger down the list, she notices his nails are in need of a trim. "After you've run the summary cards through the statistical machine, print a report on the tabulator."

"Is the statistical report the last step?" she asks.

Willem flips to the next page. "No. The final step is an alphabetical list generated from all the remaining cards in the batch. And remember, if one of the cards gets rejected or damaged, punch a new one to replace it." Willem's eyelids shut as he yawns. "I need this as soon as possible, so no stopping for lunch, I'm afraid."

"And after that?" she asks with a hopeful rise to her voice.

"After that, you might as well go home. Your father will be keeping me busy all day, so I won't have time to get another order ready." Though they are encased in concrete walls a meter thick, he takes a step closer and lowers his voice. "Reichskommissar Seyss-Inquart is going to Berlin for a meeting, and he's asked Generalkommissar Wimmer to brief him on our progress with the census before he leaves."

Cornelia knows the Ministry of Information reports to Friedrich Wimmer, the gentlemanly Austrian who oversees Holland's civil service, but she's frightened to hear her father's name uttered in the same breath with that of Arthur Seyss-Inquart, Hitler's personally appointed governor for the Netherlands.

Willem runs a hand through his hair. "On top of everything else, at the last minute your father decided to have this batch processed for a statistical correlation he wants to discuss with Wimmer this afternoon. A technician will be coming in later today, but until then, there's only you." Willem packs up his briefcase and gets ready to leave. He stops in the doorway before ascending the ramp and speaks over his shoulder. "I hope you know what a tremendous help you've been to me these past months, Cornelia."

His praise makes her cringe. She's ashamed to think the work she does at the Ministry of Information is of any help to the Nazis. Only the fear of disappointing her father keeps her from quitting. All she wants is to finish processing the cards as quickly as possible so she can get out of the bunker.

Alone now, Cornelia sets the dials on the sorting machine for the first step: sequencing the cards according to the digits punched in column thirty-two, with a summary report listing the total occurrences for each digit punched in that column. She remembers punching cards for the animal census. Column thirty-two, if she recalls correctly, corresponded to piglets. She has no way of knowing what column thirty-two on these cards represents.

With the sorting machine set up, she wheels over the cart with the boxes of punch cards. She holds one up to the light, curious. The pattern of perforations seems random, their significance a mystery to human eyes. Yet Cornelia, like an astronomer searching for stars in the night sky, understands that each prick of light shining through the card is a dot of information that, when taken together with all the others, becomes meaningful. It's a strange language, she thinks, this scattering of absences. The explorers who discovered the Rosetta stone had no idea, at first, what the shapes chiseled into granite meant, but they could recognize that the pictures represented words, that the words, when read, would tell a story. Cornelia wonders what someone from the future, unearthing this trove, will make of the thousands of pieces of paper riddled with millions of minuscule holes. Unlike the letters of an alphabet or the pictograms of hieroglyphics, the meaning of the holes depends entirely on the particular code for each job. But even if this future explorer miraculously found a matching codebook, the cards would remain mute. This is a soundless language no mouth can give voice to. It was invented for the Hollerith machine. Only the computer can make the cards speak.

Cornelia loads the cards in the hopper and presses the start button. The machine leaps to life, furiously spitting cards into various pockets. She didn't think it was possible for a job to be less intellectually stimulating than punching cards, but once she starts the sorter, there's literally nothing for her to do but sit and watch. If a pocket gets too full, the machine will shut itself off. It's her job to make sure that doesn't happen, but it doesn't take much focus. The frantic chuck-chuck-chuck of the rollers and the quick ticking of the counter fade into the background as Cornelia's thoughts return to Leah Blom.

After they finished translating the Hollerith instruction manual, Cornelia proposed that Leah continue to be her English tutor. It wasn't a lie for her to say she wanted to be more fluent in the language, and paying Leah for lessons gave her a way to help that wasn't charity. Leah, whose freelance work was drying up as fewer people were willing to do business with Jews, eagerly agreed. She insisted, however, that the sessions be fun for both of them. Instead of reviewing grammar and conjugating verbs, Leah suggested Cornelia learn the nuances of the language by reading novels written in English.

For their curriculum, Leah pulled favorite books from her own shelf: *Jane Eyre* in June, *Sense and Sensibility* in July, *The Age of Innocence* in August. The girls rode their bicycles to the beach, where Cornelia read aloud while Leah sketched and corrected her pronunciation. They hiked through the dunes, debating Jane Eyre's devotion to the wretched Rochester. They sat in cozy cafés, arguing over whether Willoughby was truly remorseful about his treatment of Marianne. They strolled through parks, sharing their frustration at Newland Archer's refusal to visit Madame Olenska in Paris. On rainy nights, when their eyes got too heavy for reading, they sprawled on Leah's bed and listened to music. By the time August gave way to September, Cornelia came to feel as if that attic room were her native land, English her mother tongue, and Leah her true countrywoman.

Cornelia is jolted from her thoughts when a red light on the sorting machine flashes. A damaged card has been shunted into a pocket by itself. Cornelia retrieves it—there's a fold in the paper—and takes it to the punch machine, where she duplicates the card. After placing the new card in the hopper, she switches off the warning light and restarts the machine. On the back of the damaged card, she carefully writes the date, the batch number, and the order number. She has written those same pieces of information on at least one card from every batch she has processed in the Hollerith bunker. At home, under her bed, she has a shoebox filled now with damaged or duplicated punch cards. She imagines a day may come, after the war, when the cards she's saved can be reunited with their codes to reveal what the Nazis were up to in the Netherlands. It's a pathetic act of resistance, she knows, but it's all she can think to do from inside the ministry.

Cornelia tucks the damaged card into her pocket and allows her thoughts to turn back to Leah, who was dismayed to learn, when she proposed they try Shakespeare, that Cornelia had read only the sonnets in school. The plays were so much better, Leah said, especially the comedies. She ran her finger along the red leather spines of the Shakespeare set her grandparents had given her and chose *Twelfth Night* for their current assignment. Scene by scene, they've been staging dramatic readings in Leah's room, complete with improvised costumes and props. It's immensely enjoyable, even on those occasions when Leah stops the performance to give Cornelia an English lesson, like she did yesterday evening.

"What does it mean, here," Leah asked, pointing to a line, "when Viola says, 'I am not that I play.' Do you understand the syntax?"

"Is Shakespeare using 'that' to mean a thing, like a role?" Leah nodded, prodding Cornelia on. "Viola is not the thing she seems to be, because she's playing the part of a boy, even though she's a girl."

"Yes, but there's more to it than that. In Shakespeare's time, remember, only men were allowed on the stage, so for the actor playing Viola to say 'I am not that I play' is doubly true."

"But wouldn't the audience forget about the actor once they started to believe in the character?"

"Not at all." Leah jumped up from the dormer bench. "Some of the humor of the play depends on the fact that the actor saying those lines is really a boy playing the part of a woman dressed as a man."

Cornelia stood up, too, animated by Leah's argument. "Maybe that was true in Shakespeare's time, but Viola hasn't been played by a man in centuries, has she? If anything, it's the other way around now. Didn't Sarah Bernhardt famously play Hamlet? I think you're reading too much into it."

Leah went back to the dormer bench. Night had not yet fallen and the window was open to the evening air, soft with coming rain. "Maybe I am, but for me, it makes the play so much more interesting to think about what it was like when Shakespeare wrote these lines. When Viola says, 'I have one heart, one bosom and one truth,' I feel she's telling us to be true to ourselves and who we love, no matter what costumes we wear or how people perceive us."

Cornelia came to sit beside Leah. "I don't remember that line."

Leah smiles wistfully. "We haven't gotten to it yet. You should read Viola's part tomorrow. I'll be the duke."

"Can I draw a mustache on you?" Cornelia asked, tracing Leah's upper lip with her fingertip.

"Sure." Leah laughed and grabbed Cornelia's hand. "But be careful you don't make me too handsome or you might fall in love with me by accident, like Olivia with Viola."

Cornelia lifted her hands to her cheeks to hide the blush that burned them. Too late, she thought. I already have.

The sudden silence when the sorting machine shuts off pulls Cornelia from her daydreaming. She removes the cards from their pockets and takes the entire batch, now sequenced according to the digits in column thirty-two, to the Hollerith to be tallied. Reading the summary report that scrolls up from the typebar, she sees that 3 is the most frequently punched digit in that column. She makes a note of that fact, then moves on to the next step. She's to run the batch through the sorting machine four more times in order to group together all cards with a hole through the digit 9 in columns thirty-three through thirty-six. Cornelia adjusts the dials to that configuration, stacks the cards back in the hopper, and pushes the start button.

It was her mother's thinking she was ill that made Cornelia realize she was in love with Leah. "Let me take your temperature,"

Helena said one night, observing Cornelia's listlessness and lack of appetite. As Helena shook the thermometer, Cornelia described the rapid beating of her heart, the dizziness in her head, the tightness in her chest. After Helena left to telephone the doctor, another possibility came to Cornelia's mind. She opened a volume of poetry she'd studied in her classics course at Haganum. It was in Greek, her own Dutch version penciled in the margins. Since everything to do with Leah happened in English, Cornelia sat down to begin a translation. As the words spun from the tip of her pen like spider's silk, she found an exact match for her own symptoms. How her heart fluttered when Leah laughed. How her mouth became dry at the sight of Leah's smile. How she started to shake and sweat when Leah looked into her eyes. How her skin felt on fire whenever Leah touched her. The poem seemed to describe the onset of a flu, but Sappho of Lesbos was no apothecary. Cornelia's teacher said that Sappho was among the greatest of ancient poets for the way she conveyed the physical manifestations of love. The diagnosis was unequivocal: Cornelia was in love with Leah.

It was like the last piece of a puzzle fitting into place. Cornelia finally understood why she'd always felt so indifferent when the girls at school mooned over boys they liked. There were plenty of boys Cornelia admired, but whenever one of them asked her to go for a bike ride or out to a café, she felt an inexplicable resistance. She'd assumed there was something wrong with her until she met Leah. In a way that confused her to think about, being near a girl who seemed like a boy allowed Cornelia to feel more like a woman than she ever had before.

A clang from the vault door echoes down the ramp, startling Cornelia from her reverie. The sorting machine is quiet. How long since it shut itself off? she wonders. By the time the technician enters, she is on her feet, busily returning all of the unselected cards to the cart.

"Good day, Mejuffrouw Vogel," he says. "How goes it with you?"

"Good, thank you, though I'm very busy, as you can see." She doesn't want to encourage conversation. The technician is a rude young man who makes her uneasy, especially when they are alone together.

The entire batch is now reduced to the subset of cards with a hole punched through the digit 9 in any of columns thirty-three through thirty-six. She is taking this last group from the pocket of the sorter when the cards slip from her hand and drop to the floor. She panics, afraid the next step might depend on these cards staying in the exact order in which they were sequenced. She crouches down, relieved to see that the cards have fanned out without getting mixed up. Gathering them together, she lifts them up to check that the edges are squared. As expected, light shines through where the holes in column thirty-six align, but Cornelia is intrigued to see there is another speck of light in this sparse constellation. The digit 4 in column forty is punched through on every card. She wonders if this is the common factor that unites the entire batch. She removes a fistful of cards from the cart and holds them up to the light. There it is, shining like a miniature North Star in an otherwise obscure sky: a hole punched through the digit 4 in column forty. If this batch is part of the census, and each card represents a person, then every person in this batch must share this one trait, whatever it is. After glancing over at the technician, she stealthily takes the damaged card from her pocket and adds this bit of information.

Determined to swiftly finish the job, she stacks the cards in the hopper of the tabulator, which tallies them and prints a summary report. The next step is to run these cards back through the sorter, selecting now for the most frequently occurring digit from the first sort, which—she checks her notes—was 3 in column thirty-two. When this sort is complete, she feeds the selected cards through the statistical machine. It will take someone who knows the codes to interpret the results, but Cornelia can see there is a strong correlation between the information represented by the digit 9 in columns thirty-three through thirty-six and the digit 3 in column thirty-two.

Once the statistical report is run, she goes to the alphabetizer to print the final list. Walking past the technician's desk, she's horrified to see him reading a copy of *Storm*, the magazine of the Dutch SS. Cornelia doesn't need to look over his shoulder to know what hateful propaganda is written there. No wonder Willem lowered his voice even when they were alone; members of the NSB are everywhere nowadays.

More eager than ever to complete this order and get out of the bunker, Cornelia starts the alphabetizer. She watches the paper advancing through the platen as the Hollerith spells out a list of names. How this works, at least, she does understand. During her training, she learned that a hole-punch through position twelve on the card, coupled with a punch in digits 1 through 9 in the same column, represents the first nine letters of the alphabet. A punch through position eleven shifts the code to the next nine letters, while a zero punch with digits 2 through 9 represents the last eight. She takes the damaged card from her pocket. Columns one through five are punched 12-3, 11-6, 12-8, 12-5, 11-5. Cornelia spells out the name "Cohen." From the printed list, she sees that "Cohen" occurs frequently in this batch.

Cohen is a Jewish name. She looks again at the hole punched through digit 4 in column forty—the one fact every card in this batch has in common. What if the category is religion and 4 is the code for Jew? A sense of foreboding rises up from the concrete floor through the soles of her feet, weakening her knees. She remembers the question she asked her father when he extolled the efficiencies of the animal census: *Doesn't that make it awfully easy for the Nazis to steal our horses?*

Chapter Seven
Rita Klein

New York City
June 1960

F or the next two days, I immersed myself in the intricacies
of Olympia Metal's business accounts, which were as arcane
and complicated as they were inefficient. Every piece of cutlery
they manufactured involved one computer code for the blank, another for the steel it was made from, another for the handle design.
There was a code for each type of spoon, for the different knife
edges, for the number of fork tines. Each code was connected to
a price, each job to a salesman for commission, each order to a
customer, each item to a supplier. The same was true for their pots
and pans and chafing dishes. On Thursday morning, Mr. McKay
stopped by my desk to check on my progress.

"I think I'm getting the hang of it, but it's pretty confusing that
each item in inventory has so many codes attached to it."

Mr. McKay nodded sympathetically. "As Olympia's business
has grown, they've kept adding more codes until it's the mess you
see here. I've been after them to streamline and modernize for
years."

"But how do you still process their reports on the old Hollerith?"

"Multiple sorts." He reached for a piece of paper on my desk and
sketched it out for me. "Back in the 1930s, Hollerith technology was
considered a miracle of efficiency, but it can only sort the punch

cards one data point at a time. Each successive sort narrows down the stack until the question gets answered. Once the remaining cards are collated and summarized, a report is printed."

"That sounds terribly tedious."

"It gets the job done," he said, shrugging. "Eventually. Be grateful you're programming for the 602, Miss Klein."

"I am," I said, turning to the next page in Olympia's bloated codebook and getting back to work. By that afternoon, Mr. McKay decided I understood the business well enough to make sense of what I'd see at the metal factory in Brooklyn—and hopefully to impress the Plunketts. He gave me an address in Fulton Ferry, enough petty cash for cab fare, and a polite suggestion that I wear pants instead of a skirt.

"I'll call Francie and let her know to expect you first thing tomorrow. You might as well spend the day there. Get a good look around. Ask every question that pops into your mind, no matter how trivial, and make note of every idea that occurs to you, even if you think it's obvious, or dumb, or impractical. Leave it to me to separate the wheat from the chaff. We'll start fresh Monday morning."

"So does this mean I have the job, Mr. McKay?"

"I can't make a final decision without the Plunketts' approval, but it's a safe bet as far as I'm concerned."

A safe bet sounded close enough to count as fate. After work, I headed up to the top of the Empire State Building to share the news with Jacob Nassy. I circled the observation deck looking for him, my disappointment growing with each glance at a face that wasn't his. Then a tourist who'd been hunched over one of the binoculars stepped back and there he was, squinting out toward the bay, a forgotten cigarette dangling from his fingers. I stood and watched him for a while. He'd been gregarious and engaging as a tour guide, but standing alone like that, Jacob's face had a haunted look, like he was seeing beyond Lady Liberty to some distant memory that still had the power to hurt him. There was a bow to his back that matched the menacing crooks of the curved suicide fencing above his head, as if he were being dragged down by a heavy burden. I had no idea what that burden might be, but I empathized with its weight.

In the back of my mind, a voice that sounded an awful lot like Miss Murphy's told me to find someone jolly and carefree who could help me forget about the past. Instead, I stepped forward until I was close enough to smell the sweat on Jacob's neck.

"Hello again."

He turned. His pupils were tiny from staring at the bright sky, the black dots ringed with green and gold. He dropped his cigarette, crushed it with his shoe, and fixed me with a searching look. "So, Little Rita, you got the job?"

"I'll know for sure tomorrow, but I think so, yes."

"Good." He pronounced the word strangely, with a guttural *G* and the *D* sounding more like a *T*. It must have been another one of those words that was the same in English as in Dutch. We started walking together around the deck, his pace perfectly matched to mine. "Tell me, Little Rita, do you like films?"

I smiled. "Going out to the movies is one of my favorite things to do."

"Then you must have seen *On the Beach* already."

"No, actually, I haven't." We were passing the gift shop. The clerk behind the counter waved good night to Jacob.

"Really? I've resisted going because I admire the novel so much, but they say the film is one of the best pictures this year." As we got in line for the elevator, he showed me a page from the newspaper, folded to feature the movie listings. "There's a seven o'clock show at the Trans-Lux on East Eighty-Fifth Street. I think we can make it, unless you prefer something else?"

In the elevator, I looked over the listings. *Hiroshima Mon Amour* was getting rave reviews, but I wasn't up for a doomed love affair. *Babette Goes to War* was playing at the Paris Theater, but I didn't want Jacob comparing me to Brigitte Bardot, even in a role for which she was fully clothed. I considered *The Rat Race,* which claimed to be a first-rate comedic romp. I waited until my ears popped to answer. "Let's stick with *On the Beach*. I don't think I've got the patience to sit through a comedy."

"That's how I feel about comedies, too. I don't like being told to laugh." Jacob offered me his arm as we crossed the lobby. His elbow was so bony I thought of the witch pinching Hansel in that fairy tale. "Do you mind the subway?"

"No, not at all. I used to take it everywhere when I was in college."

"And where was that?"

"Barnard, the woman's college at Columbia."

"College at Barnard." Jacob smiled down at me. I hadn't thought of him as especially tall until I had to lift my chin to look him in the eye. "Now I know eight things about you."

"Eight? I didn't know you were keeping count."

We squeezed together into a segment of the revolving door. Out on the sidewalk, he steered me through the evening crush of pedestrians. "Your name is Rita Klein. You are a woman. You are American. You speak German badly. You speak French well. You dislike comedies. You went to Barnard College."

"That's seven." We were waiting for the walk sign to cross Madison Avenue. "What's the eighth?"

He frowned, as if sorry to be delivering bad news. "Sometimes, you are sad."

The light changed and we were swept across the street. For the past few days, I'd been practicing that *Wizard of Oz* trick of pretending my time away was merely a vivid dream. It wouldn't work with him, I realized. Even if he never suspected the truth, I had the feeling I could stretch the widest smile across my face and he'd still see the tears dammed up behind my eyes. It was like we recognized that in each other. His Land of Oz couldn't have been anything like mine, but at some point in his life, he must have been carried away by a tornado, too.

At the subway entrance, he stopped and turned to me. "I don't mind that you are sad sometimes, Little Rita. I am, too. This is why a movie about the end of the world is a perfect first date for us."

"I didn't know that's what the movie was about, actually." What I wanted to say was that I didn't know this was a date.

"I forget you didn't read the book. All I'll say is this: our troubles will pale in comparison to a cloud of atomic radiation extinguishing the human race." He grinned, his smile a little lopsided. "Shall we?"

Jacob's sense of humor was strange but I liked it. The way he said everything, too, in that accent of his, made me feel like I was in a sophisticated European satire. I couldn't stop myself from matching his smile. "Sure, let's go."

It was after nine when we got out of the movie. Night had fallen while we were in the theater, though in Manhattan nothing really feels late before midnight. Instead of going back to the Lexington line, Jacob suggested we walk to the subway on Central Park West. The moon was full and the Bridle Path was dotted in pools of light from the old lampposts, but it would never have entered my mind to cross the park if I'd been alone. How the world opened up for a woman, I thought, when she was with a man.

"What did you think of the film?" he asked, the traffic on the Eighty-Sixth Street Transverse fading from view as we crossed East Drive.

"I can't understand all those people in Australia going on with their lives as if they weren't about to die. Why didn't they riot in the streets, or loot the stores, or quit their jobs and run off to the outback? Why keep going to work and throwing parties and following orders like that?"

He was quiet for so long, I worried he thought my questions were stupid. "But that's how it really is, Rita, when something too huge to understand happens. People become desperate for things to stay as normal as possible. I saw it myself, during the war."

"You were still in Europe then?"

He nodded, then stopped to light a cigarette. "I was nine years old when the Germans blitzed Rotterdam. My parents and I huddled in the bathtub under a pile of blankets during the bombardment. All the windows in our house shattered. Shards of glass fell on us like a dangerous rain." He blew a series of contemplative smoke rings that floated up through the lamplight. "But that is a story for another day. What would you do, Rita, if you knew the world was ending?"

The answer materialized immediately in my mind, an instinct more than a thought: I'd go get my baby. If the world was ending and nothing mattered—not my parents or what their friends thought, not how I'd earn my money or who would help me—the only thing I'd want in all the world was David in my arms.

I didn't realize I was crying until he offered me his handkerchief. "I'm sorry, Rita, I've upset you."

"No, it's just a terrible thing to think about, isn't it?" I wiped my eyes, making an effort to regain my composure. "I see your point, though, about people wanting things to stay normal. Everyone knows about atomic weapons, but if we thought about them all the time, we'd never be able to enjoy something as simple as walking through the park on a beautiful night. I guess the thing about the movie that really doesn't make sense to me is the submarine captain going back to America just so his crew can die closer to home. He should have spent every last second of his life with the woman he loved, don't you think?"

Jacob nodded thoughtfully. "In the novel, Moira drives off a cliff after he sails away."

I shivered. "I hate to think what movie we'll see on our second date."

At that, Jacob laughed. "Let's promise each other never to see another movie about the end of the world."

"It's a promise." We came out onto Central Park West. At the subway entrance, I asked if this was his train, too.

"I'm all the way downtown, so any train gets me close enough. We can ride together as far as the Port Authority, unless you'd like me to wait with you for your bus?"

"No, thanks, I'll be fine." I was sure the terminal would still be bustling at ten o'clock, even without the theatergoers shut out of Broadway because of the actors' strike. Jacob dropped one of his tokens into the turnstile for me. He'd bought my movie ticket and the popcorn we'd shared, too. The evening hadn't cost him much, but I appreciated being treated.

The people waiting on the platform were strung out in a thin line. A guy taking swigs from a bottle in a paper bag was sprawled on a bench singing some tune. After sitting through *On the Beach,* I was actually surprised not to hear "Waltzing Matilda." Jacob must have had the same thought because he started humming it.

"No, don't!" I said, laughing. "I'll never get rid of that earworm."

"Ear worm?" A warm whoosh of air announced the arrival of the train. "Is that like an intestinal worm?"

As the subway whisked us under the streets of Manhattan, I explained that "earworm" was an expression I'd picked up from a Bavarian girl at Barnard. "She used to say *Ohrwurm* for a song you can't get out of your head."

He was relieved to hear it. "Once, when I was a boy, my mother was treated for a *lintworm*. It was horrible to see."

"What's a *lintworm*?"

"The literal translation is 'tapeworm.' Is that correct in English?"

"Tapeworm, yes." I'd only ever heard of them in dogs. "How was it treated?"

"The doctor held an onion between her teeth until the smell lured the worm up her throat. I'll never forget how he reached in with his instrument and pulled it out of her mouth."

A man across from us shot Jacob a look of disgust and changed his seat. "Why would you tell me such a thing, Jacob?"

The color rose in his cheeks. "I'm sorry, Rita. Please forgive me. Sometimes I forget that everything in America is clean and good. Here, even worms are songs."

I felt bad for embarrassing him. I put my arm through his and leaned into him. "Don't worry about it. I guess we come from different worlds is all. How old are you, anyway?"

"I'm twenty-nine." He raised his eyebrows at me but knew better than to ask.

"I'm twenty-one."

"Now I know nine things about you, Little Rita." Jacob gave me that crooked smile of his. I rested my head on his shoulder until we pulled into the station at Forty-Second Street.

"This is me." I took back my arm as the train screeched to a halt and the doors opened. "Good night, Jacob."

He grabbed my hand. "If you come find me after my last tour tomorrow, I'll take you up to see the view from the hundred and third floor."

"You mean the hundred and second floor, don't you?"

The conductor announced doors closing. I dashed out onto the platform. Jacob was saying something but his words got cut off. I followed along for a few steps as the train lurched into motion.

He covered his eyes and turned his head so abruptly, I assumed something terrible was happening behind me. I looked, but there was nothing but a violinist sawing away at his strings, an upturned hat at his feet to catch the coins of appreciative passersby. By the time I looked back, the train had disappeared down the tunnel. Whatever had spooked Jacob must have been in his imagination.

The Groucho Marx show was almost over when I got home to Teaneck. Dad switched off the television and got up to give me a hug. He hadn't held me like this for months, and I breathed in his smell of Ivory soap and Old Spice aftershave.

"I was getting worried, Rita. Where've you been?"

I didn't want to ruin the moment by telling him I'd been on a date with a man. "I went to a movie after work. I should have called. I'm sorry."

"It's okay. Listen, I'm going to have a sandwich before bed. Want to keep me company?"

"I'll join you, actually. All I had for supper was popcorn."

In the kitchen, he took bologna and cheese and mustard out of the fridge while I put out slices of bread. It felt conspiratorial, like those rare nights of my childhood when we happened to meet over a midnight snack. I told him all about *On the Beach* while he ate. He finished his sandwich before I even started mine.

"Go on to bed, Dad, I'll wash up."

"Thanks." He kissed me on the top of my head. "Sweet dreams, Ritabell."

He hadn't called me that in ages. It made me feel like a good daughter again, instead of the rotten girl who'd caused her parents such grief. If the world were to end a month from now, I thought, I'd want more moments like this.

Chapter Eight
Cornelia Vogel

The Hague, Netherlands
September 1941

A re you all right, Nellie? You're so distracted today."

The two young women sit on the dormer bench with their knees pressed together. The window is open, a cool breeze carrying with it the ring of a bicycle's bell and the high-pitched cries of children in the street. A record is playing, the symphony's swell rising and falling like waves on a beach. The sun's rays, slanted toward evening, wash their faces in golden light.

Cornelia closes *Twelfth Night*, a finger holding her place. "You know I've never liked working at the ministry, but an order I processed today makes me worried I'm no better than a collaborator."

"Don't say that. You're here with me, aren't you? That's already a kind of resistance. Besides, I doubt putting pieces of paper in a machine changes things one way or another."

Cornelia wishes she believed Leah's words, but she suspects, now, what it is the Germans are looking for among all those cards being processed on the Hollerith. "Leah, can I ask, did your family register as Jews?"

"Of course." Leah hesitates, then says, "Don't tell anyone, but some of my friends didn't register. One of my professors was against the Aryan attestation from the very beginning. He used to say if only every teacher and civil servant had refused to fill it out back in 1940, we'd have a better chance against the Nazis now."

Cornelia remembers her father filling out the form. It was a simple question—are you Aryan or not? "But no one knew, then, what the Germans wanted those for."

Leah waves an agitated hand. "I don't believe that for a minute. Didn't Hitler publish *Mein Kampf* back in 1930? The whole world knew what the Nazis were up to. I'm glad for my friends who didn't register as Jews. It gives them a better chance if they decide to go into hiding. You can't tell who's Jewish just from looking, can you?"

Cornelia gazes at Leah. Her hair and eyes are dark, but so are plenty of people's. Her skin has an olive hue, as if she's found a patch of sun to lie in, but her nose isn't as long as her father's, and her hair isn't curly like her mother's. The only thing Cornelia can think is how beautiful she is.

Leah taps a finger on the cover of *Twelfth Night*. "Come on, let's get back to our lesson. You're reading Viola, which makes me the duke. But first, you promised me a mustache." Leah gets a charcoal pencil so Cornelia can draw a fringe above her lip. The sketched suggestion of facial hair shifts Leah's appearance toward the masculine, reminding Cornelia of the time she mistook her for a boy. That was only a few months ago. How strange time is, Cornelia thinks. She can hardly remember her life before Leah.

Leah puts on a hat and declares her outfit complete. "But what about you?"

Cornelia gestures at her simple dress. "Why should I change?"

"Because Viola's disguised as Cesario, remember?" Leah rummages in a drawer, pulling out a pair of trousers and a plain shirt. "Here, put these on."

Cornelia does, but the effect is nothing like when Leah wears pants. "How come they look so good on you? I feel like an imposter."

"Well, Viola is a girl dressed as a boy, so that's perfect." Leah takes a moment to adjust the shirt on Cornelia's shoulders. "Although in Shakespeare's time—"

"Yes, yes, I know. Let's read the scene." They go back to the dormer bench and pretend to be sitting in the duke's courtyard.

"Start here," Leah says, pointing to a line.

Cornelia clears her throat. "'But if she cannot love you, sir?'"

Leah lowers her voice, pronouncing her lines sternly. "'I cannot be so answered.'"

"'Sooth, but you must.'" Cornelia, having read ahead, looks into Leah's eyes. "'Say that some lady, as perhaps there is, hath for your love as great a pang of heart as you have for Olivia?'" The line echoes the pang in Cornelia's heart. "'You cannot love her; you tell her so; must she not then be answered?'"

Leah searches Cornelia's face for a moment, then looks down to read the duke's lines. "'There is no woman's sides can bide the beating of so strong a passion as love doth give my heart; no woman's heart so big, to hold so much.'" Leah lifts her eyes to see Cornelia staring at her intently. "Don't you understand it, Nellie?"

Cornelia, caught off guard, points to a phrase. "What does 'no woman's sides' mean?"

"I think the image is literal." Leah places her open hand on Cornelia's ribs. "The duke means that the sides of a woman's body are too weak to withstand the beating of a heart as passionate as his."

Cornelia's own heart is bouncing around her chest like a rubber ball. Leah leaves her hand where it is as she finishes reading the passage.

"'Make no compare,'" Leah says, "'between that love a woman can bear me and that I owe Olivia.'"

It's a warning, Cornelia thinks. Leah's telling her there's no hope.

"It's your line, Nellie."

"What? Oh, yes." Cornelia finds her place but fumbles a few words in her nervousness. "'I know too well what love women to men may owe: in faith, they are as true of heart as we. My father had a daughter loved a man, as it might be, perhaps, were I a woman, I should your lordship.'"

"'And what's her history?'"

Is it Cornelia's imagination, or has Leah tightened her grip? Either way, she's finding it hard to breathe. Her cheeks are so hot she's sure they're bright red. As soon as they finish this scene, she'll tell Leah she's coming down with a fever and has to go home.

"'A blank, my lord. She never told her love, but let concealment, like a worm in the bud, feed on her damask cheek.'" Cornelia blinks and misses a line. "'She sat like patience on a monument, smiling at grief.'" Her throat closes up; she can't speak the next words.

Leah's fingers press into the spaces between her ribs. "What's the matter, Nellie?"

Cornelia's lips tremble. An inarticulate whimper escapes her mouth.

"Here, I'll read your line." Leah glances down at the page, then looks directly into Cornelia's eyes. "'Was not this love indeed?'"

Cornelia would give anything to run away, but Leah's eyes pin her to the spot.

"Go ahead, Nellie, say it." Leah's palm slides to Cornelia's spine. With her other hand she takes Cornelia's chin between her thumb and forefinger. "'Was not this love indeed?'"

Cornelia licks her lips, tasting salt. Her limbs are weightless. Her skin is numb, or raw, she can't tell which. Her stomach is cold, her throat on fire. Leah's eyes have never looked so huge, her lashes so long, her mouth so tender. The music recedes as

Cornelia's heartbeat clogs her ears with the sound of surf. She doesn't so much say the words as bleat them. "'Was not this love?'"

Leah smiles, stretching the drawn-on mustache. "You're in love with me, aren't you, Nellie?"

Cornelia nods as best she can with her chin held fast in Leah's hand. Slowly, the distance between their lips disappears. Calm washes over Cornelia like a warm wave. She is in Leah's arms and they are kissing and it is soft and inevitable and perfect.

The sound of a bicycle's bell outside reminds them they are two girls kissing in an open window. They startle apart, laughing so hard they slide from the bench to the floor. Leah reaches over and grabs a cushion from the bed to put under Cornelia's head. "There, that's better, isn't it?"

Cornelia licks her thumb and wipes the smudged mustache from Leah's lip. "That's better, too."

"You haven't told me yet, you know. Not really. I won't kiss you again until you do."

Their faces are so close, Leah's two eyes turn into three. Suddenly, Cornelia understands Picasso's portraits of women. "*Ik hou van jou.*"

Leah's smile stretches even farther. "What's that? I'm sorry, but haven't you heard? We only speak English here."

Cornelia, giddy, shakes her head and laughs. "I love you, Leah. Now can we kiss again?"

Our second kiss, Cornelia thinks to herself as their mouths meet. By the time her mother telephones to call her home for the evening meal, she's lost count.

After changing back into her own clothes, Cornelia follows Leah down to the vestibule, where they share one last kiss, squeezed against the wall by the bicycles. A lift in Leah's tone turns her farewell into a question. "Until tomorrow?"

Cornelia throws her arms around Leah's neck. "Until tomorrow and tomorrow and tomorrow after that!"

Halfway through their evening meal, Dirk kicks his sister under the table. "What's the matter with you, Nellie? Mom asked you to pass the potatoes."

"Oh, sorry." Cornelia picks up the plate and hands it to her mother.

"Are you coming down with a cold, Cornelia?" Helena asks. "Look at her, Gerard, doesn't she look feverish?"

Gerard Vogel glances up. "Aren't you well, Cornelia?"

"I'd be fine if you all stopped looking at me." She's hardly heard a word any of them has said. In her mind, moments from the afternoon with Leah are playing over and over like a skipping record.

"She hasn't been herself since she started spending all her time with that Jewish girl upstairs," Helena says. "I wish you'd talk to her about it, Gerard."

"She's getting English lessons, isn't she?" Gerard turns to Cornelia. "How goes it with the lessons?"

"Good. Great. Leah is an excellent teacher. We're reading Shakespeare."

"You see, Helena?" Gerard turns his attention back to his plate. "She might as well learn while she can. There's no rule yet against taking lessons from Jews."

"But she's been up there all afternoon, ever since she got home from the ministry."

Gerard regards his daughter with new interest. "Do you often come home early?"

"Willem Nooteboom lets me go once I've finished the day's work." Her father scowls. Cornelia rushes to explain. "I can't start a new processing order until the control panel on the alphabetizer has been changed, and that requires an engineer."

Gerard Vogel clears his throat. "Tomorrow, when you are finished in the Hollerith bunker, come up to my office. I'll tell Mevrouw Kwakkelstein to expect you. She mentioned being very busy lately with all the requests to verify identity cards. You can help her until the end of the workday."

Cornelia swallows her fury. Shoving her hands into the pockets of her dress, she feels the damaged punch card. "That reminds, me, Father, I want to ask you about something."

"Can't it wait until I've eaten?"

"Yes, of course."

Helena is setting down a plate of cookies and a pot of tea when the doorbell rings. Thinking it might be Leah, Cornelia rushes to answer it. Dirk, alert to any excitement, is hard on her heels. Together, their hands turn the knob.

Framed in the rectangle of the open door, backlit by the head-lamps of an idling automobile, is the silhouette of a German officer. His face is in shadow, but there's no mistaking the broad-shouldered jacket and puff of jodhpurs stuffed into tall boots.

"*Goedenavond meisje, jongen.* I'm looking for Herr Vogel. Could you tell me if he is at home?"

Cornelia knows the Dutch words mixed in with his German are intended to be polite, but she hates how his accent mars her language. Dirk stands speechless, still holding the doorknob.

"Who is it?" Helena switches on the hall light, illuminating the officer's face. It is clean-shaven, with inquisitive eyes and a slender nose. It's a face better suited to a tuxedo and top hat, Cornelia thinks, than a military uniform.

"It's for Father." She turns to her mother. "Go get him."

The officer clears his throat. "The Dutch pride themselves on their hospitality, yet you haven't invited me in."

Cornelia detects an Austrian lilt to his pronunciation. "Please," she says, stepping back to make room.

As he enters, light from the hallway spills into the dark street. Two soldiers flank the automobile outside. In the seat behind the driver sits an elegantly coiffed woman. Her diamond earrings glitter as she rolls down the window and calls out, "Don't be long, Friedrich, or we'll be late for the symphony."

Gerard Vogel approaches with his hand out. "Generalkommissar Wimmer, welcome. Would you and Frau Wimmer care to join us for tea and cookies?"

"No, thank you, I can't stay long. But if I may have a word?"

"Yes, of course." Gerard ushers him in. Helena pulls Dirk away, apparently nervous about what her son might say to a Nazi officer standing in their living room. Cornelia, curious, lingers.

Declining the chair Gerard offers him, Wimmer says, "Herr Vogel, I'm here to thank you for your excellent presentation today. I've discussed the preliminary results of the census with Reichskommissar Seyss-Inquart and he is very impressed. In fact, he's invited me to join the delegation to Berlin. I'm to help the *Judenreferent*, Willi Zöpf, brief Obersturmbannführer Adolf Eichmann on the Jewish question in Holland. It's quite an honor for me, as you can imagine."

"One I am sure you well deserve," Gerard says. Her father's flattery makes Cornelia cringe.

"Thank you, Vogel. I expect the last part of your presentation, on the methodology you've developed for identifying race Jews, will be most intriguing for Eichmann. We're departing tomorrow, and I want to be certain I understand it completely in case he has any questions. Would you please explain it again?"

"Certainly. In fact, my daughter is assisting me. She works with the Hollerith. Today she processed the statistical model I designed for identifying race Jews by cross-referencing three factors: name, occupation, and lineage. Cornelia, you printed the statistical report. What did you notice?"

Her father is standing tall, proud of his accomplishment, yet Generalkommissar Wimmer is clearly the conqueror. His uniform glitters with brass badges. Outside, his wife wears diamonds and his soldiers carry rifles. Silence is not an option. Cornelia sees in her mind's eye the typebar racing back and forth across the platen. "The report showed a strong correlation."

"Not merely strong. It's practically perfect, statistically." Gerard turns back to Wimmer. "What we proved today is that a Dutch person with a typically Jewish name working in the diamond industry with at least one Polish grandparent is ninety-nine percent likely to be a race Jew."

Wimmer is delighted. "I thought that's what I remembered, but it was so wonderful I wanted to hear it again. And this methodology can be replicated?"

"Absolutely. I focused on Amsterdammers to start, but by applying similar parameters to the population at large, the Hollerith will be able to identify individuals who are statistically likely to be Jews even if they don't know it themselves."

"Ah, we've got them in the bag now, don't we, Vogel?" Wimmer rubs his hands together as if warming them in front of a fire. "Thanks to you, we'll be declaring Holland *judenfrei* ahead of schedule. Eichmann will be very pleased." He steps closer to Gerard and drapes an arm across his shoulders. "Seyss-Inquart will be meeting with the Führer himself while we are in Berlin. Can you imagine the honor of your work reaching Hitler's ear?" He looks around, his eyes resting on the landscape painting above the mantel. "I see you do not have a portrait of our Führer?"

Cornelia watches a flicker of fear cross her father's face. Isn't it enough that they've taken down the picture of Queen Wilhelmina and replaced it with a placid landscape of black cows in a yellow field?

"I've been so busy working on the census, I've hardly had a thought for anything else."

"Yes, of course, Vogel, your mind is elsewhere. Call in your son, won't you?" Her father summons Dirk, who slinks into the room, followed by Helena. "Be a good boy and go ask my driver for the gift I brought your family." They stand stiffly in silence until Dirk returns with a wrapped package the size of a serving platter. Wimmer takes it, then offers it to Helena. "Frau Vogel, will you do the honors?"

Helena tears off the paper to reveal a portrait of Hitler. It's an oil painting, not a print, and though German art students are churning them out by the hundreds, its value to Wimmer is evident. He takes down the landscape painting and sets it on the floor. "I think it will fit perfectly here, don't you?"

Helena looks to her husband, who prods her into motion with a bob of his chin. She hangs the portrait and steps back.

"*Wunderbar!* I will no longer intrude on your evening. Good night to you all." With a click of his booted heels, Wimmer takes his leave.

When the rumble of Wimmer's car engine has faded away, Dirk dashes to the fireplace and grabs the portrait down from the wall. He's about to smash it over the back of a chair when his father raises a hand in warning.

"Put that back, Dirk."

"But, Father—"

Gerard Vogel stuns his son by slapping him across the face. "I said, put it back."

"Gerard, what are you—"

"Not now, Helena. Do as I say, son."

Dirk is trembling with rage but also weeping. All it took was Hitler's image, Cornelia thinks, to bring violence into her family.

Her brother tries to hang the picture but can't snag the hook. Helena steps forward to help him. The portrait swings off-kilter above the fireplace.

"Come, Dirk," Helena says, "let's go upstairs."

Alone with her father, Cornelia's voice shakes as she says, "I can't be part of this anymore. Now that I know how my work is helping the Nazis hunt down Jews, I have to quit."

Gerard wheels on her. "You cannot, and you will not. Don't you understand the suspicion you will bring on me if you quit now, after Wimmer has met you here, in our home?"

"But I'm nothing. All I do is process the cards. Anyone can be trained to do it."

"Do you really think, Cornelia, that the Germans would allow just anyone to work with the Hollerith machines? They built a bombproof bunker to house them. They smuggle parts from America to keep them working. They pay thousands in contracts to the Watson Business Machine Company to engineer and service them. Willem Nooteboom may have requested you, but I'm the one who vouched for your trustworthiness. Don't be fooled into thinking my position gives me any clout with Wimmer. Think what will happen if he ever suspects me of treachery."

Cornelia imagines the consequences of her father's unemployment: food coupons reduced, bank account diminished, house underheated. "We'd find a way to manage without your job, Father."

He shakes his head. "I know too much for them to let me walk away. The alternative to being director of the Ministry of Information isn't staying home—it's going to jail. That holds true for both of us, Cornelia. You can't stop doing your job any more than I can stop doing mine."

Cornelia stumbles back, grabbing a chair for support. She's always thought of her father as so important. She sees now he's only as valuable as a highly trained dog. But what happens to a dog that bites its master's hand? It's put down with a bullet to the skull.

Gerard places a cool hand on his daughter's forehead. "I think your mother was right, you may be running a fever. Go rest now, Cornelia. You'll have a full day tomorrow. No more coming home early."

"But Leah—"

"You can do your lessons after the evening meal from now on."

Cornelia opens her mouth to object. He stifles her with a fearsome look. She leaves him standing by the mantel, straightening the portrait, Hitler glaring at her from over her father's shoulder.

Chapter Nine
Rita Klein

New York City
June 1960

I s that what you're wearing to work?" Mom said, pointing at my khaki pants.

"They're for the factory, Mom. I've got a dress to change into later." I waved the shopping bag containing the clothes I'd picked out for my second date with Jacob Nassy—not that my mother needed to know that. "I may go to another movie after work, so don't worry if I'm home late."

"You be careful in Fulton Ferry today." She handed me the lunch she'd packed for me, like I was a kid again heading off to Lowell Elementary. "Dad says that part of Brooklyn's no place for a young lady."

"I'm not going to be wandering the streets, Mom. Mr. McKay gave me money for a taxi."

"All the way from the Port Authority?" She nodded approvingly. "That Mr. McKay sounds like a good boss."

He would be, I thought, assuming the Plunketts approved me for the job. The taxi I hailed outside the bus terminal took me across the Manhattan Bridge into a district of brick warehouses that overshadowed narrow, cobbled streets. Other than a few idling delivery trucks being unloaded by brawny men, the neighborhood was eerily deserted. The driver dropped me off in front of a building with OLYMPIA METAL COMPANY painted on its side in letters so big they were legible a block away. I walked into a showroom where daylight spilled through massive windows, glinting and shimmering on a thousand metal surfaces like sunshine on a lake. Stainless-steel cutlery was arrayed on a felt-topped table, shiny as silver but never in need of polish. On a shelf, aluminum mixing bowls were lined up like Russian dolls, the littlest smaller than my cupped hand, the largest big enough for me to climb into. There was cookware of every sort and size, from enormous soup pots capable of serving hundreds to single-ounce sauce cups. While I waited for the salesman stationed in the showroom to finish a phone call, I contemplated my distorted reflection in the concavity of a serving spoon, my face morphing from wide to thin and back again.

"That's a wonderful choice, ma'am. The finish will hold up to the steam of a dishwasher without ever tarnishing. Are you looking to outfit a restaurant?" The salesman who sidled up to me radiated a friendly confidence that must have endeared him to a generation of clients.

"No, sorry, I'm not a customer. I'm Rita Klein, from Antiquated Business Machines."

"Ah, you're that girl Mr. McKay called about. I was told to be on the lookout for you. I'm Mr. Connelly, by the way. You wait right here, Miss Klein."

He pushed through a swinging door I hadn't noticed before. The din of machinery whooshed into the showroom in waves as it swung back and forth before sealing itself shut again. A minute later, it whooshed open and a tall woman in a checked shirt and dungarees strode into the showroom. The salesman pointed at me and she walked over, her long legs quickly closing the distance.

"Hello there," she said, taking a cigarette from her mouth with pinched fingers. "I'm Francine Plunkett, but you can call me Francie."

Her red hair and emerald eyes reminded me of Maureen O'Hara in *The Quiet Man*, though her square jaw could have belonged to John Wayne. I expected an Irish lilt to match her looks, but her gravelly voice was heavy with Brooklyn vowels. I recalled what Mr. McKay told me about how Francine Plunkett had stepped into her husband's role at the company after he died. It must take a lot of gumption, I thought, for a young widow to manage a metal factory.

"Pleased to meet you, Francie. I'm Rita Klein." I was glad I'd followed Mr. McKay's suggestion about wearing pants today. Although my summer khakis made me look a little like Annette Funicello on her way to the beach, at least I wasn't facing this intimidating woman in a schoolgirl's skirt.

She took a drag on her cigarette, regarding me like she was pricing a machine part. "How'd a kid like you learn enough about those computers to do this job?"

I straightened up to my full height, though the top of my head barely reached her shoulder. "I've taken a computing machines class at Columbia University, and I've got my certificate from the Watson Laboratory course if you want to see it."

"Nah, that's okay." The ash was about to fall from her cigarette. The salesman scurried over with a glass dish to catch it. "You must know what you're doing if you passed muster with Frank McKay. Anyway, I'm glad you're here, Rita. Jesus knows we need the help. Come on back to my office."

I followed her through the swinging doors onto the factory floor. Motes of metallic dust suffused the air like scratches in an old film reel. Twenty-foot ceilings were held up by a forest of riveted posts. The floorboards beneath my feet were wide as halved oak trees.

Men in overalls scurried around beneath coils of steel hung from overhead cranes like gigantic rolls of aluminum wrap. I could see Francie's mouth moving but I couldn't hear a word over the clanking, hissing, snapping, clattering, whining, screaming sounds of the machinery.

We headed toward a door in a wood-paneled wall that separated the offices from the factory floor. The paneling didn't eliminate the din, but it did reduce it to a tolerable level.

"Sorry about the noise, Rita. I don't even hear it anymore." Francie told me to sit down, then settled herself behind a desk so overflowing with ledger books and stacks of paper I didn't realize there was a telephone on it until it rang. "Jimmy, good." She cradled the receiver between her shoulder and chin. "That girl from Antiquated is here to go over the contract with us." She pursed her lips and sent a thin stream of smoke to the ceiling. "Whaddaya mean, you're heading up to Lackawanna?" She listened, then said, "Hold your horses, Jimmy. No matter what price they give you, don't sign anything without talking to me first, you understand?" She stubbed out her cigarette like she was smashing a spider. "Don't tell me that. You need to promise this time. Okay, then, see you tomorrow."

Francie hung up the phone. "Looks like you're stuck with me today. My brother-in-law's going to meet with a new steel supplier." She combed her hair back from her forehead with nicotine-stained fingers. "That boy'll be the death of me. Sometimes I think I should've walked away from this place when my Joey passed, but my half of the business is all the security my kids've got."

"You have kids?"

"Sure, why not? Me and Joey were married for nine years. Take a look." She excavated a framed picture from the clutter on her desk and held it out to me. I saw a round-faced boy with a shock of ginger hair and a pale girl with eyes the color of seawater. "Junior's six, and Maeve's almost eight."

How could she have kids at home while she was at work all day? I wondered. That was one of Miss Murphy's reasons for why unwed mothers could never be good parents. It seemed crazy to me I'd never thought about widows before. They were single mothers, too, with all the same challenges we would have faced. The difference, I realized, was the world around them. A woman whose husband has died might cover her face with a veil, but she never had to hang her head in shame.

My question got answered when Francie took a phone call from her mother, who, I gathered, lived with her now. "Junior knows he can't go farther than the park. If he gives you any lip, tell him I'll take away his bike. See you later, Ma."

She hung up, then focused on me. "Okay, Rita, let's get started. First thing I've got to do is get your signature on the loyalty oath."

"Loyalty oath?" I couldn't imagine why anyone would need to pledge allegiance to a metal factory.

"Now that we've got a navy contract, the Defense Department requires all our employees, even our subcontractors, to sign a loyalty oath."

"Like students have to before they can get their college grants?"

"Exactly. The military's paranoid about saboteurs and subversives, but unless you're related to Ethel Rosenberg, I wouldn't worry about it." Francie grinned at me. "I don't suppose you've been alive long enough to get yourself into any trouble the FBI would care about."

But being inexperienced is exactly why I got into trouble, I thought. When Leonard brought me back to his hotel after our magical dinner at the Rainbow Room, I only understood sex from a technical standpoint. At Barnard, Dr. Marjory Nelson's lectures on the reproductive system were famously explicit, but birth control was a mystery—not to mention illegal for unmarried women. I believed Leonard when he promised I had nothing to worry about, that he knew what he was doing, that he'd take care of everything. I may have been smart enough to program a computer, but when it came to understanding men, I was dumb as a cow.

Francie handed me an official-looking document and a pen. "As soon as you sign this, I can show you around the factory."

I took it and started to read. I didn't object to the oath on principle—I wasn't a Communist, after all—but some of the questions upset me. *Is employee married? Does employee have children? If employee is a woman, what is the reputation of parents or husband?*

I never would have thought twice about answering such questions before, but after answering no to being married, it was impossible to answer yes to having children. It was no lie to say my parents' reputation was spotless, but that only held true as long as I kept my baby a secret. It hit me that putting my mistake behind me meant I would never be completely honest about myself again. But was it really a lie to swear I had no children? I didn't have David. There would never be a framed photograph of him on my desk. I didn't even know what his name was now.

I stopped reading, flipped the page over, and signed my name. "There you go."

Francie put the form on a teetering pile. From the state of things in her office, the chances seemed good the summer would be over before anyone at the FBI ever saw my oath.

"Frank showed you the contract already, right?"

"I've read it through a number of times."

"Then you know what I'm up against here." She shook her head and sighed. "When Jimmy heard the *Constellation* was being built in the Brooklyn Navy Yard, all he saw was dollar signs. He thought he was doing a good thing going after that contract, but he was in over his head from day one. Me, too. I took bookkeeping classes in high school, is all. I've never had a solid grasp on production. Jimmy figured we had thousands of stainless-steel blanks for the cutlery in inventory ready to be pressed and polished, and the factory foreman said we had plenty of cold-rolled stainless on hand, and a fixed price from our supplier for more. It looked like our only real expense would be machining a new press plate for those galley trays, so Jimmy bid low. When he won the contract, he stopped the machines and handed around bottles of whiskey in celebration. The guys were all late to work the next day, and too hungover to be much use. It was while they were nursing their aching heads that I read every word of that contract for the first time. When I got to the specifications and saw Type 316 instead of Type 304 for the stainless, I shit myself. I mean, seriously, Rita, I had to run to the toilet, it made me so sick."

I winced for her sake. Sure, Francie came off like a tough gal, but I sensed the vulnerability behind her brash façade. "What's the difference between Type 316 and—what's the other one?"

"Type 304 stainless is what we use for everything—pots, pans, spoons, you name it. It's called A2 for short, it's so damn common. But Type 316? That's marine grade. We only use it for special orders, and we sure as hell don't keep tons of it lying around. I dragged Jimmy in here and pointed it out to him. We can still get out of this, I said. It'd cost us a lawyer's fee and a hefty fine, but what other choice did we have? I told him there was no way we could fulfill this contract without losing money, but Jimmy wouldn't listen. He argued supplying the *Constellation* would be like free advertising. We'd get so many new customers, he said, we'd make up any loss in no time. The foreman found a coil of cold-pressed Type 316 in inventory, so at least we could get production started, and now Jimmy's heading up to Lackawanna to see about ordering more." She unscrewed a thermos and poured herself a cup of coffee. "You want some?"

"Sure, thanks."

Francie rummaged around for a clean cup, filled it, and handed it to me. "The type of steel the navy specified isn't my only headache. It's the accounting, too. It's way more detailed than what I'm used to. All's I've got is a girl who comes in nights to code the day's paperwork on those punch cards. It's Frank McKay who runs the reports back at Antiquated, but he says he's too busy to give this contract his full attention, or some such bullshit. Instead, he sent me you." She lit another cigarette and took a drag, letting the smoke seep out of her nose. "So, Rita Klein, can you save my ass here, or what?"

I felt like I'd been given an exam for a class I'd never taken, but I needed her approval to clinch the job. I decided a little bluster was called for. "I'm confident I can, Francie."

"I'll take you at your word, Rita. So, where do we start?"

"How about you show me around? Mr. McKay wants me to see everything."

"Everything? You sure? Ever been in a factory like this before?" I shook my head. "It's gritty, and dangerous, too. Better put these on." She handed me a pair of steel-toed boots that were too big for my feet and a stained smock that covered my blouse. "I'm glad you're wearing pants, kid, but those khakis are gonna be ruined by the end of the day. A good pair of Levi's is what you need."

I thought of that pair of my brother's jeans. A sudden wave of nausea caught me by surprise as I remembered putting them on at the hospital. I coughed, clearing my throat. "Next time," I said, grabbing a pen and a notepad.

I spent all that day enduring the din on the factory floor, learning how a coil of stainless steel got punched into blanks, how the blanks got pressed into shape, how each spoon or fork or knife was polished and edged and decorated. I was the one who thought to tell the foreman that the navy was requiring each item to be stamped with a serial number, which would add one more step to the production process. When I noticed how they collected the skeletons left after blanks were punched from sheets of steel to sell for scrap, I reminded Francie that for the navy job, they'd have to set those aside and save them for a final weigh-in.

She wiped the sweat from her forehead with a greasy hand. "Jesus Christ, Rita," she shouted over the noise of the machinery. "I feel like an idiot for not putting all this together before."

"Don't feel bad," I yelled, my mouth close to her grimy ear. "I'm thinking ahead to how I'm going to program the computer to keep track of all the steps in the process."

"At least someone around here is thinking ahead," she said, her voice quieting as we went back into her office. "Listen, let's make this official. I'm gonna call Frank McKay right now and tell him you're all right with me."

When the factory foreman blew the whistle to signal the end of the day shift, I put away my notes and picked up my shopping bag. "Is there somewhere I can change, Francie?"

She showed me to a converted janitor's closet that she'd turned into the only feminine retreat in the entire factory, with yellow walls and gingham curtains and scented soap by the sink. I tossed my khakis in the waste basket—they were so splattered with grease I knew they'd never come clean—and stuffed the blouse into my pocketbook. After scrubbing my hands and face, I put on my dress, combed my hair, did my makeup, and stepped back into my own shoes.

"Don't you clean up cute," Francie said. "Like Cinderella at the ball. Got a date with your boyfriend?"

"Yes. Well, no. I mean, he's not my boyfriend," I stammered, my cheeks hot from blushing. "We only met Monday. Tonight's our second date."

"Two dates in less than a week?" Francie dropped into her office chair with a laugh. "Take it from me, kid, it doesn't matter how many dates you've been on. Once you know, you know. Joey proposed to me the very first time he took me out. We'd known each other from the parish since we were kids, but still. We were at the top of the Wonder Wheel, all of Coney Island lit up under us like a carpet of stars. The ride stopped and stranded us there, swinging in the night sky. He put his arm around my shoulder and said, 'Frances Rose McGinnis, I think we ought to get married while you're still an honest woman. How about it?' And you know what I said?"

"Yes, obviously."

Francie laughed again. "I was happy as a hive of bees, but I tried to match his cool. I said, 'If you think you can handle me, Joseph Patrick Plunkett, you can have me.'"

She really was like Maureen O'Hara in *The Quiet Man,* I thought. "Sounds like a fairy tale."

"No, it never was, but that boy loved me, and I loved him." She slapped her knees. "Enough of this mush. What happens next?"

"I'm going to come up with some new codes for the girl who does your punch cards," I said. "The sooner she starts using them, the better, but I'll have to test my program first. I'll call you next week."

Francie walked me out to the showroom. "Thanks, Rita." She opened her arms and surprised me with a hug. "It feels good to have someone on my side."

I thought about Francie and Joey on the Wonder Wheel as the taxi took me back to the Empire State Building. I'd felt the love she had for him as sure as a barometer sensed the weather. It got me wondering what the emotion was made of. Scent seemed as elusive as a feeling, but really it was made up of molecules. I rolled down the window and sniffed as we crossed the East River. Ocean water, car exhaust, asphalt, tree leaves—every smell my nose detected was actually a minuscule, but measurable, particle. Was love like that, I wondered—something invisible adrift in the air?

Up on the observation deck, I stepped out of the elevator, excited for my second date with Jacob. This time he was easy to spot, slouched casually against the gift shop counter, nicely dressed in a tan suit with a narrow tie. There was no hint of melancholy in the lopsided smile that lit up his face when he saw me.

"Little Rita, you look lovely."

"You look rather dashing yourself."

"Well, tonight is something special. Are you ready?"

"Sure." I'd never been up to the observatory on the 102nd floor, but I could picture that scene from *An Affair to Remember* where Cary Grant is looking for Deborah Kerr.

Jacob led me to a small elevator where an operator in a red jacket whisked us up another two hundred feet. There were fewer tourists up here, which was nice, but all that glass made me feel like I was in a tank at the aquarium. The view stretched down to Ellis Island and up past the Bronx, but I preferred the open air on the eighty-sixth floor. Jacob pointed out the exposed rivets and industrial girders as he told me how Mohawk ironworkers had balanced on beams hundreds of feet in the air during the building's construction. After we walked all the way around, I figured we'd seen all there was to see. Instead of returning to the elevator, however, he steered me past it.

"Stand here, close to me." He drew a key from his pocket and unlocked a narrow door. "Now we wait."

The elevator arrived. A few tourists got out. A few got in. The motor whirred as it descended. When no one was looking, Jacob put his arm around my waist, opened the narrow door, and pulled me inside. My shins smacked against a metal staircase. The space was so small I had to go up a step for him to shut the door behind us. When I heard the dead bolt click into place, I realized I was locked in a deserted stairwell with a man I barely knew. For some reason, though, I didn't feel afraid.

"Go ahead, Rita." Light spilled down the stairs from a window at the top. Jacob came up behind me, his hands on both railings. If I were to trip, I'd have nowhere to fall but into his arms.

At the top of the stairs, he edged around me. What I'd taken for a window was actually a glass door, which he unlocked with another key. He helped me step out onto a ledge narrower than a sidewalk, one hundred and three stories above the streets of New York City. There was no fence, not even a railing, only a low wall that barely came up to my knees. Terrified, I flattened my back against the building and squeezed my eyes shut.

"Hold my hand. I won't let go." Jacob spoke in a reverent whisper, but I heard every word. The only other thing I could hear was the sound of my heartbeat. No street noise rose this high. Even the cawing gulls flew far below us. I grabbed his hand, took a deep breath, and opened my eyes.

It was as if we were in the crow's nest atop a monumental mast. The entire island of Manhattan was the deck of our ship, all of New York Bay a slip in the vast marina of the Atlantic coast. From up here, I could imagine the island breaking free of its moorings and setting off across the ocean.

I looked up at Jacob, as amazed as if he'd orchestrated a magic trick. "This is incredible."

"It is, isn't it?" His face was bright with wonder. "I wanted you to experience this. It's the only place in the world where I feel completely at peace."

It was a strange thing to say about such a perilous perch, but I felt it, too, as if nothing painful could reach us here. I thanked the miracle of gravity for anchoring us to this moment as we circled the spire of the Empire State Building. Jacob couldn't resist spewing statistics: that we were 1,050 feet in the air; that, on a clear day, you could see all the way to New Haven, Connecticut; that the radio waves were so strong this close to the transmitter we shouldn't stay longer than fifteen minutes.

I pressed a finger to his lips. "Shush now, Jacob. Let me listen."

I reveled in the exquisite silence as the wind washed over me like the baptismal touch of some ethereal deity. I didn't realize my finger was still pressed to his mouth until Jacob pursed his lips to kiss it.

In the elevator back down, the operator gave Jacob a knowing look. "I hope she was impressed, Jake."

"She was." His hair was disheveled from the wind. I reached up to comb it with my fingers. He returned the favor, disentangling my knotted curls.

Returning to the lobby was like falling back to earth. I was about to suggest a drink at the Longchamps bar when Jacob asked if I'd have dinner with him at the Rathskeller. I said yes, of course. Catching my reflection as we descended that mirrored staircase to the basement of the Empire State Building, I didn't recognize the happy, windswept girl I saw.

We entered the restaurant to a blast of German music, the air redolent of sausage and sauerkraut. The hostess led us to a table tucked in a corner near the kitchen. I hoped the scrape of my chair covered the growl from my stomach—I hadn't realized I was starving. We were offered menus but Jacob set his on the table without so much as a glance. He took mine, too. "We won't need those, Rita. I used to work here."

I learned what he meant when the waiter appeared and greeted Jacob by name. I was introduced to Rudy, who welcomed me in

English, then launched into a conversation with Jacob in German. They spoke so quickly I was immediately lost. I recognized "hefeweizen," my mouth watering at the prospect of a tall glass of cold wheat beer, and though I heard *wurst* and *kartoffel,* the words were surrounded by so much unfamiliar vocabulary I doubted we'd be getting a humble plate of sausage and potatoes. When Rudy left, Jacob smacked his forehead, as if he'd just remembered leaving his wallet out on the parapet. "I never asked if you keep kosher, Rita."

I pictured the slices of Oscar Mayer ham in my mother's refrigerator. "No, we've never been like that. We celebrate Passover, of course, and my brother was bar mitzvahed, but except for the High Holy Days, we only go to the synagogue for social events."

"I'm relieved to hear it. I'm proud to be Jewish, of course, but since the war, I find it hard to believe in anything."

Our beers arrived, frothy and fragrant. I asked Rudy how he and Jacob knew each other.

"Didn't Jake tell you? We're brothers."

I turned to Jacob. "You have a brother?"

Rudy laughed. "Enjoy your drink, Rita."

After he left, Jacob explained. "We feel like brothers because we came to America together as part of a Jewish Aid Committee program for stateless orphans."

Hearing a grown man call himself an orphan broke my heart. I remembered representatives of the JAC raising funds at our synagogue to help displaced persons who'd survived the concentration camps. Sadly, it was easy enough to put two and two together. Jacob's parents must have perished in the Holocaust, but their son was sitting across the table from me, lifting a glass to his warm lips. I wondered how he'd survived.

"Did your parents send you into hiding during the war, like Anne Frank?"

Jacob made an impatient sound that blew the froth from his beer. "That poor girl. People think Anne Frank is a saint, but believe me, if she had come back from Auschwitz, she would have burned the page in her diary where she wrote that people were good at heart." His words struck me as harsh. I'd seen that movie while it was playing at the Palace last year. Millie Perkins couldn't quite carry the part, but the closing scene was so uplifting I left the theater feeling hopeful for humanity. But maybe he was right. Maybe it was only because her last entry was written while she still believed in goodness that her diary was so popular. "And no, Rita, we didn't hide."

Rudy returned with fresh glasses of beer and a platter of food that he set between us with a flourish. The white china was loaded with delectable morsels of meats, cheeses, and pickled vegetables along with slices of dark bread and tiny bowls of mustard. The smells were delicious, but my appetite was on hold while the subject of the Holocaust hung between us. "If you didn't go into hiding, then how did you—?"

Jacob cut me off. "Let's not break our rule, Rita."

"What rule?"

"To never speak of the end of the world." He reached across and took my hand. "Let's not talk of terrible things."

I squeezed his hand. "No terrible things."

"Tell me about yourself. I want to know everything."

No you don't, I thought, my stomach souring. If I told you everything, you wouldn't want to be here with me. "You already know nine things about me. Isn't that enough?" I bit into a pillowy potato pastry. "This is delicious, what's it called?"

After Jacob told me about the food, I steered the conversation in the direction of movies, since we had that as a common interest. I thought the platter was meant to be our shared supper, but after Rudy removed our empty plates, he brought us tender slices of veal schnitzel with a bitter salad. I was stuffed to the gills, but we weren't done yet. The schnitzel was followed by black coffee and a torte piled high with whipped cream. One of the musicians, who was a friend of Jacob's, came over on his break and pulled up a chair, cheerfully digging a spoon into our torte until the bandleader called him back. We followed him onto the small dance floor, where Jacob led me through a bouncy polka that left us both breathless. As we were leaving the Rathskeller, Rudy presented us with a box tied with string—a little something for later, he said. It made me happy to see how popular Jacob was in the Empire State Building, from the basement to the parapet.

The streetlights came on as he walked me up Broadway to the bus terminal. "Well, Little Rita," he said when we got to the Port Authority, "this evening was a success, don't you think?"

I had to laugh at his enthusiasm. "I'd say so, yes." I got more serious. "It was really special, thank you."

"Is it too soon for me to ask what you're doing next Friday?"

"No, it's not too soon, and the answer is nothing."

"Shall we see another movie? Not a comedy, obviously, but also nothing too tragic. I could get tickets for the opening of that new Alfred Hitchcock film?"

"That sounds perfect." My favorite Hitchcock was that old one of his, *The Lady Vanishes,* but I'd loved *North by Northwest.* I didn't know anything about his new film except that he wasn't allowing press screenings, so there'd be no reviews of *Psycho* before opening night.

"Until next Friday, Little Rita." The kiss he placed on my cheek felt very European, but the long pause afterward let me know he wanted more. I tilted my head back and held his eye—an invitation. He accepted, kissing me so hard I felt the shape of his teeth through his lips. To relieve the pressure, I opened my mouth. Our tongues met with a spark that shot clear down to my toes.

We kissed until the wail of a passing ambulance broke us apart. I ran, breathless, into the terminal. My heart was still fluttering as the bus swung into the Lincoln Tunnel. Even underneath the Hudson River, I could conjure the feeling of being a thousand feet in the air.

Chapter Ten
Cornelia Vogel

Amsterdam, Netherlands
May 1942

*D*ocumenten, *alstublieft, dames en heren*. Please have your documents ready for inspection."

The policeman making his way down the aisle of the train car is Dutch, not German. Cornelia doesn't consider him a Nazi collaborator. She doubts he's even a sympathizer. For all she knows, he could be a Royalist with a hidden radio at home who tunes in to the BBC every night to hear Queen Wilhelmina's speeches from London. But today, his job is to check papers for all passengers traveling from The Hague to Amsterdam. The policeman dispatches his duties efficiently, moving on after a quick glance between the face of a passenger and the photograph on their identity card. But if he deems a passenger's documents suspect? He'll have no choice but to summon his supervisor, who's likely to hustle the hapless passenger off the train and lock them up in a local police station while a telephone call is placed to the Ministry of Information to verify their identity.

Cornelia knows all too well, now, what happens next. Her father's secretary is one of the civil servants who answers the telephone when there's a question about a person's documents. Cornelia's job, after she's done in the Hollerith bunker each day, is to assist Mevrouw Kwakkelstein by locating duplicate registration forms for people under investigation. Cornelia has become as familiar with Huize Kleykamp's filing system as she is with the columns on a punch card. As she works her way from one fireproof cabinet to the next, she imagines relieved citizens whose identities have been confirmed going home to their families. She hates to think she's played even a small part in the fate of those whose identities are not verified. Even though all she's done is pull a piece of paper out of a drawer, Cornelia can't help feeling responsible for the people who are sent to one of the Nazi concentration camps in Holland, Amersfoort or Vught, or worse yet, on to Buchenwald or Ravens-brück in Germany. By the spring of 1942, Cornelia knows as well as anyone what awaits a convict in those camps, where exhaustion, disease, and cruelty so often lead to death.

Which is why the passengers on the train to Amsterdam are all on edge as they present their identity cards. Cornelia's papers are in perfect order, of course. The policeman barely glances at the photograph, fingerprints, and signature before returning her card with a curt nod. But when Leah and Lillian Blom hold out their cards for inspection, there's a letter *J* stamped so large it's visible to everyone seated nearby. The policeman settles back on his heels and pushes his glasses higher on his nose. Jews require close inspection.

"What is the purpose of your trip to Amsterdam?"

Even though Lillian has fortified herself for the journey by dressing in her smartest outfit—a fitted jacket and pencil skirt in navy wool over a silk blouse, with seamed stockings and a veiled hat—her voice quavers in fear. "We have business at the Jewish Council."

"Business?" He frowns. It's illegal, now, for Jews to conduct any business.

"Not business, pardon me, I mean an appointment. I'm regis-tering for voluntary emigration. I'm American, you see." Cornelia worries Lillian is making things worse for herself. The United States has been at war with Germany since the bombing at Pearl Harbor five months ago. "It's compulsory, the registration. I have to do it."

The passengers around them are beginning to stare. The policeman seems uncomfortable with the attention. "Do you have your travel permit?"

"Yes, of course, I'm sorry." Lillian rummages in her purse. "This is the first time I've left The Hague since permits were required. It's in here somewhere." Cornelia and Leah exchange a worried look until she finds the paper and hands it to the policeman.

"This permit is for three people. Where is Philip Blom?"

"My husband wasn't feeling well last night." Lillian pauses, then rushes on. "He suffers from migraines lately, and with the motion of the train, I thought it would be better for him to stay home today. Is that a problem?"

The policeman looks both ways along the aisle. With no other officers in sight, he is the only figure of authority in the train car. The man's voice softens. "Jews are forbidden to travel without permits, but I don't think a person needs permission to stay home." He hands the paper back to her and continues on his way. "Documents, please, ladies and gentlemen."

Cornelia lets out a sigh of relief as conversations resume among the passengers. With their identity cards put away, there's nothing now to mark Leah and Lillian Blom as different from anyone else.

"Are you sorry you came?" Leah's lips are so close to Cornelia's ear, the warmth of her breath feels like a caress.

"No, of course not."

"Good. I'm glad you took my father's ticket, Nellie. It gives me courage to have you with me. Besides, who knows if I'll ever get permission to travel again? This may be our last chance to have an adventure, before . . ." She looks wistfully out the window without finishing her thought. She doesn't have to.

"Let's not think about that today," Cornelia says. "Besides, we make our own adventures, don't we?"

Leah squeezes Cornelia's hand. As they look out the window instead of into each other's eyes, both their hearts beat faster as they think about the times when Cornelia (to her mother's dismay) purposefully misses the midnight curfew in order to stay with Leah. Those are the nights when Cornelia and Leah set their imaginations, and their bodies, free. They might pretend to be Egyptologists on an expedition to Giza, stranded together in the desert by a sandstorm. Or Cornelia might play the part of Alexander returning from battle to his beloved Hephaestion. Some nights, Leah embodies Greta Garbo as Queen Christina, imperiously ordering Cornelia to her knees. But the best nights, Cornelia thinks, touching cool fingertips to her burning cheeks, are the ones when they are simply themselves. Two girls, together, in love.

"We do make our own adventures." Leah's voice is low and sly. "But you have to admit, it's nice to be out of The Hague for once. I can't wait to take you to that café my friends told me about." She rolls her shoulders back. "I shouldn't let it get to me, all this business with papers and permits. It's just—"

"I know." Cornelia forces herself to smile. "We won't let them spoil this for us, will we?"

Leah smiles, too. "No, we won't."

Cornelia turns back to the window as the train chugs through the countryside. It's the first of May and tulips are still in bloom, Holland's fields carpeted in broad stripes of red, yellow, pink, purple, and orange. The scene is so beautiful it hurts her heart. To choose a bouquet from the hundreds bundled together at the flower market. To set those flowers in the basket of your bicycle beside a loaf of brown bread and a wedge of cheese. To ride atop the hump of a dike as a windmill pumps water from the polder. To look up at a lavender sky streaked with clouds and wonder when it will rain. Cornelia has spent so much time in her father's world, where every Netherlander is a number on a piece of paper, she sometimes forgets what it really means to be Dutch.

The Hollerith has already processed punch cards for everyone whose last name is, according to Gerard Vogel, likely to be Jewish. After sorting for profession and collating for ancestry, hundreds of unregistered Jews have been identified. These, in turn, have led to far-flung relatives who, after a lifetime of praying to Jesus, are stunned to receive a letter from the Ministry of Information notifying them they are members of the Jewish race. Many have appealed, but until they can prove otherwise, these people now have a letter *J* stamped on their identification and a hole punched through digit 4 in column forty on their Hollerith cards.

Cornelia's father would have exempted priests and nuns from the final list of race Jews, but Generalkommissar Wimmer told him not to be fooled by a white collar or a black habit. "Blood doesn't lie, Vogel," she overheard him lecture her father. "It's the ones who look the least Jewish that put us Aryans at the greatest risk for impure breeding." Cornelia didn't see how an argument about genetics applied to celibate clergy, but that was beside the point. For a Dutch person to be considered Christian or Jewish used to depend on what they believed and how they worshipped. Now, under the Nuremburg Laws—and thanks to her father—it's determined by a list generated by a machine.

The fields of tulips are marred by slashes of asphalt as they pass Schiphol Airport, its runways camouflaged by false tarmacs to confuse British bombers. Approaching Amsterdam, passengers begin to gather their things. Lillian stands to collect her overnight case from the rack above their seat. A man seated nearby gets up to retrieve it for her. "Have strength, *mevrouw*," he says quietly, handing her the bag. "You are among friends."

The train hisses to a stop under the massive shed of Amsterdam's Centraal station. On the platform, people flow past them like water around a stone as Leah, motionless, stares up at the trusses and beams. "Isn't it beautiful?" she says. "I could spend all day sketching in here."

Cornelia, glancing up, appreciates the intricate geometry of glass and steel, but Lillian is being swept away by the stream of people. She takes Leah's arm and pulls her past the German soldiers who patrol the platform, their holstered pistols an implicit threat.

The three women emerge into the turmoil of Stationsplein. Hundreds of people are crisscrossing the brick plaza like a physics experiment in perpetual motion. Trams arrive and depart, scattering pedestrians and cyclists. Bicycles are being chained to or unchained from every rack, bridge railing, streetlamp, and traffic sign in sight. Harbor gulls flap overhead while cooing pigeons scramble for crumbs underfoot. Barges ply the waters of the Open Haven. Car horns honk. Church bells peal. Clock towers chime.

"How will we ever find him?" Lillian shades her eyes with her hand. It's been a few years since the Bloms have visited their friends Meneer and Mevrouw Presser, but when Lillian telephoned to say they were coming to Amsterdam, the Pressers immediately extended their hospitality.

"There, Mommy, look." Leah points to a shack selling herring, the headless fish arrayed along a plank. She waves at a well-dressed man who is picking up a herring by its tail. "Meneer Presser, here we are!"

The man drops the fish down his throat, wipes his mouth with a napkin, and waves back. They make their way across Stationsplein toward each other. "Welcome," he says, kissing Lillian's cheek, "but where is your husband?"

Lillian explains about Philip's headache, then gestures toward Cornelia. "We've brought Leah's friend Nellie with us instead."

Cornelia smiles. "Good day, Meneer Presser."

His breath smells of herring as he kisses her cheek. "Welcome to Amsterdam, Nellie, and to you, Leah." He steps back, assessing her outfit. "But why are you in disguise as a boy?"

Leah glances down. Her shoes are flat, her trousers pleated, her jacket cut square across the shoulders. Her mother begged her to put on a dress, but Cornelia is glad Leah stood her ground. She thinks her lover looks marvelous.

"It's the fashion, *meneer*," Leah says. "Haven't you seen a picture of Marlene Dietrich?"

"So you're a fan of German actresses now?" He harumphs, then turns to Lillian. "You can leave your things at our house before going to the Jewish Council. We'll take Tram 8, just over there."

"I'd rather walk, if you don't mind," Lillian says, though Cornelia wonders if she simply wants to avoid having to show her papers again.

"In that case, we should go directly to the Council. I'll bring your things home with me and you'll come when you've finished." Meneer Presser takes the overnight case from Lillian's hand and leads them over the bridge onto Prins Hendrikkade. The commotion quiets the farther they get from Stationsplein.

Leah, whose eyes are darting this way and that to take in the architecture of the city, points to the white edifice of the Victoria Hotel, its limestone façade as decorative as a wedding cake. "Didn't we stay there once?"

Lillian looks over. "Oh, yes, when your father received his prize from the University of Amsterdam."

"See that little house there?" Meneer Presser draws their attention to a narrow building that pierces the hotel's flank like a dark splinter. "When the hotel was being built, the owner refused to sell, no matter how much pressure he was put under. Finally, the architect changed the plans to build the hotel around his house. It comforts me to remember that sometimes people refuse to go along, even though powerful interests oppose them. Come, let's cross over to the Geldersekade. It's best to stay as far from Zeedijk as possible."

At his mention of Zeedijk, Leah gives Cornelia a nudge. "That's where the café is," she whispers. Cornelia cranes her neck to look up the narrow street. Amsterdam's De Wallen district is infamous, but it doesn't look at all dodgy in the daylight.

As they pass the old city gate at Nieuwmarkt, Cornelia feels herself transported back to the Dutch Golden Age, when their tiny country managed a far-flung empire, all the world's wealth passing through its ports. Narrow brick warehouses along the canals once housed everything from Caribbean sugar to Russian pelts to Indonesian spices to Virginia tobacco. When Meneer Presser leads them up the charming cobbles of Sint Antoniesbreestraat, Cornelia pictures it populated by characters out of a Rembrandt painting. They cross over a broad bridge dotted with tables serviced by a nearby café. People are drinking coffee or sipping beer while chatting amiably and enjoying the lovely spring day.

On the other side of the bridge, Cornelia's eye is arrested by a sign attached to a nearby streetlamp. It reads JOODSCHE WIJK.

JEWISH DISTRICT. There are no fences, no barbed wire, no checkpoints, no barricades. Uniformed Germans stroll past like tourists taking in the sights rather than soldiers of an occupying army. But the sign brings Cornelia to a standstill as abruptly as if she walked into a wall of ice. She shivers, remembering.

It was the end of January, the days so short and the nights so long all of life seemed to happen in the dark. Cornelia, home late from spending the evening with Leah, saw the lamp on in her father's study. Peeking in the door, she found him standing in front of a large map pinned to the wall, a list in one hand and a pen in the other. He beckoned her in, accepting her offer of the cup of tea she'd made for herself.

"Thank you for this, Cornelia," he said, settling into an armchair, the cup balanced on his knee. "Come, sit with me awhile. I haven't had much opportunity to tell you, but I'm very pleased with the way you've been assisting Mevrouw Kwakkelstein."

Cornelia wished he wouldn't praise her for a job he knew she hated. To change the subject, she pointed at the map. "What's that you're working on?"

He sipped the tea. "Go take a look."

Cornelia stood before it. There were no street names or neighborhoods labeled, but the ring of canals made a pattern any Dutch child would immediately recognize. It was a map of Amsterdam, covered in tiny black dots. "What is this, Father?"

"I'm plotting the results."

She looked closer. In some areas, the black dots were scattered far apart. In other areas, the dots were clustered so close the map was almost black. "Results of what?"

"Of the census, of course. Obersturmbannführer Eichmann is putting more pressure on the *Judenreferent* since a conference was held in a suburb of Berlin called Wannsee. Zöpf, however, is too lazy to read my reports. He requested that I communicate my information visually from now on."

Cornelia's stomach soured at this reminder that her father's work served the interests of Judenreferent Willi Zöpf, Adolf Eichmann's appointed "Jewish expert" in Holland. "What do they mean, the dots?"

"Oh, of course, you need a key to read the map." He got up, took a piece of paper from his desk, and pinned it to the wall. Printed in block letters, it read ELKE STIP = 10 JODEN. EACH DOT = TEN JEWS.

Cornelia swallowed the acid that rose in her throat. The dots were scattered all across the city, but toward the edge of the map, on the streets east of the Centrum, they were thickly clustered. "What neighborhood is that?"

"That's the Weesperbuurt, near Plantage Middenlaan. The neighborhood starts where Sint Antoniesbreestraat becomes Jodenbreestraat. They're very populous there, and Tram 8 runs directly to the train station, which makes it ideal."

"Ideal for what?"

"For a Jewish district. No neighborhood is perfect, obviously. In Amsterdam, the Jews are too integrated to enclose a ghetto without inadvertently including many non-Jews as well, but the map makes it clear where the highest density is." He gazed fondly at the wall, as if contemplating a pleasant landscape sketch. "I published an article in *Allgemeines Statistisches Archiv* describing this methodology. In fact, I had a letter recently from a statistician at the United States census department who's planning to use my work as a model. It seems there's a need to pinpoint their Japanese population, now that the countries are at war."

What Cornelia's father described wasn't a regular part of his work under German occupation. He was actively promoting the Nazis' hateful policies. Her hands shook as she turned to confront him.

"Why are you doing this, Father? You aren't a member of the NSB. You're not anti-Semitic. Our own neighbors, my best friend, are Jewish. You know how the Nazis will use a map like this."

His voice became stern. "I don't set the policies, Cornelia. I have no control over what is done with the data I produce. You know the motto of the Ministry of Information, don't you?"

She parroted the slogan she'd heard him intone hundreds of times. "'To inform is to serve.'"

"That's right. I'm simply doing my job. The same as you."

Leah grabs Cornelia's elbow, jolting her back to the present. "It's only a stupid sign, Nellie. Meneer Presser says it's best to ignore it. Come on, we're almost there."

When they turn onto Nieuwe Keizersgracht, the mansion at number fifty-eight is the only building along the quiet canal with a queue out front. Lillian is worried she should have come earlier, but Meneer Presser says people line up every morning to make their requests of the Jewish Council. He steers Lillian past the line and up the front steps. Cornelia and Leah follow, self-conscious about the jeers from those gathered at the ground-level entrance.

"Wait your turn with the rest of us!" one calls out. "Who made you so special?"

"Mind your own business," Meneer Presser says. Fearlessly, he raps his knuckles on the imposing door. It's opened by a harried woman who points to the words printed on a placard beside the knocker.

"Chairmen only at this entrance, *meneer.*" The woman steps onto the stoop and surveys the line below. "Best to come back tomorrow, everyone. We're fully booked for the rest of the day." For a moment, Cornelia fears a riot will break out, so frustrated are the people on the sidewalk, but soon their shoulders slump in resignation and they begin to walk away. "That goes for you, too."

"But Mevrouw Blom has an appointment," Meneer Presser says.

Lillian displays a letter on stationery printed with the logo of the Joodsche Raad. "See, it's signed by Chairman Asscher."

"My apologies, *mevrouw.* Chairman Asscher said he was expecting Professor Blom today, but you've come instead?" Lillian nods. "I'll let him know you're here, but I hope you're prepared to wait." Leah is about to follow her mother inside when the woman stops her. "The building is bursting at the seams. I really can't admit anyone who isn't named in the appointment."

"I'll be all right," Lillian says when Leah objects. "You and Cornelia go on home with Meneer Presser."

Walking away, Cornelia looks back at the building. It's an exceptionally large canal house in the heart of Amsterdam, five stories tall and five windows wide, with a balustrade above the cornice suggesting a rooftop terrace. It makes sense when Meneer Presser explains it was built by one of the founders of the Dutch East India Company, who was himself a Jew. "The Bayer pharmaceutical company was using it as their headquarters here until the neighborhood was designated Jewish. The Germans offered it up to the Joodsche Raad, and the council members grabbed it." He frowns. "They enjoy its elegant trappings a bit too much if you ask me, but the truth is, the more workers they can fit into the building, the more of us they can help. I'm on their payroll myself, now that I'm teaching at a Jewish school."

Crossing over the Amstel River, Leah is inspired to draw the charming scene of bridges and boats on the water. Cornelia and Meneer Presser lean against the railing while she wanders with her sketchbook, seeking the perfect perspective. Cornelia counts the people as they walk by: women and men, workers and students, parents with children, babies in carriages. Every time she gets to ten, she feels a stab of shame as she imagines her father inking a dot on his map.

"Philip tells me you've become Leah's best friend," Meneer Presser says after a while. Cornelia blushes, knowing how much more she and Leah are to each other than friends. "I congratulate you, Nellie. It takes courage, these days, to befriend a Jew."

Another ten people cross the bridge before Cornelia answers. "I wish I could do more."

"Come, Leah," he calls. "I have my camera with me. Let me make a photograph of you two."

Leah stashes her sketchbook and joins Cornelia at the railing. Meneer Presser takes a silver and black Leica from his pocket and backs up to the other side of the bridge. Leah puts her arm around Cornelia's waist. They smile as he snaps the shutter. Then the two girls turn to each other. Their eyes meet. It seems impossible to Cornelia that anyone looking at them could fail to see the love in their gaze. She barely notices when he snaps the shutter again.

Meneer and Mevrouw Presser live in a narrow house on a quiet street near the Artis park. The girls endure small talk over tea and cookies with these middle-aged acquaintances of Leah's parents until the cuckoo emerges from its clock to give four cheerful chirps.

"When do you think my mother might be back? Nellie and I were planning to go out and explore the city."

"Why didn't you say so in the first place?" Meneer Presser asks. "Appointments at the council can last all day. They'll shut their doors before the start of Sabbath, of course, but the sun doesn't set until nine o'clock tonight. There's no need for you to wait."

His wife agrees. "The longer Lillian's there, the better. It's only when the Jewish Council can't help that they send people away. I bought fresh eels at the fish market today, but I'll wait to serve the evening meal until you return."

"Would you mind terribly if we missed it?" Leah asks. "We don't know when we'll ever get back to Amsterdam and we want to stay out as late as we're allowed."

Mevrouw Presser is obviously disappointed, but her husband says, "Here then, take a key. It rattles our nerves if the bell rings after dark. Go, enjoy yourselves, and try not to worry about the signs. The Germans can't forbid your eyes from seeing the sights, can they?"

Outside, Leah practically skips down the street. "Come on, Nellie. It's been ages since I was here, but I think I remember the way."

The girls soon realize what every visitor to the city quickly learns: no matter how carefully one studies a map of Amsterdam, its curved streets and crisscrossing canals are as disorienting as a labyrinth. The two of them get so turned around they're surprised to find themselves on Koningsplein, where the bookstore Scheltema proves irresistible. A sign in the window declares, JODEN NIET GEWENSCHT, but a magazine has been casually propped up to obscure the word *niet,* which Leah interprets as a signal of tolerance.

"You see," she whispers, "here, Jews *are* wanted." Cornelia is nervous, but no one challenges them as they browse. They find a novel by Radclyffe Hall that Cornelia's never heard of but Leah swears is positively scandalous. Despite their supposed welcome, Cornelia insists she be the one to make the purchase while Leah waits outside.

They buy croquettes from a cart and sit for a while on the pavement alongside the Singel, feet swinging above the brackish water of the canal as they snack. From there, they wander down the bustling Kalverstraat. Even though every shop window displays an anti-Jewish sign, no one looks at Leah with suspicion among the throng of pedestrians. Still, it's a relief when the narrow street leads into the expanse of Dam Square. Cornelia and Leah feel more at ease in the wide-open space—until a group of black-shirted NSBers swaggers by, saluting the German soldiers guarding the Royal Palace. Leah stumbles on an uneven cobblestone. Cornelia takes her arm and hustles her away.

Cornelia wonders if they'll really be allowed to enter the café Leah's been talking about. Afraid of the humiliation Leah will feel if they're turned away, she's about to suggest they go back to the Pressers' house when they round a corner and Leah points to the street sign. "Look, here we are!"

Zeedijk seems more sinister in the evening than it did earlier in the day. Slanted rays of sunlight glance off attic windows as shadows rise up the brick faces of the buildings. Women linger in open vestibules illuminated with red-shaded lights, ribbons of smoke rising from their cigarettes. Raucous groups of drunken louts stumble by, singing. Solitary men scurry past, chins tucked into collars. German officers patrol in pairs, heads swiveling like searchlights as they scan the street. Cornelia drags her feet, wondering if they should have heeded Meneer Presser's advice and avoided Zeedijk after all.

"Don't worry, Nellie." Leah tries to sound brave, but there's tension in her voice. "My friends say the Germans are more interested in keeping their own soldiers away from prostitutes than they are in harassing the Dutch. Oh, there it is."

Café 't Mandje is only as wide as the door and one window. Cornelia thinks the Little Basket is a suitable name for such a tiny place. She's heartened to see there's no sign declaring that Jews aren't wanted. In fact, according to Leah's friends, Café 't Mandje is a place that welcomes all kinds of people, no matter how different— even women like us, Leah told her, though Cornelia is so convinced their love is unique she can't believe there's anyone else quite like them.

"Come on, let's go in," Leah says, tugging on Cornelia's sleeve. Jukebox music and lively conversation spill into the street as she pulls open the door. Cornelia steps into a narrow entry squeezed between a half-dozen barstools to their left and a wall to their right. She blinks, overwhelmed by the visual onslaught. Every inch of the walls is covered in photographs and magazine clippings. Above their heads, men's neckties and women's brassieres swing from the ceiling. Business cards and printed coasters are tacked to every beam. A vase of flowers is perched atop the beer taps, the blooms reaching up to the arms of a brass chandelier. Catching her reflection in the mirror behind the bar, Cornelia thinks she looks conspicuously provincial compared to the other patrons. There are artistic types dressed in colorful silks and flowing scarves. There's a woman wearing a leather cap, a man with a flower tucked behind his ear, an elderly gentleman reciting poetry to no one. A group around the jukebox is dancing, the couples impossible to discern among the gregariously linked arms.

"And who do we have here?" The bartender is a woman with a friendly face, a man's necktie, and slicked-back hair. She leans across the bar to extend her hand.

Cornelia instinctively takes it. "I'm Nellie, and this is my friend—"

"Lee." Cornelia is surprised to hear Leah introduce herself this way. Perhaps she's afraid her name sounds too Jewish? "I'm her friend Lee."

"Well, hello there, Nellie and her friend Lee. I'm Bet. This is my place, and you are welcome here." Her strong grip has pulled Cornelia between two women perched on bar stools, threatening to topple them. They steady themselves and laugh, clapping Cornelia on the back.

"Be careful Bet doesn't take you for a ride on her motorcycle, you may never come back," one woman says.

The other nods vigorously. "That happened to me once, do you remember, Bet?" She turns, her lips inches from Cornelia's ear. "We were gone for a week. The patrons ran the bar themselves until she finally brought me home."

The bartender throws back her head and laughs. Letting go of Cornelia's hand, Bet caresses the woman's cheek. "You loved every minute of it, didn't you, darling?"

She swats Bet's hand away. "You never stop flirting, do you?"

Bet smooths her hair with the flat of her palm. "You wouldn't have me any other way."

Cornelia doesn't understand how they've all become such intimate friends in a matter of moments, but the feeling is utterly genuine. Bet pours Cornelia and Leah glasses of pilsner without even asking. When a new crop of people come crowding in the door, the girls edge their way past the bar to a tiny table that's no more than a shelf projecting from the wall. Cornelia is giddy as Leah puts her arm around her waist and kisses her right there in front of anyone who cares to look. When Cornelia glances around, the elderly gentleman gives her a wink without missing a line of his poem. The music stops and everyone around the jukebox groans in protest. A new record drops that's met with a cheer. Couples of all kinds turn to one another. Leah holds out her arms. "Dance with me, Nellie."

They've held each other in this exact same way in Leah's bedroom, swaying to the phonograph, but dancing together in public is intoxicating. No wonder Leah wanted a new name tonight. They are new to the world, and to each other, in this little café. "It's like a Queen's Day party here!" Cornelia says, to which Leah replies, "You're my queen, Nellie, today and every day."

They stay for hours. When they get hungry, they order the only item on the menu: a rather questionable pea soup that's somehow the most delicious thing Cornelia has ever tasted. Bet stops by from time to time for a chat. At some point, they find themselves singing with the women who have abandoned their bar stools and joined them. Through it all, the jukebox keeps playing, the couples keep dancing, the poet keeps reciting.

"Listen up, everyone, curfew is in one hour!" Bet calls out, working her way through the crowd. "If you're leaving, leave now. If you're staying, you'll be locked in with me until the morning." She comes up to Cornelia and cups her chin in her hand. "If it weren't for this friend of yours, I'd ask you to stay."

"Hey, be careful there." Leah makes fists as if to defend Cornelia's honor, then they all crack up laughing.

"You two are sweet kids. Come again soon, won't you?" Bet gives them each a kiss on the cheek. "Hurry home now, the *moffen* come down hard on girls out in De Wallen after curfew."

Outside, no streetlights are lit and every window is blacked out. The old city, so charming and baroque in the daylight, has become gothic in the dark. Pedestrians glide furtively down the Zeedijk as if in a scene from a film noir. Leah and Cornelia take tentative steps until their eyes adjust to the silver moonlight. Linking arms, they walk toward Centraal station as fast as they can.

People are converging on Stationsplein, some on foot, others on bicycles, all hurrying to catch the last trains and trams before curfew shuts the city down. The German soldiers patrolling the square are menacing, the sound of their bootheels on the brick pavement as loud as the clomp of shoed horses. "Hurry along now, *Fräulein*," one calls out to Cornelia. Mistaking Leah for a boy, he adds, "I'm sure your young man's eager for you to warm his bed." His companion laughs, then shouts, "What's a nice girl like you doing out at this hour anyway?"

"Visiting my *Oma*," Cornelia calls back, instinctively responding in German. "*Gute Nacht, Jungs.*"

Tram 8 is ringing its departure bell. Cornelia and Leah leap aboard just in time. They drop into their seats, arms still linked, as the tram begins to move. A man across the aisle hisses at Cornelia. "You should be ashamed of yourself, flirting with the *moffen* like that."

Cornelia opens her mouth to reply, but Leah shushes her. "It's not worth it," she whispers.

Cornelia has no chance to say she was only distracting the soldiers. She didn't want them to ask for their papers. She couldn't stand the thought of Leah opening her identity card to expose that letter *J*.

The tram makes quick work of the distance they walked that afternoon. At Meijerplein, Leah says, "Here's our stop." The girls panic for a moment as the tram pulls away. It's nearly impossible to see street names in the dark. Cornelia fears they're lost, but after a couple of wrong turns, Leah locates the Pressers' address. They quietly let themselves in. Lingering in the dark vestibule, Leah finds Cornelia's lips with her fingertips. Between kisses, she whispers, "This has been the best night ever, Nellie. Thank you for going with me, for being with me."

"I'll always be with you, Leah. Always."

They jump apart as Meneer Presser swings open the interior door. "Ah, there you are. Come in, please."

They follow him into the living room, where Lillian is doing needlework in a circle of lamplight. She sets aside the fabric in her lap and gets up to clasp Leah in a tight hug. "I've been worried sick about you."

"I'll bid you good night now," Meneer Presser says. "My wife has made up the *opklapbed* in my study for you girls. It's at the end of the hallway upstairs. You can find it for yourselves, yes?"

"Certainly, thank you, *meneer*," Cornelia says.

When the three of them are alone, Lillian holds Leah at arm's length. "I suppose it's good you went out, though. I waited at the Jewish Council for hours to meet Chairman Asscher, and then I had to go to another building on Lijnbaansgracht where they have their emigration office. I found out there isn't any emigration going on at the moment, but I did get us on something called the Exchange List. It costs a fortune, but it qualifies us to be exchanged for German prisoners of war, probably with the

British in Palestine. There's a chance we could be traded to the Americans, but for that, the Germans would probably demand a ransom, too. Of course, my father will pay any amount in the world to get us back to New York. In the meantime, we're all exempt from being called up for labor service, see?"

Lillian shows them a blue stamp on her identification, along with two other stamps Leah and Philip can add to theirs. There's a twitch at the corner of her eye and a gleam of sweat across her forehead. Though the news is good and she's kept her voice steady, Cornelia is worried about Lillian's mood.

"But how did you pay for these, Mommy? I thought we already turned over our bank account to Lippmann Rosenthal."

Lillian's voice catches in her throat. "An art dealer who works for the bank is coming to our house on Monday to appraise my Van Gogh. If he deems it worth what we owe, he'll take the painting and we'll stay on the list."

"No, Mommy, not your poppies!"

Lillian sets her mouth in a grim line. "A pretty piece of canvas can't be worth more than our lives, Leah. Now, before you go upstairs, give me your jacket."

"Why? It isn't ripped."

"Neither was mine." Lillian shows Leah what she's been sewing. On the front of her jacket, in the exact place where a person would place a hand over their heart, is a piece of bright yellow fabric cut in the shape of a six-pointed star. In the center of the star, printed in script that parodies Hebrew, is the word *Jood*.

Cornelia is horrified. Her mind flies to medieval portrayals of Jews in ghettos. This can't be happening here, not in their civilized country, not in the twentieth century.

"Go on, Leah." Lillian's voice is soft and sad. "Give it to me."

Reluctantly, Leah removes her jacket. Lillian cuts another star from a strip of printed fabric. Spreading Leah's jacket on her lap, she pins it in place. The yellow is bright. The star is big. She threads a needle and begins to sew.

"You mean—" The words squeak through Leah's closed throat. "You mean we have to walk around like that from now on?"

"The Jewish Council was just notified the rule goes into effect tomorrow." Lillian's chin begins to tremble. "They're frantically distributing stars before anyone gets in trouble. I was lucky to buy enough for both of us to travel safely."

Leah points a trembling finger. "You won't catch me dead wearing that thing!"

"You'd rather they haul you off to prison so you can die there?" Lillian shouts, then covers her mouth, stifling a sob. "Please, don't upset me any more than I am."

Leah kneels at her mother's feet. "I'm sorry, Mommy. It's going to be okay tomorrow, you'll see. Remember how nice that man was on the train this morning? I bet everyone will be extra nice to us when we wear those stars. I'll pretend mine's a boutonniere, and you can think of yours as a corsage. Remind me what kind of corsage you were wearing at the reception in New York where you and Daddy met?"

"It was a Dutch iris. Your father said it reminded him of home." Lillian blinks back tears. "Go on upstairs, the two of you. I'll be fine."

"But—"

"Really, please go. I need to be alone for a while."

When Cornelia pulls back the curtain around the *opklapbed,* she thinks how they might have pretended the narrow bed hidden by drapes was a sleeping berth on the Orient Express. Now it seems more like a coffin. Once Cornelia is beneath the blanket, Leah switches off the lamp and gropes her way under the covers, clinging to Cornelia like a frightened child.

Cornelia runs her fingers through Leah's hair, soothing her. Eventually, Leah falls into a fitful sleep. But Cornelia can't sleep. She's infuriated that the Germans are forcing every Dutch Jew to wear that star. What's the point of slapping a symbol on their clothing when any policeman inspecting identity cards can see by the letter *J* if someone is Jewish?

That's it, she realizes. This is the next step. The Hollerith sits hidden in a secret bunker. The punch cards are a mystery to human eyes. The Ministry of Information keeps its files under lock and key. Only policemen and soldiers can demand to inspect someone's identification. But anyone walking down the street can see a yellow star.

A wave of dread sweeps over Cornelia. Her father designed the census, but those black dots on the map in his study are based on information she helped create. She may be a tiny cog in Nazi Germany's great machine of destruction, but there's no denying that her energy, like a gust of breeze on the sail of a windmill, helps turn the gears. She might as well have sewn that star on Leah's chest herself.

Saving inscrutable punch cards for some future reckoning of Nazi crimes will do nothing to help Leah in the here and now. She needs to find a way to use her access and understanding to save the one person who has become her whole world. Cornelia racks her brain until, near dawn, a plan forms in her mind.

Chapter Eleven
Rita Klein

New York City
June 1960

Congratulations, Miss Klein. Mr. McKay told me you've officially been hired for the position."

"Thanks, Gladys, but I wish you'd call me Rita."

When I first met Gladys, I'd assumed purple was her signature color, but over the past week I'd learned it was the overall effect she went in for. So far, I'd seen Gladys in blue, yellow, and pink. On this Monday morning, she was resplendent in shades of orange from head to toe, like a walking sunset.

"All right, Rita. I've got your employment papers ready for you."

I filled out the tax forms she gave me for the Internal Revenue Service and the State of New York, then turned to the document that would make me a salaried employee of Antiquated Business Machines for the next three months. I looked up at her, disappointed.

"I'm sorry," she said. "I guess I spoke too soon. Mr. Pettibone lowered the salary because you're a woman."

"I'm sorry, too. I know you were hoping I'd set a precedent." Seventy-five dollars a week wasn't bad, but it was less than they'd budgeted for a man. Of course, men were assumed to be supporting families—that's why they were paid more for the same jobs. Then I thought of Francie. She supported herself and her kids and her mother, too. I bet every woman at Antiquated depended on her paycheck just as much as the men in Olympia's factory.

"They never pay us what we're worth, but who does?" Gladys shrugged. "Don't get me wrong, Rita, I like it here. At least Mr. McKay and Mr. Pettibone treat all the girls with respect. Compared to the crap I've put up with from other men I've worked for—"

Mr. McKay's entrance cut her off. "Good morning, Miss Klein. If Gladys has got you squared away, I'm eager to hear about your day at Olympia."

"Go ahead, Rita, I've got everything I need."

"Thanks, Gladys. I'll see you at lunch, okay?"

Mr. McKay tilted back in his chair and listened as I offered my observations about the metal factory. I told him how Francie's brother had gotten the company in over their heads by mistaking the kind of steel they needed to fulfill the contract, and that the foreman hadn't been aware of the navy's requirement that every item be stamped with a serial number. "That's going to add an extra step to the production process they didn't plan on. I also noticed that their press machine needed to be shut down for an adjustment whenever they switched the steel from A2 to Type 316. Until it started back up, there was a worker standing around idle. Oh, and they won't be able to sell their skeletons for scrap until the contract's fulfilled, which will cut into their cash flow."

"You're not painting a pretty picture, Miss Klein. I've had my doubts about the wisdom of the *Constellation* contract from the beginning, but it's not our place to advise the businesses we service. At least you were able to head off a couple of potential problems. Hopefully, they'll be in full production soon. Olympia's profit margins have been thin for years now. We'll know soon enough if this aircraft carrier will sink the company."

He smiled at his pun, then offered me a cigarette. This time, I accepted. He raised an eyebrow in surprise but gallantly held out his lighter. "Sounds like you made the most of your time in Brooklyn, Miss Klein. Francie was certainly impressed. So, what ideas have you come up with?"

I checked my notes, even though I didn't need to. I'd been thinking about this all weekend. "Olympia already has multiple computer codes attached to every inventory item, and now I'll have to create even more codes for the navy contract. The 602 can do multiple sorts in a single operation, but I'm afraid so many different codes will make it cumbersome for us to efficiently produce weekly progress reports."

"I agree with your assessment of the problem," Mr. McKay said. "What do you propose as a solution?"

"Well, I was thinking about creating master codes for each of the items they're producing for the navy. That would make it easier for Olympia to code the punch cards on their end, but we could instruct the computer to break down each item into its constituent parts as needed for the reports."

"I like the way you're thinking," Mr. McKay said, crossing a leg and taking a drag off his cigarette. "How about you get started on a planning chart? You can work at that desk by the window, and I've cleared off a chalkboard for you with a diagram of the 602's control panel."

"Oh, okay." I was surprised to be sent off to work independently already. "I do have a question, though. If I create master codes for the navy job, how will you integrate that information with their old Hollerith system?"

"Olympia's old system is my purview. Leave it to me to figure out how to reconcile our two approaches."

I spent the morning consulting the 602 instruction manual and reviewing Olympia's codebooks. I was about to begin a planning chart when Gladys stopped by my desk. "Joining us for lunch, Rita?"

"Sure, thanks." I'd been eating a bagged lunch in the break room with the other girls since my second day at Antiquated. Gladys made sure I felt welcome, but they'd all been working together for so long, they quickly fell into conversation with one another as if I weren't there. That day, their gossip turned to someone's cousin who'd gotten herself "in trouble." My ears perked up, expecting the topic would lead to talk of unwed mothers' homes and ruined futures. Turned out, the story had a different ending: the girl's mother brought the child into their family, claiming it was her youngest baby instead of her eldest daughter's bastard. From the knowing nods around the break room table, I realized this was a familiar story.

My sandwich stuck in my throat. Had Miss Murphy ever considered this solution to the problem of a teen pregnancy? I wondered. I was too old for such a scheme to have fooled anyone, but some of the girls at the Hudson Home were still kids themselves. It rattled around in my brain for the rest of the day, like a misplaced decimal in a math equation—tiny enough to be overlooked, but enormously consequential.

At five o'clock, Mr. McKay, hat on his head and briefcase in hand, stopped by my desk to say good night. Even though he didn't seem especially busy, he'd given me a wide berth all day. I didn't want to run to him with every question that popped into my head, but I hadn't expected such indifference.

"Before you go, can I ask a question about my planning chart?" I hoped I didn't sound as frustrated as I felt. "I want to make sure I'm on the right track before I begin diagramming the control panel."

He raised his hands to stop me. "Developing programs for the navy contract is your bailiwick, Miss Klein. I wouldn't have hired you if I didn't have faith in your abilities."

I appreciated his faith, but he knew my abilities were limited. I decided to approach the problem fresh in the morning. Before leaving the office, I stopped in the ladies' room. Standing shoulder to shoulder with the rest of the girls as we all combed out our hair and touched up our lipsticks felt nice, like being back in a dormitory. As I met my gaze in the mirror, I realized I was feeling less like an imposter with every passing hour.

On Tuesday morning, I found a series of notes on my desk from Mr. McKay. He must have gotten here early, I thought, squinting at his tiny handwriting. He'd made a few corrections to my planning chart that turned the efficient process I was developing into an elegant one. I looked up to thank him, but he was facing one of his blackboards, his back turned to me. I shrugged. If Mr. McKay preferred an epistolary collaboration, who was I to question it? Besides, it could have been worse. I thought about the times in my computing machines class at Columbia when the professor ignored my raised hand to call, instead, on a guy who confidently presented one of my ideas as his own. Consoling myself with the thought that the professor's praise rightfully belonged to me did nothing to ease my silent fury. Bosses were notorious for taking credit for their subordinates' work, but Mr. McKay seemed intent on keeping his name as far from Olympia's navy contract as possible.

The planning chart had to be complete before I could diagram the control panel, but then I'd have to test the program to be sure it worked—and testing always revealed problems that needed to be fixed. It was a logical process but a recursive one, without a clear beginning or end. I ate lunch at my desk that day, and the next, too, determined to show Mr. McKay that his faith in me wasn't misplaced.

When Mr. McKay tapped me on my shoulder after lunch on Thursday, I hoped it was to further explain the note he'd left on my desk that morning. Before I could ask about it, though, he said, "I'd like you to meet my wife and son, Miss Klein."

Mrs. McKay was a regal woman whose beauty surely meant she'd never be insecure about her husband working in an office full of women. Their son shook my hand, told me his name was Max, announced that he was twelve years old, and said it was a pleasure to make my acquaintance.

"I'm pleased to meet you, too, Max," I said, amused by his formality.

"I don't usually leave this early," Mr. McKay said, "but we're going to the British Exhibition at the Coliseum this afternoon, then we have tickets for Madison Square Garden to see the Military Tournament and Tattoo."

When I asked what that was, Max piped up. "It is an enormous show with motorcycles and military maneuvers and marching bands with bagpipes!" He pronounced his words with a lisp that led me to assume he had some kind of impediment. When Mrs. McKay excused herself to go freshen up, Max started to follow her, but his father caught him by the shoulder and said quietly, "*Bleib hier, mein Sohn.*" Max stayed put. Though the language revealed that what I'd taken for a speech defect might have been an accent, it left me wondering why in the world they were speaking German.

I worked late that day, losing track of time as I stood at the chalkboard, completing the wiring diagram. When I finally looked around, I was surprised to see everyone else had gone home—except Gladys, whom I found at her desk in reception. Today she was blinding in white, with a damask jacket patterned with ivory flowers over a linen sheath. Her espadrilles seemed too informal for the office, but the macramé matched, as did the string of pearls shimmering around her neck. I thought the silver eye shadow was a stretch, but her nude lip was perfection.

"All done, Rita?"

"I didn't realize what time it was. I'm sorry for keeping you."

"It's fine, I had some letters to finish up." She covered her typewriter and began gathering her things.

"Gladys, I was wondering, have you ever noticed Mr. McKay speaking German to his son?"

"Of course. The boy was born there."

The picture of a German boy that popped into my mind didn't match up with Max's brown skin and kinky hair. "I don't understand."

Gladys put down her pocketbook and leaned against the desk, relishing the chance to tell me the story. "Mr. McKay dated Max's mother while his army unit was stationed in Germany. Max showed me a picture of her once—blue eyes, blond braids, the whole Aryan ideal. From what I gather, Mr. McKay didn't know she was pregnant when he sailed for the States. By the time she wrote to tell him he had a son, he was already married. He and his wife both wanted the boy to come live with them in Harlem. They felt it would be better for Max to be raised in a community where he'd fit in, instead of some German town where he was sure to stand out. But his mother refused to give him up until last year."

"What happened last year?"

"She got engaged to a man who mistreated the boy. Probably an ex-Nazi, the country must be crawling with them. Anyway, she put Max on a flight to New York right before the wedding. It was the best thing she could do for the boy, if you ask me. He worships his father, and Mrs. McKay treats him like he was her own flesh and blood."

The story of a mother giving up her son struck a chord in me, sure, but what I thought about most was the courage it took for an unmarried woman to keep a child who didn't even look like her for as long as she had. I followed Gladys into the corridor and waited while she locked up the office. "You know a lot about it, don't you?"

"When Mr. McKay and Mr. Pettibone get to talking, they forget I can hear them from reception. Not that I'm snooping, mind you, but I can't very well shut my ears, can I?"

You could shut the door, I thought—but didn't say.

On Friday, I told Mr. McKay I was ready to wire the control panel for the 602. Instead of keeping his distance, he jumped out of his chair.

"Do you mind if I check your diagrams first?"

"Please, I'd appreciate it."

He went over every curved line and calculation on the chalkboard, finding and correcting a couple of mistakes. I wished he'd taken this much interest earlier; it would have saved me hours of work and a few headaches, too.

"There you go, Miss Klein. If you get the panel wired today, I'll show you how to set up the 602 to run a test program on Monday."

"Thanks." I turned to go back to my desk, then spun on my heel to face him. "I know you're busy, Mr. McKay, but I wish you were working more closely with me on the navy contract."

"I would if I could, Miss Klein." He frowned. "As soon as I heard the Defense Department was going to be involved, I told Pettibone we'd need to hire someone else to handle the job."

"I don't understand. Are you a pacifist?"

"A pacifist?" He shook his head, incredulous. "Come with me."

I followed him across the office to the conference room. "Here's the thing," he said, closing the door behind us. I imagined Gladys with her ear to the keyhole, listening in. "I can't have my name associated with that navy contract in any way, shape, or form." He lit a cigarette and sent a stream of angry smoke toward the ceiling. "I risked my life fighting Fascism in the war, but according to J. Edgar Hoover, I'm not American enough to help make spoons for sailors."

It finally dawned on me what he was referring to. "But why would the FBI care that you had a child with a German woman?"

"How do you know about Max?" His surprise settled into resignation. "Thanks to Gladys, I suppose. Well, it's obviously not a secret." He took a deep drag, smoke swirling around his face. "I'm sure Hoover hates miscegenation as much as he does homosexuals, but I doubt my son is mentioned in my FBI file. No, Miss Klein, the truth is, I was a Communist right up until Stalin signed that nonaggression pact with Hitler. Before the war, lots of Blacks were sympathetic to their cause. They had recruiters on street corners all over Harlem. Back then, solidarity among the races sounded pretty good compared to segregation and lynching. I see now, of course, that Communism is a sham, but the FBI doesn't care that I've changed my mind. Once a Red, always a Red, as far as they're concerned. If I'd signed that loyalty oath, they would have dredged it up all over again. It could've damaged our whole company. I didn't even dare tell Francie Plunkett." He leaned forward and crushed his cigarette in the ashtray. "So now you know, Miss Klein, what are you going to do?"

"Do?" I hoped he wasn't worried I'd denounce him. As far as I was concerned, his politics were none of my business. "Could you keep looking over my work and leaving me notes, like you've been doing? That wouldn't get you in trouble, would it?"

From the way he rolled his shoulders back, I could tell he was relieved. His confession was a risk for him, sure, but all it did was remind me I'd lied on that oath, too.

"No, that should be fine. Don't mention this to Francie, though, okay?"

"You got it, Mr. McKay."

All the real work of control panel programming was in the diagramming; plugging wires into the panel was time-consuming but easy enough. Instead of staying at my desk or eating in the break room that day, I headed to Bloomingdale's on my lunch hour to get something special for my date with Jacob. The belted madras shirtwaist I bought practically emptied my wallet of cash, but it was payday, finally, and I figured I deserved a splurge. Besides, Jacob was taking me out. All I'd need was bus fare home.

It was about quarter to five when all the girls left in a group, eager to start their weekends. Mr. McKay went to his partners' meeting in Mr. Pettibone's office, though from the smell of cigars and the clink of glasses it seemed to me more like a happy hour. I ducked into a stall in the ladies' room to change into my new dress. Washing up, I checked my watch. I still had a few minutes. Jacob had called me at work that morning to say he'd gotten tickets for the six o'clock screening at the Baronet. No one was allowed to enter the theater after *Psycho* started playing, he said, so we couldn't be late.

I stepped back from the mirror and cinched my belt one notch tighter. I was finally as slender as I'd been before I went away. It eased my mind to know Miss Murphy had told the truth about that, at least. It had just taken a few weeks longer than I'd expected.

A bark like a wounded dog's escaped my mouth as I counted back twenty-three days to when David was born. The image of his tiny face suddenly filled my vision like a close-up on a movie screen. My stomach churned all over again with the sick feeling that something was terribly wrong. I gripped the edge of the sink and stared down my reflection in the mirror. What would Miss Murphy say to that girl? Your son has a better life than you could ever give him. And you—you have your whole life ahead of you. What more do you want?

You know what I want, the girl in the mirror whispered, her eyes rimmed in red. I want to hold my baby.

A toilet flushed. Gladys appeared beside my reflection swathed in green like an exotic plant. "Are you okay, Rita?"

I pressed my hand to my stomach. "Just cramps, you know how it is."

"Not anymore I don't." She smiled at me. "Poor thing. Whoever said youth is wasted on the young was never a woman. That's a nice dress. Do you have a date tonight?"

I nodded. "We're seeing that new Hitchcock movie. What about you?"

"I'm going to *West Side Story* at the Winter Garden, now that the theater strike is over." She took out a lipstick the same shade of pink as the flowers peeking through the palm fronds on her skirt. "One of the distinct pleasures of being a woman my age is that there are so many confirmed bachelors who can't conceive of going to a Broadway show on their own. I haven't paid for a ticket in years."

"Oh?"

"Don't sound so surprised, Rita. You thought I was a spinster, I suppose. Well, I'm not in the market for a husband, if that's what you're wondering. My favorite moment of the night is putting the man in a taxi at the end of it." I didn't dare ask at what point in the night that taxi was called for. Gladys gave me a sidelong look as she capped her lipstick and snapped her pocketbook shut. "Are you sure you're all right?"

"I'm sure." I don't think she believed me, but she left me on my own to splash cold water on my face and fix my makeup. Even if I could figure out the logical flaw in Miss Murphy's argument, it didn't matter anymore, I reminded myself. It was like realizing you'd made a mistake after turning in an exam—too late to change the answer.

I found Jacob pacing in the lobby. "We'll have to hurry, Rita." He grabbed my hand and pulled me through the revolving doors without even stopping to compliment my dress. We dashed down the couple of long blocks to Park Avenue to catch the Lexington line up to Fifty-Ninth Street. When I pressed up against him in the crowded train, he took advantage of our proximity to plant a kiss on my cheek. "Hello, by the way," he said, a little breathless.

"Hello to you, too."

I'd been looking forward to buttered popcorn, but there was no time to stop at the concession stand. We barely made it into our seats before the lights went down. There wasn't much action for the first half hour, but I found myself engrossed nonetheless. The hotel room where Marion met her married boyfriend—well, divorced, technically, but still, there was something unsavory about it—got me thinking about my night with Leonard. That man on the movie screen was in town on business, too. Soon he'd fly back to wherever he'd come from and leave Marion alone again, feeling ashamed of herself for loving someone who kept her hidden like a dirty secret.

In the dark theater, I wondered what I'd ever meant to Leonard. Was the prospect of sex with a naïve college girl really so compelling to a man that he'd travel to New York City and pretend to have feelings that weren't true? Leonard had lied about his marriage and his family, and for what? Ten minutes of grunting? It infuriated me to think how many men were in hotel rooms like that one on the screen, zipping their pants and walking away untouched, while women were left to face the consequences.

The pace of the film picked up when Marion stole the money she thought would enable her boyfriend to finally marry her. Once she was on the road, though, it seemed like every man in the world felt entitled to put her under surveillance just because she wasn't acting like a respectable lady. What kind of woman pulls over for the night by the side of the road or buys a car without caring what color it is? That moment where the mechanic and the car salesman and the patrolman all line up to watch her walk away made me so angry. What gave them the right to judge her? Sure, she was stealing thousands of dollars in cash, but they didn't know that. As far as they were concerned, she was simply a woman moving through the world in a way they didn't like.

When Anthony Perkins showed up, I gave Jacob a nudge of recognition because he'd starred in *On the Beach,* too. I leaned over and hummed a bar from "Waltzing Matilda" until he playfully pinched my arm to make me stop.

The hotel manager Perkins played was strange, what with his collection of taxidermy animals and that horrible mother of his, but it was nice how he made Marion a sandwich while they talked things over. I was relieved when she realized she'd made a terrible mistake stealing that money. She'd thought it would solve her problems, but deep down she knew she couldn't buy integrity—certainly not with stolen loot. It was as if she'd been in a fog of bad decisions, each mistake compounding the last, until she made up her mind to do what was right and everything became clear.

Once she decided to go home and face the consequences, I figured the rest of the film would be about her trial or something. Her taking a shower seemed, at first, like a classic literary device signaling the washing away of sin. Then that terrible screeching music started and the hotel manager's crazy mother pulled back the curtain and began stabbing her. I screamed right along with everyone else in the theater. When Marion fell to the floor of the bathroom, her naked body was so vulnerable and alone, I started to cry. It was senseless and cruel for Hitchcock to kill her off like that. Just because she loved a man who wouldn't marry her, did that mean she deserved to die?

"Get me out of here, Jacob," I said. We weren't the only ones hustling up the aisle of the theater after that shower scene. What surprised me was how many people stayed in their seats.

Out on the street, Jacob couldn't stop apologizing. "I had no idea what the film was about. I'm so sorry it frightened you, Little Rita."

"Why do you always call me that?" I snapped. "You think I'm so small and helpless?"

"What? No, I thought . . . never mind, you're upset. Why don't we stop off for a drink somewhere?"

We were heading west on Fifty-Ninth Street. I considered asking him to take me to the expensive Oak Room at the Plaza to punish him for such a disastrous date. I was pretty sure he'd do it, but that wouldn't have been fair to his wallet, and after all, the movie wasn't his fault. Instead, I pointed to a little Irish hole-in-the-wall we were passing. "Let's go in here."

We tucked ourselves into a dark booth with a high back. The lights were dim and the air smelled of malt and French fries. The patrons over at the bar all seemed to be nursing glasses of Guinness, but I wasn't in the mood for black beer. I ordered a martini and Jacob did the same. When the bartender brought them over, he dropped off a menu, too.

"What do you recommend?" I asked.

"You can't go wrong with the fish and chips, miss. I took myself down to Fulton Street this morning to pick out the cod, and me wife's batter is an old family recipe handed down through the generations."

I wasn't sure I believed his malarky, but I ordered a basket of fish and so did Jacob. When I lifted my glass to take a sip, I caught a glimpse of my watch. It wasn't even seven o'clock. "Well, Jacob, our track record for terrifying movies remains unbroken."

He laughed nervously. "I apologize, Rita. The first review ran in this morning's paper, but I purposely didn't read it."

"Don't worry about it." I covered the back of his hand with my own. "I'm okay now."

"You were crying." He turned his hand up so we were palm to palm. "That attack was terrible to see."

"I felt so sorry for her." I thought of that stream of blood circling the shower drain and shivered.

"It was upsetting for me, too, that sudden violence. The terror in her face when that crazy woman pulled back the curtain—" He took back his hand to wipe his forehead with a napkin. "That's a feeling I know."

I took another sip, the cold gin warming my throat. "What you said about Anne Frank and Auschwitz . . ." I hesitated. I could practically hear my mother's voice telling me not to go poking around in the past, but I screwed up my courage and asked, "Were you there, Jacob?"

"I was." He took a large swallow. I watched his Adam's apple rise and fall and thought that might be all he'd say about it. He set the glass on the table and stared down at the olive. "I was thirteen the night I went down that ramp. I was tall for my age or I wouldn't have lived to see the morning." A picture seemed to have appeared before his eyes. He blinked, as if advancing the slide in a projector, then looked at me. "I was transported there in April of 1944. I survived that hell until December, when the Russians started closing in. Everyone knew that Hitler was doomed, but the Nazis still wouldn't let us out of their clutches. Thousands of prisoners were evacuated back to Germany in the dead of winter, poor Anne Frank among them. Some froze in train cars. Others marched through the snow with no shoes on their feet."

I shivered. "Did you march, too?"

"If I had, I wouldn't be here with you now. I hid myself, right there in the camp. I managed to stay alive until liberation."

I'd seen the newsreels—emaciated people, striped uniforms, mass graves. It seemed impossible that the handsome man I was sitting across from had experienced such unimaginable cruelty. "What about before you were sent to Auschwitz?"

He drained his glass, gulping down the olive whole. "My family lived for over two years in Rotterdam after the bombardment. It wasn't so bad, at first. I didn't really mind going to a Jewish school, but I hated wearing that hideous star. Eventually, though, we got a notice to turn ourselves in to the police. At least Camp Westerbork was still on Dutch soil. My parents and I were together there for a while."

Our baskets of fish arrived, looking as delicious as they smelled, but my appetite had disappeared. Jacob handed the bartender his empty glass. I hadn't even finished my first drink but it was already going to my head. I guessed I'd find out pretty soon if Jacob could hold his liquor.

"We keep breaking our pact, Jacob."

"What pact?"

"Not to talk about the end of the world."

He laughed, a hollow sound that lacked joy. "You're right. All I want when I see you across the table from me is to think about how pretty you are. I never meant to ruin our date by speaking of such terrible things."

"How about we blame Alfred Hitchcock and enjoy our fish while it's hot, okay?"

His martini arrived. He used it to make a toast. "Damn you, Alfred Hitchcock."

We clinked glasses. "Damn right."

He got gregarious after that second drink but he didn't order a third. He put his arm around my waist as we walked through the city streets, the summer evening too young, yet, for the romance of streetlights. When we got to the Port Authority, I asked if he'd heard about the British Exhibition.

"Is that at the Coliseum by Columbus Circle? Yes, certainly, I remember seeing Prince Philip's picture in the paper at the opening last week."

"Well, I think we should have another date to make up for tonight, don't you? Would you like to go tomorrow, together? It opens at eleven."

The smile that stretched across his face raised the temperature of my heart. He kissed me sloppily and then stepped back, laughing with genuine joy. "I'll see you at the feet of Columbus, Little Rita."

I really didn't mind when he called me that. It was kind of sweet, actually.

Chapter Twelve
Cornelia Vogel

The Hague, Netherlands
January 1943

I t's rare, lately, for the Vogels to find themselves together at the breakfast table. Gerard, under constant pressure to meet the next deadline, often leaves for work while his children are still asleep. Dirk, who's now attending Zandvliet Lyceum on the Bezuidenhoutseweg, has taken to folding his breakfast bread into a sandwich that he eats while biking to school. Helena is usually in the kitchen cleaning up by the time Cornelia comes down for her coffee and *ontbijt*. On this January morning, however, when Cornelia enters the dining room, her gathered family is a cozy sight. She takes her seat among them, committing the moment to memory: her father finishing the last bites of his buttered bread; Dirk dipping a spoon into a jar of jam; Helena stirring yogurt into her muesli. A pang of nostalgia pierces her heart at the enormity of what she's risking for Leah's sake.

Not just for Leah, she reminds herself. It's more than that now. Since the night of yellow stars in Amsterdam, Cornelia has been purposefully making mistakes when processing Hollerith orders. It's not enough to stop the Nazis—that would bring too much suspicion on her—but she does occasionally slow down their relentless effort to identify and deport every Jew in the Netherlands. But today she's not thinking about all the people in Holland whose documents are stamped with a letter *J*. Today, she's only thinking about one.

A shoe nudges her shin beneath the table. "Wake up, Nellie."

"I'm awake, Dirk. Pass me the milk, would you?"

"Let me pour it for you." Dirk stands to lift the spout of the pitcher above his sister's coffee cup. "Enough?" She nods, touched by her little brother's act of kindness.

Helena smiles at her son. "That was nice of you."

Dirk shrugs. "She would have spilled it, wouldn't she? Hey, Nellie, maybe you should do a puppet show about Egypt." He points to her hands, laughing. "Your fingers look like mummies!"

Cornelia rolls her eyes, though the way her mother has wrapped each blistered fingertip in gauze does make them look mummified. She's sure it's excessive, but once Helena gets out the first aid kit, there's no arguing with her.

"A burn is nothing to take lightly, Dirk." Helena turns to her daughter. "I wish you wouldn't go to work today, Cornelia. You should soak your hands, and I'd like to change those bandages."

"You can change them when I get home. Father, would you take me?" Cornelia spreads her wrapped fingers wide. "I'm not sure I can manage my bicycle."

Gerard Vogel tips his head back to drain his cup. "I'm leaving now, Cornelia. I'm sorry, but I can't wait for you."

She swigs her coffee and pushes her empty plate away. "I'm coming."

Though curfew has lifted, it's still dark as night outside, the winter sun hours yet from rising. Her father wheels his bicycle out of the garden house, through the gate, and into the alley. He holds the handlebars steady while Cornelia sits on the rack over the rear tire. "Ready to ride?" he asks, as if she's a little girl again.

She knots her scarf against the cold. "Ready."

Gerard attaches the dynamo that acts as a headlamp, then stands on the pedals to put the bike in motion. The extra weight of his adult daughter elicits a grunt of effort. It's been a long time since Cornelia has hitched a ride on his bike this way. It brings to mind a childhood memory of her father taking her to primary school after she'd sprained her ankle. The man who was always so strict at home became playful as he swerved his bike in wide arcs up the street, calling out to Cornelia to hold on tight. She did, gathering fistfuls of his coat in her hands, her laughter trailing behind them like soap bubbles from a child's wand.

This past summer, Cornelia was the one doing the hard work of pedaling with a passenger. In June, the Nazis made it illegal for Jews to own bicycles, so Leah started sitting on the rear rack of Cornelia's bike whenever they ventured out. As the months elapsed, however, there were fewer and fewer places for them to go. The Germans declared the dunes along the shore verboten, and all the parks were closed to Jews. Bus drivers and tram conductors, seeing the yellow patch of fabric sewn to Leah's clothing, denied them entry. Jews were banned from so many streets in The Hague that navigating the city on foot became as complicated as running a maze. Even on the streets where Leah was allowed to walk, she had to contend with the stares of passersby whose eyes were invariably drawn to the star on her chest.

With the coming of winter, Leah and her parents practically became prisoners in their own home. The telephone company, provided with a list of Jewish customers, disconnected their number. The post office stopped servicing any address identified as Jewish. All correspondence now came through the Jewish Council, which added mail delivery to its long list of duties. These deliveries, however, were rarely welcome. Each weekly printing of the *Joodsche Weekblad* was full of distressing information: A new

rule against shopping at the fish market. A ban on mixed marriages. An earlier curfew just for Jews.

Through it all, Lillian kept on believing the sacrifice of her
Van Gogh would spare them the Jewish Council's most dreaded
delivery of all—a call-up notice directing the family to report for
"labor service" in Germany. That changed yesterday, when the
buff-colored envelope containing their notice was slipped through
the mail slot of the Bloms' front door.

Cornelia learned the news when she came home from work.
As she crossed the garden, Leah tossed a crumpled note down
from the balcony.

> *They've given us two days to pack our bags and turn ourselves
> in to the police. Don't come upstairs tonight, Nellie. My parents
> are too upset. Come see me tomorrow, to say goodbye.*

By the time she looked up, her vision blurred by tears, Leah
had disappeared inside. Cornelia stuffed the note in her pocket,
already certain of what she had to do.

Balancing on the back of her father's bike as he pedals through
the morning darkness, their path illuminated by the dynamo's
wobbly circle of light, Cornelia wonders if she'll have the nerve
to pull off what she has planned. She rests her head against her
father's back, hoping his strength will soothe her, but the change
in position throws off his balance.

"Sit up straight, Cornelia."

After turning off Scheveningseweg, Gerard Vogel approaches
Huize Kleykamp at full speed, not even braking as they cross
the moat. Entering the glare of the guard post's spotlight, he
simply lifts his fingers from the handlebar to acknowledge the
soldiers stationed there. They raise stiff arms as he rides past.
Cornelia isn't sure if her father has forgotten she is on the back

of his bike or if he doesn't want to waste the time it would take for her to be inspected by the guards. Either way, she sails past, too, unchallenged and unexamined—just as she hoped.

In the courtyard, Cornelia hops off so her father can park his bicycle, wondering how he justifies being hailed with a Nazi salute. She supposes he accepts the soldiers' deference as his due. After all, he invented the Dutch identity card. Why should he have to show one to prove who he is? It occurs to Cornelia that her father could get away with transporting anything into or out of Huize Kleykamp, from a sack of forged documents to a ticking time bomb. Not that he'd ever do such a thing. He's so obsessed with his work, she doubts he's capable of even the thought of sabotage.

"Are you going to stand there daydreaming or are you coming inside?"

"I'm coming, Father."

Cornelia has never known Huize Kleykamp to be so quiet. Their footsteps echo as they pass the galleries where ranks of file cabinets stand like sleeping sentries, their treasure trove of documents secure. There's a hum of conversation from the cafeteria, where the night guards have congregated around urns of coffee, but the elegant villa is still unstaffed by the civil servants who will soon arrive to do the ministry's work—except for Mevrouw Kwakkelstein, of course, who is already at her desk outside Gerard Vogel's office.

"Good morning, *meneer,* and Cornelia—oh, what's happened to your hands?"

"My clumsy daughter burned herself last night making a pot of tea." Gerard frowns at Cornelia. "I'm still not certain how she managed it."

"I told you, Father, my apron got caught in the flame when I reached for the tea tin." She turns to Mevrouw Kwakkelstein. "It was silly of me, but I was in a rush to boil the water before the gas was turned off."

Mevrouw Kwakkelstein nods. "It is frustrating that the gas is on for such a short time each day."

"Gas isn't on all the time anymore?" Gerard Vogel looks puzzled. "That I hadn't realized."

Of course he didn't realize it, Cornelia thinks; her father never spends time in the kitchen. Mevrouw Kwakkelstein, who is obviously thinking the same thing, catches Cornelia's eye and winks. "Yes, it's quite annoying, *meneer,* but that's the war for you. Are your hands terribly hurt, Cornelia?"

"It's not as bad as it looks. My mother gets carried away whenever she has the chance to play at being a nurse. I did blister my fingers when I grabbed off the apron, but at least my dress didn't catch fire."

"Or the curtains, or the house." Gerard Vogel sighs. "What are we to do with you, Cornelia?"

"Accidents happen." Mevrouw Kwakkelstein unscrews a thermos of coffee and pours her boss a steaming cup. "Is there anything else I can get for you, *meneer*?"

Gerard Vogel's attention shifts away from Cornelia as he checks his watch. "Have you prepared my proposal regarding the updated population information from Camp Westerbork?"

"Yes, I typed it up in triplicate, as you requested."

Cornelia's ears prick up. Westerbork is the transit camp in the northern province of Drenthe where Jews are being taken. "What proposal?"

"That's none of your concern, Cornelia."

"But, Father, if it involves population information, I'll end up processing the punch cards eventually, won't I?"

Outside, the sun is beginning to dilute the inky sky to a watery gray. The villa is still quiet. Gerard Vogel has a hot cup of coffee warming his hands. His daughter is an attentive and intelligent audience. Mevrouw Kwakkelstein, with a conspiring glance at Cornelia, says, "It would be helpful for me, too, if you would explain it again, *meneer*."

"Well, it's simple enough. Generalkommissar Wimmer expects me to keep the Jewish population list up-to-date, but as you know, people are constantly departing the country, often hundreds at a time. Once they emigrate, I need to remove their names from the list, but the flow of information is completely disorganized and beset with delays. I'm proposing to the *Judenreferent* that a punch card be created for every person who has emigrated at the point of departure. That way, when the cards arrive here, we—you, Cornelia, in fact—can immediately process them on the Hollerith. The more efficiently we cull the names of the departed, the more accurate our information will be."

Cornelia reels from the implication of his words. Everyone knows Jews are not "emigrating" from the Netherlands. They're being forcibly deported from Westerbork to so-called labor camps in Germany or Poland or Czechoslovakia. Cornelia is sickened that her father's role in the Nazi campaign to rid Holland of Jews includes not only identifying people in the country but tallying their expulsion from it.

"Yes, that's what I thought, *meneer*, but I do have a question." Mevrouw Kwakkelstein looks puzzled. "Will you be expecting Mevrouw Plank to send punch-card operators to Camp Westerbork? I imagine her girls would object to such an unpleasant assignment."

Gerard Vogel shrugs, as if such pedestrian matters are beneath his consideration. "That would be one way, I suppose, but Zöpf's office must have girls he can provide?"

"You can ask his secretary, Fräulein Slottke. She's coming this afternoon to review the proposal."

"But I asked you to get me an appointment with Willi Zöpf."

"He was unavailable, *meneer*, but Gertrud Slottke is a very impressive woman. I'd venture to say she's the one who does the real work of the *Judenreferent*."

"Be that as it may, if Zöpf is too lazy to meet with me himself, I see no reason to waste my time with his secretary. You'll speak with her, please."

"Of course, *meneer*. I'm sure Fräulein Slottke and I can work out the details."

"Very good, *mevrouw*. Cornelia, I'll be working late this evening. You should take the tram home." With a single nod of his chin that serves as farewell to both women, he retreats to his office. The room feels bigger in his absence.

"You must be more careful, Cornelia," Mevrouw Kwakkelstein says. "Your father depends on you, as do I."

"I'll be fine, really, but I was hoping you could give me some advice."

"Naturally." Mevrouw Kwakkelstein gestures to the chair beside her desk.

Cornelia leans close, speaking quietly. "My identity card was in the pocket of my apron when it caught fire. It's incinerated. Nothing but ashes."

"You don't have identification?" She looks shocked as Cornelia shakes her head. "How did you get past the guards this morning?"

"I came in with my father. They never stop him to ask for papers, do they? But I'm not sure how I'm going to get home this evening."

"But why would you have your identity card in your apron?"

"It was starting to look a bit tattered, so I thought I'd make a cover for it, like yours." Last week, Mevrouw Kwakkelstein showed off the neat little sleeve she'd sewn for her card. "I was on my way to the sewing basket to find a piece of fabric the right size when I stopped to light the gas. It was an accident, but I'm afraid to tell my father. He'll be so disappointed in me."

Mevrouw Kwakkelstein nods sympathetically. "With all the pressure he's under, I'd hate to worry him about something so trivial." She smiles at Cornelia. "How about I approve a replacement for you right now? That way you'll have a new identity card by the time you go home this evening."

"Thank you so much, *mevrouw*. I hesitated to ask, but that would be a perfect solution."

"Do you have a photo?"

"Yes, I brought it with me." Cornelia takes a passport photo out of her satchel, her face pictured in the obligatory three-quarter pose. Typically, Mevrouw Kwakkelstein compares the information submitted with an application for a replacement identity card— photo, fingerprints, signature—against the duplicate registration in the files before approving a request. For Cornelia, though, there's no need for all that. She simply takes a form and rolls it into her typewriter, the three sheets of paper and two of carbon thick behind the paper bail. "Now, remind me of your birth date?"

A minute later, she pulls the completed form out of the typewriter, tears off one of the carbons for her records, signs and stamps the other two, and attaches Cornelia's photo with a paper clip. "There, all approved. You can submit the form on your way to the Hollerith bunker. You know the office?"

"Of course, and please, allow me to save you the bother of picking it up this afternoon. It's the least I can do to repay your kindness."

"Thank you, that would make my day easier. I have no idea how long I'll have Fräulein Slottke on my hands. I can do your fingerprints before you go home, if you like. I have an ink pad here."

Cornelia's morning coffee regurgitates in the back of her throat. Swallowing hard, she wriggles her mummified fingers. "I think that might have to wait."

"Oh, yes, of course." The telephone on Mevrouw Kwakkelstein's desk rings. She waves Cornelia off as she picks up the receiver. "Certainly, *meneer,* right away."

Downstairs, the villa has come to life. The file cabinets are unlocked now, the metallic screech of their sliding drawers blending with the tapping of typewriters and thwacking of stamps to create a bureaucratic symphony. No one questions Cornelia as she approaches the room where clerks equipped with colored inks and laminating machines create replacement identity cards. Pausing in the hallway, she places the pad of her bandaged thumb on her passport photo, slides it from under the paper clip, and secrets it up her right sleeve. Entering the room, she trips over the threshold and goes down on one knee, dropping the form. Reaching for her injured knee, she shakes something from her left sleeve, which flutters to the floor.

A clerk she's never met before rushes over to help her gather the dropped form. Getting to her feet, she looks around as if missing something, then points to a passport photo on the floor. "Perhaps you could pick that up for me as well?" The clerk does, handing her the image of a girl with a boyish face. She clips the photo to the form bearing her name. "Thank you for your help. May I leave this with you now? I'll come back this afternoon on Mevrouw Kwakkelstein's behalf. When will it be ready?"

"I should think by four o'clock, Mejuffrouw . . . ?" He raises his eyebrows, waiting for her to give him her name.

"Nellie." She pulls her mouth into a wide smile. "You can call me Nellie."

In the Hollerith bunker, the day passes with excruciating slowness. Cornelia obsessively checks her watch, only to see mere minutes have crawled by since her last look. Afraid the technician who reads *Storm* will become suspicious, she puts the watch in her pocket. Her mind casts itself forward to tonight, when this will all be over, but she's afraid to tempt fate by imagining the happy result of her subterfuge.

Two days ago, during her last visit with Leah and her parents, the Bloms were arguing, as usual, about what their family should do as the Nazis tightened their net around Holland's Jews. Lillian reiterated her faith that the Exchange List would protect them— after all, she asked, pointing to the empty space above the mantel where her poppies had once hung, hadn't they paid enough for it? "Perhaps we'll have to move to the Jewish district in Amsterdam," she conceded, "but I'm sure it's only a matter of time before the Germans exchange us for some prisoners of war. If it's more money they're after, my father—"

"Yes, Lillian, we all know your father would pay any price, but I doubt those stamps on our identity cards are worth the paper they're printed on." Philip Blom paced the living room, lecturing his wife and daughter as if they were students in his class. "The Germans imagine they can concentrate all of European Jewry in their camps, but they'll soon realize there's no ghetto vast enough to hold our millions. For centuries, our people have survived despite Crusades and inquisitions and pogroms. The *razzias* in Amsterdam are a tragedy, certainly, but the Jewish Council is doing its best to preserve the core of our community so we can recover after the war. If we are called up for labor service, we'll have to go along and hope for the best. If we resist, we become criminals, subject to the harshest penalties. Believe me," he said, dropping into his chair, "our chances are better if we cooperate."

Leah, who'd been nervously chewing her nails throughout her father's speech, jumped up. "You're both delusional if you think the Nazis are to be trusted. Hasn't Nellie told us how they're using that machine to locate each and every one of us? You know their policy is to make Holland *judenfrei,* free of Jews. Please, I'm begging you, let's try to go into hiding. I have friends with contacts in the Resistance. Maybe they could find a place for us on a farm somewhere."

"But I heard the Resistance separates family members when people go into hiding." Lillian's eyes filled with tears as she took Leah's hand and brought her over to Philip's chair. "I couldn't stand for us to be apart. Whatever we do, we have to stick together. Promise me, both of you."

Philip pulled his wife onto his lap. "I promise we'll stay together, *liefje*, no matter what happens."

As Cornelia robotically tabulates punch cards, she wonders if Philip and Lillian have changed their minds since getting their call-up notice yesterday. It pains her that the plan she's come up with doesn't include Leah's parents, but she can't be expected to save everyone, can she?

At lunchtime, Cornelia manages to choke down a sandwich in the cafeteria. Her stomach churns as the afternoon drags on. When next she checks the time, she's stunned to see it's almost four o'clock. The order she's processing isn't finished yet. Desperate to get out of the bunker, she turns the wrong dial and jams the alphabetizer. A buzzer sounds as a warning light flashes on.

"Not again!" The technician throws down his magazine and runs over to remove the cover plates and check the wiring. "God give me leprosy," he curses in frustration. "You might as well leave, *mejuffrouw*. Due to your ineptitude, this won't be fixed until tomorrow."

Cornelia's head feels filled with helium as she emerges from the bunker. What if the clerk has figured out who she is and what she's done? What if he telephoned her father or the police? But the clerk from this morning is not in the office when she picks up the completed identity card. On her way out of the ministry, she secrets her new identification in a slit she's cut in the lining of her coat. Despite the cold, perspiration drips from her brow as she approaches the guard post. When the soldier on duty asks if anything is wrong, she tells him her father is sending her home because she's feeling ill.

"And who is your father?"

"Meneer Gerard Vogel, director of the Ministry of Information."

"Yes, of course." He waves her on. "Good health to you, *Fräulein*."

Night comes early in January, but despite the darkness, Cornelia has hours to endure at home before she can see Leah. There's a regulation, now, against Jews having non-Jewish visitors. Thanks to their yellow stars, everyone knows which houses are occupied by Jews, and there's no telling which of their neighbors might be tempted to denounce the Bloms in exchange for a reward. Cornelia will have to wait until the midnight curfew has shuttered the residents of their street behind blacked-out windows before she can sneak the single step to Leah's front door.

A knock at her bedroom startles Cornelia, but it's only her mother with the first aid kit to change her bandages. It's been close to three years since the German invasion, and Helena Vogel's movie-star looks are showing the strain. Cornelia knows her mother is tired of unreliable gas and limited food coupons and empty shelves at the market. She is tired of worrying about her rebellious son and arguing with her intractable daughter. She is tired of waiting up at night for a husband who cares more about winning the Germans' respect than keeping his wife's affection. Cornelia has been so caught up in Leah's plight that she's spared no thought for her mother's woes. I'll be a better daughter from now on, she silently pledges, as soon as this is over.

"Listen, Cornelia," Helena says, dabbing each burned fingertip with cream and blowing gently, "I don't want you going upstairs to the Bloms' tonight."

"But I have to, Mama. Leah is expecting me."

"I know it's terrible, what's happening to the Jews. I have pity, of course, but there's nothing we can do. If you won't be more careful for my sake, then think of your brother. He looks up to you. Surely you don't want to lead him into trouble?"

"No, of course not." Cornelia knows full well that boys barely older than Dirk are being swept off the streets and sent to work camps in Germany.

Helena is quiet as she wraps her daughter's fingertips in gauze. When she's done, she puts the tiny scissors back in the first aid kit and takes both of Cornelia's hands in her own. "You're a loyal friend, Cornelia, but if Leah really cared about you, she'd want you to stay away."

Cornelia gazes into her mother's eyes, so like her own. She's come close, many times, to confessing what Leah really means to her. She's rehearsed how she'd explain that she and Leah are in love the way men and women love each other, the way her mother loves her father. But how can she put into words the way it feels when she and Leah are together? Thinking of it makes Cornelia's mouth go dry. All she manages to say, in a small squeak of a voice, is, "I have to see her, Mama. I can't help it."

The crescents of her mother's fingernails bite into Cornelia's wrists. "I've read that Jews can hypnotize Gentiles into doing their bidding, but I never believed it until now."

"But, Mama—"

"I don't want to hear it." She releases her daughter's hands as if flicking off filth. "I know you'll do as you please no matter what I say. I'll leave it to your father to talk some sense into you."

When it comes time for the evening meal, though, Gerard Vogel still hasn't come home from work. The three of them eat in tense silence, Dirk's eyes darting back and forth between his mother and sister. As soon as she's done washing dishes, Cornelia retreats to her room to get ready.

Normally, she wears only a nightgown and robe when going to Leah's at night, her idea being that she can claim to be stepping outside to check the weather if a patrolman spots her on the stoop. Tonight, though, she dresses in her warmest winter clothes: knit stockings, wool skirt, flannel blouse, thick sweater. She's pulling on a worsted jacket when Dirk slips through her door.

"Were you and Mama fighting about Leah again?"

Cornelia nods. "She doesn't think I should see her anymore."

Dirk frowns, his young face solemn. "Mama blinds herself to what's happening. I didn't even know some of my classmates were Jewish until they had to go to a different school. Our teacher moved me forward to sit at one of their desks, but I thought we should leave their seats empty so we wouldn't forget them."

"Did you suggest that?"

He hangs his head. "No, I never said anything."

Cornelia hugs him tight. "You have a brave heart, Dirk, never forget that."

"Not as brave as yours, Nellie." He hugs her back until he remembers he's a teenager. Pushing her away, he looks at how she's dressed. "You have something planned, don't you?" When she doesn't deny it, he rushes on. "Let me help."

Dirk's help would make things easier, she thinks—then she remembers her mother's worried face and hesitates. "Are you sure? It could be dangerous."

He rises to the balls of his feet, eager. "I want to do something, Nellie, please."

"Okay." Cornelia takes him by the arm and sits him on her bed. "After Father comes home, can you stay awake until he's sound asleep in bed?" Dirk nods. "Once you're sure he's asleep, I want you to go open the garden house. Get my bicycle ready by the door, then unlock the gate and come back inside. You have to do all this in the dark, without making any sound. Can you do that?"

He nods, his eyes shining with excitement and fear.

"Once you're back in your room, turn out your light and crack open your window so you can keep watch out back. Early in the morning, someone will come down the fire ladder and go to the garden house. If you see any trouble—" Cornelia isn't sure what her brother should do.

"I'll coo, like a dove." He makes the sound. It's utterly convincing.

"That's good, Dirk. The moment curfew is lifted, someone will go through our back gate and ride away on my bicycle. Then you must run down and lock the gate and close the garden house before anyone notices. Can you do all that?"

"Yes." Dirk takes his sister's hand, tenderly touching her bandaged fingertips. "Is it you who's running away, Nellie? Are you joining the Resistance?"

"Hush now." She kisses him on the head. "The less you know, the fewer lies you'll have to tell."

Cornelia sends him to his room and waits a while longer, claustrophobic in her warm clothes. Impatient, she lifts a corner of blackout fabric from her window. The street is as dark and quiet as the inside of a tomb. All the doors of all the houses are shut tight. The patrolman is nowhere to be seen. It's time to go.

Cornelia grabs her satchel and pads silently downstairs, carrying her shoes by their laces. She slips into the vestibule just as her father comes into the kitchen from the garden, finally home. She holds perfectly still as he calls out for Helena. She listens to her mother's begrudging footsteps as she is roused from bed to serve up her husband's evening meal. Cornelia waits until she hears the clatter of plates on the dining room table before stepping into her shoes and pulling on her coat. She readies the key Leah gave her. They won't notice, now, her silent leaving.

Chapter Thirteen
Rita Klein

New York City
June 1960

"What can I get you, dearies?" It seemed like the barmaid had been imported from Britain right along with the pub, her thick accent reminding me of Julie Andrews onstage in *My Fair Lady*.

"Two pints of bitter." Jacob read in the paper that's what Richard Nixon drank when he toasted Prince Philip's birthday here last week.

"A half pint for me," I said, "and something to eat?" We'd been waiting to get into the Red Lion Inn for nearly an hour and I was starving.

"How's about a couple of Scotch eggs with your bitters?"

I said that sounded fine, though I had no idea what to expect of a Scotch egg. I figured it was a euphemism for something else, the way hot dogs had nothing to do with canines. Quick as a flash, two glasses of amber beer appeared on the counter in front of us. We were taking our first sips when the barmaid plunked down a basket lined in paper containing what looked like two deep-fried baseballs. "When you're ready for more, dearies, you shout out for Hebe. That's what everyone calls me. Means 'goddess of youth,' don't you know." She turned to the next person shouldering up to the bar. "And what'll you have, lovie?"

Jacob and I had been exploring the British Exhibition since eleven o'clock that morning, marveling at everything from antique clocks to jet engines. We'd seen a life-size reproduction of Queen Elizabeth's bedroom, a vehicle fitted out with a kitchen for camping, and a scale model of the Swan Hunter shipyard featuring, weirdly, a miniature Statue of Liberty. It was after one o'clock when we got on line for the Red Lion Inn. Now that our Scotch eggs were in front of us, my hunger made me brave enough to cut one open. I was surprised to see an actual yolk nestled in its pocket of sausage and breading. We each picked up a half, touching them together as if making a toast.

Jacob took a huge bite. "*Lekker.*"

He'd been teaching me a few Dutch phrases and I knew by now that *lekker* meant "delicious." Dubious, I nibbled the Scotch egg. It wasn't bad. For the first time all day, we stopped talking, dedicating our mouths to food and drink instead of words.

From the moment we'd met at Columbus Circle, our kiss sheltered by my umbrella from the morning's rain, we'd been talking nonstop. Inside the Coliseum, I asked Jacob to tell me more about his family while we window-shopped along a facsimile of a London arcade.

"My parents and I were born in Suriname, but we moved to Rotterdam when I was a baby so I don't remember anything about it."

"Suriname?" The country's name was familiar to me from geography class, but I misplaced the continent. "Where in Africa is that?"

Jacob tutted impatiently. "Suriname is a Dutch colony in the Caribbean situated between the two Guyanas." That helped me picture where it was in South America, but I still didn't understand why the Dutch had colonized it, let alone how a Jewish family ended up there.

"Portuguese Jews settled in Suriname after being expelled

from Queen Isabella's realm," he said. "The territory was still ruled by Britain then, but our community grew larger under the Dutch. The name of Nassy has been known in Suriname since 1666."

That was impressive to me, especially since my own family history went no further back than the orphanage where my parents met. For all I knew, a miasma had evaporated my four grandparents somewhere between Ellis Island and the Orphaned Hebrews Home, leaving two only children and a single surviving aunt. I wasn't even sure if Ida was related to my mom's side or my dad's.

"But how did Jews get to Suriname in the first place?"

We stopped in front of a millinery shop displaying feathered fascinators and tasseled smoking caps while he explained the complicated history of his parents' homeland. I tried to map the story Jacob was telling me on an imaginary globe, but I got confused by the crisscrossing migrations of persecuted Jews from Spain to Portugal, across the Atlantic to Brazil, then back to the Netherlands. Once Jacob connected the settlement of Jews in Suriname to the Dutch West India Company, though, I felt on slightly firmer ground.

"Then you know what happened next." Jacob ushered me into a replica of the historic Lloyd's Coffee House.

"I have no idea." I ordered mine with milk and sugar. Jacob took his black.

"The Treaty of Breda. The famous trade."

"What trade?" I asked.

He looked at me like a disappointed tutor. "How do you think New Amsterdam became New York?"

I hoped the scent of coffee would jog my memory. It didn't. "Remind me."

"In 1667, the Dutch swapped Manhattan to the English in

exchange for Suriname. It's hard to believe now, but at the time, the Dutch thought they were getting the better deal. Surely you learned this?"

His professorial tone was beginning to irritate me. "Colonial history isn't essential to the study of mathematics and computing machines, Jacob."

"I've been lecturing you, Rita. I apologize." He put down his coffee and gave me his full attention. "Have I told you yet how pretty you look today?"

That's more like it, I thought. "Maybe, but you can always say it again."

After we finished our coffees, we visited the Vickers booth in the industrial section, where I showed off my recently acquired knowledge of steel manufacturing until I could see he was getting bored. "Let's find that pub, okay?" I threaded my arm through his. "The coffee woke me up, but now I'm getting hungry."

The rain had stopped and the sky was blue when we came out of the Coliseum that afternoon. The open arms of the Merchants' Gate beckoned us into the greenery of Central Park. On the Sheep Meadow, Jacob spread his raincoat over the damp grass and we stretched out in the sunshine. He surprised me by taking off my shoes and rubbing my feet. No one had ever touched me like that before. When he pressed his thumbs into my soles, I couldn't stifle the moan of pleasure that rose in my throat.

People lounged all around us, shed of jackets and sweaters and shoes in the summer heat. Birds called. Squirrels chattered. Someone strummed a guitar. I wanted nothing more than to enjoy the moment, but its perfection was poisoned when I saw a young mother lift her infant from its carriage.

"Are you all right, Rita?"

I blinked, hard, my hand pressed to my heart. "I'm fine, Jacob, but I should be heading home."

"Yes, of course. Do you want to take the subway to the bus terminal?"

"No, let's walk. Father's Day is tomorrow and I still need to find my dad a present." I slipped my shoes back on. "Thank you for that, it felt really nice. What word would you use in Dutch?"

He helped me to my feet and shook out his raincoat. "We'd say *lekker.*"

"Isn't that for food?"

"Anything that is pleasing to the senses is *lekker.* Beautiful weather. A refreshing swim. Holding your hand—" He took mine as we headed toward the Artisans' Gate. "Holding your hand is *lekker,* Little Rita."

Strolling down Seventh Avenue, we passed a haberdashery with silk ties in the window. Such an exclusive little place was bound to be expensive, but I wanted to get my dad something special. I'd deposited my first paycheck that morning before catching the bus to Manhattan. Though I'd left most of it on deposit at the Central Bergen Savings and Loan, I'd kept twenty dollars in cash. The nine-dollar Italian tie I chose was a little wider than the ones Dad usually wore, but I was certain he'd appreciate its quality.

"I've seen advertisements for Father's Day sales in the newspaper," Jacob said as we turned on Forty-Third Street toward Eighth Avenue, "but I don't know the history of this holiday."

"I think it's something retailers made up to sell products, but it is a nice reminder to appreciate your dad." I immediately regretted my words. Father's Day must be a painful time for an orphan of the Holocaust. Wanting to make up for my insensitivity, I said, "Listen, Jacob, would you like to come over for lunch tomorrow? My brother, Charlie, and his wife, Debbie, will be there, and I'd like you to meet my parents." I almost bit my tongue. Inviting him to meet my parents might make him think I was getting too serious, but he was genuinely pleased.

"Thank you, Rita. I'd like that very much. I usually visit Rudy's family on Sundays, but I'm sure he won't mind. I'll stop by the Rathskeller on my way home tonight to let him know I'll be with you."

"Say hello to him for me, won't you?" I brought Jacob into the Port Authority to show him which bus he should take. After we checked the schedule and decided on a time, I promised to meet him at the stop on Teaneck Road. He held me so tight as he kissed me goodbye I lost my breath.

"*Tot morgen, liefje.*" He smiled at my puzzled expression. "Until tomorrow, darling."

Mom wasn't happy that I'd invited my new friend from the Empire State Building, Jacob Nassy, to join us for Father's Day. "You could have asked first, Rita. You know I don't like having strangers over."

I figured she was feeling self-conscious about our threadbare furniture. "Trust me, Mom, a man who survived Auschwitz isn't going to care about the state of our couch cushions."

"He was in Auschwitz, really?" Dad said. "How old did you say he was?"

Over supper, I told my parents more about Jacob. Explaining his origins in South America led me to ask my dad if he knew the Dutch had traded Manhattan to the English for a country called Suriname.

Mom thought that was the silliest thing she'd ever heard, but Dad leaned back in his chair, staring thoughtfully at the ceiling. "Wasn't that part of the Treaty of Breda?"

"That's right, Dad. It was news to me, though. Jews have been living there since the seventeenth century, can you believe that?"

We ended up getting out Hammond's *Complete World Atlas* and studying the map of South America at the kitchen table while Mom made supper. On the double-page map of the Western world, I traced with my finger the international migrations Jacob had described. The route between Brazil and the Netherlands caught Dad's attention.

"That reminds me," he said. "The first Jews to settle in Manhattan were on their way from Recife to Amsterdam when their ship was captured by pirates. They had nothing but the clothes on their backs when they finally managed to make landfall in New Amsterdam. Peter Stuyvesant didn't want to let them stay, but he was overruled by the Dutch West India Company."

"Did you learn all that in school, Dad?"

He shook his head. "The superintendent of the orphanage, Mr. Grossman, used to lecture us about Jewish history sometimes. Do you remember, Adele?"

"Don't talk to me about that man." She wiped her hands on her apron and joined us at the table. "I'll never forget the time he beat that boy bloody right in front of us. What was his name?"

Dad squinted for a moment, then lifted his eyebrows. "Sam Rabinowitz. I remember because we were in the same dormitory. He ran away from the home after that."

"That's right. Wasn't his sister that bald girl? I think she ran off after him." Mom smiled and tapped the center of his forehead with the tip of her finger. "The things you have in that brain of yours, Irving."

He caught her finger and pretended to nibble on it. I hadn't seen my parents this playful in ages. It made me so happy I almost cried. You see, I told myself, you haven't ruined their lives after all.

On Sunday, Jacob got off the bus carrying a bouquet of flowers. I held out my hands, assuming they were for me, but he stepped into a hug, keeping the flowers for himself. It turned out they were intended for my mother. She accepted the bundle of tulips awkwardly.

"Oh, my, how beautiful. Rita, go find something to put these in, will you?" Mom wasn't the type of housewife to keep a collection of cut-crystal vases. I returned with a glass pitcher half-filled with water. Even in that humble container, the bouquet was so fresh and colorful, its presence on the coffee table made everything else look even shabbier by comparison.

I'd spent the entire morning helping Mom clean the apartment, but besides tucking a quilt over the couch cushions and cutting some threads from the unraveling rugs, there wasn't much more we could do to spiff up the place. For his part, Jacob pronounced our apartment *gezellig,* which he said meant "cozy and welcoming." He soon made himself at home on the quilt-covered couch with a plate of babka on his knee and a cup of coffee in his hand. The way he crossed his legs, I couldn't help but notice his worn-out shoes. They were freshly polished—he must have had them shined at the bus station—but the stitching that held the uppers of his Oxfords to their soles was so loose I was surprised they hadn't separated yet. I caught Dad's eye. He'd noticed, too.

"Jacob, I wonder if you'd do me a favor before you leave today and take a pair of shoes with you. I've got a pile of boxes down in the stockroom that I can't even give away. I'm pretty sure there's something in your size, don't you think so, Rita?"

"I think I saw some loafers in a twelve. You are a twelve, aren't you, Jacob?"

He looked bashfully down at his feet. "I suppose so."

"Well, like I said, son, you'd be doing me a favor."

I worried we were embarrassing Jacob. To change the subject, I said, "I meant to tell you, my father knew all about the Treaty of Breda."

"Well, just the main idea," Dad said. "I'm still curious about the details."

Dad soaked up every word of the history lesson Jacob launched into. I opened the atlas on the coffee table and we all got on our knees to flip through its pages. When we turned from South America to Western Europe, that divided Germany was smack in the center of the map.

"Rita told us you were in the camps," Mom said quietly. "You don't have to talk about it, Jacob, but I wanted to say how sorry we are."

"Thank you, Mrs. Klein. There's much I prefer to forget, but I don't mind speaking about it in general. I was in Auschwitz for the last ten months of the war. Before that, I spent over a year here." He pointed to the northeast corner of Holland. "Westerbork wasn't a concentration camp like you see in the newsreels. It was filthy and crowded and cold and we were always sick and hungry, but a person was still a human being there. Most didn't stay long, though. Every week, a train would come to take away a thousand people or more. Some went to Ravensbrück or Buchenwald, others to Bergen-Belsen or Theresienstadt. Most went to Auschwitz or Sobibor. We had no idea what awaited us at the other end of that journey."

Mom took his hand, tears welling up in her eyes. "You poor thing."

The solemn moment was interrupted by my brother's voice calling up the stairs. "Hey, we're here! Come give us a hand, will ya?"

Charlie and Debbie had stopped by Tabatchnick's to pick up the order Mom had placed that morning. They were loaded down with a bag of rolls, a platter of deli meats, and containers of chopped liver and coleslaw and potato salad and pickles.

"And we brought this." Debbie held up a bakery box tied with red-and-white twine. "It's that cheesecake you liked so much on Memorial Day." She handed it to my dad with a kiss on the cheek. "Happy Father's Day."

It was my first time seeing Charlie since I'd been back. He

caught me up in a hug that squeezed the breath from my lungs. "How's it going, kid? I hear you're a fancy working girl now." He put me down and stepped back to look at me. "You got skinny again, Rita. Does that mean I can have my jeans back now?"

I'd been wondering if Charlie had any idea why I'd really gone away. Apparently not. I punched him in the arm. "Don't talk to me like that, Charlie."

"Ouch." He pretended to be hurt, then he noticed Jacob. "Oh, hey, I didn't know you had a fella." Charlie went up to him, hand outstretched. "I'm Rita's big brother, Charlie."

"Jacob Nassy. A pleasure to meet you."

"Say, what's that accent? Debbie, come here. Say something, Jake."

"Hello, Debbie." Jacob glanced at me, eyebrows raised. I shrugged. "It's a pleasure to meet you."

"Charmed, I'm sure." Debbie curtsied, then giggled. "You sound like Omar Sharif. Where are you from, Jake?"

"It's Jacob." I stepped between them. "And he's from Holland."

"You mean the country with all the tulips?" Debbie asked. Jacob nodded.

"I guess that explains the flowers," Charlie said. "I was wondering where Mom got them."

"Come on, everyone," Mom called from the kitchen. "Lunch is ready."

I was ashamed of the worn-out Formica of our kitchen table, but Jacob seemed to like the closeness of the six of us sitting shoulder to shoulder, arms reaching across like poker players in a casino as we helped ourselves. I loaded my plate with coleslaw and heaped my hard roll with pastrami and mustard. Jacob, I noticed, preferred the tongue, which I'd never really liked. No one wanted the chopped liver except my father, who spread it thickly on slices of rye.

"Now, Jacob, I want you to know everything I ordered from Tabatchnick's is kosher."

"Thank you, Mrs. Klein, but that doesn't matter to me."

"Oh, really?" Mom said. I could tell she was miffed. Paying for kosher from Tabatchnick's was a splurge. "I just thought, after everything you've been through, you'd be more religious."

"What's he been through?" Charlie asked. I kicked him under the table. "Ouch. What?"

Despite the occasional clueless remark from my brother, it felt good having my family all around me again. Before I knew it, Mom was replacing the platter of cold cuts with Debbie's cheese-cake.

"Charlie, don't you think we should share our news?" Debbie was making eyes at my brother like he'd invented penicillin or something.

"I thought you wanted to wait until we were done with dessert."

"Wait for what?" Dad asked. "What is it?"

"Well, first of all, here's your gift." Charlie produced an envelope from his back pocket.

"I have a present for you, too, Dad." The Italian tie was nicely wrapped but still in my bedroom. Everyone would have had to get out of their chairs for me to go get it. I kicked Charlie again. "I didn't know we were doing this now."

"Cut that out, would ya?" Charlie handed the envelope to Dad. "Here you go. Happy Father's Day."

Dad opened the envelope and pulled out a pair of tickets. "Floyd Patterson and Ingemar Johansson at the Polo Grounds, tomorrow night!" He reached over to clap Charlie on the shoulder, smiling from ear to ear. "I can't believe you got me tickets for the heavy-weight championship."

"They're from me, too," Debbie piped up, but no one paid her any attention.

"Well, one of those tickets is for me, Dad, unless you'd rather go with someone else."

"Are you kidding, Charlie? What better Father's Day present than to go to the fights with my son." He got up and stood behind Charlie's chair to kiss him on the head. "Really, thank you." He kissed Debbie's head, too. "Thank you both."

"They're floor seats, a few rows back from the ring. Close enough to taste blood, right, Dad?" Charlie turned to me. "What'd you get him, Rita?"

My brother was a good guy, but he never could resist upstaging me. I wasn't all that eager, now, to gift my father a boring old tie. "Never mind."

Jacob squeezed my hand, then leaned over to whisper in my ear. "I'm sure he'll treasure the tie you chose."

I could have fallen in love with him right that minute. The fight was only one night, I told myself. Dad would wear the tie for years to come.

"Don't forget about our news, Charlie."

"Yes, Debbie." Mom tried, and failed, to hide her exasperation. "What's your big news?"

"I'm pregnant!" She popped up from her chair like a jack-in-the-box. "We're going to have a baby!"

I don't think Charlie or Debbie noticed the way Mom, Dad, and I all froze for a second. Jacob felt it in my hand, I'm sure, the sudden surge of sweat followed by an uncontrollable tremor. I could tell from the way my cheeks went cold that all the blood had drained from my face. I sat stone-still, afraid I might hurl the cheesecake against the wall if I so much as moved a muscle.

My parents reanimated themselves, hugging Debbie and embracing Charlie. Mom patted Debbie's flat little tummy. Dad shook Charlie's hand. It was surreal to see them laugh and smile after the way they'd reacted when I gave them the exact same news. Apparently, the ring on Debbie's hand had the power to magically transform tragedy into joy.

"You're going to be an aunt, Rita!" Charlie frowned at me. "What's the matter, aren't you happy for us?"

I managed to choke out a congratulatory sound. Who cared about being an aunt, I wanted to say, when I was already a mother?

"Mazel tov." Jacob stood up to reach across the table. He pulled me to my feet, too. "Rita, where can I find the toilet?"

Wordlessly, I led Jacob to the bathroom. Charlie and Debbie and my parents were still yammering away in the kitchen when he came out. I grabbed the keys for the store. "Let's go look for those shoes my dad was telling you about, okay?"

Jacob followed me downstairs. As soon as we were alone in the stockroom, he stroked my arm. "What's wrong, Rita?"

What would it be like to confide in him? I wondered. I imagined the relief of spilling my secret to someone who'd sympathize with my side of the story. But so many fictions depended on my silence, it was impossible to imagine the words coming out of my mouth. "Nothing. I was surprised, is all. Come on, let's find you some shoes."

While Jacob poked through the boxes for something in his size, I went over to dust off the old fluoroscope Dad used to keep out in the store to X-ray children's feet. He'd moved it to the stockroom after the State of New Jersey banned them. I hoped the radiation they emitted wasn't really all that harmful, since Charlie and I had played with it all the time as kids. Curious, I plugged it in. It buzzed and hummed back to life. I stepped up and looked through the viewing tubes at my wriggling toes. The bones glowed white as ghosts.

"What's that?" Jacob asked. I lifted my head and blinked. He was holding a shoebox.

"It's for looking at your feet. It uses X-rays. Try on your shoes, then you can see how they fit."

Jacob unlaced his battered Oxfords and slipped on a pair of kiltie loafers. The tasseled shoes looked good on him, casual yet debonair. He stepped up to the fluoroscope and looked through the viewing tubes, amazed at what he saw. When he was done, I unplugged the machine. The sudden quiet felt solemn.

"Little Rita." He took my face in his hands. "I can see you are sad again."

He didn't ask for explanations or try to cheer me up. All he did was look at me. The emotions I'd been damming up came bursting out. I mashed my face against his chest, sobbing. He cradled me in his arms and let me cry for as long as the tears kept coming.

"I'm sorry, Jacob. I get like this sometimes—"

"I understand." He kissed my forehead. His lips felt cool. "Are you ready to go back upstairs yet?"

I shook my head. "I'm not feeling well. I think it's best if you go now."

We walked up the street. The next bus was fifteen minutes away. My eyes were sore and my head was pounding. I couldn't imagine standing on that public corner for so long. "I have to get back, Jacob."

"Thank you for inviting me, Rita, and thank your parents, too. I enjoyed meeting them." He pulled his eyebrows together and asked, tentatively, "When will I see you again?"

What he was really asking, I thought, was whether he'd see me again at all. I asked myself the same question. What the hell I was doing with this guy? Everything he liked about me was based on a lie. The longer this thing went on between us, the deeper the hole I was digging myself into. I knew damn well what would happen if I ever did confide in him. Just imagining the affection in his eyes turning to disgust made me sick to my stomach.

"I don't know. This is all moving so fast, Jacob. I need some time to myself, to think things over."

He seemed dismayed, but all he did was wrap me up in a hug tight as a straitjacket. I wriggled away. He caught my elbow. "Please say you'll come up to the observation deck after work on Friday. We won't go anywhere if you don't want to. But I'm afraid . . ."

"Afraid of what?"

A wave of panic washed over his face. "Afraid of not having anything to look forward to."

He really was a sweet guy, I thought. He deserved so much better than me. "Sure, I'll come up on Friday if you want me to, but I don't know how I'll feel."

He let go of my elbow and stepped back. "It doesn't matter, as long as I know I'll see you again. *Tot vrijdag,* dear Little Rita."

I left him standing there at the bus stop and walked away. I was back home before I realized I'd forgotten to kiss him goodbye. Charlie and Debbie were gone, thank God. I went into my room, threw myself down, and started crying all over again. Mom came in and sat on the edge of the bed. I was afraid she'd be mad at me for being so rude, for not playing along, for acting suspicious. Instead, she stroked my hair with all the gentleness her hand could muster.

"What's done is done, Rita," she said. "What's done is done."

Chapter Fourteen
Cornelia Vogel

The Hague, Netherlands
January 1943

In one fluid movement, Cornelia shuts her own front door and opens the one beside it, moving unseen from the home where her family lives to the house where her heart resides.

With the Bloms' bicycles gone, their dark vestibule is empty except for the ghost of a coat hanging from the wall and the hump of a rucksack on the floor. Cornelia is about to put her keys in her pocket when she remembers she won't be wearing her own coat home again. She's hanging them on a hook when there's a rush of motion in the darkness. She loses her breath as she's tackled back against the closed door.

"Oh, Nellie, I thought you'd never come."

Leah's kisses are so deep and desperate, Cornelia has no tongue left for shaping words. When Leah starts tugging at Cornelia's clothes, she turns her head to the side so she can speak. "What about your parents? What if they turn on the light?"

"They're not here, Nellie. It's only you and me. It's our last time." She unbuttons Cornelia's coat, pushes up her skirt. "I'm Napoleon back from battle. You are my Josephine. Hush now, darling."

Cornelia is pulled to the tiled floor, her hands trapped in

the sleeves of her coat. Cold air raises gooseflesh on her thighs as Leah rolls down her stockings. A hand searches under her sweater for a breast. A finger parts her lips. Cornelia surrenders to the onslaught. Soon, her cries rise up the stairs on the vapor of her breath.

Leah's face is once again beside Cornelia's, their cheeks touching. She whispers, "You're trembling, Nellie."

"I must be cold, but I can't feel it."

"Let me warm you." Leah shimmies out of her trousers and straddles Cornelia, rhythmically rocking until she climaxes with a shudder.

Cornelia kisses her lover's neck. "You've conquered me, my emperor."

Leah sighs, then shivers. "It is cold, isn't it?"

She pulls Cornelia to her feet and blindly helps rearrange her clothing. Cornelia's shoes are left behind as they tiptoe upstairs in stocking feet. In the Bloms' dining room, a single bulb burning in a lamp seems so bright, Cornelia squints.

Leah wraps her arms around Cornelia from behind. "I hope I didn't scare you, Nellie."

"You did scare me a little." Turning, she puts her hands on Leah's face. "But I forgive you."

Leah covers Cornelia's hands with her own. Feeling the gauze, she steps back. The bandaged fingers are an alarming sight. "Nellie, what happened?"

"It's nothing to worry about. Here, I'll show you." She removes the bandages one by one, revealing her pink fingertips. "I burned them last night when my apron caught fire, but it was all worth it. Look—" Cornelia dips her hand into the slit in the lining of her coat, then stops. The room around them is in worse disarray than usual. A pile of books has spilled across the floor, a lamp has been toppled, a chair overturned. "Wait, Leah, where are your parents?"

"They're gone." Leah's mouth turns down, her chin quivering. "Come upstairs, Nellie."

Stuffing her hat and scarf into her coat pockets, she follows Leah to her room. Together, they pass through the beaded curtain that once promised far-off adventure. Tonight, the strings of bamboo seem like the bars of a birdcage. Candles are guttering in glass jars while a record spins soundlessly on the phonograph. Leah lifts the needle and drops it back at the beginning. The notes of her favorite Chopin nocturne sound melancholy in the smoky air. Leah's face is pale, her hair disheveled, her clothes rumpled. In Amsterdam, she cut a dashing figure; tonight, Leah looks as pathetic as Jane Eyre after running away from Thornfield.

"They won't do it, Nellie." Leah sits on her bed, beckoning Cornelia to her side. "My parents won't go into hiding. We fought about it for hours last night. I couldn't change my father's mind." She stares at her hands as if reading her own palms. "Mommy made him go out this morning to see the Jewish Council's agent in The Hague to remind him we're on the Exchange List. They contacted the council's headquarters in Amsterdam. Chairman Asscher couldn't do anything about our call-up notice, but he did say he could get us housed somewhere safe. Apparently, there's a group of important Jews living in a château at Barneveld. He even wrangled travel permits for the three of us. He insisted we bring our luggage and come to Amsterdam right away." She looked mournfully at Cornelia. "My parents left this afternoon."

Cornelia grabs Leah's hand. "Thank God you didn't go with them."

She brings Cornelia's knuckles to her lips. "I packed my rucksack, but at the last minute I refused to go. Mommy didn't want us to be separated, not even for a night, but I couldn't leave without saying goodbye to you. I promised I'd turn myself in tomorrow to join them."

"No." Cornelia slides to the floor and kneels, a supplicant. "Leah, you can't turn yourself in. I told you what's happening—"

"Shush, Nellie." Leah looks down at her, tears dripping. "What choice do I have? At least Chairman Asscher says my family will be safe in Barneveld."

"Leah, listen to me. No Jew is safe. Do you know what happens when they're deported from the country? They're stricken from the population lists."

Leah frowns. "What does that mean?"

"It means any Jew who leaves Holland is never expected to return. I don't know what's happening to people after they're deported, but I know this: Your father is wrong. Your family can't wait this out. It means—" She reaches up to take Leah's face in her hands. "It means once they have you, my darling, I may never see you again."

Leah folds forward, her head on Cornelia's shoulder. "But what can I do, Nellie? I can't abandon my parents."

"If they knew the truth, they'd want what's best for you, wouldn't they?"

"My mother needs me, you know that. Besides, going into hiding is too much of a risk."

"What if you didn't have to hide?"

Leah lifts her head, confused. "How could that happen?"

"If you had papers that were perfect, you could travel, openly, to the port at IJmuiden, maybe. There are boat captains who'll smuggle people across the North Sea for the right price." She gets to her feet and grips Leah's shoulders. "If you got to England, you could contact your grandparents. They'd help you and your mother and father, too. Don't you see? Saving yourself is the best thing you can do for your whole family."

Leah's eyes brighten with the glimpse of freedom Cornelia

offers. "My mother left me some jewelry to barter, and I have some money, thanks to you." Leah points to the box into which Cornelia deposited her tutoring fees. "My grandparents would move heaven and earth to bring me to New York and rescue my parents, but how can I get to them, Nellie?"

"With this. Look." Cornelia reaches into the lining of her coat and hands Leah a brand-new Dutch identity card.

Leah puzzles over the sight of her own face next to Cornelia's name. "I don't understand."

"I said mine was burned when my apron caught fire. I needed a good excuse to ask Mevrouw Kwakkelstein to authorize a replacement. Remember when we traded passport photos, as keepsakes?"

Leah points to her bulletin board. "Sure, I keep your picture right there."

"Well, I switched my picture for one of yours. Other than that, it's completely legitimate. No one will ever question it. You can sign my name, here, in your own handwriting, and the fingerprints are still blank on the card, so they can be yours."

Leah is stupefied. "But what about you, don't you need identification?"

"Mine is down in my room. I only pretended it was burned. Besides, I'm Gerard Vogel's daughter. The guards don't even inspect me anymore."

"You really did all this for me?"

Leah's hair has grown as long as a girl's. Cornelia tucks a lock behind her ear. "If we'd been allowed, I would have married you to keep you safe, you know that, don't you? But see, I've given you my name after all."

Leah touches the photo of her own face. "Cornelia Vogel. Is that really who I am now?"

"As far as the world's concerned, yes."

Leah stands, hugging Cornelia close. "You never even asked."

"Asked? But there was no time. Once you said you'd gotten your call-up notice—"

"Not about this." Leah places the identity card on her drawing table. "I mean, you never asked if I'd marry you."

"Oh, well." Cornelia's mind is still on plans of escape, but she realizes Leah's mood has shifted. "That's because you should have been the one doing the asking."

"Why, because you think I'm the boy?"

"If there were a stage where only women were allowed to act, you know you'd play the man's part."

"As long as I'm being cast as a gentleman." Sweeping a pretend hat from her head, Leah goes down on one knee with a bow. "My lady, will you marry me?"

It's just pretend. It can't be real, not between the two of them. Yet Cornelia's heart beats so hard it hurts her ribs. "You know I would, of course, yes."

"Then repeat after me." Leah twists the signet ring from her finger. "I am my beloved's."

Cornelia has never uttered truer words. "I am my beloved's."

Leah slides the ring onto Cornelia's hand. "And my beloved is mine."

"My beloved is mine," Cornelia says.

Leah stands and kisses her slowly, as if they have their whole lives ahead of them. The moment couldn't be more sanctified if they were before an altar. Then Leah stomps her foot on the floor, frightening Cornelia.

"What was that for?"

"I was pretending to break a glass—never mind, it's something from a Jewish wedding." She gazes at Cornelia. "If I were to offer you my name, would you take it?"

"Nellie Blom." No wonder women change their names when

they marry, she thinks. Even this pretend ceremony has made her feel like an entirely new person, as if Cornelia Vogel is a skin she's shed. "I love the way that sounds."

"Come, then, let's make it official." Leah leads Cornelia to the drawing table, where she pulls her own identity card from her pocket and places it beside the one Cornelia has made for her. She takes a craft knife from her jar of colored pencils. With the skill of a draftsman, she cuts a slit above the photograph on her card and tugs it from behind the laminate with tweezers. Then she reaches up for the passport photo of Cornelia on her bulletin board. Leah trims it to size, tucks the picture behind the lamination, and secures it in place with a dab of glue.

"You gave me your name, Nellie. Now I've given you mine."

A mixture of elation and dread envelops Cornelia as she takes the card. As a forgery it's amateurish at best, but held at arm's length, the transformation is convincing. To see her own face coupled with Leah's name lights a fire in Cornelia's heart, but seeing that letter *J* beside her picture sends ice through her veins. She flushes hot, then cold, then hot again.

"Nellie, what's wrong?" Leah sits her down, gives her some cold tea to drink, pats a silk scarf to her sweating forehead. "What happened?"

"Oh, Leah, it's just that—it's all so perfect, and now—you have to—"

"Go, yes, I do. But look, we're one now, don't you see? I'll carry your name to London and safety, and you'll . . ."

Cornelia holds the identity card that names her as Leah Blom to her heart. "I'll treasure this, always, as a reminder of our vow."

"Promise we'll find each other again after the war, Nellie. That's all the vow I need you to make."

"I promise."

Leah takes a long look around the room. "This will all be *gepulst,* won't it?" They both know it will only be a matter of days before the moving company of Abraham Puls empties the Bloms' home. Even if Leah returns someday, the place will have been stripped bare, their possessions sold and their furniture carted off to Germany.

"At least I can keep your drawings safe until we see each other again," Cornelia says.

They take all the drawings off the walls, tucking them between the covers of Leah's sketchbooks. Cornelia places the identification Leah made for her on top of the stack. They turn to each other. Neither has to say that time is running out. The clock knows it, and so do they.

"Leah, listen. I wore all these clothes for you. If you're dressed like me, any neighbor who sees you riding away will think I'm going to work early. The garden house is open. The back gate is unlocked. You can bicycle out of The Hague and be on your way to freedom. Come now, let's change."

Cornelia strips to her underwear. While Leah dresses in Cornelia's clothes, she puts on one of Leah's old nightgowns and a wool robe.

"I look ridiculous," Leah says, lifting the skirt's fabric.

"Pretend you're in a Shakespeare play," Cornelia says, hugging her tight. The curve of Leah's ribs through her skin are like whale bones in a corset. Cornelia remembers that first glimpse of Leah, when for a moment she saw a cocksure young man. Leah's feminine curves have melted away, but in her distress she's more of a girl than ever. "When all is right in the world again, you'll be revealed as your true self."

The clock ticks quickly now. They hide Lillian's jewelry in the lining of Cornelia's coat and fill her satchel with coins. Leah lifts the needle from the phonograph and blows out the candles. Cornelia picks up the pile of sketchbooks. Together, they part the beaded curtain and leave the attic behind.

In the kitchen, Cornelia sets the sketchbooks on the counter as they gather food for Leah's journey. Wordlessly, they gaze into each other's eyes for the last time before switching off the lone lamp.

"I guess this is—"

The trill of the doorbell seizes their hearts like an electric shock. It's short, barely a ring, and yet the sound is an explosion in their ears.

"They've come for me." Leah's voice is shrill. "It's too late, Nellie."

Cornelia steps out onto the balcony and listens for Dirk's signal. No dove's coo. The garden, at least, is safe. She steps back in. "It's probably someone in the street playing a trick on you." With shaking hands, she covers Leah's head with her hat, wraps her scarf around Leah's neck. "Hurry now, to the garden house. Ride away the minute curfew is lifted. I'll go to the front door and take care of it, whatever it is."

"Darling, I—"

"I know. Hurry."

Leah goes out to the balcony, throws her leg over the railing, reaches with her foot for the fire ladder's rung. Moments later, her shadow flits across the lawn and into the garden house. Everything is silent. No one shouts or blows a whistle or shines a light. Cornelia closes the door to the balcony where Leah once watched a pretty girl turn cartwheels on the grass.

With shaking hands, she gathers the sketchbooks in her arms. Maybe it is a churlish neighbor playing a mean trick on a Jewish house. Maybe it's Dirk, warning her to hurry. Maybe it's her mother, having found her bed empty. She thinks of everything it could be, to give herself the courage to go down those dark stairs.

In the vestibule, she almost trips over Leah's rucksack, huddled on the floor like a troll guarding the entrance to its cave. Blindly stepping into her shoes, Cornelia reaches for the handle, holding the sketchbooks against her chest like a warrior's shield.

A shock of cold air hits her as the door swings open. For a second, she believes the dark street is empty. Then a uniformed figure materializes on the stoop. Behind him, there's a lorry, its headlamps off, the truck bed concealed beneath an arch of canvas. A second officer appears, a circle of brightness from the flashlight in his hand illuminating a sheaf of papers. He dips his head, examines the list, then looks at Cornelia frozen in the doorway.

"You must be the daughter, Leah Blom."

"No, I'm—" She swallows the words she can't say. "But the call-up notice was for this afternoon."

"New orders," says the one with the list. "For your convenience, we now come to your door. Meneer and Mevrouw Blom are already checked off. I need to see your identification."

Cornelia's mind races. The keys to her house are within reach. Maybe her father can save her. He's friends with Wimmer, valuable to the *Judenreferent*. Seyss-Inquart appreciates his work. Even Adolf Eichmann knows the name of Gerard Vogel.

It's no use. Cornelia has already broken the law. Involving her father will only incriminate him, not rescue her. Anything she says now will result in Leah being hunted down and her own family being destroyed. There's only one thing Cornelia can do to save the ones she loves.

She lifts her chin. The officer plucks the identity card from atop the pile of sketchbooks. He shines his light on the face of the girl pictured there, the girl named Leah Blom. He moves the circle of light to Cornelia's face. They match.

He brings his arm down like an ax on the sketchbooks. They crash to the ground, Leah's drawings scattering on the stoop and blowing down the street like leaves from a paper tree.

"Come on, quickly now."

Cornelia takes a step forward before the other officer stops her. "Don't forget your rucksack, *mejuffrouw*," he says. His language is Dutch, his tone paternal. "And wear your coat. It's a cold night."

Cornelia's heart claws at her throat as she puts on Leah's coat. The flashlight finds the yellow star, setting it aflame.

The officer prods her. She shoulders the rucksack and stumbles up the fender into the truck bed. The canvas flap shuts. The engine jerks into gear. The lorry rumbles past all the windows of all the houses, every one of them blind to what's happening in their street.

Chapter Fifteen
Rita Klein

New York City
June 1960

What's done is done. It was the kindest thing my mother could have said, really. It was about time I stopped tormenting myself. I'd signed the papers and left him behind. David had been with his new parents, his real parents, for close to a month. I had to accept that he belonged now to the doctor and nurse who were giving him love and a home. Like planning a computer program, I thought it through a hundred different ways. The only outcome that resulted in a happy future was the one where I let go of his memory. I suppressed the image of David I carried in my mind's eye until it settled into a stone in the pit of my stomach. My intestines wove around it like a basket, the better to carry its weight.

What's done is done. The phrase became my mantra. I said it as I walked up Cedar Lane on Monday morning. I muttered it on the bus ride to Manhattan. I let the thought ricochet through my brain as I finished wiring the control panel to test my program on the IBM 602.

When I was ready, Mr. McKay showed me how to insert the control panel, set the knobs and dials, and start the machine. He hovered nearby while I stacked a test set of punch cards in the hopper and pressed the start button. The typebar began hammering away. It wasn't long before Mr. McKay tore a printed piece of paper from the platen. Processing a report on a computer was like preparing Thanksgiving dinner, I thought—weeks of planning and days of work to create something that was finished in minutes.

"That was fast," I said.

"We were lucky today. The 602 usually takes more persuading."

I spent a couple of hours reviewing the test report to make sure the program ran the way I intended. As far as I could see, it did. I asked Mr. McKay to double-check.

"Leave it on your desk. I'll take a look in the morning. Even if you need to make a few tweaks, I'd say your idea of using master codes has been proven correct, and on the very first try. Impressive, Miss Klein. Olympia should start using the new codes right away. Did you write up instructions?"

I nodded. The whole idea of using master codes was to make it as easy as possible for the girl who punched cards at Olympia, so the instructions were pretty simple.

"Good. She'll have to go back a few weeks to get the work they've already done correctly coded, but from here on out the *Constellation* reports should be smooth sailing." He paused to smile at his pun. "I'll have Gladys send a messenger to Brooklyn to deliver the instructions. Why don't you give Francie a call to let her know?"

Francie's Brooklyn accent was even stronger on the telephone than in person. "Thanks, Rita. I needed some good news. Things around here are going from bad to worse. You heard me tell Jimmy not to agree to anything with Lackawanna Steel without talking to me first, didn't you?"

"Sure I did, Francie." I shifted the receiver to my left ear so I could pick up a pen and take notes. "Why, what happened?"

"He went ahead and signed a supply contract without even calling me." She snorted in anger. "That idiot got bamboozled into ordering even more Type 316 stainless than we need to fulfill the *Constellation* contract just to get a lower price per ton."

"I'm sorry to hear that."

"I've been dealing with his crap for years now. Joey could handle him, but every time I try to put my foot down, Jimmy waves his degree from Fordham in my face. I ask him, while you were gallivanting around business school, who was holding things down in the factory after the old man died, huh? My Joey is who. He was always smarter than his little brother, but he never got the chance to go to college. What's it like?"

I'd lost the thread of her conversation. "What's what like?"

"College."

I put down my pen and shifted the phone back to my right ear. "It's pretty great, especially at a women's college like Barnard. It makes such a huge difference, clearing all the men out of the room. It's like our voices are at a pitch men can't even hear sometimes, you know? But in a class where everyone's a woman, I could always speak up."

"Sounds nice. Maybe Maeve will have that kind of chance. It's too late for me, that's for sure."

"Don't say that. Lots of people go back to college, Francie. The New School specializes in adult education."

"Nah, I don't really wanna be a student again. All I ever wanted was to take care of my family, but life ain't fair, is it? Like today—guess where Jimmy is right now."

"Where?"

"Out golfing with some banker who's thinking of investing in a restaurant." For the first time since I'd known her, Francie sounded truly defeated. "What I wouldn't give to be out on a golf course on a gorgeous day like this, or better yet, at Jones Beach with my kids. Sometimes I wonder if I'm throwing my life away here, Rita."

"You deserve a day off at least, Francie."

"You're damn right about that."

"It's too bad you don't run the place yourself."

"You want to know what's too bad?" Francie's Brooklyn vowels turned into growls. "That some drunk asshole ran my Joey off the road and left me alone to deal with all this shit." She took in a shuddering breath. "Hey, don't mind me. It's one of those days."

I wanted to tell her I knew how she felt, that some asshole had derailed my life, too. "Hang in there, Francie. Look out for that messenger, and call me if you have any questions."

"Sure thing, kid."

On Tuesday morning, I found a few notes on my desk from Mr. McKay. It didn't take long to make the changes he suggested. After testing my program again, I found myself suddenly idle. I couldn't produce a navy report on the 602 until I had a stack of correctly coded punch cards to process, so I offered to help run Olympia's regular accounts on the old Hollerith. It was monotonous work but oddly meditative. First, I narrowed down results through multiple sorts, then summarized them on one machine before printing them on another. Mr. McKay taught me how to wire a Hollerith control panel, too. By the end of the week, he pronounced me as proficient on the old machine as any of the quartermasters he'd served with in the army. I was certain he was exaggerating, but I was grateful he'd given me a new task that kept my mind occupied.

What's done is done, I reminded myself that Friday afternoon as I rode the elevator to the eighty-sixth floor of the Empire State Building. I hadn't heard a word from Jacob since I'd sent him away last Sunday, not a card or a note or even a phone call at work. I'd asked for space to sort out my feelings, but I hadn't expected him to take me so literally. After a week of lonely silence, I decided to stop sabotaging our relationship. I was so afraid he'd hate me if he knew my secret, but what if I really did forget I'd ever had a baby, like Miss Murphy had promised? It wouldn't be a lie for me not to tell him about something I didn't even remember. By a stroke of luck, I'd found a man who let me cry in his arms without demanding I explain my sadness. A man who'd known horrific suffering yet still had a tender touch. A man who believed we had been brought together by fate. A man who, though different from me in almost every way, felt like coming home. I walked around the observation deck searching for Jacob's skinny silhouette, eager to tell him I'd be his, if he still wanted me.

Jacob was nowhere to be seen. I waited until the next tours started, thinking he might be on a break, but those commenced—in English, French, and Italian—with no Jacob Nassy. I hadn't bought a ticket for the 102nd floor but the elevator operator recognized me and took me up for free. I paced as anxiously as Cary Grant waiting for Deborah Kerr, but true to script, the one I was looking for didn't appear. I hung around the secret door to the 103rd floor for thirty minutes, twice as long as anyone was supposed to expose themselves to those radio waves, but no one came down from the parapet.

My heart sank right along with the elevator to the bottom of the building. I couldn't believe Jacob was standing me up. All I'd asked for was time to think things over. Apparently, he'd been doing some thinking of his own. He'd obviously come to the conclusion I wasn't worth the wait.

Fine, then, I thought, leaving the lobby. Good riddance to bad rubbish, as my mother would say. The last thing I needed in my life was an orphaned Holocaust survivor whose back bent under the weight of bad memories.

The revolving door opened onto Fifth Avenue, noisy and hectic. I didn't step out.

Maybe Jacob was hurt. How could anyone who'd seen *An Affair*

to Remember not have thought of that? He could be lying unconscious in a hospital or home sick in bed. But where was home?
Other than meeting him in the Empire State Building, I had no
way of finding Jacob Nassy.

I went back around the revolving door again. Of course, I
thought: his friend the waiter. I'd go down to the Rathskeller
and talk to Rudy. Jacob had every right to avoid me—if he was
smart, he'd want nothing to do with me—but I couldn't go back
to Teaneck without at least finding out if he was okay.

It was still early for a Friday night, but the Rathskeller was filling
up. The waitstaff scurried around as the band got started, jaunty
drumbeats backing bass notes from the tuba. I asked the hostess
to seat me at the same table Jacob and I had shared two weeks ago.
Alone with the menu, I suddenly felt self-conscious. Why was I
even doing this? Jacob was a grown man who'd survived the Nazis,
for God's sake. He didn't need little me to save him.

"Rita, thank goodness you're here." Rudy pulled out the chair
across from mine and sat down. "I didn't know how to get hold
of you. I looked in the directory for the building, but you weren't
listed with any of the companies."

"I'm a temporary worker at Antiquated Business Machines.
Why, Rudy, what is it?"

"I'm sorry to tell you this, Rita, but Jake is in the hospital."

Even though I'd just been thinking of Deborah Kerr, I couldn't
believe it was true after all. "What happened?"

A customer at a nearby table whistled to get Rudy's attention.
"Can you stay until I get a break? I'll bring you something to eat,
on the house. Sit tight for a while, okay?"

I said yes, of course. Rudy hustled to the other table to take their
order. After a while, he brought me a cold hefeweizen and a basket
of pretzels but said he couldn't take his break until the first seating
turned over. I doodled in my notebook to look busy while I sipped

the beer and nibbled the pretzels. I wished Rudy would tell me what hospital Jacob was in. I could have been there visiting him by now. My head was clouded with alcohol and anxiety by the time Rudy finally beckoned me to follow him into the kitchen.

For such an enormous restaurant, the kitchen was surprisingly compact. The smells of cooking and frying and searing and baking filled the hot and steamy air. The serving counter was a buzz of activity: line cooks shouting out orders, tickets flapping above plates sizzling under heat lamps, waiters shuttling back and forth. Everywhere I looked there was stainless steel. I wondered if Olympia had supplied any of it.

"Let's sit over here." Rudy dragged his chair close to mine at the staff table and opened his mouth, but still he hesitated to speak.

"Please, won't you tell me what's happened?"

"Jake had an accident with his sleeping pills. At least, I hope it was an accident." Rudy took a pack of cigarettes from his shirt pocket, tapped one out for himself, and offered one to me.

"I don't understand." "Accident" meant slipping in a bathtub or tripping on the stairs. What kind of accident, I wondered, does someone have with sleeping pills?

"Jake has dark moods, Rita. I've seen it ever since we met at the displaced persons camp. When we qualified for American visas under that program for war orphans, Jake almost refused. He still didn't know for certain what happened to his parents, though we had to assume the worst. He got the crazy idea that declaring himself an orphan would somehow seal their fate. He wanted to wait, but we were fifteen already, and the program was only for children under sixteen. I convinced him to come with me while we had the chance."

It broke my heart to think of Jacob all alone in the world. Suddenly, the memory of Miss Murphy taking David out of my arms rose in my mind. I shoved it back down.

"You would have thought Jake had murdered his parents himself, he felt so guilty for leaving them behind. His mood lifted once we got on the airplane, though. Who could be sad flying above the ocean like that? Our first years here in New York were so busy, he didn't have time to wallow in his memories. We were fostered by a family until we turned seventeen, then we moved into a boardinghouse sponsored by the Jewish Aid Committee. We went to school during the day and worked here in the kitchen at night. I was satisfied with a high school diploma, but Jake kept on taking classes at the New School. There's nothing he can't learn—but I guess I don't need to tell you how clever he is.

"Anyway, when I married my girl, I moved out of that boardinghouse, but Jake never did. Even after he started giving tours and making more in tips than I did, he stayed in that same shitty room down in the Bowery, as if he didn't think he deserved any better." Rudy took a long drag on his cigarette, letting it out in a slow stream of smoke. "I remember when he got word from the Red Cross that they identified the transport his father was on. It went directly from Westerbork to Sobibor. Jake suspected his father had died, of course, but it was horrible when the Red Cross confirmed it. What was worse for him, though, is there was no trace at all of his mother."

I let my cigarette languish in the ashtray. "Poor Jacob."

"It was a terrible blow for him." Rudy stubbed out his cigarette. "Each room in that boardinghouse had a gas ring for cooking. After he got the news about his parents, Jake turned his on but didn't light it. He was unconscious by the time the landlady came in to check on the smell."

Tears spilled out of my eyes as I pictured Jacob splayed out on the floor. "My God, Rudy, I had no idea."

"Why would you? When he's in a good mood, you'd never guess he was capable of something like that. Anyway, the JAC has a hospital fund that paid for a week in the psychiatric unit at Mount Sinai. Jake's not the only one who's been through what we went through to suffer up here." Rudy tapped his temple. "His doctors made him move to a different boardinghouse that had a hot plate instead of gas, and prescribed sleeping pills so he could get enough rest. He started giving tours again. He even celebrated my son's bris. He was on an even keel, as they say, until he met you."

"What do I have to do with it?"

"After he met you, he became happy. Happier than I've ever seen him. It made me nervous, how happy he was." He looked at me, his eyes haunted. "He didn't seem happy anymore when he stopped by our place Sunday night, after spending the day with your family. He said he was fine, but I had a bad feeling, Rita. The next morning, I went by his room. He didn't answer, but I have his spare key. I found him in bed, so still and pale I thought he was already dead. I yelled for someone to call an ambulance. I should have called his doctor first. By the time they took him away, it was too late."

"Too late?" My heart clawed its way up my throat. "What do you mean, too late?"

"They took him to Bellevue."

Bellevue. In the newspapers, whenever someone did something crazy, they were invariably reported as having been sent to Bellevue. So far that summer, I'd read about the teenage boy who threw a neighbor girl off the roof of their apartment building. The ex-con out on parole who stabbed yet another woman in Central Park. The subway worker who called in a false bomb report. All sent to Bellevue. I remembered that scene in *The Lost Weekend*: an open ward populated by alcoholics and mental patients who screamed and struggled while orderlies built like boxers wrestled them into straitjackets. I shuddered to think of Jacob among those criminals and addicts.

"It took a few days, but I finally got hold of his doctor at Mount Sinai," Rudy said. "He's arranged for Jacob to be discharged, but Bellevue will only release him into someone's custody. I would have gone myself, but I can't afford to miss work. I hate to think of him there one hour longer than necessary, but we need the wages, what with the baby and all. But now he doesn't have to wait until the restaurant is closed on Sunday. Maybe you could get him out tomorrow?"

"Me?"

Rudy took my hand. "Yes, you. You could get him out tomorrow and stay with him overnight. Then I could come on Sunday to help."

I felt very small and afraid, but responsible, too. "You think this happened because of me?"

"Not because of you, Rita, no. You are wonderful. After he met you, I was hoping he'd let himself be happy for once in his life. Maybe it really was an accident. Maybe he couldn't sleep and lost count of the pills he took. But Jake is hurt, here." Rudy put his hand on his chest. "I don't think his heart knows the difference anymore between happiness and pain."

"Psst, Rudy." Another waiter tapped him on the shoulder and pointed to the chef, who beckoned him, glowering.

"I have to go." He stood, waiting for my response.

"I'll get him out tomorrow."

"Good. Take this." He gave me the key to Jacob's room at the boardinghouse, then scribbled some numbers on a page in his serving book that he tore out and handed to me. "Here's my telephone, and Jake's address, and also his doctor at Mount Sinai, in case they give you any trouble at Bellevue."

I folded the note around the key and put it in my pocketbook. "Thank you for telling me all this, Rudy."

He shrugged. "Jake may not like it, but what's the point of being ashamed to speak of such things? Our secrets do us no good if we end up buried under the weight of them."

That night, I packed my pink suitcase with whatever I'd need for the weekend, including clothes for work on Monday. I told my parents Jacob had come down with the flu and that I was going to take care of him. When Mom warned me to be careful, I knew she wasn't talking about catching a virus. I told her not to worry, that I'd learned my lesson. Dad didn't understand why I needed to play nursemaid to a grown man until I reminded him why Jacob was all alone in the world. I hardly slept, worried about what I'd find at Bellevue the next morning.

Chapter Sixteen
Cornelia Vogel

Camp Westerbork, Netherlands
February 1943

N ext!"
The man in line behind Cornelia gives her a shove. "It's your turn."

Cornelia has been dozing on her feet. Like a horse, she thinks, shaking herself awake. As the fog in her head clears, sound comes crashing back into her ears. Sleet sizzles on the roof. Feet shuffle across the floor. Suitcases drag. Babies wail. People's voices rise to the rafters and reverberate, individual shouts and pleas subsumed by the general din. Above it all is the cacophony of typewriters, hundreds of keys on dozens of machines tap-tap-tap-tapping like a factory of frantically hammering elves.

When Cornelia imagined what awaited her at Camp Westerbork, she pictured black-booted soldiers wielding truncheons and snarling dogs baring their teeth. Instead, the lines of anxious people surrounded by piles of luggage remind her of the chaos in a shipping terminal as passengers scramble to board a boat.

"I said next, please." A young woman with a head of brown curls impatiently beckons Cornelia. She picks up the rucksack at her feet and trudges across the Registration Hall. The desk toward which she is heading is one tiny island in an archipelago of desks. Seated behind each, a person is taking information.

Seated in front, a prisoner is giving it. Despite the cold outside, the air is stifling from the nervous heat of hundreds of human bodies. As she drops into her chair, Cornelia unbuttons her coat—Leah's coat—revealing the nightgown underneath.

The clerk rolls a large index card into her typewriter and looks up. Her dark eyes widen as her expression escalates from harried to alarmed. "Where is your star?"

"My star?" For a misguided second, Cornelia wonders why she is being asked about her astrological sign. Then she looks around and sees that her nightgown is the only visible garment lacking a yellow star. All the people on line have stars on their coats, shirts, jackets, and dresses. The children have them sewn to their sweaters. Scanning the hall, she sees that all the clerks, too, are branded with a star. Even the guards have them pinned to their uniforms. In this sea of stars, Cornelia's unadorned breast flashes like a beacon. "It's just a nightgown, not a dress."

The clerk shakes her head, tossing her curls. "Be that as it may, you should get one sewn on at the tailor shop. Keep your coat buttoned until then. I'm Etty Hillesum, by the way. I work for the Jewish Council. We help with registration here, among other things."

Cornelia grasps the hand Etty holds out to her. How odd, she thinks, to be welcomed to prison with a handshake. "I thought the Jewish Council was based in Amsterdam."

"We are. I mostly work here at Westerbork, but I have a permit to travel back and forth," Etty says.

"But—" Cornelia swivels her neck to look around the hall. "Where are the Germans? Don't they run this camp?"

"If they did, life here would be a thousand times more terrible." She continues in a lower voice. "Believe me, the prisoners who are transferred from Amersfoort weep with gratitude. Commandant Gemmeker is German, of course, and the soldiers in the watchtowers, too, but it's the long-term residents who maintain order at Westerbork."

"Long-term residents?"

"German refugees who've been here since before the war. Ironic, isn't it, that Jews who fled the Nazis would end up working for them? The way they throw their weight around, you'd think they sympathized with Hitler. But they've lost everything they left behind, too, and they live better while they're here. Their main incentive, though, is being exempt from the transport list."

Cornelia is having trouble taking in Etty's words. "Please, is there any water?"

"Here, have some of this." She pours tea from a thermos and pushes a cup across the desk. "Did you come directly from Amsterdam? I hear conditions at the Hollandsche Schouwburg are dreadful."

"No, I was arrested in The Hague." Cornelia, drinking deeply, struggles to piece together the past two days. The lorry didn't go far before its canvas flap opened at Scheveningen prison. Everyone with her in the truck was locked together in a large cell. Others kept arriving throughout the day until they were packed as tightly as commuters in a tram. There was one sink for water and a toilet in the corner around which the women formed a screen with their shawls. No meals were given out, but most people seemed to have brought food to eat. An elderly man, pitying Cornelia, shared an apple and some cheese. As day passed into night, rucksacks became pillows and coats blankets as the prisoners carpeted the floor with their bodies, strangers curled close as spouses. Cornelia, exhausted but sleepless, tuned her ear to the distant sound of surf breaking along the beach. Her brain, paralyzed with anxiety, allowed one thought to surface: that those waves might be the last sounds she'd ever hear of her birthplace.

The next morning, they were herded out of the cell before dawn and taken in lorries to the train station. Cornelia recalls the scene with wonder. Their group stood on the platform with their luggage waiting to board the first scheduled train to Amsterdam, just like the other passengers at the station—except for the armed soldiers shepherding them aboard.

"I never got on a train without a ticket before." Cornelia is surprised that, among all of her experiences, this is the one that felt most strange.

"No, they don't give tickets to Jews." Etty is taking the opportunity of their conversation to massage her fingers. "The Germans have an account with Dutch Railways. The soldiers tell the ticket agent how many third-class seats to charge them for."

Cornelia succumbed to sleep as soon as the train started rocking along its tracks. By the time the jolt of a switch point woke her, a pale sun had risen behind gray clouds. Through bleary eyes, she saw they were passing the same fields as when she'd traveled to Amsterdam with Leah, the tulips now shriveled to dormant bulbs beneath tracts of frozen mud. Pulling into Centraal station, she saw so many flashes of yellow, Cornelia thought for a moment a border of flowers had been planted along the platform. She rubbed her eyes and looked again. It was Jews, hundreds of Jews, each marked with a star.

"May I have some more tea?"

Etty refills the cup. "Did you pack a thermos? It's quite crucial here."

"I don't know." Cornelia hasn't gone through Leah's rucksack yet. To explain her ignorance, she says, "My mother packed for me."

"Well, let's hope so. If not, you can try the Welfare Department, but I'd be surprised if they had one to spare. Now, let's see your identification."

Cornelia's heart jumps into her throat. Her picture is so clumsily glued in place, the card will never hold up to scrutiny. Then she reminds herself that close inspection of her identification is unlikely—after all, there's no incentive for someone to counterfeit being a Jew. She reaches into her pocket and hands it over.

Etty glances at the identity card without comment and begins typing, copying the name and birth date before asking, "Now, Leah, what is your occupation?"

"My occupation? Why do you need to know that?"

"We try to place people in jobs where they can be most useful, though to be honest there's rarely much of a match."

Cornelia is stumped. Leah is an illustrator, but Cornelia can't draw so much as a stick figure. Saying she's an English translator would be true to her abilities, but she's afraid of attracting suspicion for expertise in an enemy's language. There's no use mentioning the Hollerith when hardly anyone even knows what it is. "I do clerical work."

"Like typing?" There's a hopeful lilt to Etty's question.

"No, I—" She looks around, ashamed that the work she did at Huize Kleykamp helped create the lists that ensnared all these people. "I mostly do filing."

Dutifully, Etty types "file clerk" next to the word "occupation" on the index card and continues. "You mentioned your mother. Are you here with your family?"

"No." Cornelia swallows back a sudden rush of tears as she pictures her parents and brother gathered around the breakfast table, her own seat empty. But she isn't Cornelia Vogel anymore, she reminds herself. She's Leah Blom. "My parents are on the Exchange List. My mother is American, you see."

"American, really? My mother's Russian. I guess that makes us both unique, doesn't it? Where are your parents now?"

"I think they went to a barn somewhere—no, that's not right. Maybe it was a château?"

Etty stares at her. "Is your father Professor Philip Blom?" Cornelia nods. "I saw your parents in Amsterdam a couple of days ago. I remember distinctly because Chairman Asscher himself intervened on their behalf. They've gone to Barneveld. Why aren't you with them?"

"They were in Amsterdam, like you said, when I was arrested in The Hague."

"Well, when we're finished here, I'll take you to have your case reviewed. Hopefully, you can be transferred to Barneveld with your parents. Now, let me get your mother's name and their birth dates?"

Cornelia's stomach turns. Is this how I'll be found out? she wonders. She takes a deep breath. Her eyes drift shut as she turns her brain into a memory machine. Think: What day did you help Leah pick out a birthday present for her mother? How many candles did Lillian blow out on her cake that evening? What was the date of the dinner party you attended for Professor Blom's fiftieth birthday? Cornelia recites the dates she's come up with, hoping they aren't wrong.

Etty types the information on the index card, which she then pulls out of the typewriter. Picking up a pencil, she adds a note about Barneveld, then writes down Cornelia's new address. "I'm assigning you to barrack sixty-five. It's for unmarried women." She nods at Cornelia's hand. "You're not married, are you?"

Cornelia touches the signet ring Leah placed on her finger. "No, I'm not."

"Very good." Etty rolls a small square of green card stock behind the paper bail. "This will be your camp identification. You must always keep it with you. I've typed your name and barrack number on it, see? Here's your identity card back. Now, bring your things and follow me."

Wending their way around the desks, they reach the back of the hall, where there's a raised platform, like a stage, on which stands a table laden with file boxes stuffed with index cards. Men in shabby suits affixed with faded yellow stars buzz about the platform like bees around a hive, pulling cards out and shoving them in.

"What are they doing?"

Etty takes Cornelia's elbow and steers her past the stage. "Those are members of the camp's Registration Department."

"I thought you said the Jewish Council registered people."

"We do, though I sometimes wonder why we bother. The Registration Department, like everything else around here, is the opposite of what it seems. They use the cards we type up to create the transport lists." Etty's voice breaks as she adds, "I hear the next quota is over a thousand."

She leads the way down a corridor clotted with people, some sitting on chairs and chatting idly, others leaning against walls and staring into space. The doors along the corridor are closed, but a window in the wall reveals a counter behind which some bureaucrat is apparently stationed. Etty positions Cornelia in front of the counter.

"Now, Leah, I want you to explain that your parents are on the Exchange List and that you should be transferred to Barneveld. You can report to your barrack as soon as you're finished speaking with Fräulein Slottke."

Cornelia's knees buckle as Mevrouw Kwakkelstein's words ring in her memory: *Gertrud Slottke is a very impressive woman. I'd venture to say she's the one who does the real work of the* Judenreferent. "Wait, Etty, did you say Slottke?"

"Yes. Gertrud Slottke reviews all cases." She lowers her voice to a whisper. "The Registration Department thinks they're all-powerful, but Slottke has the final word on every transport." Etty pulls Cornelia back to the counter and calls out in German, "Fräulein Slottke, do you have a moment to consider a case?"

The hollow clomp of heels precedes Gertrud Slottke's appearance behind the counter. She's obviously middle-aged, but her white face is strangely smooth, as if neither smile nor frown has ever creased its skin. Her nose is as narrow as a bird's beak, her thin lips held in a straight line by a downward tug at the corners of her mouth. A braid of unnaturally red hair is wound around her head. She's wearing a brown jacket over a white blouse buttoned to her jugular notch. Cornelia wonders what's so odd about her outfit until she notices the conspicuous absence of a yellow star.

Fräulein Slottke's small eyes light first on Etty. "What case?"

"Leah Blom here will explain everything," Etty says, retreating down the corridor. "Good day to you, *Fräulein*."

The woman's eyes shift to Cornelia. Her face remains impassive as one eyebrow twitches. "Let's start with your identification."

Cornelia panics as she tries to recall if her father ever mentioned Fräulein Slottke entering his office. Picturing the photograph of their family on his desk, she's terrified to imagine what could happen if the secretary to the *Judenreferent* realizes Gerard Vogel's daughter has sacrificed herself to save a Jew.

Praying the woman won't recognize her, Cornelia places the identity card on the counter with a shaking hand.

Fräulein Slottke compares the photograph to Cornelia's face. "I see you attempted to alter this."

"No, I—"

Slottke raises a single finger, silencing Cornelia. "That makes no difference now. Your attempt obviously failed. Now, tell me about your case, Leah Blom."

Cornelia's tongue is stiff in her mouth as she explains about Barneveld and the Exchange List. Fräulein Slottke listens without comment.

"Your German is excellent. You are well educated, I take it?"

"I was at Leiden University until—" Cornelia snaps her lips shut. Leah attended school in Delft, not Leiden.

Fräulein Slottke taps a fingernail on the identity card. "And you have no other documents to support your case?"

"Not with me, no."

"I'll need to keep this, then, while I investigate. I'll write you a receipt." Fräulein Slottke steps back into her office, where she sits down at a desk. On a nearby typing table, Cornelia is stunned to see a punch machine with a stack of rectangular cards beside it. She leans in to look around. There's only the one machine; beneath it, the bit bin is empty.

Fräulein Slottke speaks without turning her head. "Step back from the counter."

Cornelia does, her mind churning. Those punch cards, she is certain, can have only one destination: the Hollerith bunker at Huize Kleykamp.

Fräulein Slottke returns to the window. "Here is your receipt. I will summon you back after I have looked into your case. In the meantime, I'll add a note for the Registration Department that you are unavailable for transport." She dismisses Cornelia with a wave of her hand.

Cornelia's legs feel like columns of water as she retraces her steps through the Registration Hall. It's beginning to empty out as people disperse to their assigned barracks. Etty, busy interviewing another prisoner, gives a quick wave as Cornelia passes by. At the entrance, a sneering official with a frayed star pinned to his blue cape demands to see Cornelia's camp identification. "The unmarried women's barrack? I know it well." He winks obnoxiously, then beckons to a teenage girl in overalls who is passing by with an empty wheelbarrow. "You there, escort this woman to the spinsters' hut."

"Sure thing." The girl, with ruddy cheeks and wild blond hair, comes closer. "Throw your luggage in here, why don't you."

A puddle of water sloshes in the tub of the wheelbarrow. "I can carry my rucksack," Cornelia says, stepping outside.

"Go ahead, toss it in." She tilts the wheelbarrow to dump out the standing water, but Cornelia still hesitates. The girl glances at the official, whose attention is momentarily elsewhere, then covers her mouth to speak quietly to Cornelia. "Please don't get me in trouble with the Order Police. They're not such bastards as the Green Police, but you don't want to get on the wrong side of them. Besides, I want to hang on to this, but I'm not officially part of the Flying Column so I won't be allowed to push it around empty."

Cornelia, utterly baffled, sets Leah's rucksack in the tub.

"All right, then, follow me."

That morning, when the scheduled train from Amsterdam to Groningen stopped at the station in Hooghalen, the cars full of Jews were disengaged and a locomotive attached to bring them directly into Westerbork. The prisoners, disembarking in the freezing rain, were herded into the Registration Hall without the chance to look around. Now, with the clouds wrung dry and the sun not yet set, Cornelia takes in her surroundings for the first time.

With its plywood buildings and dirt lanes, Westerbork seems more like some shabby colonial outpost than a wartime prison camp. Men sit on upturned barrels smoking pipes. Dispirited pedestrians trudge along while unparented children wander aimlessly. A woman in a filthy fur coat wrestles with a baby carriage that keeps getting stuck in the mud. The only uniforms she sees are those of the Order Police, whose blue capes and brimmed hats lend them an air of authority incongruent with their yellow stars.

The girl with the wheelbarrow, who is performing her assigned task with the utmost leisure, narrates their route to barrack sixty-five. "See those little houses? They're for the long-term residents. They're all Germans, not to be trusted."

"But aren't they Jewish, too?"

"Everyone's Jewish here, even the priests. That doesn't mean we're all in the same boat." The girl gestures with her chin. "That big building is the central kitchen. I tried to get a job there peeling potatoes but instead I got sent out to the fields to dig them up."

Cornelia has had nothing more than an apple and some cheese in the last two days. "When is the evening meal served?"

"Evening meal!" The girl laughs. "There's only one meal a day here, and it won't be dished up again until tomorrow. They run out sometimes, so you'll want to line up early. Once you've gotten your share, you take your mess kit back to your barrack to warm it up and eat." She pauses to point out another building. "That there is the bathhouse. We're supposed to get a shower every week, but I haven't had one in a month. There's the boiler house, for the steam heat, though you'd never know it from how freezing the barracks are. You can fill your thermos with hot water at those taps, at least. You have any friends back home who care about you?"

Cornelia chokes back a sob. "I think so."

"You better write and tell them to send you a package quick. Make sure you ask for tea. You won't forget me when you get it, will you? I'm Greta, by the way. Greta Speelman. My mother and I are in barrack sixty-two, so we're practically neighbors. My papa's in the S-hut, though."

"The S-hut?"

"The punishment barrack. It's the one with extra barbed wire all around it. He got caught riding a tram without his star, so now he's a criminal, on top of being a Jew."

They've emerged from behind the boiler house onto a broad road dotted with anemic trees, down the center of which runs the train track. Here, Cornelia has her first unobstructed view out to the fence surrounding the camp. Lines of barbed wire—painful looking, even from a distance—are closely strung between posts as tall as the barracks' rooftops. Beyond the fence is one of the watchtowers, square and squat atop thin legs. She pictures the soldier stationed there lining her up in his rifle sights and cringes.

"This is the Boulevard des Misères." Greta points to the tracks. "Be careful you don't get caught on the wrong side of camp when the train comes in. I once spent a whole day starving in my barrack because I couldn't get across to the kitchen."

Cornelia wonders how this "Road of Misery" through a German camp for Dutch Jews got a French name, but she has a more pressing question. "Does the train come often?"

Greta looks at her as if she's asked if the world is round. "The transport arrives every Monday and departs every Tuesday. You can set your watch by it."

"But today is Friday, isn't it?"

"I'm not talking about those little trains that bring people in." Greta's mood becomes somber. As if reciting a memorized line, she says, "The transport comes empty, like a hungry snake, and leaves with its belly full."

Her words send a shiver down Cornelia's spine. Crossing the tracks, she steps smack into a puddle, soaking her shoes. Greta looks down. "Shit for you, hey? You'll never get those dry before April, I'll bet. Potato diggers get these." She lifts a leg to show off a clunky wooden clog. "Not much for fashion, but they keep my toes dry."

Greta leads her past a row of identical barracks—long, squat wooden structures—until they arrive at number sixty-five. Cornelia lifts the rucksack from the wheelbarrow, relieved to find it's damp but not soaked. Greta promptly sits herself down in the tub and lights a hand-rolled cigarette. "Hey, there's no rush, you know. Give me a minute before I have to make my-self look useful."

While Greta smokes, Cornelia turns a full circle. Everything she sees is the color of dirt. A final beam of sunlight pierces the low clouds before dropping beneath the horizon. From a nearby barrack, she is amazed to hear singing. The voices are baritone, the key minor. She doesn't recognize the tune, which is more like a chant than a song.

"We call that barrack over there the Holy Land," Greta says. "They say this is the only night of the week the rabbis stop arguing."

A cat has appeared. It slinks between Cornelia's feet, caressing her ankles with its tail. "What's special about tonight?"

"What are you, a baptized Jew? It's the Sabbath."

Cornelia remembers those Friday nights when she joined Leah's family for their evening meal. For the Bloms, Shabbat wasn't an elaborate ritual. Lillian simply draped a lace shawl over her head while she waved her hands above a couple of candles and chanted a melodic prayer. Even so, Cornelia saw how the Hebrew words imbued Leah's nervous mother with serenity and strength. She wishes now she'd accepted the Bloms' invitation to attend Passover. At the time, she said she didn't want to intrude, but in truth she was self-conscious about being the odd one out. The realization that she's now a foreigner in this involuntary city of Jews is disorienting. She crouches down to pet the cat, which bangs its head against her shin. "How did you end up here, puss?"

Greta pinches out the butt of her cigarette, tucks it into her pocket, and clambers out of the wheelbarrow. "Don't forget, you promised to share your packages with me. Hey, what's your name, anyway?"

"Cor—" She turns the sound into a cough. "Leah. Leah Blom."

"I'll keep a lookout for you, Leah." Greta grabs the handles of the wheelbarrow and heads back toward the Registration Hall.

Cornelia pets the cat once more before shouldering the rucksack and entering what the obnoxious guard called the spinsters' hut.

The interior of the barrack is as bleak as its exterior: plywood ceiling supported by crisscrossed timbers, plank floor caked in mud, small windows opaque with grime. But like everything else at Westerbork she has encountered so far, barrack sixty-five is not what Cornelia expected. Instead of a stark and regimented prison ward, it is as chaotic and cluttered as a bazaar. Each bunk seems to be a stall, its wares of clothing, books, boots, and plates arrayed as if ready for bartering. Clothes hang from lines strung between bunks like goods in a flea market. On the lowest tier of a bunk, Cornelia sees a woman reclining with a book, while the second tier is being used as a table by a woman who eats standing up. The third tier is crammed with suitcases; Cornelia assumes it is unoccupied until a teenager pushes past her and climbs to the top, muddying the blankets of both bunks below. The woman on the bottom showers her with half-hearted curses. It can't be helped. There are no ladders.

Rows of metal bunks three tiers high unfold before her eyes with the dizzying repetition of an Escher illustration. Cornelia counts twenty bunks to her right before the diminishing perspective of the barrack makes it impossible to differentiate one from the next. She doubles that for the bunks to her left, then triples that for the three tiers. One hundred and twenty women living together in the space of a dairy shed—and that's only as many as she can see. One hundred and twenty persons identified by the Ministry of Information as members of the Jewish race. One hundred and twenty names printed on a list by the Hollerith alphabetizer. And which twelve dots on her father's map, she wonders, represent these hundred and twenty women? To him, these people are as abstract as perforated cards processed by a computer. Here, they're more than six thousand kilos of muscle and bone. Would it change his point of view to know his own flesh and blood was among them?

Women jostle past her as she makes her way farther down the aisle. In the center of the barrack, her progress is blocked by a group standing hip to hip. Peering over their shoulders, Cornelia sees they are huddled around a cast-iron stove, frying potatoes on tin plates. The smell makes her mouth water, but it's the babble of their voices that sparks her interest. Instead of Dutch, she hears Portuguese, which is not surprising given the ancestry of so many Jews in the Netherlands. But there are other tongues, too, that she can't place right away. An unexpected thrill cuts through her exhaustion and hunger as she tunes her ear to their polyglot speech. An older woman holding a plate of cold potatoes begs for a turn at the stove in Greek. She is rebuffed by a pair of stout women who mutter to one another in what sounds like Turkish. How have the speakers of these far-flung languages come to be housed together in the spinsters' hut of Camp Westerbork? Cornelia wonders.

"You look lost." A woman is speaking to her in good old-fashioned Dutch. "I'm the matron of this barrack. Were you assigned here?"

"Yes." Cornelia shows her the camp identification.

The woman barely glances at it. "You came in today?" Cornelia nods. "That's the second group to arrive this week. Lucky for you, someone just went into the hospital, otherwise you would've been the drop that makes the bucket overflow. I've got a bunk for you over here."

In the time it takes to walk past the stove to the far end of the barrack, the matron has pointed out the toilets ("There's always a line, so plan accordingly") and the washroom ("Sinks only, showers are at the bathhouse"). The bunk she indicates is far from the stove ("Too bad about the heat, but at least it's quiet") and on the third tier ("Go on and toss your things up there before someone else claims it").

She stands with hands on hips while Cornelia clumsily clambers to the top. Her bunkmates aren't in their beds, so no one curses as the structure sways. She slings the rucksack onto a thin mattress that stinks of sweat and urine. There's no pillow or sheet, only a disheveled blanket. Cornelia thinks of her cozy bed at home and despairs. Then she pictures Leah bicycling toward freedom and summons her courage.

"Come with me to the matron's room. They've brought over the evening coffee urn, and I've got a piece of bread you can have. I'll get you a mess kit, too." She strides off, her outstretched arm clearing a path.

Cornelia drinks the bitter water the matron calls coffee, eats the stale slice that counts as bread, and takes possession of a mess kit that's in dire need of scrubbing. After waiting in line long enough to learn that the Greek woman is a refugee from Salonika, she uses the toilet and cleans herself up as best she can. The narrow spaces between the bunks are transformed into dressing rooms as women ready themselves for bed. The woman on the bottom, who is at home now, offers Cornelia a space below the bunk for her shoes, so at least she doesn't leave a muddy trail as she climbs up. She hopes she won't have to use the toilet at night—that descent would be treacherous in the dark. The woman on the third tier of the bunk beside her is close enough to touch, but instead of greeting Cornelia she turns away.

The advantage of being on top, Cornelia realizes, is that she can sit up without hitting her head on a bunk above her. For the first time, she unclasps the buckles on Leah's rucksack. Whatever it contains now comprises the entirety of her possessions. There are clothes, of course: trousers, blouses, sweaters, three pairs of wool socks, five sets of cotton underclothes, one bra, a menstrual belt and some pads. No dresses or skirts. Cornelia has taken Leah's name; now she'll be impersonating her style, too.

There is a thermos, she's grateful to see, and a couple of tins of sardines. Cornelia wishes she'd thought to look for food in it before. She's so hungry she's about to pry open a tin when she sees in the bottom of the rucksack a package of *speculaas*. She unwraps the spiced cookies and eats one in a single bite, saliva squirting at the first tang of clove. She forces herself to stop after two more so she'll have some tomorrow. Further rummaging reveals a jar of jam, a box of tea, and a roll of *zoute drop*, the salted licorice that Leah loves and Cornelia detests. A perfect gift for Greta, she decides.

Leah has also packed drawing charcoal and a sketchbook. There are two novels—the copy of *The Well of Loneliness* they bought together in Amsterdam and Leah's favorite, *Jane Eyre*—as well as the volume of Sappho's poetry that Cornelia inscribed to Leah on her last birthday. An envelope contains a collection of photographs: Leah's parents on their wedding day. Her father's parents, now deceased, admiring their baby granddaughter. Her mother as a child in New York City. Cornelia's heart hitches when she sees the next picture. It's her and Leah on the bridge in Amsterdam, the love in their eyes as easy to spot as a lighthouse beacon. She keeps that photo out while she repacks the rucksack and pushes it to the bottom of the bunk. She holds the picture in her hand, gloved now against the cold, as she lies down for the night. Leah's face is the size of Cornelia's thumbnail, but every detail is dear to her.

Lights-out comes suddenly, but the noise and commotion only increase in the dark. As exhausted as she is, Cornelia gets little rest. The mattress is too thin to blunt the wire webbing beneath it. As the stove cools down and the radiators fail to warm up, Cornelia regrets not putting on trousers and a sweater under the coat she hugs around her frigid body. She regrets not putting on an extra pair of socks. She regrets not eating another cookie.

But even though she is freezing, and heartsick, and hungry, and afraid, she doesn't regret taking Leah's place.

Like the ripples from a thrown stone, Cornelia wonders if, by stepping into the stream of Leah's fate, she may have diverted its course. No one knows exactly what happens to the Jews who are sent away from Holland, but the fact that their names are deleted from the population list is enough for Cornelia to be certain deportation is to be avoided at all costs. If she is to survive, she must stay here at Westerbork. To do that, she must find a way to keep herself off the transport list. And the key to that, in some way Cornelia has yet to reckon, lies with Gertrud Slottke.

Chapter Seventeen
Rita Klein

New York City
June 1960

I'm sorry, miss, we got nobody here by that name." The nurse spoke to me from behind glass embedded with wire, as if she were a bank teller fortified against bandits.

"Yes, you do." I tamped my voice down. I knew from watching other people plead their case that yelling did no good at Bellevue psychiatric hospital. "The nurse I spoke with earlier knows who I'm talking about. She said all she needed before he could be released was a call back from his doctor at Mount Sinai." Pins and needles shot up my leg. I hadn't realized, before I got up, that my foot had fallen asleep. "I was checking if she'd heard from him yet. Can I talk to her, please?"

"She's on her lunch break now."

"Can't you help me, then?"

"That's what I'm trying to do, miss, but I'm telling you I don't see no Jacob Nancy on my list here."

"Nassy, not Nancy. N-A-S-S-Y."

"Oh, why didn't you say? Let me have a look around. I'll call you up to the window when I got some news for you."

I had no choice but to drag my numb foot back to my seat. I'd been in the waiting room for three hours now. Jacob was somewhere inside this fortress, but it was like prying gold from a dragon trying to get him out. The woman I'd been sharing the bench with all morning sidled closer and offered me a tangerine. "This your first time, honey?"

I nodded, accepting the fruit, its orange skin bright as sunrise in that dull room.

"Fourth for me. My pop hasn't been the same since my mom went home to Jesus. He's a good man, honest to God he is, it's just the whiskey makes him crazy. He goes missing every now and again, but he doesn't always end up here. Until I get that postcard from Bellevue telling me to come get him, I worry he's floating in the East River." She patted my arm. "You gotta be patient, honey."

The nurse at the reception window called out a name. "Speak of the devil," the woman said, getting to her feet and gathering her things. "You eat that up now, you don't want your blood sugar getting low."

I dug my thumbnail into the tangerine to peel the skin from its flesh. The scent freshened the air like a spritz of perfume. I lingered over each segment, the sweet tang dancing on my tongue. It really was ironic, I thought. A month ago, I'd abandoned my boy, bereft of parents, at one hospital. Now I was at another, begging to be given custody of an orphaned man.

"Jacob Nassy?" It was the nurse back from lunch.

I circled my ankles to make sure my feet were awake. "Yes, here I am."

"Come this way." She beckoned me through a locked door. I grabbed my suitcase and followed her down a hallway lined with gurneys and wheelchairs, some occupied, others empty. Metal grates over the windows cast graph-paper shadows on floors and faces alike. At the far end of the hallway, a uniformed officer lounged behind a battered desk. An orderly, muscular and clean-cut, stood casual guard over a man slumped on a bench. A white-coated doctor, stethoscope slung round his neck, made notes on a chart. This was apparently where patients were handed over to the people who came to claim them. I wondered when they'd bring Jacob out.

The nurse showed some paperwork to the doctor, who glanced at it before scribbling a signature. She nodded to the orderly, who dropped a huge hand on the shoulder of the slumped man. Gathering the fabric of the man's shirt in his fist, he hauled him to his feet. "He's all yours, ma'am."

I hadn't even recognized Jacob. His face was gaunt, his mouth slack. Purple crescents drooped beneath his puffy eyes as if he'd lost a prize fight.

"I don't expect he'll give you much trouble," the nurse said. "He was agitated when he first got here, but we've kept him calm since then, isn't that right?"

The orderly nodded his head. "Mr. Nassy's been a regular lamb."

The nurse pressed some pills into my hand. "If his agitation returns when the sedation wears off, give him one of these. Best thing you can do is tuck him in bed and let him sleep for a couple of days." She patted Jacob's arm. "Remember what the doctor told you, Mr. Nassy. Think happy thoughts."

I clutched Jacob's skinny elbow. He was like a somnambulist as I guided him down the hallway and out onto Thirtieth Street. Between my suitcase in one hand and Jacob's elbow in the other, I couldn't even flag a taxi. Fortunately, there was a call box on the corner of First Avenue. I spoke to the dispatcher, reading off the address on Ludlow Street that Rudy had given me. A few minutes later, a Checker cab pulled up. "Discharged from Bellevue, huh?" the driver said. "That's tough. Here, let me give you a hand." He helped Jacob into the backseat, where he sat limp with his eyes closed while we drove to his boardinghouse.

It took some cajoling, but I got Jacob up to his room. Closing the door behind us, I almost choked on the hot, stuffy air. "Sit down for a minute, okay?"

He dropped into a battered armchair while I opened the only window as high as it could go. It faced a brick wall but at least it let some fresh air into the place. It really was a depressing room, I thought, looking around. Besides the armchair, the furniture consisted of an old armoire, a lumpy bed behind a threadbare curtain, a rickety table, and a couple of chairs. There was a cold-water sink on the wall and a hot plate on a counter. The bathroom must have been down the hall. I asked Jacob if he needed to go.

"Rita?" He raised his eyes to mine for the first time that day.

"Yes, Jacob, it's me." I knelt in front of his chair and looked up at him. "I'm here."

He ran his fingers through my hair. "You saved me from that place. I thought I was hallucinating when I saw you. The medicine they gave me—" His voice cracked. "I saw things I hope I never see again."

I didn't mention the pills in my pocketbook. I walked him down the hall to the bathroom and waited for him outside. After he came out, I asked for a minute to myself. I stared at the white tile walls while I sat on the toilet, wondering what I'd gotten myself into. When I opened the door, Jacob was standing there in his stocking feet, a bar of soap in his hand and a towel and robe over his arm. "I'm going to take a bath, if that's all right? I've got to wash that place off of me."

"Of course. Have you eaten today?"

He looked confused by the question. "I really don't know."

"How about I go get us some lunch at that deli on the corner while you're in the bath, okay? Maybe some soup?"

"Sure." He knitted his eyebrows together. "There's money in the bottom drawer of the armoire, in the blue socks."

"Don't worry about it, Jacob. You go ahead and get cleaned up."

I walked up to Houston Street, where I telephoned Rudy's wife to leave the message that Jacob was out of Bellevue and back home. After picking up a paper at the newsstand, I went into Katz's Deli for a container of chicken soup, a loaf of rye, a side of jelly, and a couple bottles of chocolate soda. I had everything set out on the table in Jacob's room by the time he came in, wrapped in his robe with the towel around his neck.

"Where are your clothes?" I asked. He'd gone into the bathroom fully dressed.

"I threw them down the incinerator shaft." He sat at the table and stared at the soup.

"Won't you try some, Jacob?"

He spooned the broth into his mouth, avoiding the pieces of chicken. "I think I need to lie down now."

"Of course, I'm sorry. The nurse said you needed your rest."

He practically fell into bed. I lifted his legs and spread the blanket over him. "You have a good sleep, and no bad dreams, okay? Promise me."

Jacob took my hand and kissed it. "I promise, Little Rita."

I boiled some water for tea, then put his uneaten soup in the pot to heat up later. I looked for something to read, but aside from depressing novels by Nevil Shute, most of his books were in languages other than English. I settled down in the armchair and spent the afternoon paging though the newspaper. I looked to see if the State Department had made any progress securing Francis Gary Powers's release, but news about the U-2 spy plane incident seemed to have disappeared from the papers as completely as its pilot into a Soviet prison. I was glad to see that Mayor Wagner was sticking to his guns and refusing to give the American Nazi Party a permit to rally at Union Square on Independence Day. I read a long article about the Army Corps of Engineers taking over nine thousand acres of land that had been granted to the Seneca Indian Nation by George Washington himself so they could build a dam to protect Pittsburgh from flooding. I couldn't believe Argentina expected the United Nations to support their demand that Israel return Adolf Eichmann. It seemed the country didn't appreciate foreign agents kidnapping one of their citizens—even if he was a monster responsible for the murder of millions.

Jacob turned over in bed. It was the most movement I'd seen from him in hours. His face was still gaunt, his eyes still circled in purple, but his mouth was soft, his forehead smooth. I hoped he was having nice dreams.

I opened a soda I'd been keeping cool in the sink and went back to the paper. The word "Hollandia" in a dateline caught my attention. It turned out to be the capital city of an island near Australia called Dutch New Guinea—another colony of the Netherlands, like Suriname, I hardly knew existed.

"Little Rita." Jacob was watching me through half-open eyelids.

I sat on the edge of the bed, holding his hand between both of my own. "How are you feeling?"

He didn't sob or wail. All he did was look at me as rivulets ran along his cheekbones and pooled in his ears. I started crying, too, water sliding silently down my face. "Jacob, tell me, did you do this because of me?"

"No, please, don't think such a thing." He dragged breath into his lungs. "Sometimes I feel like I am a ghost in this life. I can see it happening all around me, but it's as if it's on the other side of a screen. Nothing touches me. With you, though, I felt myself coming to life. Walking through the park in the moonlight. Being with you on the parapet. Your lips when we kissed. Everything brought me such happiness, Rita. Then I remembered I don't deserve happiness. Why should I have it when there is so much suffering in the world?"

Jacob started crying in earnest then, pain radiating off him like heat above a summer sidewalk. I wasn't supposed to let him become agitated. I would have given him one of those pills, but I didn't want to let go of his hand. All I could do was sit with him until the tears thinned to a trickle.

"You survived something unimaginable, Jacob, but you deserve to be alive." I brushed his dark hair back from his face. Exhausted as he was, his skin still had a healthy tan—from all those hours spent on the observation deck, I supposed. "You shouldn't punish yourself for something you had no control over."

He sighed and shook his head. "This is what the doctors say to me. Rudy says it, too. He has a wife, you know, and a child now."

"I know. I went to see him yesterday, when I couldn't find you. He told me where you were. He gave me your key."

"Is that how you came to rescue me? I thought I summoned you by magic."

I smiled. "Maybe you did."

He closed his eyes and rested his head on the pillow. "Rudy likes you. He says you're good for me. He thinks it would make me happy to become a husband and a father."

He wasn't proposing, but the idea of marriage floated above our heads like an escaped balloon. It's supposed to cure me, too, I wanted to say. Miss Murphy taught us that becoming a wife and a mother would be our reward for surrendering the children we didn't deserve to keep.

"I can't imagine it, Rita. When I think of the millions who perished, happiness feels like betrayal. I'm sorry, that sounds crazy, I know."

"No, it doesn't, but that's all in the past. It's a beautiful summer day and we are both alive and that's all we have to think about right now."

"Yes, yes, happy thoughts." His voice got edgy, impatient. "I try, really I do, but even in my better moods, I can never forgive myself for deserting my mother."

I knew Jacob felt guilty about saying he was an orphan, but

how could he believe he deserted his mother? "I don't understand. Weren't you in the camp together?"

"Yes, we were in Westerbork together, my mother and father and me. We were exempt from the transport list while my father appealed our status. We weren't members of any synagogue, and we had no birth certificates on file in the Netherlands to document that we were Jews. My father held out hope while Calmeyer's office considered our case."

I stopped myself from asking who Calmeyer was. Jacob squeezed my hand, his words coming in a whispered rush as he ventured deeper into the past. "It didn't save my father from being sent away. He was only saying goodbye to a friend, but Schlesinger saw him on the Boulevard des Misères. It was forbidden to be on the Boulevard once the train cut the camp in two. For that offense, Schlesinger added my father's name to the list. The Green Police pushed him into one of the freight cars. The train was gone before a member of the Flying Column told my mother what happened. We didn't know where he was going or if we would ever see him again. After the war, the Red Cross told me there were over three thousand people on that train to Sobibor. One survived. It wasn't my father."

I had no idea who Schlesinger was, or what he meant by Green Police or the Flying Column, but the death camp at Sobibor evoked a nightmare of gas chambers and crematoria.

"I'm so sorry, Jacob. I can't imagine carrying such a weight on my heart." But I could, I thought. I did. Jacob's father had been murdered by Nazis. My son had been adopted by loving parents. The situations were worlds apart. I knew this with utter clarity in my mind, but my heart was a muscle incapable of reason. All it knew was what it felt, and what it felt was loss.

"I'm glad you can't imagine it, Rita. I would never wish it on anyone. But it isn't my father's fate that haunts me. I know he is dead. I know how he died. I know who to blame for his murder. I grieve, but I don't drive myself insane wondering what happened. But my mother—" A lump rose in his throat that he struggled to swallow. I watched, helpless, as his pain dragged him to an even deeper place.

"I'm sure it was a comfort to your mother to have you with her after your father went away." Went away. I was angry at myself for couching it in such euphemistic terms, but I couldn't speak the words for what had really happened.

"I was all she had left. I was young enough, at Westerbork, to stay in the barrack with her. She was in the bunk above me. Every night for months, she'd reach down to hold my hand while I slept. And then—"

I wrung out a washcloth in the sink and wiped his cheeks. The nurse would have told him to hush, to go back to sleep, to stop thinking about it. "Tell me, if you want to," I whispered. "I'm listening."

With his voice as flat as someone reading the phone book, he told me what had happened. It was the fifth of April 1944. The train that day included a combination of destinations, he said, with third-class passenger cars bound for Theresienstadt coupled to freight cars carrying people to Bergen-Belsen and Auschwitz. There were about a hundred Romanians, too, the women and children going to Ravensbrück and the men to Buchenwald. The scene along the tracks was chaos. Romanian families wailed as husbands and fathers were separated from wives and children. Green Police swung their batons, threatening anyone who stepped out of line. The Flying Column pushed wheelbarrows full of luggage and invalids. Schlesinger bicycled up and down the Boulevard like a madman, checking names and approving last-minute changes to the lists. Gemmeker strolled along, observing, hands behind his back and his hound at his heels.

Jacob and his mother were on the list for Bergen-Belsen. A member of the Order Police was counting people off as they clambered up a stepstool into a freight car. Jacob was right behind his mother when the count for their car reached fifty.

"The Order Policeman said that was enough, that I would go to the next one." Jacob looked at me, his eyes wet and red. "She was up in the car already. I was still down on the tracks. I stood on my tiptoes and stretched as high as I could. We touched fingertips. Then he pulled me away. She started screaming and wailing. I was afraid she'd be punished. 'I'll meet you there, Mama,' I said. 'Don't worry, I'll meet you there.' The policeman slid the door to her car shut. He wrote the number fifty in chalk on the outside of it. The next car was already quite full, but he hoisted me into it. Then an argument broke out between him and another Order Policeman, the two of them shouting and pointing and waving their lists. Schlesinger came to settle it. I remember him crossing out a name on one list and writing it on the other. Then they shut the door to my car, too."

They traveled for three days and three nights, he said. Twice, the train stopped along the way. They felt the bump of cars being uncoupled for other destinations. Each time, they expected to be released. Each time, the train continued its journey. When the doors finally opened, they were not in Bergen-Belsen. They were in Auschwitz.

Jacob spoke as if hypnotized as he described the blinding lights, the barking dogs, the ramp, the selection. Children went with women to the left, but the men he'd traveled with brought him with them to the right. The people who'd gone to the left were murdered in the gas chambers that night. The people who'd gone to the right were stripped, shaved, registered, tattooed. His new friends showed off their bloody numbers as if they'd won a prize. We have been chosen for labor, they said. We have a chance to survive.

It was getting dark in that dingy room with its view of a brick wall. Jacob stopped talking for a while. I switched on the lamp, heated up some soup, brought the bowl to him in bed, made him eat. I'd heard survivor testimony like this before, at fundraising events at our synagogue, but those people had been grown men and women. Jacob was only thirteen at the time. I thought of my brother, Charlie, at his bar mitzvah. He'd never looked like more of a boy than when his voice cracked as he declared himself a man.

"I've asked every agency I can think of, from the Red Cross to the Jewish Aid Committee, but there is no record of what happened to Rebekah Nassy after arriving at Bergen-Belsen." Jacob's voice was hoarse. He'd come to the end of an exhausting story.

"You need to rest, Jacob. Go to sleep now."

He clutched my arm, suddenly wide awake. "Where are you going, Rita?"

"Nowhere, darling." I loosened his fingers. "I'm staying right here, all night. See?" I pointed to my pink suitcase, the only pop of color in that dismal room. "I even brought my pajamas."

I changed while he went down the hall to the toilet, then I did the same. When I came back, he was on the armchair wrapped in a blanket. "No, Jacob, don't be silly. I want you to lie down."

He got up reluctantly. "But you can't sleep in the chair."

"Well, neither can you."

"Little Rita." He looked at me like a lost puppy. "Will you sleep beside me tonight?"

I knew he was too exhausted to mean anything other than sleep. "Yes, Jacob, I will."

His bed was narrow, but he was skinny and I was small. We fitted ourselves together, his arm under my head, my cheek on his shoulder. His body gave off a particular scent, like rusted metal mixed with autumn leaves. I wrinkled my nose at first, but soon I found his smell a comfort. As he relaxed into sleep, I crossed my leg over his thigh and matched my breath to his.

Chapter Eighteen
Cornelia Vogel

Camp Westerbork, Netherlands
February 1943

Thanks, Leah." Greta pops a licorice into her mouth. "At least I can say I got something for my birthday."

"Today's your birthday?"

"As of six o'clock this morning, I'm seventeen years old." Her cheerful face falls a little. "My mother forgot, but I can't blame her. One day's like the next here, isn't it?"

Cornelia holds out the roll of licorice. "It's not much of a present, but here, please, have them all."

"Me too!" A child has appeared beside Greta's bunk, hand outstretched and grasping.

"Just one." Greta places a licorice in the child's palm, then grabs Cornelia's elbow. "Come on, Leah, let's get out of here before we're swarmed with little beggars." Potato diggers aren't required to work on Sunday afternoons, and Greta has offered to play tour guide. It's cold out but not raining, the clear sky a wash of watercolor blue. Cornelia is bundled up in both of Leah's sweaters under her coat, the yellow stars on her chest layered three deep. Her shoes are finally dry after she learned how to ask, in Turkish, for permission to tuck them under the stove while the women fried their potatoes. During the hour she stood in their circle, she picked up enough vocabulary to understand that these

Ottoman women were in a Dutch prison because they'd been traveling abroad when Turkey stripped all Jews of citizenship. With no country to return to, they ended up in Hitler's clutches.

Except for two trips to the central kitchen, where Cornelia lined up yesterday and today for her share of chopped kale and cold potatoes, she hasn't ventured beyond the spinsters' hut. Despite listing her occupation as file clerk, she's been assigned to the barrack's cleaning crew, an impossible job given that the toilets are always occupied, the sinks are all clogged, and the floors become filthy within minutes of being swept. "It's worse in the summer," the matron warned. "The wind blows so hard it's like a sandstorm. Dirt gets everywhere. If you're smart, you'll ask your friends to send you a pair of goggles."

"How do people get packages here?" Cornelia and Greta are trudging along the Boulevard des Misères. Pairs of Green Police patrol the empty stretch of track. An Order Policeman rides by on a bicycle, blue cape fluttering. Members of the Flying Column—prisoners assigned to haul luggage, Cornelia has learned—sit in their empty wheelbarrows, faces turned toward the weak winter sun. Some children run past, jostling an old man on crutches, who yells at them to get back to the orphanage. "Are we allowed to write letters requesting things?"

"Sure, but they all get read by the censors before they're sent. If you write anything about the camp, anything at all, you might as well put your own name on the next transport list. Just keep it short. Say you're feeling well and everything's fine, then ask for what you need."

They stop at the boiler house so Cornelia can fill her thermos from one of the taps. She was surprised, at first, at the leniency of letting prisoners help themselves, but Cornelia is beginning to understand the way Westerbork works. By providing hot water, by encouraging Jewish prisoners to get packages from their

Christian friends, by letting everyone wear their own clothes instead of requiring uniforms, Commandant Gemmeker can placate thousands of otherwise miserable people while saving a fortune on uniforms, food, and tea.

After showing Cornelia where to find the post office, Greta takes her around to the Welfare Department, where the Jewish Council distributes donated items. Greta's in need of new socks, and today she's in luck. She leaves with a hand-knitted pair that come up to her knees. Next, she shows Cornelia the laundry where prisoners can leave their clothes to be cleaned. "They give you an itemized receipt, but don't be surprised if some things go missing. Same goes for the tailor shop. I hear the cobbler's trustworthy, though, in case you need your shoes repaired. And if you've got any money, you can go to the store." Greta gives her a sidelong glance. "Have you got money, Leah?"

"I don't have any with me, but I think my parents have an account with Lippmann Rosenthal."

"That's perfect then! Their representatives manage the bank here." Greta leads Cornelia past the bathhouse toward a large field. A dozen boys are chasing a soccer ball across the muddy pitch, while groups of girls engage in calisthenics. Cornelia hears shouts, snippets of song, even peals of laughter. The scene reminds her of a schoolyard until she looks up and sees the barbed wire fence and the looming watchtower.

What is the purpose of this surreal place? she wonders. Westerbork is obviously not a concentration camp, designed to abuse and degrade. It's not even a prison camp meant to punish the incarcerated. It's a warehouse, she realizes, like those canal houses in Amsterdam where the riches of the world were once hoarded. Except this warehouse is stocked with human beings who have been numbered and shelved like goods ready for export. What does it matter to Commandant Gemmeker if the items in his stockpile play soccer or drink tea or send letters while they are here, as long as there is enough inventory available to meet the weekly transport quota?

"Come on, I want you to see something." Greta grabs Cornelia's hand. Together, they run across the field toward the edge of the camp. The cold air stings their cheeks, but the movement warms their muscles. "There, take a look at that. Beautiful, isn't it?"

Beyond the barbed wire, soft flanks of heath and dune undulate westward. Fuchsia clouds burn against the amethyst sky. Tree limbs darken into abstract shapes as the sun plummets toward the horizon. The last streaks of sunlight burnish the gold in Greta's hair. "You see, Leah? For all of Hitler's power, he can't stop the earth from showing us God's glorious creation."

Cornelia is humbled at the exultation in Greta's expression. Then the sun is swallowed by the heath, and the amethyst sky hardens to purple. The joy leaves her face as Greta shivers in the cold. "We better get back to our barracks before dark."

That night, Cornelia is settled in her bunk, clad in every warm piece of clothing she possesses. She is determined to write a letter before lights-out, but it's difficult to focus. Tensions are running high in the spinsters' hut. Arguments break out, visitors come and go, secrets are traded, warnings are given, hands are wrung, tears are shed.

"What's happening?" Cornelia asks.

The woman in the next bunk rolls toward her with a sigh. "It's Sunday night."

Cornelia shrugs. "So?"

"The train comes tomorrow. The transport list is being made up. Everyone is worried about being selected."

"Are you?"

The woman shakes her head. "I'm a teacher at the orphanage

the Jewish Council set up here, so I have an exemption—for now, at least. I figure I'll be safe until they start sending children to do labor service." She leans across the space between their bunks, warming now to the topic. "Some of these women would do anything to avoid the train, if you know what I mean, but the only man in the Registration Department with the power to keep you off the list is Schlesinger, and he's already got a wife *and* a girlfriend." She snorts. "He thinks he runs this place, but even he can be overruled by Fräulein Slottke, and of course Commandant Gemmeker has the last word, doesn't he? A month ago, a boy ran off and hid when his name was called for the transport. The Order Police found him soon enough, but Gemmeker was so angry, he had fifty people grabbed up at random and thrown on the train to teach us all a lesson."

No wonder everyone here is so cooperative, Cornelia thinks. Despite the seeming liberality of their prison, beneath the surface runs the same current of arbitrary violence that reduced Rotterdam to rubble. Cornelia shares a *speculaas* with the woman, who grabs the cookie and rolls back over.

Cornelia covers her ears with the knit hat she found in the pocket of Leah's coat. She has the sketchbook open on her lap and a piece of charcoal in her gloved hand. In exchange for a promised share in her first package, the matron has excused Cornelia from her cleaning duties tomorrow so she can go to the Registration Hall to ask the bankers of Lippmann Rosenthal if it's possible to withdraw any money from the Bloms' account. She's hoping they'll give her a bit of Westerbork currency—colorful pieces of paper that are worthless anywhere else but that she can use to buy postage for the letter she's trying to write.

She resists the urge to scrawl a desperate note to her father begging him to rescue her. No matter how valuable his work is to the Germans, she knows there's nothing he can do for a daughter who has helped a Jew evade arrest. Cornelia has already heard the story of the NSBer who came to Westerbork determined to liberate his Jewish wife. He assumed being a Dutch Nazi would give him clout. Instead, he was arrested himself. A week later, he and his wife did leave Westerbork together—on the next transport to Auschwitz.

Besides, the authorities think they've arrested Leah Blom. As long as they believe that's true, no one will go looking for a girl with a boyish face traveling under Cornelia's name. But she needs to know what her parents think has happened to her—and she'll need their help, too, if she is to survive this place. Certain her mother will tear open any envelope addressed to her missing daughter, Cornelia decides the best approach is to write a letter as if from Leah to herself. She sets pencil to paper, printing each letter to camouflage her handwriting.

Dear Nellie,

I write to inform you that I am now a resident of Camp Westerbork in Drenthe. My address is Barrack 65. Please don't worry about me. It isn't so bad here. I have a shelf above my bunk where I keep my books, and I've made a friend who's showing me the ropes. The food is very plain, though, and everyone appreciates whatever help they can get from their friends. We are allowed packages, and I'm hoping you might send me some things? I would really appreciate tea and biscuits and a pot of butter. Oh, and I've been told that goggles are necessary for the summer sandstorms. I also wish I had a proper notebook to write in, and some lead pencils, too. As you can see, a piece of charcoal is better for drawing than writing.

Cornelia's head is aching from the psychic dissonance of pretending to be Leah writing to herself for the purpose of getting her own mother's help. She decides to keep it short.

> I'm sorry our English lessons were cut short. I miss you terribly, but it comforts me to picture you in the house we shared for all these years. My best to your parents and to Dirk, also.
>
> **Your friend, Leah Blom**

The next morning, a representative of Lippmann Rosenthal is pleased to inform Leah Blom that her family does, indeed, have enough on deposit for her to make a withdrawal. Cornelia leaves their office with enough Westerbork money to post her letter. On her way out of the Registration Hall, she passes Fräulein Slottke's counter. The window is open. Not knowing when she might be excused from her cleaning duties again, Cornelia decides to join the line of supplicants in the hallway.

While they wait, she's startled to hear sirens wail. Cornelia asks what's happening. The man ahead of her mutters, "The siren means the gate is opening to let the transport in."

Sure enough, a train's steam whistle is soon accompanied by the cha-chunk cha-chunk cha-chunk of carriages rolling along tracks. When the locomotive belches to a stop with a squeal of brakes, everyone in the hallway flinches. A sense of dread envelops Cornelia like a foul odor.

"But please, *Fräulein,* you see right here I have an exemption stamp." The man in front of Cornelia has finally made it to the counter. "I am working in the hospital for Dr. Spanier. He assures me my job is indispensable, and yet I hear from a friend that my name is on the list for tomorrow. I'm here to ask—"

Fräulein Slottke's placid expression never changes. When she's heard enough, she simply raises her hand. The man's words evaporate in his mouth as if she's cast a magic spell. "You do have an exemption, but your wife does not. Your friend's information is incorrect. It's your wife's name that is on the list for tomorrow." She waits a moment while her words sink in. "Now, you may choose to let her go on her own while you stay here, but I wonder if you wouldn't prefer to voluntarily accompany her?"

The man's knees sag; only his elbows on the counter keep him from dropping to the floor. "My wife? She's on the list?"

"For tomorrow, yes." Fräulein Slottke pushes a piece of paper and a pen across the counter. "If you volunteer, I will instruct Schlesinger that you and your wife are to travel together in the same train car."

The man doesn't seem to understand, but Cornelia can't tell if that's because his German isn't very good or because the information is too horrible to comprehend. "You put my wife on the list?"

Fräulein Slottke clucks her tongue impatiently. "I had nothing to do with it. The Registration Department handles the lists. Commandant Gemmeker has ordered them to fill a quota of one thousand, but I believe there is room on tomorrow's train for about a hundred more. Now, will you allow your wife to commence her labor service in Poland all alone, or will you accompany her to Auschwitz?"

The man's shoulders slump. "Is there nothing I can do to remove her from the list?"

Fräulein Slottke's small eyes meet his. "*Nichts.*"

His face is blank as he takes up the pen, signs his name, and walks away. Fräulein Slottke carries the piece of paper to her desk, where she adds it to a small pile. Though Cornelia is frightened by what she has witnessed, she forces herself to step up and take the man's place. Leaning over the counter, she sees the punch machine is exactly as it was on Friday, the bit bin beneath it still empty. No one here has used it.

"And what do you want?" Fräulein Slottke's red braid twists around her head like a flame—appropriate, Cornelia thinks, since her face seems carved from wax.

"I'm Leah Blom. You were reviewing my case. My parents are at Barneveld?"

"Let me see your identification."

"You took it, *Fräulein.*" Cornelia produces the receipt.

The smooth forehead crinkles ever so slightly. "This is dated three days ago. I don't have any information for you yet. You'll please wait until you are summoned before coming here again." Since the line ends with Cornelia, she reaches for the shutters to close her window.

"I see you have a punch machine for Hollerith cards." The words leap from Cornelia's mouth.

Fräulein Slottke's arm ceases its motion. Cornelia detects a twitch at the corner of one eye. "What would you know about that?"

Cornelia has been turning this over in her mind since she first learned Gertrud Slottke was here at Westerbork. The long-term residents survive by making themselves indispensable to the commandant in the management of the camp. If she is to survive, Cornelia must also find a way to make herself indispensable. Asking Fräulein Slottke for any favor is a risk, but it's a risk she needs to take now, today. A hungry train is on the Boulevard des Misères waiting to be fed. How long before Cornelia finds herself on its menu?

"My neighbor in The Hague was trained as a punch-card operator." Cornelia's mouth has gone dry. She coughs and continues. "She brought one of those machines home once, so she could practice. I myself became quite good at using it."

"Your neighbor is a punch-card operator?"

"Yes. She works at some government ministry. We used to study together sometimes. Anyway, thank you for your consideration, Fräulein. I'll wait until you summon me before I return." Cornelia takes a step back from the counter.

"You know how to use that thing?" Gertrud Slottke's voice pins her in place.

Cornelia blinks away the memory of Mevrouw Plank criticizing her incompetence. "Yes, I do."

Fräulein Slottke's small eyes narrow farther. "Come back here tomorrow, after the train has departed." She scrawls some words on a piece of paper. "Give this to your barrack matron. As soon as the train departs, you understand?"

"Yes, Fräulein Slottke."

Cornelia's heart is beating so fast she practically runs out of the Registration Hall. On the Boulevard, she stops short at the sight of the train. It stretches from the front gate nearly to the rear fence. The barracks on the other side are blotted out by the line of cars, one linked to the next like the sections of a centipede. Cornelia counts twenty-six cars all together: a second-class compartment up front, a few third-class carriages, then a series of freight cars. For a moment, Cornelia assumes the freight cars are intended for luggage—after all, the Germans have plundered every Jewish household in Holland. Then she realizes that, to meet a quota of one thousand, every car on this train will need to be filled with people.

An Order Policeman rides along the length of the train, ringing his bicycle's bell to warn people back from the tracks. Remembering what Greta said about being stuck in her barrack all day, Cornelia posts her letter, fills her thermos, and lines up at the kitchen for her portion of food. Avoiding the train as much as possible, she carries her mess kit along the Boulevard to the far fence, where people are darting in front of the engine to get to the other side. Waiting until there are no Order Police or Green Police in sight, she makes a dash for it.

The winter night comes early. Cornelia tries to pass the time reading, but the woman on the first tier has come down with bronchitis. Every time she coughs, the bunk sways like a ship at sea, causing Cornelia to lose her place on the page. Giving up on *Jane Eyre,* she decides to make a list of the Turkish vocabulary she's learned so far. She focuses her mind by defining each word in every language she knows, but just as the tumult of the barrack begins to recede from her consciousness, she's stabbed by a cramp. She digs through Leah's rucksack for the menstrual belt and a pad, then clambers down to line up first for the toilet, then to wash out her underwear. No wonder the sinks are clogged and disgusting, she thinks, adding her blood to a basin. Lights-out comes as she's returning to her bunk, making the difficult climb perilous.

Alone in the dark, miserable and aching, Cornelia curls up on the narrow bunk. Exhausted as she is, sleep proves impossible as worries ricochet across her brain. What if Fräulein Slottke investigates her identity and discovers it's Gerard Vogel's daughter, not his neighbor, who is incarcerated at Westerbork? If his position at the Ministry of Information is compromised, who will protect her family?

Cornelia must have fallen asleep eventually, because she's roused from a dream before dawn by someone shouting. A member of the Order Police, his face illuminated by a flashlight, is reading from a list, pronouncing names loudly and clearly. After each name, there is a gasp and a cry from somewhere in the barrack. Bunks creak as people rise in the dark like ghouls from the grave. Cornelia has counted a dozen names when her bunk shakes and sways. The woman on the first tier, the one with bronchitis, has been called. It doesn't make sense. How can a sick woman perform hard labor in Poland?

"Pack up your possessions, ladies." The Order Policeman speaks in German, not Dutch. Cornelia wonders if the Turkish women understand him; she's certain the old Greek lady doesn't. "All work details are delayed except for kitchen helpers and the Flying Column. Everyone else, you are to stay in the barrack until the train has departed. No one is to step outside until you hear the siren."

The summoned women shuffle in the darkness, gathering their things. They're allowed to bring one sack, one rolled blanket, and whatever clothes they can wear. Bunkmates blindly offer scarves and mittens and hoarded food for the journey, while neighbors stealthily claim every abandoned pair of shoes or bar of soap. Cornelia grabs a tin of sardines and scrambles down to give it to the sick woman. In return, the woman's fingers grope in the darkness as she fastens a thin chain around Cornelia's neck. "I'm afraid they'll take it from me," the woman croaks. "It was my mother's. Please keep it safe."

When everyone is assembled, the Order Policeman marches them outside. Cornelia climbs up to her bunk, heartsick. She touches the necklace. There's a charm dangling from the chain. Cornelia traces its shape with her fingertip, counting six sharp points. Feeling the ridges of an inscription on the back, she realizes she never learned the name of its owner.

The woman in the next bunk reaches over to tug her sleeve. "What do you know about the labor camps in Poland?" Cornelia knows nothing for sure, though she's certain they're terrible and wretched places. "I heard a rumor that the Germans use some kind of gas to kill anyone who can't work," the woman whispers. Cornelia tells her not to be ridiculous. "Well, unless they're taking your bunkmate to a convalescent spa, she's as good as dead."

The matron switches on the lights an hour later. The women avoid one another's eyes as they collect their morning ration of watery coffee, bread smeared with margarine, and a vitamin C tablet. The bottom bunk is quickly claimed by the woman on the second tier as a place to store her luggage. "You can put your rucksack down here, too," she tells Cornelia. The offer strikes her as callous, but Cornelia takes her up on it nevertheless, anticipating the meager comfort of straightening her legs while she sleeps. She takes off the necklace to examine the inscription on the back of the Star of David. It is lettered in Hebrew. Whether it spells the woman's name or some verse, Cornelia can't tell. The thought crosses her mind that Hebrew is yet another language she could learn here.

Those who don't work in the kitchen or for the Flying Column spend the next few hours in agitated boredom, relieved not to have been called for transport and guilty for being relieved. It's one o'clock in the afternoon before they hear the camp siren wail its farewell to the train. A strange elation animates them at the certainty they've avoided the belly of the serpent for another week. Bursting forth from their barrack, most rush across the tracks to line up at the kitchen. Following along, Cornelia sees items scattered up and down the Boulevard: a single glove, a child's doll, a woman's shoe, a crutch, an overturned baby carriage. There are letters, too, folded pieces of paper being trodden into the mud. Cornelia picks one up, dries it off, and tucks it into her pocket. She'll buy a stamp for it, she decides, the next time she goes to the post office.

Cornelia is hungry, but Fräulein Slottke insisted she come as soon as the train has departed. Having fortified herself with the last of her cookies and stopping only to fill her thermos, she forgoes the kitchen and heads to the Registration Hall. There are no scattered desks or typewriters today, no clerks like Etty interviewing arriving prisoners. Instead, chairs have been arranged in rows. The Registration Department has cleared their file boxes from the stage to make room for an array of music stands. Apparently, there will be some kind of performance tonight. A concert, she discovers, picking up a printed flyer and recognizing the name of a renowned violinist whom Cornelia never knew was Jewish. Prisoners are even invited to purchase tickets for ten Westerbork cents apiece. Such entertainment can only be authorized by one person. Cornelia is incredulous. More than a thousand people have just been transported to a dreadful fate in a far-off land, yet tonight Commandant Gemmeker insists on music?

Fräulein Slottke's window is closed, so Cornelia knocks on the nearest door. It's opened by an ugly man whose blond hair juts out from under a flat cap. His riding breeches and tall boots imitate the silhouette of a German soldier, which is what Cornelia takes him for until she sees the shriveled bit of yellow fabric pinned to his lapel. He looks her up and down as if deciding whether or not she's pretty enough to flirt with. Concluding in the negative, he pushes past her with a scowl. That must be the famous Schlesinger, she thinks. As much of a bully as he's known to be, Cornelia has the feeling Gertrud Slottke is not intimidated by him in the slightest.

"There you are, Leah Blom. Sit here." Fräulein Slottke indicates the chair in front of the typing table. The punch machine is exactly where it's been since Cornelia first saw it. The stack of Hollerith cards is still beside it, but the table is now crowded with a stuffed file box and a thick sheaf of papers. "These are the Jewish Council's index cards for everyone Schlesinger's department selected for today's transport, and this is the list they used to confirm who got on the train. Both are organized alphabetically, but you may find additional names on the list for which there are no cards, or maybe a card for someone who was taken off the list at the last minute, so you

have to cross-check every one. According to these instructions . . ."
An uncharacteristic frown knits her eyebrows as she stares at what
Cornelia recognizes as a processing order. With an impatient flick
of her wrist, she tosses it on the typing table. "But I shouldn't be
explaining anything to you. You've told me you know how to operate
this machine. Let's see if you were telling the truth."

Fräulein Slottke turns her back and goes to her desk. The only
sounds in the office are the scratching of her pen and the occasional
thwack of a stamp. Cornelia takes a breath and examines the processing order. The cards are to be double-punched alphabetically
for last name and first name, then coded numerically for birth date
and departure date. In addition, every card in the entire batch is
to be punched at digit 1 in column forty-five. There is no code to
explain its meaning, but Cornelia understands this last hole-punch
must signify "emigrated from the Netherlands." Once these cards
have been sorted, collated, and processed by the Hollerith, every
person in this batch will be culled from the Jewish population lists.
Cornelia touches the Star of David dangling from her neck. Whatever awaits the Jews of Holland at the place called Auschwitz, the
woman who gave her this necklace cannot possibly survive it. She
already knows the code for "emigration" really means "deportation."
Could it be that "deportation" is simply a euphemism for "death"?

"So, Leah Blom, do you understand what to do or not?" Fräulein
Slottke doesn't turn her head, so she doesn't see Cornelia wiping
tears from her eyes.

"I understand, yes."

"You'd better get on with it, then."

"Yes, *Fräulein*." Cornelia checks the first name on the transport list, then pulls the corresponding index card from the box
to confirm spelling and birth date. She sets a punch card on the
plate of the machine, checks the processing order once again, and
begins. It takes her a few moments to remember the twenty-six

codes for alphabetical double-punching. When she completes the punch card, she sets it aside, puts the Jewish Council's index card at the back of the box, and checks the name off the transport list.

Nearly three minutes have elapsed. There are over a thousand more cards to punch. Even if she picks up her pace, she estimates it will take her over forty hours—not counting breaks—to accomplish this on her own. It's already two o'clock in the afternoon on Tuesday. Not wanting Fräulein Slottke to have unrealistic expectations, Cornelia clears her throat and explains that it will be Saturday before she expects to finish punching all the cards.

Fräulein Slottke looks at Cornelia for a long moment. "I continue to be impressed by your German, Leah Blom. It's a pleasure to hear my mother tongue pronounced so perfectly. You say you can finish by Saturday?"

"If I work on this all day, every day, between now and then."

"In that case, I'll inform your barrack matron that you now work exclusively for me. And let's not waste your time standing on line at the kitchen. I'll order a meal brought to you here. Have you eaten today?"

A growl from Cornelia's stomach answers before she does. "No, Fräulein."

"I'll arrange it before I leave for The Hague. I won't be back until Saturday. I'll tell Schlesinger's secretary to lock up this office at six o'clock. She'll let you back in tomorrow morning at eight."

Fräulein Slottke makes some phone calls to put her promises into action. Cornelia has only punched ten more cards when a kitchen worker appears carrying silver cutlery rolled in a linen napkin and a china plate loaded with a leg of roasted chicken in addition to warm chopped kale, crispy fried potatoes, and a large apple polished to a shine. The worker is surprised when Fräulein Slottke indicates the plate is not for herself, but for the Jewish girl at the typing table.

"I'll be leaving now." Gertrud Slottke makes a show of stashing every piece of paper, pen, and stamp from her desktop in a drawer, which she locks with a key on a chain that's threaded through a buttonhole on her jacket. She ties a scarf around her head and pulls a pair of leather gloves from her coat pocket. "I am entrusting you with an important task, Leah Blom. I hope you won't disappoint me." She slaps the gloves against her palm. "If you do, I'm sure I could find a place for you on the next train to Auschwitz."

Cornelia's appetite is curdled by fear, but her head is getting light. She won't be able to work if she doesn't eat. Alone in the office, she chews each mouthful deliberately until the plate is clean, then washes it down with a cup of tea from her thermos. She uses the toilet down the hall—no lines, and so clean! Refreshed by a splash of cold water on her face, she returns to the office and makes slow but steady progress until Schlesinger's secretary comes to lock up.

In the empty Registration Hall, the violinist is onstage, warming up for tonight's performance. At first, Cornelia thinks he's running scales, but then she recognizes the Sabbath song she heard her first night at Westerbork. She turns to listen. Their eyes meet. His are glassy with tears. Then the front doors swing open. His bow arrests its caress of the strings. A man's voice calls out in German, "Ah, good, you're rehearsing. I have high hopes for the concert tonight. I've invited some dignitaries from Amsterdam to attend." The violinist stretches his face into a false smile and breaks into a jaunty melody that makes Cornelia think of Bavarian beer gardens. Head down, she slinks along the wall, hoping to remain invisible to the cocky Nazi who can only be Commandant Gemmeker.

Outside, a cold rain is spitting from the slate-gray sky. Cornelia refills her thermos at the boiler house before dodging puddles back to the spinsters' hut. It turns out her father was right all

along, she thinks. It is entirely possible to punch cards all day—
especially if one's life depends on it.

Wednesday and Thursday are interminable in their boredom
yet swift in their monotony. Cornelia's fingertips have gone numb
but her pace has picked up considerably. On Friday morning, she
wakes up optimistic that she'll be able to finish by the end of the
day. Because Gertrud Slottke's note excuses her from any other
work assignment, she's looking forward to having tomorrow free
to practice her Turkish. She's hoping, too, that one of the rabbis
will agree to teach her the Hebrew alphabet. She plans to ask
tonight, after she goes to Greta's barrack for a visit.

The Registration Hall this morning has been transformed
from a concert venue back into a chaotic ship's terminal. The
Jewish Council is out in force, registering hundreds of people.
She spies Etty at a desk, furiously typing. The prisoners, dazed
and weeping, don't line up so much as huddle in mounds. Among
those sprawled on the floor, she sees bandaged arms, legs in plas-
ter casts, heads wrapped in gauze. Cornelia stops in front of a
nurse holding an intravenous bottle of fluid above an unconscious
woman on a stretcher. Shocked, she looks back at Etty, who has
just finished registering a boy who slumps in his chair, rocking
and muttering to himself. Etty jerks her head, then gets up and
crosses the Registration Hall. Cornelia follows.

"Horrible, isn't it?" Etty says when they meet up behind the
stage. "They came in last night. The *Judenreferent* has ordered all
Jewish hospitals and asylums to be emptied."

"Is there room here for all of them?" Cornelia has learned by
now that the camp hospital is the most desirable address in all
of Westerbork. Staffed by Jewish doctors and nurses who once
worked at the best medical institutions in the country, its heated
barrack, clean cots, and warm blankets are the stuff of legend.

"Maybe. Maybe not. Either way, they probably won't be here

for long." Etty's pale face gets even whiter. "Last month, the Green Police went along with the Germans to raid the Jewish psychiatric hospital in Apeldoorn. The inmates were loaded into lorries and driven back here to Westerbork. A train was waiting on the Boulevard. They were put directly on the transport before we even had a chance to talk to them. You should have heard the screams." She swallows a sob. "Sometimes I think it would be simpler to put myself on the train than to witness this week after week."

"Don't say that, Etty." Cornelia takes her hands. They're cold and shaking. "You were so kind to me when I arrived. I can't tell you what it meant to me."

Etty blinks the tears from her eyes. "I suppose we do what we can. It won't matter in the end. One day it will be my turn."

"Don't you have an exemption for working for the Jewish Council?"

"For now I do, but how can I be happy to be exempt from what so many others have to suffer?" She squeezes Cornelia's hands. "It does me good to talk to you, Leah."

"Me too, Etty. Listen, maybe we could swap language lessons sometime, my English for your Russian? It would take our minds off things, at least."

"Sure, but aren't you going to Barneveld?"

Cornelia shakes her head. "I don't know about my case yet. Fräulein Slottke assigned me to work in her office. That's where I'm going now."

"You work for her?" Etty looks at her curiously. "Be careful, Leah. Gemmeker and Schlesinger underestimate her, but Gertrud Slottke is the most dangerous person here. Never forget that."

Cornelia eats her lunch quickly that day, eager to complete her work before Schlesinger's secretary locks up the office. She's fallen into a kind of trance, names and numbers morphing into abstract symbols as she goes from one card to the next. She double-punches 0-2, 11-7, 12-5, 12-5, 11-3, 11-4, 12-1, 11-5 without recognizing the last name spelled out by those letters of the alphabet. Then she begins on the first name: 12-7, 11-9, 12-5, 0-3, 12-1. The code for the letters G-R-E-T-A.

Greta Speelman. For a fleeting moment she allows herself to hope there's more than one girl here with that name. She checks the birth date. This Greta Speelman's birthday was last Sunday, the day Cornelia gifted her a roll of licorice. She cross-checks the transport list. The next two entries are also Speelmans. From their birth dates, Cornelia guesses they are Greta's parents.

Cornelia doubles over, gagging on the bile that fills her mouth. The Star of David swings from the chain around her neck. It takes three days for the transport to reach its destination in Poland, she's learned. The woman who gave her the necklace has arrived at Auschwitz by now. Sick as she is, Cornelia's certain there's no labor the woman could survive, but Greta? She's a young, strong girl who can dig potatoes and handle a loaded wheelbarrow. She'll be all right, won't she?

When she can sit up without fainting, Cornelia lifts the punch card from the machine with the reverence of a minister offering the host. Once these cards are processed on the Hollerith at Huize Kleykamp, Greta Speelman's name will disappear from the Jewish population list. Cornelia places Greta's completed punch card on the stack with the others, checks her name off the transport list, and moves her index card to the back of the file box.

Suddenly, nausea overwhelms her. Cornelia runs to the toilet, heaving until her stomach is empty. She finagled a job in Slottke's office for her own survival, but as a result, she's once again become a tiny gear in the Nazis' machinery of persecution. But if she walks out now and never returns, she'll be sacrificing her life without saving anyone else's. Etty said it would be simpler to put herself on the train than to witness its horror week after week, but without a witness, who will be left to remember the names of the departed?

Cornelia rinses her mouth and returns to Slottke's office. There's nothing she could have done to save Greta, but at least she can memorialize her. As if writing an epitaph, Cornelia punches a duplicate card for Greta Speelman. When it's finished, she holds it up to the light to gaze at her friend's constellation. Then she tucks the card into her bra, near her heart, under her blouse, beneath the star.

Chapter Nineteen
Rita Klein

New York City
June 1960

We made love in the morning before I opened my eyes. It started with a quiet exploration, as if our limbs and lips were still dreaming. When Jacob hesitated to go further, I took him in hand, learning his contours and introducing him to mine. With Leonard, sex was something that happened to me. Now it was a power I held, strong enough to bring a man back from the dead. I was sore at first, but Jacob's tenderness was an aphrodisiac that opened me to pleasure. Afterward, I pressed my ear to his chest, listening to his heartbeat settle into the steady rhythm of a muscle doing its work of keeping a body alive.

Jacob fell back to sleep. I stretched my toes and extended my fingers, careful not to disturb him. For the first time in months, my body felt like it really belonged to me. Last August, it had betrayed me by becoming pregnant. Then it turned inward, nurturing the baby, leaving me to deal with the consequences. After giving birth, all it could feel was the part of itself that was missing. But this morning, in this narrow bed, beside this skinny man, my body was mine again.

Jacob snored and shifted. I slipped quietly out of bed, pulled on my panties, and put on his robe. It was only as I padded down the hall to the bathroom that I realized my stupidity in taking such a risk. Just as I started to panic, though, I saw a smear of blood on the toilet paper. I was having my period, my first since David was born. A wave of relief washed over me, followed by a cramp that felt, weirdly, like grief.

Back in his room, Jacob was up and dressed in trousers and an undershirt. I'd pictured us spending the morning in bed, but he'd already stripped it of sheets. "On Sundays we get clean linens," he explained sheepishly. "We have to put our old ones out in the cart before the laundry service comes."

"Okay," I said. We stood stiffly apart for a moment, then he opened his arms and I stepped into them. He hugged me close, kissed my neck, murmured a few words in Dutch that I was sure meant something like "Good morning, my darling." I wondered if he'd seen any blood on the sheets. I wondered if he thought it was my first time. I wondered if it was his first time, though that seemed farfetched. I wondered a lot of things as we stood like dancers after the music has stopped.

He took the sheets with him when he went to the bathroom. While he was gone, I got dressed, put a percolator of coffee on the hot plate, and set out a breakfast of bread and jelly. When he came back and saw the table, he kissed me again. "Thank you, Little Rita."

"How do you say 'You're welcome' in Dutch?"

"*Graag gedaan.*"

The guttural sounds were impossible for me to pronounce. I finally gave up and said "*De rien*" in French. This got us talking about the cultural differences between the polite English "you are welcome," the generous Dutch "gladly done," and the haughty French "of nothing." We didn't talk about the sex or our relationship or what it all meant. It was as if our progression from friends to lovers was as inevitable as an apple falling from a tree: a consequence of gravity that needed no explanation.

I sipped coffee and picked at the crust of my bread, queasy from cramps and uncomfortable sitting on the lump of toilet paper I'd wadded up in my panties. Jacob, however, was ravenous, which I took to be a healthy sign. Maybe those pills he took were an accident, I thought. Maybe he just needs someone to take care of him. Maybe if he had something in the future to look forward to, he'd stop dwelling on the past.

He reached across the table for another slice of bread. For the first time, I saw his tattoo. I'd tried to feel it in the dark last night, but his forearm was smooth to the touch. Now it was washed in morning light from the open window, the numbers stark and purple against his golden skin. How can a person forget the past, I thought, when it's written on them for life?

I glanced up. He was looking right at me. "I'm so sorry, Jacob, I didn't mean to stare."

"Go ahead, Rita, it's nothing for me to feel shame about." He kept his arm extended so I could satisfy my curiosity. I ran the pad of my thumb over the five digits, wondering why the numbers seemed so oddly familiar. Then it hit me.

"Serving-ladle blanks," I murmured, "marine-grade stainless."

"What are you talking about?"

I'd been embarrassed before; now I was mortified. "Oh God, Jacob, please forgive me."

"Forgive you for what?" he asked, pulling back his arm.

"It's just—" I hesitated, but what harm could there be in explaining? "Your number is the exact same as the inventory code at Olympia Metal for serving-ladle blanks in marine-grade stainless steel. I actually saw the item in my mind's eye when I looked at your tattoo."

He shrugged, unperturbed. "I suppose there are only so many numbers in the world. Eventually they repeat themselves."

"I guess so." It sent a shiver down my spine to see human flesh stamped with what looked to me like a computer code. "It's just so uncanny."

"In Auschwitz, they treated us like things, not people." Jacob put down his slice of rye. "Once we were registered and given a number, our names vanished. Every morning at roll call, the guards had a list, and every number on that list had to be accounted for. If one person was missing, he had to be found, and then the count started all over again. If a person died, his body had to be presented to the guards so they could strike off his number. It was torture, standing outside in every kind of weather for hours like that."

"I'm sorry I brought it up, Jacob." Happy thoughts, I reminded myself. He should be thinking happy thoughts. "Rudy said he'd stop by today, won't that be nice? I thought we could go for a walk in that park on Chrystie Street."

But Jacob was lost in his memories now. "When we were assigned to work details, it was never by name, only by number. They sent us as slaves to the factories that were built inside the camp. We had to earn our keep, they used to say, but they spent less on our keep than a farmer does on slop for pigs. I didn't know it at the time, but the businesses were invoiced for our labor. It wasn't enough to work us to death. The Nazis had to profit from us, too."

I tried to think of something happy to say, but my analytical mind involuntarily turned to the immense challenge of managing the labor of thousands of prisoners. Jacob's talk of invoices and profits suggested a system like the one at Olympia. "Tell me, Jacob, did they have computers at Auschwitz?"

"Computers?" He shrugged. "I have no idea. They did have a power plant and electric fences and a railroad spur and five crematoria. It really was the most modernized hell you can imagine."

I took his hand and brought it to my lips for a kiss. "No talk about the end of the world, remember? Listen, we don't have to wait for Rudy to go out. We could take a walk in the park now, together, before it gets too hot."

"What would a computer do in such a system?"

"Please, I don't want you thinking about all that, Jacob."

"No, I ask because I want to understand your work, Rita."

He was obviously still thinking about Auschwitz, but I figured telling him about it was the easiest way to get us out of his stuffy shoebox of a room and into the fresh air. Anyone who didn't understand computing machines typically got bored within the first five minutes of my explanation.

"Okay, well, at Antiquated I program control panels that direct the computer how to process various kinds of business reports. Depending on how the panels are wired, the machine sorts and collates and tabulates and calculates whatever information you put into it, then prints a list of results. The lists can be about anything—how many items are left in inventory, or comparing this year's output to last year's, or totaling up commissions, or generating invoices—whatever you ask it to report on."

"How do you ask a machine to do something?"

Maybe this topic wasn't so bad after all, I thought. At least his focus wasn't on his tragic past. "Well, everything has a code. The codes are punched through cards where every hole represents a digit. Inventory codes are almost always five digits, like your tattoo. Anyway, when those cards go through the computer, wherever there's a hole, the machine makes an electrical connection that sparks a wire on the control panel—"

He sat up straight, suddenly animated. "So what you are telling me is that my number from Auschwitz is like a code for a punch card?"

"Yes, that's how the computer processes information, from the punch cards." I pictured again that stainless-steel ladle. It really was uncanny.

"Rita, listen." He got up and began pacing the room. Tall as he was, he could only take four strides before turning around. I got a little seasick watching him go back and forth, back and forth. "Over the years, I've tried everything to find out what happened to my mother." He covered his heart with both hands. "Of course, it is most likely that she died in Bergen-Belsen, I know that, but I can't accept it completely as long as there is any doubt. The Nazis deported over a hundred thousand Jews from Holland. Only a few thousand survived, but there were survivors. What if my mother managed to survive, too? If she is alive somewhere, she must think I'm dead, otherwise she would have looked for me."

"But wouldn't the Red Cross have told her about you?"

"Maybe she asked before they knew where I was, or after I left, or maybe she was too afraid of the answer to ask at all. Maybe she's waiting somewhere for me to find her." He grabbed two fistfuls of hair and pulled them away from his skull. "I can't stand it, not knowing for sure."

I got up and wrapped my arms around him. Stupid, stupid girl, I said to myself. Look what you've done, getting him all worked up when he should be resting and calm. "I'm so sorry, Jacob, I've upset you."

"No, Rita, you don't understand." He stepped back and held me at arm's length. "The organization that sponsored me and Rudy, the Jewish Aid Committee, they have their archives here, in New York, on Forty-Second Street. I've spent countless hours there, searching for some clue about my mother, but there was nothing. Now you tell me about computer cards and prisoner numbers and it reminds me of a report about a woman at Bergen-Belsen who saved punch cards. They weren't for a computer, though. It had a different name."

"Was it Hollerith?"

Jacob's eyes opened wide. "Hollerith, yes, that's it! This woman saved Hollerith punch cards with prisoner information, but I don't remember anything else. I didn't understand it. But you, Rita— you would understand it."

"Do you want me to go look at this report?"

"Yes, yes, that's what I want." He was making me nervous now, pacing and gesticulating, his voice rising in pitch and volume. "Don't you see? This is why we met."

"I don't know about that, Jacob."

"Believe me, it was *beshert*. When I saw you on the observation deck, I told myself to leave that poor, sad girl alone. But I didn't. I couldn't. Now I know why."

"Please, sit down. Let's talk about this calmly." I practically forced him into a chair, but he popped back up and started pacing again. I don't know what I would have done if Rudy hadn't shown up. We managed to lure Jacob outside, but his agitation only grew once he was beyond the confines of his room. While Jacob walked ahead of us at the park, Rudy asked when he'd last had his medication.

"He hasn't taken a pill since Bellevue. He said he hated the medicine, that it made him see things."

"Well, he has to relax. Go up to his room and crush a pill in a bottle of soda or something, okay? I'll bring him back after he's worn himself out."

Rudy caught up with Jacob and linked arms with him, leading him around the park. I stopped by a drugstore first to get myself a box of Tampax, then at Katz's for a few bottles of Coke and some knishes. Up in Jacob's room, I opened one of the Coke bottles and dissolved a pill in it. I felt terrible betraying him like that, but I figured the doctors knew best. When he and Rudy came in, we all had a cold drink and a warm knish. Over the next half hour, Jacob went from wild to mild to dopey. After a wobbly visit to the bathroom, he dropped into bed. The pill had done its work.

Rudy offered to stay, but I told him I'd be happy to spend

another night. Since he didn't start until the dinner service on Mondays, he promised to come back first thing in the morning so I could go to work. He put a hand on Jacob's shoulder. "Goodbye, my brother, I will see you tomorrow."

"*Tot morgen, jongen,*" Jacob muttered.

When we were alone again, I sat on the bed and unbuttoned Jacob's shirt, wiping the sweat from his chest and neck with a cool cloth. A strange image superimposed itself over the sight of my hand holding the washcloth. I saw my baby's new mother bathing his tiny body, her hand sponging his chubby legs and round tummy. Then my vision shifted and I saw not a helpless newborn but a haunted man.

"Rita." He reached for my hand and kissed it. "You are here."

"Yes, I am. Go to sleep now, sweetheart."

He nodded drowsily, then forced one eye open. "You will go to the archive tomorrow, won't you?"

"I'll go on my lunch hour, I promise. Now get some rest."

Reading some old report was the least I could do. I'd do whatever it took to put his fears to rest and help him heal. Maybe I would learn something useful. Maybe it was fate that had thrown us together that day, a thousand feet in the air.

Chapter Twenty
Cornelia Vogel

Camp Westerbork
September 1944

Time behaves strangely in captivity. The eighteen months since Cornelia's arrest are an eternity that has flown past in the blink of an eye. Her memories come in flashes, like scenes from a book in which the signatures have been ordered at random, each turn of the page shifting the story into the future or back to the past. On this first day of September, she is following the same rutted path along the Boulevard des Misères that she has trod hundreds of times before. The only thing that differentiates this moment from others weeks or months in the past is the weather. Instead of being soaked by a chill autumn rain, or bitten by a hard winter's sleet, or soothed by the sweet fragrance of spring, she is wilting in the late-summer heat. Dirt sticks to every inch of her sweaty skin. At the post office, Cornelia removes her goggles to wipe the dust from their lenses. The pale circles around her eyes give her the look of an inquisitive owl.

"Any packages for Blom?"

"Blom, did you say?" The man behind the counter glances over his shoulder at a table where a number of open boxes are piled up. Poking a finger at one of them, he says, "I haven't had time to inspect it yet. You'd best come back tomorrow."

Last year, after the Nazis dissolved the Jewish Council and

sent thousands of its employees to Auschwitz, Commandant Gemmeker needed new management for the post office. He gave the job to the bankers from Lippmann Rosenthal, who were sitting around idle after expropriating the wealth of Holland's Jews into Hitler's coffers. The bankers are a misery to deal with. They stopped allowing outgoing mail, keep everything addressed to departed prisoners for themselves, and so thoroughly pilfer each package that by the time it is placed in a recipient's hands, there is little left but packing straw. Cornelia sees the flaps have been torn open on the box he indicated. She has apparently interrupted his thievery. If she walks away now, there will be nothing when she returns.

"I'm afraid Fräulein Slottke is expecting me to work tomorrow," she says. This is a lie. Gertrud Slottke has been absent from Westerbork since the beginning of August, but Cornelia is hoping this miserable banker doesn't know that. "She won't like me having to leave her office to come back here."

"Ah, well, you didn't say *Leah* Blom." The man grabs the box and thrusts a clipboard at her. "Sign here and you can have it."

Everyone in Westerbork has learned that the woman they know as Leah Blom is under the particular protection of Fräulein Gertrud Slottke. The other prisoners call her Slottke's bitch behind her back, but it's an epithet uttered without malice, as if she were simply a dog at Slottke's feet, no different from the hound who trots at Commandant Gemmeker's heels. A vague twitch in her gut as she signs Leah's name is all that remains of the guilt Cornelia once felt for the special treatment she receives. To get packages that haven't been pilfered, to eat a full meal on the days she slaves away in Slottke's office, to be exempted from the transport list—this is the full extent of the favor she enjoys as Slottke's bitch.

To make up for it, Cornelia spreads her paltry privileges as widely as she can. She shares the contents of every package. The meal she eats during the day allows her to gift a bunkmate her slice of evening bread. And when she overhears a name she recognizes while the transport list is being discussed, she conveys a warning so the person has a chance to appeal, or at least say their goodbyes. The one thing she has never done is ask Gertrud Slottke for a personal favor. Making herself indispensable to avoid being deported—to Cornelia, that is simply survival. To benefit herself any further would cross the line between self-preservation and collaboration.

With her goggles back in place and her package under her arm, Cornelia retraces her path along the Boulevard des Misères toward the spinsters' hut. The measly trees provide little shade from a white sun that burns the blue from the sky. Stepping over the rails, Cornelia suddenly becomes disoriented. Sweat soaks her armpits, yet she shivers as if buffeted by a winter wind. Time and space collapse as her vision slides down a dark tunnel. The transport train materializes in front of her eyes. People populate the Boulevard like filmed images projected on a screen. Her ears pick up the sounds of their shouting and crying and saying farewell. She sees bewildered children lifted into freight cars, surgical patients carried from the hospital on stretchers, the doors closing on a woman nursing the infant she'd given birth to that morning. She can't tell if the scene is real or a mirage until she reaches out to touch the rough wood of the freight car. Her fingers fall through empty air.

"*Mejuffrouw,* are you unwell?" A man has taken her arm. Cornelia closes her eyes, then opens them again. The train has vanished. The Boulevard is again deserted. She focuses on the man beside her. Beneath the sweat and grime, she recognizes his face. He is the famous violinist. Cornelia last saw him play a few months ago, when the orchestra accompanied a performance in the Registration

Hall. With some of the most talented entertainers in all of Europe imprisoned here, Commandant Gemmeker ordered a cabaret production complete with costumes, sets, and original songs. He was so pleased with the result, he invited Reichskommissar Seyss-Inquart himself to attend. The cabaret was a hit, playing three performances to sold-out crowds of conquering Nazis and doomed Jews. After completing punch cards for the 732 people who'd been transported to Auschwitz that week, Cornelia, desperate to forget her misery for an hour, bought herself a ten-cent ticket for closing night.

The violinist's fingers tighten their grip. "May I accompany you back to your barrack?"

"Thank you, yes." Cornelia's head still swims, but with his support she takes one step, then another, until she is in motion again. Though she doesn't remember telling him where she lives, or even her name, the violinist leads her to the door of barrack sixty-five.

"It's been my pleasure to assist you, Leah Blom," he says with a bow. "May I ask—have you heard anything about another list being drawn up?"

"No, I haven't." A month has now passed since the last hungry train snaked out of camp. Everyone in Westerbork is on edge, teetering between dread and relief.

"Let us hope we have come to the end of the transports, then. Good day to you, *mejuffrouw*."

Cornelia watches him disappear into the dusty haze before stepping into the stifling barrack. She rubs her throbbing forehead as she carries her package down the aisle of the spinsters' hut. Most of the bunks are empty now, the relentless transports having shrunk the population of the camp to the point where Cornelia now has all three tiers to herself. She sleeps on the bottom, hers the only shoes beneath the bed, and uses the third tier when she needs what passes here for privacy. Her tree house, she calls it, climbing up.

Sitting cross-legged, she unscrews her thermos and takes a long drink of tepid tea before focusing on the package. As always, Helena Vogel has addressed it to Leah Blom, still unaware that the imprisoned girl with whom she has been corresponding for over a year is really her own daughter. Cornelia digs through the straw to find a packet of tea leaves and a loaf of *volkorenbrood* that's so stale it will have to be soaked in hot water and eaten with a spoon. There are also, miraculously, three pears. Cornelia holds one to her nose and breathes it in before sinking her teeth into its juicy flesh. In seconds, there is nothing left but its stem.

She closes her eyes, savoring the taste of fruit on her tongue. Suddenly, time slips backward. The weather shifts from hot to cold. The taste in her mouth changes from pear to apple. It is the tart apples that came in the very first box addressed to Leah Blom, back in February 1943, during Cornelia's second week at Westerbork. She remembers the note that accompanied those apples word for word.

Dear Leah,

My daughter went to stay with relatives in Vlissingen. I hope you won't be upset I opened your letter to her. Since you were such good friends, I send you this package for her sake. In it you will find apples, notebooks, and pencils. I will pass along your letter when Cornelia returns, but I can't say when that will be.

Best wishes, Helena Vogel

Even though the words were impersonal, seeing her mother's handwriting consoled Cornelia's heart. She was puzzled by the mention of a visit to Vlissingen until she thumbed through the pages of the notebook. Even though it seemed blank, she noticed a word or two lightly erased on many of the pages. Squinting, she managed to make them out. Read together, they became a message.

I peeked out the front window when I heard the engine but it was too late they were already putting you in the truck I am so sorry Leah but you will be glad to know I saw my sister get away on her bicycle mother is upset and father is furious but I am proud of her she will be fighting for you and so will I be brave your friend Dirk

Cornelia began to cry, imagining her brother plying such spy-craft. By honestly telling their parents what he thought he saw, Dirk led them to believe Leah had been arrested and Cornelia had left to join the Resistance. They must have been covering up her absence by saying their daughter had gone to stay with relatives. The enormous relief she felt knowing that Leah had gotten away did nothing to blunt the arrow of homesickness that pierced her heart.

Cornelia is recalled from her memories by a fly that has buzzed in through a broken window. She swats it away, then rummages through the packing straw to make sure she's found everything. Believing her daughter to be risking her life in the Resistance apparently softened Helena's feelings for the Jewish girl who was once her neighbor. Over the past year and a half, she has sent a variety of foods: sausage, butter, fruit, nuts, carrots, jam, honey. There was ground coffee, once, the scent transporting Cornelia to mornings at the breakfast table with her family. Helena also sent a scarf and mittens last winter, fresh cotton underclothes this past summer—even the precious pair of goggles.

At the bottom of today's package, Cornelia finds a note from her mother. She caresses the scrap of paper as if rubbing it could magically whisk her home.

Dear Leah,

I hope this finds you well. As I've had no reply to my last two boxes, however, I can only assume they are no longer reaching you. Unless I hear that you received this package, it will be the last one I send.

Good luck to you, Helena Vogel

The prospect of being cut off from her mother throws Cornelia into a panic. Damn those bankers and their rule against sending letters. She'll have to risk asking Schlesinger's secretary to mail a postcard for her, so Helena knows her packages are being delivered. Cornelia pockets the remaining pears, grabs the *volkorenbrood,* and climbs down from her tree house.

The second tier of the bunk is where Cornelia stores her possessions. The things in Leah's rucksack have been supplemented over time by the items in her packages and cast-offs from departing women until the mattress sags under the weight of it all. Thievery is common, but Cornelia doesn't begrudge the occasional sweater or shirt that goes missing. The things that are most valuable to her aren't worth stealing. Cornelia looks over her shoulder before stashing the note in Leah's rucksack, which is now stuffed with punch cards.

Every day that Cornelia has worked in Slottke's office, she has continued her practice of bearing witness by punching at least one duplicate card. Greta Speelman's was the first in a collection that has grown to hundreds. Cornelia's neighbor in the spinsters' hut, who worked in the orphanage, is here, transported to Poland along with dozens of children. The rabbi who helped Cornelia translate the inscription on her Star of David is here. Meneer and Mevrouw Presser are here, having been put on the train so soon after arriving, Cornelia never knew they'd been in Westerbork until she punched their cards. The Greek woman from Salonika is here, and one of the Turkish women, too. There's a card for the surgeon who refused to follow Nazi orders to sterilize Jewish men in mixed marriages. There's a card for the journalist who described every transport as a shipwreck, its scale of misery so vast only a natural disaster could capture its scope. There are cards for nameless babies whose age in months or weeks could only be guessed. Etty Hillesum is here, too, having volunteered to be transported on the same train that carried her parents and brother to Auschwitz.

Cornelia cinches the rucksack shut. She hasn't added a punch card to her collection since she processed the list for the last train that departed at the end of July. Daring to hope the transports have ended, she settles her goggles over her eyes and heads out of the spinsters' hut with the loaf of bread under her arm. She recrosses the dusty roads of the camp to go share her food with Lillian and Philip Blom.

Cornelia had been imprisoned at Westerbork for eight months when Gertrud Slottke suddenly announced she could be excused from punching cards for an hour to greet her parents. Cornelia's heart stopped as she pictured her father at the main gates, demanding that his daughter be released. Her shocked face prompted Fräulein Slottke to explain. "The Barneveld Jews have been transferred here. Their train is arriving now. Go on, Leah Blom, before I change my mind."

The aristocracy of Dutch Jewry arrived from Barneveld accompanied by a towering pile of random items salvaged from their previous lives. Cornelia darted through the crowd of people on the Boulevard des Misères, searching for Lillian and Philip.

When she spotted them, befuddled and afraid, she ran up and grasped their hands. Before they could ask what in the world she was doing there, Cornelia whispered, in English, "Leah got away. She is safe. I was arrested in her place." They were on line in the Registration Hall before Philip and Lillian fully comprehended what had happened. All they'd known was what they'd heard through the Jewish Council: that their daughter, Leah Blom, had been arrested in The Hague and was imprisoned at Westerbork. Lillian, too overwhelmed with gratitude to speak, clung to Cornelia, weeping. Philip placed his hands on her shoulders as if granting a chivalric title. "You are our daughter, now and forever."

The barrack occupied by the Barneveld Jews is the most inhospitable in all of Westerbork, crammed as it is with everything from rolled-up Persian rugs to antique furniture to silver tea sets whose worth is zilch in this place where the only commodities of value are a bite of fresh food and an exemption from the transport list. Cornelia wends her way through the maze of useless possessions to the bunk where Philip Blom is reclining with an open book on his chest. As she gets closer, she sees the book rise and fall in time with his snores. Since arriving at Westerbork, the once-lauded professor of history has sunk into a depression so deep he is practically mute. Lillian Blom, on the other hand, has tapped into a surprising well of American optimism. With Cornelia's help, she keeps Philip fed and dressed in clean clothes. Every morning, she leads him outside for a short walk, unshakable in her belief that he'll be back to his old self once they're set free.

"Sweetheart, it's so good to see you." Lillian hugs Cornelia close, then nods at the loaf under her arm. "You've had a package?"

Cornelia takes off her goggles. "Yes, here, I brought this for you."

Lillian accepts the bread but senses something is wrong. She pulls Cornelia into a quiet corner. "What's the matter, Nellie?"

Cornelia savors the sound of her name. It's a gift to her sanity to have someone here who knows who she really is. "My mother wrote that she's not receiving my letters. This might be our last package unless I can get word to her somehow."

"I'm so sorry. I sympathize with her, you know. We're both mothers who don't know where our daughters are."

"I'm sure Leah's in London right now, or on her way to America."

Lillian hugs Cornelia again. "Thanks to you, Nellie. Now, let's see if we can't tempt Philip into eating something." She breaks off a hunk of bread, puts it in the bowl of her mess kit, and softens it with hot water from her thermos.

Cornelia wakes Professor Blom, cajoling him to sit up by waving the pear under his nose. He gobbles the fruit, practically swallowing it whole. After Cornelia wipes the juice from his chin, Lillian spoon-feeds him the *volkorenbrood* mush. As soon as the food is finished, though, he slides back down on the mattress and rolls onto his side.

Lillian walks Cornelia out of the barrack, nibbling and licking her pear to make it last. "You've been our savior here, darling. I don't know what we would have done without you."

"You've saved me, too, Lillian, by being my family here."

"Let's say we saved each other then." She pinches the signet ring on Cornelia's finger. Though she recognizes it as the ring her own father gave Leah, she's never asked how Cornelia came to wear it. "After the war is over, I want you to come to America with us. I think you and Leah could be happy in New York. There's a neighborhood called Greenwich Village where the two of you would feel quite at home."

Cornelia isn't exactly sure what Lillian means, but there's a knowingness to her voice, and a kindness, too, that touches her heart. "I'd love to go to America," she says, indulging in some optimism of her own. Prisoners can see with their own eyes the

British bombers flying toward targets in Germany. There are rumors that Allied troops have landed in France. Every Jew in Westerbork expects the Nazis to be routed by year's end. She pictures her reunion with Leah, imagines her gratitude to Cornelia for saving her parents' lives, anticipates the home they will share in this magical Manhattan village.

"Are you all right, dear?" Lillian wipes a tear from Cornelia's face. Her fingertips leave a dirty streak across her cheek.

"I'm fine. Everything is going to be fine." She takes Lillian's hand and kisses it before putting her goggles back on. "I'm off to get a language lesson from one of the Surinamers. I'll see you both tomorrow."

There is a lightness to Cornelia's step as she walks along the Boulevard. In her mind, she's reviewing the Sranan vocabulary she's learned so far. She's fascinated by the language, which developed from a dialect of blended English and Portuguese spoken by enslaved Africans. Her mind is so occupied that she pays no attention, at first, to the automobile driving up the dusty road. But an automobile is an unusual sight on the Boulevard. When it stops in front of the Registration Hall, Cornelia slows to look. What she sees turns her optimism into dread.

A red braid. A white face. Gertrud Slottke has returned to Camp Westerbork.

Move, Cornelia tells herself. Walk away before she sees you. But Fräulein Slottke has already spotted her pet. She levels her gaze at Cornelia and curls her forefinger. Cornelia can no more resist her summons than a well-trained dog can ignore his master's whistle.

"Leah Blom, how fortunate that you should be passing by." Fräulein Slottke closes the car door and steps out of its dusty wake as it drives away. "I'll need you in the office tomorrow."

Cornelia's job is unique in Westerbork. Needing her in the office can mean only one thing. "Is—is there to be another transport?" she stammers.

"Two, in fact, back-to-back. The first is going to Poland. It comes tomorrow and will depart on Sunday. The second will leave the next day for Theresienstadt. The combined quota is over three thousand."

Cornelia feels as if she's being buried by an avalanche. Not again, she thinks, not anymore. Over one hundred thousand people have already passed through the camp. Merely four thousand remain imprisoned at Westerbork. Are the Germans so maniacal they will not rest until they've swept Holland clean of every Jew, as if they were so many crumbs on a kitchen counter?

"Schlesinger's department was only notified yesterday," Gertrud Slottke continues. "It will take a miracle to get everything finalized in such a short time. I want you to start punching cards as soon as we have the transport list. I'll expect you first thing in the morning, Leah Blom."

A lock of hair comes loose from her braid as Fräulein Slottke walks away. Cornelia hallucinates a red snake slithering down her back. Slottke does not turn around as she begins to speak again. To Cornelia's eyes, the words seem to come from the forked tongue of the snake. "You'll be glad to know your parents will be going with the Barneveld Jews to Theresienstadt. Compared to the labor camp at Auschwitz, they say it's practically a resort."

A spark shoots through Cornelia's legs. She runs after the woman, catching her as she reaches the entrance to the Registration Hall. "*Fräulein,* please, may I ask, is my name on either transport list?"

"Of course not. You will remain here. How else could you punch three thousand cards?"

"Then please, I beg you, let my parents stay with me. I wouldn't be able to work, thinking of them on that train."

Gertrud Slottke tilts her head. Her face betrays nothing as she weighs Leah Blom's request. "But I've already assured you they are going to a most agreeable destination."

It's true that Theresienstadt in Czechoslovakia is rumored to be safer than the camps in Poland or Germany, but Cornelia knows better than to trust in rumors.

"I've never asked you for anything before, *Fräulein,* not once in all this time. Please."

Gertrud Slottke looks down her narrow nose at the girl who has somehow made herself essential to the efficient execution of her duties. "Very well, Leah Blom. You will come to the office tomorrow prepared to work, and I will take your parents off the list."

Cornelia drops to her knees in the dusty street. "Thank you, *Fräulein.*"

Gertrud Slottke's lip twitches slightly before she disappears into the Registration Hall. She doesn't see Cornelia vomit up the contents of her stomach before stumbling away to tell Lillian and Philip they are safe. A stray cat slinks around the corner of the building and begins to feast on the partially digested pear.

The next morning, Cornelia is in Fräulein Slottke's office, her fingers on the keys of the punch machine, as promised. The list for Auschwitz has been set in stone, it seems, making it safe for Cornelia to begin coding punch cards the moment the train pulls into camp, its line of freight cars frighteningly long. By the next day, the snake's belly has been filled with 1,039 people. Mere hours after that train leaves, another slithers up the Boulevard. This will be for Monday's transport to Theresienstadt. When Cornelia sees that it, too, is made up of filthy freight cars, she is sure that keeping Philip and Lillian here at Westerbork was the right thing to do.

The list for this train is twice as long as the one for Auschwitz. It takes the combined efforts of the Green Police, the Order Police, and the German soldiers under Gemmeker's command to force 2,074 people into freight cars packed with up to ninety bodies each. The transport list includes all remaining Jews of dubious racial origin, including her Sranan tutor from Suriname. The entire staff of the hospital is deported with the single exception of Dr. Spanier and his family. The cast of the cabaret is shoved on board, and every member of the orchestra, too, their instruments abandoned on the Boulevard. All the baptized Jews still residing in the camp are deported, Bibles left in the dust. The Barneveld Jews are herded on board like beasts, their rugs and furniture and silver tea sets all left behind. Finally, late in the afternoon, the engine sputters and sighs as it gathers enough steam to haul the train, heavy with human cargo, through the gates and out of the camp.

For the next nine days, Cornelia leaves Fräulein Slottke's office only to sleep. She is so overwhelmed and exhausted, she adds only two punch cards to her collection: one for her Sranan tutor, the other for the famous violinist. By the time she punches the last of the 3,113 cards, her head is pounding, her eyes are burning, her fingertips are blistered. This is the end of it, she is certain. There can be no more transports after this. Rumors are swirling that the Allies have taken Antwerp. The liberation of Holland can't be far off. When Cornelia feels the vibration of an arriving train, she's certain it has come to bring prisoners in, not take anyone away. After boxing up the completed punch cards and emptying the overflowing bit bin, she clears her throat to get Fräulein Slottke's attention.

"Yes, Leah Blom?"

"I've finished, *Fräulein.* I was wondering, now that there are so few people left in Westerbork, might my parents and I move into one of the little houses together?"

Fräulein Slottke blinks. "That won't be possible, Leah Blom. You are coming with me."

Cornelia's knees seem to disappear. Her legs fold, dropping her back into her chair. "Coming where, *Fräulein*?"

"The *Judenreferent* has declared the Netherlands *judenfrei*. Our work here is done. I'm being transferred to Bergen-Belsen. The Labor Office there is a much more significant operation. They have a whole Hollerith installation, with a sorter and a tabulator, as well as a dozen punch machines. I'll need you, Leah Blom. Go pack your bag. Our train leaves tomorrow."

Cornelia's vision is sliding down the tunnel. Her skin is slick with sweat. She struggles to speak. "But how can you . . . after everything I've . . . why would you do this to me?"

Fräulein Slottke allows her eyebrows the luxury of lifting. "What have I done except feed you, employ you, exempt you from transport? What did I do when you asked me to take your parents off the list?"

Cornelia realizes Fräulein Slottke is waiting for an answer. Her voice squeaks from her throat. "You took them off."

"I did. And now they are back on. In addition to carrying a passenger car for staff and soldiers, two hundred and sixty-seven prisoners are on tomorrow's list for Bergen-Belsen. You and your parents will be housed with the Dutch Jews at the Star Camp. You should be quite comfortable there."

Cornelia has managed to keep Lillian and Philip safe for all this time. She'll never forgive herself if she fails them now. "But you only need me. You don't need my parents. Won't you let them stay here in Holland, for my sake, please?"

There is a long pause as Fräulein Slottke looks at Cornelia with amazement, as if a dog has learned human speech. "You have apparently forgotten that you are not in a position to tell me what I do or do not need." She lifts a sheaf of papers from her desk. "I have tomorrow's transport list here. There is a freight car attached to the train that will be decoupled at Hanover and sent on to Auschwitz. Your parents will accompany you to Bergen-Belsen, or I will put them on the list for Auschwitz. The choice is yours, Leah Blom."

Chapter Twenty-One
Rita Klein

New York City
June 1960

When you were serving in Europe after the war, did you ever hear of Hollerith computers being used in Nazi concentration camps?"

"In the camps?" Mr. McKay looked up from the control panel he was wiring. "No, but now that you mention it, it wouldn't surprise me if they were. The Germans were obsessed with computing machines. Most were made by Dehomag—that was IBM's German subsidiary before the war—but they were essentially the same as our old Hollerith. Everyone in the Quartermaster Corps was grateful, actually. When it became our job to manage their economy, it helped us tremendously that so much of it was already computerized. The army opened a school right there in Germany to train us to use them."

"Is that where you and Mr. Pettibone met?"

Mr. McKay nodded. "Late in 1945, yes. After the training course, we lost track of each other until we were both stateside again. Most of the American troops couldn't wait to get home after the war, but us Black soldiers were in no hurry to come running back to Jim Crow. I stayed in Germany until 1948."

That must have been when Max was conceived, I thought, counting back the years. The ease with which Gladys had told me about

Mr. McKay's illegitimate son was another reminder that everything was different for men. His reputation wasn't damaged by some wartime dalliance any more than Gregory Peck's was in *The Man in the Gray Flannel Suit*. I pictured Leonard grilling hamburgers while his kids splashed in the swimming pool I imagined he had in his suburban backyard. He'd created a child out of wedlock, but except for a one-time dip in his bank account, nothing had changed for him. Even Jacob hadn't stopped to worry about getting me pregnant.

"Did you see any of those camps yourself? I only ask because of my—" I'd never called Jacob my boyfriend out loud. "Because of a man I know who was in Auschwitz."

"Poor guy. My unit didn't liberate any of the camps, but we did get assigned to Dachau for what the army called 'logistical support,' by which they meant a job too horrible for the white troops to do."

"What was the job?"

His lip curled in disgust. "Grave digging. Re-digging, actually. All I'll say is that it required a large consignment of bulldozers. Anyway, this is ready. Would you give me a hand, Miss Klein?"

That morning, Francie had sent over a batch of punched cards using the new codes, so I'd finally been able to run a preliminary production report for the *Constellation* items. Mr. McKay, meanwhile, had written a control panel program for the 602 that would instruct it to compare Olympia's regular accounts with the navy contract. The old punch cards he usually processed on the Hollerith fit in the hopper, of course—IBM hadn't changed those specifications in decades—but the 602 was a more temperamental machine. It wasn't long before lights flashed and a buzzer sounded as it spit out a card it didn't like.

"Goddamn it," Mr. McKay muttered. He removed the damaged card and handed it off to one of the punch-card operators, who prepared a duplicate. After a little finessing, he got the 602 going again. "You're such a diva," he said, patting the machine tenderly.

The comparison report made it painfully apparent what a disaster the navy contract was for Olympia's overall business. In order to meet production deadlines and deliver goods to the *Constellation* before it launched, Olympia was delaying orders from other customers, who, Mr. McKay said, only stayed with them out of loyalty or inertia. "Given the chance, some of those customers are bound to look for alternatives. If they do, they'll soon realize they can get the same products faster and for less from newer factories in the Bronx."

"Poor Francie," I said. "She's going to take this hard."

"I daresay she will, but that's her problem, Miss Klein, not yours. Remember, you work for Antiquated. Your job is to produce accurate reports, not save Olympia from their own mistakes." He shook his head. "I am worried about them falling behind on their payments, though. We've been billing them quarterly for years, but I'm going to tell Gladys to start invoicing them every month. I don't want to be left holding the bag if Olympia declares bankruptcy."

"Do you think it could come to that?"

"The numbers don't lie. Never mind the risk of losing frustrated customers. The more they focus on supplying the navy, the more regular inventory languishes unsold in the warehouse. You can see it for yourself, Miss Klein."

I understood the cost of unsold merchandise—that's why Dad was always having sales on marked-down shoes—but looking at that list of inventory codes followed by numbers of units reminded me of Jacob's tattoo. It was horrible to think of human beings processed by a computer like so many pots and pans.

More eager than ever to put Jacob's mind at ease, I walked over to the Jewish Aid Committee on my lunch hour. Their address on Forty-Second Street wasn't far from the Empire State Building, but I hadn't realized, until I saw the Art Deco façade, that they were in the News Building. Inside, I traversed the compass points set in terrazzo as I walked around that huge revolving globe in the center of the circular lobby. After circumnavigating the world, I checked a directory on the wall to locate the offices of the JAC.

I'd imagined the archive would be a maze of shelves I could wander around in, but it turned out to be nothing more than a cramped room with an oak desk and a brass lamp. There was a window cut into the wall opposite the desk, behind which an elderly gentleman with horn-rimmed glasses and a scholarly beard sat with his nose so deep in a book I had to cough to get his attention. When I told him what I was looking for, he handed me a set of bound volumes as big as wallpaper catalogs without so much as getting up from his stool.

"These are the indexes. What you need to do is cross-reference your search terms. Look for items that are indexed under both Bergen-Belsen and—what was that other word?"

"Hollerith."

"Once you have those item numbers, bring them to me. I'll go back and get them for you."

I struggled to carry the indexes to the desk, but it didn't take long to find what I was looking for. There were thousands of entries indexed under "Bergen-Belsen" but only a few dozen under "Hollerith." After a few minutes of cross-checking, I found the one item that contained both terms. According to the description, it was a five-page document called the Blom Report. A real needle in a haystack, I thought, as I wrote down the item number and brought it up to the window.

"This might take me a while to track down," the archivist said, sounding terribly inconvenienced. He heaved himself off the stool, opened a door behind him, and switched on a bank of fluorescent lights. I glimpsed long rows of metal shelving crammed with banker's boxes. I hoped he wouldn't be too long. I was stretching out my lunch hour as it was, and I still needed to eat. All I'd had for breakfast was a cold knish at Jacob's that morning.

Fifteen minutes ticked by before the archivist reappeared to hand me a single, slim folder. "You can read it over there," he said, pointing to the desk.

The Blom Report was indexed with eleven search terms, listed alphabetically: "Bad Arolsen"; "Bergen-Belsen"; "Blom, Leah"; "Central Location Index"; "Displaced Persons"; "Hollerith"; "International Tracing Service"; "Jewish Aid Committee"; "Silver, Edith"; "Silver, Joseph"; and "Slottke, Gertrud." Though the report itself was only five pages, I figured the single-spaced type ran upward of three thousand words. I had my pad and a pen ready, but after reading the first few paragraphs, I realized the impossibility of taking adequate notes in the time I had left. I brought it back to the archivist to ask if they had a photostat machine.

"We just started leasing one from Xerox. I can take it over to the office and have the girl make you a copy, but I have to charge you ten cents a page."

It was worth every one of the fifty cents it would cost me. "And this, can you copy this, too?" Paper-clipped to the report was an old Hollerith punch card, an example, apparently, of what it described.

"Sure, it'll copy whatever the girl puts on the scanning plate." He waited, staring at me.

"Yes, fine, I'll pay sixty cents."

"I need it up front." I dug two quarters and a couple of nickels out of my change purse and held the coins out to him. When he returned, I snatched the copied pages from his hand, folding them to fit in my pocketbook. "Oh, I meant to ask, do you have any information on the report's author?" I unfolded the pages and looked again. "Edith Silver."

"Edith Silver?" For the first time, the man perked up. "You mean Mr. Joseph Silver's daughter?"

"I don't know. From what I read so far, she worked for the Jewish Aid Committee after the war?"

"That's Miss Silver, no doubt about it. Joseph Silver, her father, is on our board of directors. I wish you'd said so from the beginning. She volunteers here." He picked up a telephone that was hidden below the counter. "Hello, yes, is Miss Silver working today? Oh, right, thanks." He hung up and gave me a business card. "She'll be here tomorrow afternoon. You can call that number if you want to ask for her."

Even though I was running late, I couldn't resist stopping at a hot dog vendor on my way back to Antiquated. When he asked what I wanted, I said yes to mustard and relish but no to the onions. My mouth watered as he slapped it together. "Come to think of it," I said, "make that two."

I figured Jacob would want to read the report with me, so I left it in my pocketbook all afternoon. I was standing at the chalkboard working on a new control panel diagram when Gladys interrupted to tell me I had a phone call.

"Someone named Rudy? He's holding on line three. Sounds like a foreigner. You want me to brush him off for you?"

"No, thanks, Gladys, I'll take it." I went to my desk and picked up the phone. Rudy told me he'd left Jacob napping in his room after a morning of fresh air and sunshine. "He has his alarm set. He'll come meet you at the Empire State Building at five, in the lobby. That okay with you, Rita?"

"Sure, that's fine. We can have dinner together before I go home." I'd told Jacob that morning I needed to get back to Teaneck tonight for a change of clothes. The truth was, though, I wasn't sure how I'd handle it if he wanted to have sex again. My period was still going strong, but it wouldn't last forever. I wondered if I could drop a hint that he should get a prescription for condoms.

The idea made me blush, but one of us had to be realistic, and it looked like that was going to be me.

"Rita, listen," Rudy said, "he had a good day, but I still don't trust him to be alone at night."

The implication hung in the air between us for a moment. "I'll bring him home with me, how's that?"

"Oh, that's a fine idea!" I could hear the relief in his voice. "Should I go back up to his room and tell him?"

"Don't wake him if he's asleep. Maybe put a note under his door? And ask him to bring my suitcase, too." I hung up, then telephoned my mother. I told her Jacob was recovering from the flu but that he still needed looking after. "Can he stay with us tonight? In Charlie's room, of course."

"I guess it's better than you staying there," Mom said. "How's his appetite?"

"Not great. He's had some soup and bread is all. Oh, and knishes from the deli."

She clucked her tongue. "As skinny as that boy is, he needs a more substantial meal. I'll go down to the butcher and get a brisket. Do you suppose he likes kugel?"

"I'm sure he does, Mom. You don't think Dad will mind him sleeping over, do you?"

"Are you kidding? He'll love having another man around. They can watch President Eisenhower talk about his trip to Japan on television together."

Jacob looked adorable standing in the lobby of the Empire State Building with my pink suitcase hanging from his arm. As we walked hand in hand to the Port Authority, I pretended we were a husband and wife who'd met up after work to go home together. In my fantasy, we had a one-bedroom apartment with parquet floors and high ceilings and big windows. Maybe I should give up on the idea of going back to college, I thought. Like Mr. Pettibone said, if you were smart and ambitious, you didn't need a fancy degree to get ahead in this world. If I could manage to turn my summer job at Antiquated into a permanent position, between us we'd have plenty of money for rent.

Jacob wanted to look at the Blom Report right there on the bus to Teaneck, but I said I'd rather read it together later that night. I was worried it might agitate him, and I didn't want to be stuck in a tunnel under the Hudson River while he pulled at his hair. Instead, I asked him to tell me about his morning. He and Rudy had taken the ferry out to Staten Island and back again, he said, then wandered along the East River piers, watching the tugboats pilot ocean liners in from the bay. Afterward, Jacob napped soundly without taking any pills. He felt so good when he got to the Empire State Building, he'd gone up to the observation deck to ask his supervisor if there was a tour available.

"You're going back to work?" I was alarmed he was getting ahead of himself.

"Not tomorrow, anyway. The first tour he has for me is on Wednesday. He wants me to work late—he's expecting a crowd to watch the fireworks."

"Is that happening already?" I knew Macy's always sponsored their big fireworks display ahead of Independence Day, but June 29 seemed awfully early.

"Yes, it is. I was hoping you could meet me there, so we could watch them together?"

"That sounds nice, Jacob, if you really think you'll be up for it."

He squeezed my hand. "I'm sure I'll be feeling like my old self again by then."

"You'll feel even better once you've had my mother's cooking."

Mom took immense satisfaction in seeing Jacob polish off a second helping of pot roast, after which they enjoyed a spirited argument about the relative merits of raisins versus sultanas in noodle kugel. Over dessert, Dad asked if I'd help kick off the Independence Day sale in the store on Saturday. I told him I'd be happy to. When Mom interrogated Jacob about his flu symptoms, I cut her off by saying he'd recovered from his fever but was still fatigued. She took the hint, dismissing Jacob and my dad.

"Rita and I will clean up in here. Why don't the both of you go watch television?" When we were alone at the sink, she asked, "Is it getting serious between you two?"

"I don't know yet, Mom." I took a plate from the dish rack, dried it, and put it away. I didn't confide in her about Bellevue, but I did say he wasn't a very happy man. "I mean, his past is pretty terrible, isn't it?"

"We all have a past, Rita. You just have to put it behind you and stay focused on what's ahead."

"Is that what you did, after the orphanage?" The words slipped out, surprising us both.

Her hands, submerged in soapy water, grew still. "The first time I ever rode in a taxi was the day my father took me to the Orphaned Hebrews Home. He said it was a special treat for a special day. I hadn't been happy like that since Mama died. It felt like birds chirping in my chest. Then he brought me into that castle and dumped me there." She started scrubbing a plate so hard the water splashed. "You tell me, Rita, what's the point in dwelling on that?"

Mom and Dad didn't like talking about growing up in the orphanage, and somehow Charlie and I had always known not to ask. But I felt like I'd found a crumb in some fairy tale forest. I decided to follow its trail. "You never told me how she died."

"You've heard of the influenza epidemic?"

"Back in 1918, wasn't it?"

She nodded. "That's your answer."

I had never ventured so far into her past before. I took one more step. "Where did your father go?"

Mom gave the dripping plate to me. "How the hell should I know? I never heard from that bastard again." She thrust her chin forward, like a boxer preparing to take a punch. "I was nothing more to him than the dirt he wiped off his shoes."

"But if you knew how it felt to be abandoned like that—"

"But what?" She stared me down, daring me to ask.

I looked over my shoulder and lowered my voice. "How could you send me away to that home?"

"You're the one who caused that mess, Rita. I'm just grateful that baby will never know his mother didn't want him."

But you're the one who made me give him up, I thought. You never asked me what I wanted.

Mom took the dish from my hands. "Go and watch television. I'll finish the dishes."

The president was still talking about his trip to Japan as I sat next to Jacob on the couch. He took my hand. "Your fingers are so cold, Rita," he said, rubbing them.

After Eisenhower signed off from the White House, Mom came out of the kitchen to signal Dad. "Let's give these kids some space, Irving. Jacob, I've got Charlie's room all made up for you. We'll see you in the morning."

Once they'd gone into their bedroom, Jacob turned the volume on the television down low. "Can we read that report now, Rita?"

It broke my heart to see the look in his eyes, like he expected to find some hidden treasure in those single-spaced pages. I guessed it didn't matter how old a person got—a child always yearned for his mother. I took the report out of my pocketbook and handed it to him. "I need to close my eyes for a while. Would you read it to me?"

Jacob's hands trembled as he unfolded the pages. I rested my head against the back of the couch, my arms cradling the stone in my stomach. He cleared his throat and began.

Chapter Twenty-Two

THE BLOM REPORT
Prepared by Edith Silver
November 1945, New York City

BACKGROUND

In April 1945, the New York–based Jewish Aid Committee (JAC), which had established an office in London during the war, was particularly anxious to inspect conditions at the recently liberated camp Bergen-Belsen, which was known to us as an exchange camp where many Jewish prisoners had foreign nationality or international connections. The JAC was also aware that the population of the camp had expanded between December 1944 and January 1945 to include thousands of Jewish prisoners transferred from Auschwitz and other camps in Poland ahead of the Russian advance. These people, in particular, were in dire need of assistance.

Bergen-Belsen was, at the time, under British military authority, which was overwhelmed by the humanitarian needs at the camp. However, because of their antipathy toward Zionism and their government's political stance regarding the Mandate for Palestine, the British resisted what they considered interference from Jewish relief organizations. When an application by the JAC to inspect Bergen-Belsen and offer help to its Jewish population was denied, I managed to attach myself to a unit of the British Red Cross that was about to be sent to the camp.

We arrived at Bergen-Belsen on April 30, 1945, two weeks after liberation. The horrific conditions I observed are described in more detail in the previous reports I submitted to the JAC. In those first days, I lent a hand in any way I could, especially in the field hospital, where Red Cross nurses and British medical students dressed wounds, administered medications, and fed survivors what they called a "Bengal mixture" of nutrition designed for people suffering from extreme malnourishment and starvation.

Soon after my arrival, a team of medical personnel set out to inspect administrative structures at the camp to determine if they were safe for use by the military. Any building determined to be too disease-infested for use would be burned. Wanting to learn all I could about the administration of the camp, I volunteered to act as their secretary. It was during this inspection that the events I will detail in this report commenced.

DISCOVERY

Upon entering the building that had housed the Labor Office, or Arbeitsdienst, we found the shelves bare, the desk drawers turned over, and the file cabinets empty. It seemed the administrators of the camp had escaped days before liberation with as many records of their crimes as they could carry. The rest was incinerated. In the yard outside, the ashes of an enormous bonfire were still evident. Despite the disarray, the medical personnel saw no evidence of infestation and deemed the structure usable.

As we were leaving the building, I heard a sound from under the floor, a tapping or knocking that arrested my attention. Upon further inspection, a trapdoor was found. The lock was broken with a crowbar and the hatch was lifted. Imagine our shock when we saw a woman clinging to the steps, holding a stick with which she had been tapping on the trapdoor. She was extremely emaciated, though not as skeletal as many of the survivors I had seen. She flung her arm across her face to shield her eyes from the light. Two men carried her up from the basement and laid her on the floor. At first, I thought she was covered in dark bruises, but I soon realized she was filthy with coal dust. Beneath the smudges, her complexion was extremely pale and her lips were cracked and bleeding. A soldier assisting the medical team suspected her of being a Nazi left behind in their hasty evacuation, as she was clothed not in a prison uniform but in torn trousers and a tattered sweater, until I pointed out the faded yellow star indicating a Jewish prisoner. (We had observed at Bergen-Belsen that the prisoners in the so-called Star Camp wore their own clothing, while the prisoners who had been transferred from Poland wore threadbare striped uniforms.) I asked the woman her name, but she did not speak and continued to cover her eyes.

Upon a cursory inspection of her clothing and skin, she appeared not to be infested with lice, and thus was unlikely to have typhus. She did, however, smell strongly of urine and also of feces, indicating that she suffered from diarrhea, as did so many of the prisoners. I offered her water from my canteen, which she took eagerly. I had learned from the Red Cross nurses how dangerous it was to allow malnourished and dehydrated patients too much food or water at a time, so I soon withdrew the canteen, much to her consternation. While I attended to the woman, a member of the team descended into the basement with a flashlight. Noticing electric lights hanging from the ceiling, he called up for someone to find a switch. Once the lights were on, I left the woman reclining as comfortably as possible and joined in the inspection of the basement, curious to understand her ordeal.

The basement was a storeroom for coal to fuel the stoves that heated the Labor Office. There were also some crates of

potatoes that were in a shocking state of decay but had apparently sustained the woman during her imprisonment. There
were two buckets in a corner, one empty, the other filled with
excrement. There were also some boxes of administrative supplies, including blank death certificates and other stationery
printed with the words "Bergen-Belsen" in that medieval type-
face so beloved by the Nazis.

I returned to care for the woman, who would need to go
through the "human laundry" before I could bring her to the
field hospital for nutritional rehabilitation. She was in an almost
catatonic state as I helped carry her on a stretcher to the former stables where the "human laundry" had been established.
When we arrived, she suddenly flung out the arm that had been
covering her eyes and grabbed blindly for my hand, which she
clutched with all her feeble strength. To my shock, she croaked
four words in English: "Please don't leave me."

The more educated German and Dutch Jews in Bergen-Belsen
had some knowledge of English, and there were many with a
connection to Britain, but this woman's accent was perfectly
American. I promised to stay with her through the laundry
process, which I had not witnessed firsthand before. The British
military had pressed German nurses into service for the job to
spare their own Red Cross workers from exposure to typhus
and other diseases. It seemed a fitting punishment that the
enemy should take on the disgusting and dangerous work of
washing survivors, but the sight of German men and women intimately touching the naked bodies of people who had suffered
so much at their hands was intolerable to me. Still, the work
had to be done. First the nurses stripped the woman, tossing
her clothes on the burn pile. Next, she was lifted onto a metal
table—there was a row of them down the entire length of the
stable—where they got to work washing her as thoroughly as a

baby. As the coal dust and filth was rinsed away, a signet ring on her hand was revealed, as well as a Star of David pendant on a thin gold necklace. I have no doubt both items would have been stolen by the nurses if I weren't keeping watch.

After she was clean, they insisted I step aside as they dusted her in DDT powder. I protested that she had no sign of lice, but it was a mandated step in the process they dared not skip. Afterward, she was wrapped in a sheet and sent outside, where dozens of people, their skin white with DDT powder, were waiting to be taken to a barrack or the hospital. There were no stretchers available, but she seemed able to stand now and had even taken a few steps, so I asked if she felt strong enough to walk with my help. "Where are we going?" she said, again in English. I told her I would take her to the Red Cross hospital where I worked, and that she would get food there and medical care. She slung her arm across my shoulders and let me support her waist. In this way, I half-carried her to the field hospital, sneezing from DDT powder.

I stayed with her while she was settled in a cot and given water to drink and a bowl of Bengal mixture to eat. She became listless and I had to spoon the mixture into her mouth. Her lips, as I mentioned, were terribly chapped. I had in my pocket a little tin of lanolin that I used for my skin. I dabbed my pinky into the tin and spread the lanolin across her lips. This seemed to soothe her and she subsequently fell asleep.

Over the next two days, I visited her as often as I could, curious to learn who she was and how she had come to be in the basement of the Labor Office, but I always found her asleep. On the third day, she was awake and lucid, though still quite weak. When I asked her name, she hesitated for so long, I wondered if her ordeal had affected her memory. Finally, she said, "My name is Leah Blom."

Leah told me she was Dutch, and that she had been transported from Westerbork in Holland to Bergen-Belsen in September 1944 along with her parents, Lillian and Philip Blom.
I offered to try to locate them, but she said they had died of
typhus over the winter. When I asked how she came to speak
such excellent English, she became confused, saying first that
a friend taught her before correcting herself and saying that
she'd learned the language from her mother, who was American. As to why she was in that basement, she told me she was
assigned to work in the Labor Office with something called
a Hollerith machine. During the typhus outbreak, Fräulein
Gertrud Slottke, a German administrator in the Labor Office,
decided she should sleep in the basement there rather than
in the lice-infested barrack of the Star Camp. Leah said that
each morning, Fräulein Slottke would unlock the hatch to the
basement and she would come up with a bucket of coal to start
the fires in the stoves, then bring up potatoes to cook for the
German secretaries who worked in the Labor Office. Her own
ration was one potato each morning, but she supplemented
that with whatever food the office workers tossed in the garbage throughout the day. Each evening, she was allotted a
serving of rutabaga soup before descending to the basement
with a bucket of water, which she used for washing as well
as drinking. There was one other bucket that served as her
toilet facilities. She had a blanket but no other bedding. She
had no control over when the lights were turned off. To guard
against sabotage or theft, Fräulein Slottke locked her in at
night. "Each time I went down there," she told me, "I felt like
Euridice condemned to Hades."

Days before the British liberated the camp, Leah said, the
company Dehomag came with trucks to take away the Hollerith
machines. All that day, Fräulein Slottke ordered files and punch

cards and lists and codebooks to be burned. That night, Leah was locked in the basement as usual, but the next morning no one came to let her out. The Germans had fled, leaving her behind, forgotten. She rationed her water for as long as possible, but eventually it ran out. She had no idea how many days had passed, and she had lost hope of ever being rescued until she heard feet stomping on the floor above her. With the last of her strength, she crawled up the steps and knocked on the hatch.

When I compared her account to the timeline of British liberation of Bergen-Belsen, I realized she had been forgotten in that basement for at least twenty-eight days. Her survival was miraculous. If not for the potatoes, which had some moisture as well as calories, she would surely have perished. I felt personally responsible for her care and spent as much time with her as possible while she recovered. When she told me that she had studied linguistics, I asked what other languages she could speak. In addition to Dutch and English, she listed German and French as fluent modern languages. She had studied classics, too. Latin helped her speak a bit of Italian and gave her a foundation for understanding some Portuguese, while her classical Greek enabled her to communicate in a rudimentary fashion with Jewish refugees from Salonika. She understood the Hebrew alphabet well enough to read Yiddish and had picked up some Russian during the time she spent in Westerbork, she said, as well as learning a bit of Turkish and a South American dialect called Sranan.

Not only was I amazed at her intellect, but I immediately saw how useful she could be to the JAC in our work. More immediately, she could help in the hospital. Most of the British nurses spoke some schoolgirl French, but this was useless when dealing with Jews who spoke Yiddish, German, or Russian. Leah's skill as a translator could not be capitalized on while she was still so weak, however. In order to speed her recovery, I had her transferred to my personal care. I moved her into my quarters, which were quieter and more comfortable than the field hospital, and supplemented her Bengal mixture with my own rations, which her digestion could now tolerate. I also requisitioned new clothes for her from the vast stores of stolen goods the Nazis had warehoused in a hut they called, for some reason, Canada.

Within a fortnight, Leah Blom began assisting me as a translator. People were streaming into the camp from across Europe, and each new arrival needed to be interviewed before being provided with documents. Some of the Dutch Jews were making arrangements to return to the Netherlands to search for their families, but as Leah's parents had already perished, I was able to persuade her to stay on with the Red Cross through the summer as Bergen-Belsen was transformed into a displaced persons (DP) camp.

THE DELEGATION

In June, a delegation arrived, under the auspices of President Truman's investigation into the conditions of displaced persons in Europe. The head of the delegation was Mr. Earl Harrison. Assisting him was my father, Mr. Joseph Silver. The Harrison Report is well-known; I will not repeat its findings here. Of concern to this narrative was my father's request that I join the delegation while they toured other DP camps. I impressed upon him how crucial it would be for us to have a translator to help conduct interviews with survivors. I suggested Leah Blom for the job, and he agreed to arrange for the travel documents she would need to accompany us. When I proposed this to Leah, she became very agitated, saying she was concerned about some cards she had managed to save. She insisted I take her back to the Labor Office, which had been repurposed into headquarters for the Harrison delegation.

Leah Blom led me into the basement. Finding a crowbar, she began prying lath from the ceiling to reveal the floor joists. As the lath was pried away, thousands of rectangular cards with tiny holes in them began to rain down on us (see attached example). Leah explained that the Labor Office in Bergen-Belsen had a punch card for each prisoner in the camp. These cards were fed through a Hollerith machine to create the lists that were used for roll call, and also to update Berlin on the "daily strength totals" in the camp so that Eichmann's Jewish Division could orchestrate the movement of prisoners throughout their concentration camp system. Leah explained that whenever a prisoner died, escaped, or was executed, their name was stricken from the roll, at which point their card became obsolete and was thrown away. For months, she had secretly preserved these cards by hiding them in the cavities between the joists. Mixed in with the cards from Bergen-Belsen were other cards that she had brought with her from Westerbork, she said.

Leah claimed her trove of cards contained evidence of Nazi war crimes, though as far as I could see they had no evidentiary value. There were no names written on them. In fact, nothing was written on them at all. They were coded with numbers by means of holes punched through the paper. I brought in one of the British intelligence officers, but he said it was the registration files that were useful for tracing prisoners, not these cards. The Red Cross had begun to compile the Central Location Index to help survivors find family members, but when I showed a nurse working on the index one of the punch cards, she expressed no understanding or interest in it.

Leah was very depressed by this, and I worried she would lose her motivation to help our investigation. My father had mentioned to me an effort called the International Tracing Service (ITS) that was gathering archival materials about Nazi atrocities in a place called Bad Arolsen. I proposed to Leah that if she helped us complete the investigation for our report, which was due at the end of August, I would personally take her to Bad Arolsen, where she could donate her cards to the ITS. She agreed, after which we spent hours in the basement of the Labor Office retrieving thousands of punch cards and packing them into a footlocker, which I added to our luggage. During the course of the next two months, Leah proved to be an invaluable member of the delegation. However, Mr. Harrison felt that relying so heavily on a Jewish survivor for the translation of testimony might give the impression of bias. As a result, her contribution was omitted from all internal JAC memoranda and her name redacted from the final report to President Truman.

CONCLUSION

Once the delegation's report was complete, I kept my promise to Leah Blom. After loading the footlocker of punch cards into a borrowed car, we drove through the American occupation zone to Bad Arolsen, a town miraculously untouched by the ravages of war, where I secured us accommodation in a comfortable hotel. On the following day, we went to the SS training school that the ITS had repurposed into an archive of Nazi war crimes. Unfortunately, when Leah tried to donate her collection, the archivist had the same reaction as the Red Cross nurse: the punch cards were meaningless. Leah tried to explain how, with the Hollerith machine and the right codes, the cards could be used to generate a list of prisoners by number and birth date that would document their fate. The

archivist, who'd never heard of a Hollerith machine, said the
ITS was creating a system based on names, not numbers. She
thanked us for our offer but declined to accept Leah Blom's
collection of punch cards.

After one last night in Bad Arolsen, Leah Blom disappeared.
She left no hint of her destination, though I assumed she was
making her way back to the Netherlands. I subsequently re-
joined my father on his return to New York, where I focused on
fundraising to support the DPs still in Europe. This document,
which I have written on my own initiative in the interest of historical accuracy, is the only narrative describing Leah Blom's
work on our behalf.

J acob was bleary-eyed from staring at the small, dense type. "But why would the archivist reject Leah's cards?"

"Without a correctly programmed computing machine, the cards don't mean anything. Look." I showed him the last Xeroxed page. Jacob stared at the image of the Hollerith card as if the intensity of his gaze could pry meaning from the pattern of punched holes.

"But what if one of those cards was my mother's? I know her birth date. Couldn't we find her based on that?"

"Only if we knew which columns were designated for birth dates, or which codes meant which countries. Then an engineer would have to program a control panel based on those codes, and he'd need a computing machine to process them. I'm sorry, Jacob, but none of this is helpful." I felt bad being so blunt, but I saw now this quest was a fool's errand. Jacob was tilting at windmills if he believed there was a trace of his mother in the pages of this report, let alone in Leah Blom's lost batch of punch cards. "I know you hoped for more. Please don't let this get you down."

"I guess I expected miracles, but there are no miracles here."

"Do you want to go to the Jewish Aid Committee tomorrow to meet the author, Edith Silver? It's possible she might have something to tell us."

"What's the use?" He tossed the report on the coffee table and strode off to the bathroom. I waited nervously, not knowing which version of Jacob would come back to my mother's couch. When he did take his place beside me, I held my breath until he spoke, his voice soft and sad.

"I appreciate you helping me understand the report, but honestly, I've known for years my mother is lost to me forever. It's about time I accept this fact, or I'll never be able to live my life or look to the future. Thank you, though, Little Rita, for everything you've done for me."

I crawled onto his lap and put my arms around him. "I think I'd do just about anything for you, Jacob." Sitting on his lap, I felt his reaction to that. He kissed me, his tongue searching for comfort in my mouth while his hands slid up my thighs. "Not in my parents' house, though," I said, laughing quietly. "Let's put you to bed before we get in real trouble, okay?"

In the morning, Jacob was already at the kitchen table when I came in for breakfast. Mom was dishing eggs onto his plate while he and Dad discussed Eisenhower's speech from last night, which was printed in the morning paper.

"Sit down and have some coffee, Rita," Mom said, pouring me a cup. "The president's got a good head on his shoulders, don't you think so, Irving?"

"The Republicans were idiots to push through the Twenty-Second Amendment," Dad said. "They were afraid of another Roosevelt, but now we're gonna be stuck with Nixon as our candidate because Ike can't run again. What was it the president said last night about the use of atomic weapons?"

Jacob turned the page. "Here it is. 'Since 1953, it has been clear that the accumulation of atomic weapons stockpiles, whose use could destroy civilization, made resort to force an intolerable means for settling international disputes.'"

"Can't we start our day with a more uplifting topic?" I asked. "I thought we had a deal, Jacob."

"Of course. Let's see what else is happening in the world." Jacob rustled the paper. "Maybe you'd like to hear about the typhoon in Manila?" He was teasing me, his mouth hitched up in that crooked smile of his. I was glad to see the dark circles under his eyes had finally disappeared. Maybe letting go of false hope had brought him some peace after all.

I swatted his arm. "Try again." He turned the page and I pointed to the dateline HOLLANDIA, NETHERLANDS NEW GUINEA. "I've been meaning to ask you why the Dutch colonized an island off the coast of Australia populated by Papuans."

"I'll explain the history of the Dutch East India Company in the Spice Islands," Jacob bantered, "if you can tell me how a volcanic archipelago in the Pacific Ocean became America's fiftieth state."

"Don't talk to me about Hawaii," Mom said. She was still upset about having to replace her souvenir American flags last year after statehood for Alaska and Hawaii made the forty-eight stars obsolete. "Now listen, Rita, Jacob was saying he's not scheduled to work until tomorrow. 'What are you going to do with yourself all day?' I asked. He didn't know, so I invited him to the B'nai B'rith luncheon at the synagogue today."

I looked at Jacob skeptically. "You want to go to a luncheon with my mother?"

"She asked me to speak about my experiences, to help raise money for Israel."

"Oh, Mom, don't make him do that."

"I only asked. No one's forcing him to do anything."

"I'd like to do it," Jacob said. "Let me repay your mother for her kindness to me."

"What's it to you, Rita?" Dad said. "You've got to work anyway."

If you had seen Jacob at Bellevue, you wouldn't be asking me that question, I thought. But I did have to work that day, and so did Rudy, which meant the alternative would be for Jacob to spend all those hours alone. "Promise me you won't push yourself, Jacob. Remember, you're still getting over a flu."

"I took his temperature this morning," Mom said. "He's perfectly fine."

I looked at my parents, so eager to make a friend of this stranger. It made me wonder, if Jacob ever proposed marriage, would it be because he wanted me for a wife or because he wanted my parents for his own?

When he walked me to the bus stop later, I asked again if he was sure about speaking at my mother's luncheon. "Don't worry about me, Little Rita." He kissed me goodbye. "Just hurry home."

Jacob seemed reconciled to everything now, but having seen how agitated and depressed he could become, I wasn't sure his equanimity would last. On the way to Manhattan, I decided I'd go see Edith Silver after all. If she had nothing to add, I wouldn't even mention it to him, but I wanted to be certain this whole episode of the Blom Report was wrapped up once and for all.

There was something I needed to wrap up for myself, too. I'd realized last night I couldn't count on Jacob to think about getting a prescription for condoms. Besides, it was my destiny that was on the line, not his, and I needed to control it myself. I racked my brain until I remembered the name of that doctor with the reputation among the girls at Barnard for providing expensive abortions. If he was willing to do that for the right price, I figured he'd be willing to prescribe birth control to an unmarried woman. In the lobby of the Empire State Building, I shut myself up in a phone booth and found the doctor's name in the directory. I asked the nurse who answered for the next available appointment, saying I was a college student with a problem I couldn't talk to my family doctor about.

"Is this a time-sensitive matter?" I knew what she was hinting at, but I said yes anyway. "I can squeeze you in this Friday at three o'clock, but don't be late. The doctor is heading out to the Hamptons for the holiday weekend right after that." I promised to be there early. "The initial consultation is fifty dollars, in cash. Can you pay that, Miss Klein?"

"Yes, I can." I was grateful I had enough to cover the exorbitant fee, though it annoyed me to think Jacob could have gotten condoms for a few bucks. It was as if simply being born a woman came with added costs. I rode the elevator up to Antiquated, nervous at the prospect of dealing with yet another doctor who'd undoubtedly look down on me. It would be worth whatever I had to put up with, though, to safeguard my future. I reminded myself I was a legal adult who earned her own money. From now on, I wouldn't let my parents or Dr. Nelson or anyone else tell me what to do.

I was finishing a sandwich at my desk when Mr. McKay asked me to go to Brooklyn to bring my latest report for the navy contract to Francie—and to hand-deliver our new invoice, too.

"Make sure she understands she'll have to pay within thirty days if she wants us to keep processing their accounts," Mr. McKay said. I felt bad for Francie, but why shouldn't Antiquated protect itself, I thought, as I hailed a taxi for Fulton Ferry.

"Every month, really?" Francie shook back her red hair and lit a cigarette. The piles on her desk had grown even more precarious. When she pulled the checkbook out from under a stack of invoices, it nearly caused an avalanche. "Well, here, take this with you. I can't afford to lose Frank now, or you, either. How's it going?"

I reviewed my report, which showed that Olympia was on track to fulfill the navy contract without incurring any penalties— though at a much greater cost than what they'd bid. "At least you'll be eligible for an initial payment as soon as you make your first delivery."

"Thank you, Jesus," she muttered. "The foreman's got all the spoons stamped, pressed, polished, and weighed. He's having them packed today. Jimmy will be thrilled to finally get some of that government money."

"Where is he?" I hated to ask, but I was starting to wonder if Francie's brother-in-law was a figment of her imagination.

"He's having lunch at Fraunces Tavern with his golfing buddy. He said he'd be back later, but I'm not holding my breath." She blew out a stream of smoke. "That boy's a fool even before his first martini."

I stuck around Olympia for another hour out of curiosity, which was satisfied when Jimmy Plunkett came stumbling into Francie's office reeking of cigars and gin. He was shockingly good-looking, with jet hair and sapphire eyes and an athlete's physique. If his older brother had half his looks, it was no wonder Francie had fallen for him.

We were introduced, but after a sloppy kiss to the back of my hand, he ignored me as he launched into a sales pitch aimed at his hapless sister-in-law. The banker-cum-restaurateur he'd been wooing on the golf course was so impressed with Olympia's prospects since they'd secured the navy contract that he wanted in.

"In?" Francie frowned. "What do you mean, in?"

"In as in . . ." Jimmy burped. "In partnership. He wants to buy a third of the company, for cash!" He reached out as if to swing Francie in a dance step, but she held him back.

"What third, Jimmy? You've got fifty percent and so do I."

"Exactly! We each sell—" His brow wrinkled.

"Sixteen and a half percent," I said.

"Right, we each sell sixteen percent, then we're all equal partners. We'll use his cash to keep this place going, but together we'll still have controlling shares. He's got some great ideas about expansion, though. Why open just one restaurant, he says, when you can supply hundreds? We'll talk it over later, okay? I gotta hit the can."

Jimmy lurched through the door. "Wait up," she called, following him out. "I got some questions for you."

Finding myself alone in her office, I took out that business card the archivist had given me, found the phone on Francie's desk, and called the Jewish Aid Committee. When Edith Silver got on the line, she bluntly asked if I was the one who'd requested her report yesterday. "I am, yes. I was hoping you could tell me a little more about it? I'm asking for a friend. His mother was in Bergen-Belsen but there's no documentation about her fate."

"You read my report?" There was an edge to her voice that made me wonder if talking about this was upsetting her.

"We did, yes."

After a long pause, she said, "Can you be in the lobby of the News Building by four o'clock?"

"Sure." I'd have to take a taxi directly from Brooklyn, but hopefully Mr. McKay wouldn't mind if I didn't come back to the office today.

"Fine, see you then." She hung up before I could ask how I'd recognize her.

I'd just left a message at Antiquated and called for a cab when Francie came back in. "Sorry you had to see that, Rita." She dropped into her chair like she'd run a marathon. "That boy'll be the death of me."

"So you've said. What do you think of this offer?"

"It doesn't feel right." She took out her cigarettes but the pack was empty. "I don't think Joey would've wanted me to give up ownership of the company to some stranger."

"What would Joey have wanted for you, Francie?"

"You really wanna know?" Her emerald eyes flashed like cut

glass. "All my Joey ever wanted was for me to put my feet up once in a while, and that's the damned truth."

I sat down and looked her square in the eye. "Do you want to know what I think, Francie?"

"Yeah, I do."

I took a deep breath. Mr. McKay would say it wasn't my place, but I couldn't hold back. "I think you should offer to sell out completely. Let Jimmy and this banker be equal partners, fifty-fifty. Get your money and walk away from this place. Take your kids to the beach. Take a class if you want, or get a different job if you need to, or sit on the couch watching television." I scooted closer and dropped my voice to as close to a whisper as I could in that noisy place. "The way things are going, Olympia could be bankrupt by next year. Maybe this banker can turn it around, but if I were you, I wouldn't risk it. He can probably afford to lose his investment. You can't."

There were real tears in her eyes as she grabbed my hand. "Thanks for telling it to me straight, kid. I'll think about it."

The woman standing by the rotating globe in the lobby of the News Building looked the right age to be Edith Silver—I figured she'd be about forty by now—but she didn't fit my preconceived notion of a society do-gooder with a philanthropist father. She was dressed in linen slacks and a paisley blouse, like one of those sketch artists in Washington Square Park. Her tousled hair was loosely tied with a silk scarf that trailed down to her waist. Her brown eyes, when she spotted me coming toward her, were as soulful as a folk singer's.

"Miss Klein?" She held out a hand whose nails were blunt and unpolished.

"Rita Klein, yes. Thank you so much for meeting me, Miss Silver."

"Edith, please. I reread that old report this morning. It brought back a lot of bad memories."

"I'm sorry about that." I stood stiffly by the globe as Africa gave way to the Atlantic, wondering if she intended to have our whole conversation in the lobby. "But the thing is, I work with computing machines, and I was curious to hear more about this collection of punch cards. You didn't say what happened to them after they were rejected by the archive in—where was it?"

"Bad Arolsen. Look, I can spare you half an hour. Let's talk over a drink. Where are you going after this?" When I told her the Port Authority, she suggested the Oyster Bar at Grand Central. "Then it'll be an easy walk for you to the bus terminal, and I can catch the Lexington line down to Astor Place." I agreed, smiling to myself about how right I'd been to place Edith Silver in Greenwich Village.

Grand Central Station, with that winged statue of Mercury standing guard over the old Tiffany clock, was as out of place among the skyscrapers of midtown as some remnant of European history. The ceiling inside was so grimy I could hardly make out the constellations, but the concourse still had a sense of grandeur. We found seats along the Oyster Bar's counter and ordered a couple of whiskey sours.

"So, what more can I tell you?"

I popped a maraschino cherry in my mouth, then launched into as concise an explanation as possible of Jacob's quest and how he'd gotten the notion that my knowledge of computing machines might enable me to find some clue in the Blom Report that he'd missed when he first read it. "I already told him those cards aren't enough by themselves, but I was surprised Leah Blom didn't take them with her, after all the trouble she went through to save them."

"Leah was terribly upset after Bad Arolsen." Edith's gaze seemed lost among the glazed tiles of the Guastavino ceiling. "She took the rejection hard."

"You can't really blame the archivist, though. Even now, hardly anyone understands what computing machines can do, much less how they work."

"How did you learn so much about them?" Edith asked, focusing again on me.

I told her about being a mathematics major at Barnard and the Watson Laboratory computing course I'd taken.

"That's impressive," she said. "Math was never my strong suit. I went to Bennington for literature."

"Is that the women's college in Vermont?"

She nodded, a nostalgic look softening her face. "It's so beautiful there. My parents hadn't even heard of it when I applied, but I convinced them it was the only place for me."

We got into a conversation comparing Barnard to Bennington. The half hour she'd allotted to our meeting came and went. I didn't even realize the bartender had brought us a second round until I lifted my glass to finish my drink and found it full again.

"Here's to finding what you're looking for."

I clinked my glass to hers. "Thanks. My friend Jacob says he's not going to obsess about finding his mother anymore, but until he knows for sure what happened to her, I don't think he'll ever give up hope."

"Rita, listen." Edith leaned in and spoke softly. "When the Red Cross got to Bergen-Belsen, people were still dying by the hundreds every day. The British soldiers were too afraid of typhus to enter the barracks. They left giant pots of soup at the entrances and let people fight it out among themselves. Everyone was crazed with starvation. Each morning, the survivors would carry out the bodies of people who'd died in the night. They had to be buried quickly before they spread disease. The military could hardly count the dead, let alone keep a record of their names or prisoner numbers. The best estimate is that twenty-three thousand people perished in the three months following liberation. If your friend hasn't heard anything about his mother, the only logical conclusion is that hers was one of those anonymous bodies."

My hand shook as I drained my drink. Edith threw hers back, too. When the bartender stopped by, Edith told him we were through. He took what we owed from the bills she'd put on the bar. "Keep the rest," she said, getting off her stool. "I'll walk you out, Rita. I need some fresh air."

The air on Vanderbilt Avenue wasn't exactly fresh—the afternoon had gotten hot and humid, with anvil clouds threatening rain—but it did me good to be outside. Those two drinks I'd downed so quickly were going to my head. "Thanks for meeting me, Edith."

"I'm sorry I wasn't more help to you," she said, shaking the hand I held out to her.

"I was hoping to be the heroine who saves the day," I admitted, "but I guess those punch cards were all buried in some German garbage dump decades ago."

Edith dropped my hand and plucked at her collar. "Anyway, tell your friend I'm sorry for his loss."

"I will. Here." I fumbled my notepad out of my pocketbook and wrote down my number. "If you think of anything else, maybe you'll give me a call?"

She took my note and put it in her pocket. "Are you sure you're all right to walk to the bus terminal?"

"Once I get going, I'll be fine." My tongue felt thick in my mouth.

Edith looked skeptical. "Remember to stay on the north side of Forty-Second Street."

"Don't worry, I know better than to go near Bryant Park." I lifted my hand in a little wave. "Good night, Edith."

"Goodbye, Rita."

I managed to get to the terminal without tripping over any

curbs. Once I was on the bus, though, I practically passed out, snoring all the way to Teaneck. I was still a little wobbly walking down Cedar Lane. When I got home, Jacob was in the kitchen with an apron tied around his waist getting a cooking lesson from my mother. I guessed those drinks had made me cranky because I muttered, "Whose boyfriend are you, anyway?"

Jacob took off the apron and came over to me. "So, I'm your boyfriend, am I?"

Blushing, I walked into his arms. "You know you are."

I decided then and there I wouldn't even tell him I'd met Edith Silver. The things she'd said about Bergen-Belsen were too terrible to repeat. I wanted his focus to stay on what was ahead of him, not what he'd left behind.

Mom smiled at me from over his shoulder. See, her expression said, didn't I tell you everything would be all right? As if it never happened, I thought, closing my eyes and resting my forehead on his chest.

Chapter Twenty-Four
Edith Silver

New York City
June 1960

I should've walked that girl to the bus terminal, Edith Silver thinks, losing sight of Rita among the pedestrians on Forty-Second Street. Then Edith reminds herself what her analyst keeps telling her: you can't save everyone. Besides, she'd have to run to catch up to the girl by now. If she's still preoccupied with it later, Edith decides, she'll call the number Rita gave her to make sure she got home all right.

Edith reenters the station and goes down to the subway. Waiting on the platform, she tries to dispel those awful memories of Bergen-Belsen with a vigorous shake of her head. All she manages to do is make herself dizzy. She checks her watch, then leans out over the tracks to look down the tunnel. She never should have agreed to meet that girl today. At the very least, she shouldn't have had that second drink. She's worried she'll be late, that Carol won't be there when she gets home, that she'll miss her last chance.

The train pulls in with a blast of hot air. It's rush hour by now and the car is crowded. Edith winds up on her feet, hanging from a strap.

There is no last chance, she scolds herself. It's over. It's been over for months, ever since Carol packed up and moved out. Edith has been pretending that the few things Carol left behind—books on the shelf, records in the stereo cabinet, her favorite mug hanging from a hook above the kitchen sink—mean she isn't really gone for good. But today she's coming to get those last things, and once they're boxed up and taken away, it'll be as if Carol never lived with her at all.

Edith gets increasingly anxious about the passing minutes as the local train makes every stop. When she finally comes up from the subway at Astor Place, she's tempted to run but keeps her pace to a quick walk, not wanting to arrive all sweaty and out of breath. Crossing Washington Square Park, she hustles past the out-of-towners consulting their maps and fiddling with their cameras. Coming up Washington Place, she sees Carol sitting on the stoop of the town house that, for that past thirteen years, Edith has thought of as not her property but their home.

"Hey." Carol stands up and Edith's stupid heart skips a beat. She remembers the first time she saw Carol, on the beach at Cherry Grove, grains of sand glittering on her golden skin, blond hair sparkling in the sun. Edith tried to play it cool, but she was a goner the second Carol lowered her sunglasses and flashed those big blue eyes of hers.

"Hey." Edith edges past her on the stoop and unlocks the door. She could have spared herself this if she hadn't insisted Carol return the key. "Sorry I'm late."

"You're not late. I was early." Carol picks up the roll of twine and the cardboard boxes, folded flat, that she brought to accomplish the task at hand.

"Got someplace to be?" Edith regrets the snark in her tone.

"Nope, just finished my cases a little sooner than I expected today."

They're in the vestibule now, a cramped space small as a closet. How many nights did they stumble into its cozy embrace, barely able to keep their hands off each other until they were safely sheltered from the view of the street? It feels like hundreds to Edith, though if she really thinks about it, only a handful of times come to mind. In the living room, they stand awkwardly for a moment in front of the cold grate of the fireplace, its mirrored overmantel reaching all the way to the ceiling.

"How are José and Esmeralda doing?" Edith doesn't know, anymore, the story of each and every child Carol is managing in foster care, but there are some old cases she still cares about.

"Oh, this'll make you happy." Carol smiles. This would be much easier, Edith thinks, if she weren't so gorgeous. "Their mother was released from the sanitarium in April. She moved back in with her folks, and she's been holding down a job for about a month now. I think I'll be able to get her custody of the kids again soon."

Edith forgets her petty feelings for a minute as she genuinely wishes Carol luck.

"Thanks," Carol says. "Well, I guess I better get to it."

"Need some help?"

"Do you have any packing tape?"

Edith finds the tape and puts together boxes while Carol wanders around, collecting the books and records that belong to her. The town house felt extravagantly spacious when it was the two of them; for one person it's ridiculously big. There's the large eat-in kitchen down on the garden level, with French doors out to the patio. On the first floor, eight-foot-tall windows let light flow through the living room into the dining room. There are three bedrooms on the second floor: the one they shared, one for guests, and the one they pretended was Carol's when relatives came to visit.

As Carol fills the boxes, Edith notices a few things they bought together, but she tells herself to let it go. She even helps by wrapping the mug in newspaper, secretly picturing the shape of Carol's lipstick print on its rim.

"Do you mind if I go up to the attic? I don't think I've got anything up there, but I should probably check."

"You don't want to ever have to come back here again, is that it?"

"Edith." Carol puts her hand on Edith's arm. "Please don't be like this."

"Like what? I'm not like anything. Come on, I'll go up with you."

Edith hardly ever ventures up to the low-ceilinged rooms intended for children and servants that, for decades, have only been used for storage. The furniture, a jumble of antiques Edith inherited from her grandmother along with the house, is draped in dusty sheets. A few years ago, after a leaky faucet went undetected for months, Edith had a plumber install valves so she could shut off the supply of water to the bathroom up here. She keeps the radiators turned low in winter, and in summer she opens the windows so heat won't build up. Edith knows she ought to convert the space to an apartment—most of the town houses around Washington Square were long ago divided into two, three, even four units—but she doesn't like the idea of strangers in her building.

Once, when Carol was having trouble finding a foster family willing to take three siblings, Edith suggested she bring the kids home to live with them. They could clear out those attic rooms and get the plumbing working again. Edith imagined hearing little footsteps above their heads when one of the kids got up at night for a glass of water. Carol said Edith was sweet to suggest it, but she couldn't risk bringing children into their house, not even for one night. She'd lose her job if anyone at her agency suspected she and Edith were more than spinster roommates.

"See anything?" Edith asks as Carol sticks her head into one doorway after another.

"No, nothing. Wait, what's that over there?"

"That old coat tree? Must have been my grandmother's. It was here when I moved in."

"Oh, that's right. I thought maybe we got it at a flea market or something. I only noticed because we've been looking for one for our place."

Edith thinks of the ways she can hurt Carol for making that remark. None of them will make her feel any better. She navigates the crowded room and carries the coat tree out into the hallway. "Take it."

"I can't do that, Edith."

"Really, I want you to." Edith wishes she could stop the tears from spilling out of her eyes, but she can't, so she lets them drip. "I want you to be happy, Carol, more than anything in the world. Consider it a housewarming gift."

Carol knows better than to wipe the tears from Edith's face. Her touch, no matter how gentle, will only sting. "Thank you."

"Can you manage to get it down the stairs?" Edith drags the cuff of her blouse across her eyes. "I'm going to stay up here and look for something."

"Sure. I'll call a taxi and have the driver help me with those boxes. I'll see you around, okay, Edith?"

"See you around, Carol."

Edith tries not to hear Carol clomping down the stairs with that coat tree, or the taxi honking its horn out on Washington Place, or the front door slamming shut after Carol calls up a final goodbye. She goes back into one of the attic rooms and pulls a sheet off an old footlocker. Over a decade of dust swirls up in the air like a genie released from a bottle. Edith hasn't so much as touched the thing since she returned from Germany in 1945. It was that girl's showing up today that got her thinking about the woman she once raised from the dead. "Don't turn around!" Leah had teased that last night in Bad Arolsen. "If you look at me, I'll have to go back to Hades forever."

Edith kneels in front of the footlocker, undoes the clasps, and lifts the lid. Packed in tight bundles, protected for fifteen years from too much heat or cold or light, are thousands of Hollerith cards punched through with millions of tiny holes.

Edith sits back on her heels, remembering.

One of the officials traveling with the Harrison delegation drove a rusty Ford Köln that had been kicking around Frankfurt since the 1930s. After they finished their tour of the DP camps, Edith convinced her father to lend her the car for a couple of days. Though she'd initially proposed the trip to Bad Arolsen to secure Leah's help, over the course of the summer Edith realized she'd fallen in love with the brave and brilliant young woman with the beautiful green eyes. Edith had no intention of declaring her feelings, and no expectation that Leah would reciprocate them, but her heart was set on spending these last few days together. Edith's father wanted to send a man along for protection, but she'd insisted on getting away with Leah, just the two of them. He accused her of being reckless, adventuresome, rebellious—but Edith held firm, and as always when his daughter wanted something badly enough, he'd given in.

She and Leah packed a change of clothes, loaded the footlocker into the rear seat, and set out toward the spa town of Bad Arolsen. Driving through the American occupation zone simplified things for Edith, who could show not only her passport but an official State Department letter, too. Leah's papers were more tenuous. As a displaced person, she had no passport, but between the identification the Red Cross had provided her in Bergen-Belsen and the travel documents she'd been supplied by the Harrison delegation, the only real holdup they encountered at the checkpoints was from soldiers whose flirting bordered on harassment.

When Edith and Leah arrived in Bad Arolsen that evening, it was like being transported back in time, not only to the Baroque period of the spas and castles that dotted the town, but to an era of peace and elegance, before the chaos and destruction of war. In their beautiful hotel, they marveled at the immaculate sheets, the elegant furniture, the wallpaper patterned with peacocks. Each took a turn bathing in the clawfoot tub filled with that rarest of luxuries: gallons of hot water.

At the hotel's restaurant that night, candlelight reflected off silver cutlery that had somehow survived the war's insatiable appetite for metal. The only indication of scarcity was a limited menu featuring schnitzel made with chicken instead of veal. But the Riesling was of a collectible vintage, the spätzle was rich with eggs, and a wedge of lemon glowed like a rare jewel on the rim of the Meissen plate.

"Tomorrow," Edith said, "after we drop off your cards at the archive, I was thinking we might go for a swim at one of the spas. Would you like that?"

Leah's mind seemed to have wandered someplace far away. "A swim, yes. I haven't had a swim since the last time I was on the beach at Scheveningen."

Edith was as pleased as a parent to see Leah finish every bite of her dinner. A waiter cleared the table, asking a question in German, which Leah answered. As he stepped back, Edith noticed his eyes flick toward the little Star of David on Leah's necklace. Edith and her father were circumspect about advertising their religion, but Leah seemed to consider it a point of pride to voluntarily display the symbol she'd been forced to wear by the Nazis.

"What was that about?"

"He asked if we wanted coffee and dessert," Leah said. "I told him we'd take it in our room."

"Oh, okay, if that's what you want, but I was hoping we could take a walk through the town after dinner."

"I'm sorry, Edith, I'm not up for it."

Leah was sick the minute they returned to their room. Edith rubbed her back while Leah retched into the toilet. When the waiter arrived, Edith sent away the coffee and cake and asked for mint tea instead.

"I'm so sorry," Edith said. "I should have realized the food would be too rich for you."

"That's not it." Leah's chest rose and fell as her breath came in rapid bursts. "I can't stop thinking . . . I don't understand—"

"Don't understand what?"

"How there could be people in the world eating cake and drinking wine while we were starving to death in that hell."

Leah wavered then. Edith's open arms broke her fall. Leah clung to Edith as if she were a rope thrown down a well as Edith carried her to bed. "Hush now, you need your rest."

But Leah was determined to speak. "I wasn't with Lillian when she died, or Philip, either. I'll never forgive myself for failing them, but Slottke had started locking me up by then. The first day no one came to open the hatch, I thought she'd found out about the cards and was punishing me. By the next day, I realized she'd left me there to rot. It was so dark down in that cellar. I was so alone. I didn't know how much it hurt to be so alone."

"You poor darling," Edith cooed, wiping Leah's hot cheeks with a cool cloth.

"My mind played terrible tricks on me, Edith." Leah's voice was a rasping whisper. "I almost went crazy down there, all alone in the dark."

She started crying then, waves of weeping that crested and fell like a receding tide. When Leah was finally wrung dry of tears, Edith held the cold mug of mint tea to her lips. Leah gulped it greedily.

"How did you stay sane until I found you?" Edith imagined Leah in the cellar shuffling through languages in her mind like cards in a deck, conjugating verbs or reciting vocabulary, anything to keep her mind from cracking.

"I don't know. I almost didn't. Then God saw me." Leah rested her head against Edith's shoulder. "I was barely human anymore. I remember crawling on my hands and knees in the dark, gnawing on potatoes like a rat or a mole. I couldn't tell if I was awake or asleep. I wasn't a person. I didn't know my own name. I was so small, like an ant or an atom. It was as if I'd stopped existing. I was terrified I'd vanish, like a forgotten thought. Then, shining through the dark, there was an eye." Leah pinched the Star of David between the tips of her fingers and looked up at Edith, her face filled with wonder. "It wasn't anything like that old man on the ceiling of the Sistine Chapel, but I knew it was the eye of God. He saw me, Edith. Like the beam of a lighthouse searching for a soul lost at sea, He saw me. He knew everything I felt. He knew all my pain. He knew my despair. He saw me and He loved me and I was part of Him and I knew I would never be alone ever again. He couldn't stay long. There were so many of us for Him to look after. But in all the universe, for that one moment, it was me He saw."

Edith didn't realize she was crying until Leah reached out to dry her eyes. No word she'd ever heard a rabbi utter was as miraculous as Leah's vision. "You're an incredible woman, do you know that, Leah?"

She shook her head. "What I am is exhausted, Edith."

"Go to sleep now, darling," Edith said, stroking Leah's hair. They curled up together, still in their street clothes but shed of shoes and stockings, and let sleep come.

Edith woke to a kiss on her forehead. "Thank you for taking care of me last night."

Her heart beat so hard from Leah's kiss, she was shocked the bed wasn't shaking. Edith feigned nonchalance by replying in French. "*De rien.*"

"But it wasn't nothing. It meant everything to me."

They had bread and cheese and coffee brought to their room. Leah ate, and kept it down. The sun was high and hot later that morning when they arrived at the building where the archives of the International Tracing Service were being assembled.

"I'm looking forward to going to the spa after this," Leah said.

Edith smiled. "It'll be good for you, Leah. Good for both of us."

It broke Edith's heart to see Leah slip into despair when the archivist rejected her cards. Even an afternoon of floating in mineral water at the spa didn't lift her spirits. They hardly spoke over dinner that night, a simple vegetable stew with potato dumplings. Edith took Leah's arm as they walked silently through the town afterward, its lampposts creating pools of light along the cobbled streets. "I've gone far enough," Leah finally said. "Can we go up to our room now?"

As Leah got undressed for bed, her numb disappointment gave way to nervous agitation. "What was the point of it all? I told myself I was doing something good saving those cards, that I was bearing witness somehow—oh, it all sounds so stupid now. I can't even pretend I did it for any reason but my own selfish survival."

"You did what you had to do, Leah." Edith cupped her face in her hands. "Please, don't blame yourself for surviving."

"You don't blame me, do you?"

"Of course not, darling. You're blameless." Edith hesitated. "And so beautiful."

Leah didn't say anything back, just stared at her, green eyes open wide. Edith was worried she'd said too much. When Leah kissed her lips, she resisted the thrill that shimmied through her body and pulled back. "Are you sure?"

Leah nodded, her head moving decisively up and down.

With their second kiss, Edith allowed herself to believe in miracles for the second time in as many days. She had never dared hope her feelings might be reciprocated, but now that it was happening, she assumed she would be the experienced one. Leah, however, needed no tutoring. She was ravenous to touch, to taste, to handle every inch of Edith's body. Edith had never been so passive before—not with her roommate at Bennington, not among the friends she'd made in Greenwich Village, not with that Red Cross nurse in London. In Leah's hands, though, she was clay to be sculpted and shaped. She drifted, finally, to sleep in Leah's arms.

When Edith woke alone, she assumed Leah had gone for breakfast. Then she realized Leah's travel documents were missing, along with her clothes. Edith got dressed and ran down to see if the car was gone, too, but the Köln was still parked in the courtyard of the hotel. The concierge explained that her companion had roused him at dawn to be taken to the train station. She must be halfway to Essen by now, he said.

Edith dragged her broken heart back up to the room they'd shared. What had she expected, that they'd cross the Atlantic together and live happily ever after? Of course Leah had run away from her. How could she ever put the horror of that basement behind her if Edith was a constant reminder of what she'd endured? It seemed fitting that all she had to remember Leah by was that footlocker of useless punch cards. But as Edith packed up to go, she found she couldn't leave the cards behind. She drove back to Frankfurt with the footlocker in the backseat of the Köln. She brought it to New York with her on the ship. She hauled it to the town house she'd inherited from her grandmother. She carried it up to an unused attic room, covered it with a sheet, and closed the door.

Edith shuts the lid of the footlocker and goes downstairs to lock the front door. Carol's scent lingers in the vestibule, but she doesn't allow herself to breathe it in. In the kitchen, Edith pours herself a glass of wine and takes it out to the patio. She stands there for a long time, looking up at the patch of sky over her little rectangle of Manhattan. It's not dark enough yet for stars but the moon is out, a plump oval on its way to becoming full.

For fifteen years she's kept the memory of that night in Bad Arolsen fossilized in amber. Then out of the blue, Rita Klein appears like some prophetic messenger, asking about those cards. She's had to let Carol go. Maybe it's time she let go of those cards, too. Back in the kitchen, Edith takes the piece of paper with Rita's number out of her pocket and dials the telephone.

"Hello, Rita? Yes, it's Edith Silver. I wanted to make sure you got home all right. Oh, good, yes, I agree, that second whiskey sour was a mistake. Listen, if I did have those punch cards, do you think you could use them to find out about your friend's mother? Oh, no, that's right. No, I don't have the codes. You can't do anything without them?" She stretches the phone cord so she can sit down at the kitchen table. "But if you did have the codes, what then?"

Edith feels again how her heart stopped when she got that letter in 1946 from the State Department. It said she had been named as a reference on an immigration application by a Dutch war refugee named Leah Blom. Could she confirm that the applicant had worked for the Jewish Aid Committee helping displaced persons in Europe? If so, please sign and return the letter to the address provided. Instead, Edith called the State Department and asked to speak with the bureaucrat who'd sent it. She wanted to know if Leah Blom had given an address here in the States on her application. On the other end of the line, she heard paper shuffling. "Yes, ma'am, here it is. Leah Blom listed One West Seventy-Second Street in New York City as her intended permanent residence."

How many times over that next year had Edith stood on Central Park West looking up at the Dakota, wondering which window was Leah's? Dozens, she supposed, but she never crossed the street to ask. She was afraid the sight of her here, in this new country, would trigger Leah's horrific memories of Bergen-Belsen. It would have to be Leah's choice to seek her out. The most Edith dared do was put herself near where Leah lived and leave it up to fate to cross their paths. Fate never did. After she met Carol, Edith stopped trying to tempt it.

Now, thanks to Rita Klein, Edith has a reason to see Leah. She can introduce her to Rita, return the cards, let them get on with their impossible task. Who knows, maybe they will find a clue in those millions of tiny holes. Either way, Edith will finally be free of that seed of hope that, if she's being honest with herself, always held back a corner of her heart from Carol.

"Well, here's the thing, Rita. I do have the cards. Yes, really. I brought them home with me from Germany. Anyway, I think I know how we can get the codes. How about I meet you tomorrow? The Longchamps bar in the Empire State Building? Five o'clock is fine with me. I'll see you then."

Edith's heart is fluttering like a schoolgirl's as she hangs up. You can't save everyone, she reminds herself. But what if this time, she's really saving herself?

Chapter Twenty-Five
Rita Klein

New York City
June 1960

I didn't recognize Edith Silver when I first walked into the bar. I was looking for a long scarf, but her hair was brushed smooth and pinned back. Instead of slacks and a blouse, she wore a black sheath dress that showed what a nice figure she had. The patent leather pumps on her feet looked Italian—and expensive. Her face, which I caught in profile before she saw me, was transformed with crimson lipstick and black eyeliner. I hadn't realized, yesterday, how beautiful she was.

"Hello, Edith." She must have gotten to the bar early; her drink was almost finished. It looked pretty, like a sunset, and I decided I'd ask the bartender for the same.

"Rita, there you are. I've been waiting." She drained her drink and slid off her stool. "Come on, let's go."

I dashed after her out onto Fifth Avenue. "Wait, where are we going?"

She was on the curb with her arm up to hail a taxi. "To see Leah Blom."

I was too shocked to ask any of the questions that flashed through my mind as I followed her blindly into the backseat of a cab. Edith told the driver to take us up to Central Park West and Seventy-Second Street. I sat back, stunned at this sudden turn of events. Yesterday, the Blom Report was an obscure document about a long-lost collection of obsolete punch cards. Now it had sprung to life as magically as a golem under a rabbi's spell.

"But, Edith, I don't understand. Are you telling me the same Leah Blom you wrote about in your report lives right here in the city?"

Edith shifted in her seat to look at me. "She does. She has for fourteen years now. I've never seen her in all that time, though. I figured she wanted to put the past behind her, but since you showed up, it seems like she could help someone in the present. Anyway, I hope she'll feel that way about it. I really don't know how she'll react to us showing up unannounced."

Edith's nervous energy wafted off her like a perfume. I got nervous, too, thinking about what it could mean to Jacob if Leah Blom did remember the computer codes from Bergen-Belsen. When Edith had telephoned last night, I'd lied and told Jacob it was Gladys calling about something at work. He was so exhausted from spending the day with my mother, he didn't question it. Until I knew for sure there was at least a chance, however slim, that those punch cards might actually lead to some answers about his mother, I decided to spare him the mental strain of unfounded hope. We had ridden the bus into the city together that morning, kissing goodbye out on Eighth Avenue, with plans to meet tonight on the observation deck to watch the fireworks. Whatever I was about to learn about Leah Blom, I'd tell him about it then.

"Here you are, ladies," the driver said. The Dakota was an imposing building to approach, what with its dormers and spires and reputation for celebrity. I understood now why Edith was dressed so formally for this visit. She told the uniformed doorman that we'd come to see Miss Leah Blom. He retreated into the sentry box that flanked the entrance, leaving us to cool our heels on the sidewalk.

"Miss Blom says to send you on up," he said when he emerged, opening the gate to the building's courtyard. "It's that elevator there, across from the second fountain."

We walked through the exquisite courtyard, where splashing water drowned out the hubbub of traffic. The elevator was operated by an ancient lady dressed all in black. When Edith told her who we were visiting, she said, "Ah, yes, Mrs. Gottlieb's granddaughter."

We could have walked up faster than that old-fashioned elevator rose, but eventually we arrived at a carpeted lobby the size of Jacob's entire room. With its wall sconces and mahogany wainscoting, it perfectly fit my image of an English manor house. The elevator operator escorted us to a double door, half of which swung open when she rang the bell. A woman about Edith's age stepped out, her hair so short it could have been cut by a barber. She'd apparently been lounging at home; her clothes were as casual as pajamas.

"Visitors for you, miss." The ancient lady waited for a signal from the occupant that our presence was, indeed, wanted.

"Thank you, Adela." Once the elevator doors had closed, she focused on Edith. "The doorman gave me your name, but I'm not sure I heard it correctly."

Edith peered over her shoulder into the apartment, of which only the expansive foyer was visible. "I'm Edith Silver, from the Jewish Aid Committee. I'm here to see Leah Blom. Is she home?"

The woman in the doorway lifted an eyebrow. "So you really are Edith Silver." She smiled and extended a hand. "I'm Leah Blom."

I expected a tearful reunion, but Edith blinked in confusion. "I'm so sorry, I must have made a mistake. I was looking for someone else."

"I know who you're here for. Come inside, there's a lot to explain."

We followed her through an immense parlor with a fireplace at either end into a library where woodwork paneled the walls all the way to the crown molding. Light streamed in through massive windows, the greenery of Central Park filling the panes as if the tree branches had been woven into drapes.

She gestured to the sofa. "Please, have a seat. I still don't know your . . . companion?"

Edith's mouth opened and closed like she was a fish gasping for air, so I introduced myself and started babbling away. Leah went to a bar cart and began mixing drinks while I narrated how Jacob's search for his mother had led me to Edith. "She thought you might be able to help us, but—" I looked from her to Edith and back again. "I guess not you, exactly?"

Leah handed us each a glass filled with blood-red liquid. "Negronis, do you know them? My grandmother swears by the digestive properties of Campari." She returned to the cart, got her own glass, and sat on an ottoman facing us. Looking right at Edith, she asked, "Is the only reason you're here because of those punch cards?"

Edith blinked as if waking from a dream. "Not the only reason, no."

She and Leah looked at each other for so long I wondered if they were having some sort of telepathic conversation. Then Leah lowered her head and took a sip of her drink. "The woman you're looking for, the woman you—" Her voice caught in her throat. "The woman whose life you saved at Bergen-Belsen, her name is Cornelia Vogel."

"Cornelia Vogel?" Edith said the name as if it tasted sour in her mouth.

Leah nodded. "Her last name means 'bird' in Dutch. I've never called her Cornelia, though. I've always called her Nellie."

"But I knew Leah Blom. She told the Red Cross who she was. I don't understand."

Leah got up and began pacing the room, as if the story she was about to tell propelled her into motion. "My mother's family came from Germany, originally, in the 1860s. Her grandfather had trained as an engineer. Here, he was an inventor. The royalties on his patents paid for all this." She waved her arm around the room. I thought she was only talking about the apartment. I hadn't appreciated, before, the paintings on the walls. The canvases, which hung one above the other all the way to the ceiling, ran the gamut from dark Dutch portraits to pointillist picnics to gauzy ballerinas. There were some bold modernist paintings, too, one of which was obviously Picasso, while another could only be O'Keeffe. I would have expected the sheer wealth to intimidate me, but the paintings were arranged so intimately that the room felt less like a museum and more like an artist's atelier. There was one conspicuous absence, though: a rectangle of exposed woodwork where no frame hung.

Leah followed my eyes to the empty spot. "We keep that space open in memory of Mommy's Van Gogh. She was forced to give it to the Nazis."

"Can't you sue to get it back?" I asked.

"If the painting ever surfaces, we'll try, but it hasn't been seen since the bank appraiser took it off our wall in 1942." A cloud of sadness emanated from Leah. "My mother was raised in this very apartment. She brought me here often to visit my grandparents. This place was like an elegant dream to me while I was growing up in The Hague."

"I don't understand." Edith went to stand by the fireplace, setting her drink down on the massive mantel. "I've heard all this before, except it was *her* mother she was talking about."

"Nellie was with my parents at Westerbork, and then in Bergen-Belsen. At first, she was protecting them for my sake, but I believe the three of them really did become a family."

"But why would Leah—I mean, why would she have your name?"

"Come sit with me," she said, leading Edith to a window seat. "Nellie was my neighbor, but also my friend." Leah touched the top of Edith's hand. "My *particular* friend. Do you understand?"

Something in Edith's expression relaxed, as if a puzzle piece had been put in place. "So, you were . . . ?"

Leah nodded. "The whole story would fill a novel. I'll give you the short version, okay? When my family was called up by the Nazis for deportation, Nellie pretended her identity card was ruined so she could have a replacement made for me. Here, I'll show you." She went over to a rolltop desk in a corner of the library, got something out of one of the drawers, and brought it back to Edith. "See? My picture, but her name, and no *J* for 'Jew.'"

"Wait a second," I said. They both looked up as if they'd forgotten I was there. "Are you saying this woman Edith met at Bergen-Belsen isn't even Jewish?"

"She wasn't, then. Her parents were Calvinist," Leah said. "That changed, though, while she was in the camps. Nellie converted to Judaism after the war."

I'd gone to a conversion once, for a high school friend who was marrying a Jewish boy. I remembered her being questioned by the *beit din*: Why would you want to become a Jew? Do you not know our people are persecuted, harassed, oppressed, and despised? At the time, the questions seemed pro forma, but imagining a victim of the Holocaust responding to a court of rabbis brought tears to my eyes. Yes, she must have said. Yes, I know.

"But she wore a Star of David the whole time I knew her," Edith said.

"She still wears it. A woman at Westerbork gave it to her before being sent to Auschwitz. I don't think Nellie's ever taken it off since." Leah paused for a moment, then continued her story.

"I used this identification to escape from Holland. I got myself smuggled to England on a herring boat. From there I was able to telegraph my grandparents. They booked me passage on an icebreaker to Nova Scotia. According to my papers, I was a Dutch citizen named Cornelia Vogel, so that's how I entered the United States. By the time victory in Europe was declared, I was in this very room, listening to President Truman on the radio."

I was engrossed in Leah's narrative, but Edith was losing her patience. "I still don't understand how Leah—I mean, Cornelia—ended up in Bergen-Belsen."

"You have to believe me when I say I never knew what Nellie did for me, not until it was all over." Leah took a deep breath, as if coming to the point in the story that was hardest for her to tell. "What happened was, while I was getting away using her name, she got arrested in my place. We were neighbors, like I said. Her family lived downstairs, and mine was upstairs, but we were in the same house. It was still dark when I snuck out back, through the garden. I didn't know the police were waiting in front. When Nellie opened the door, they assumed she was Leah Blom. She could have told them who she really was, but it would have meant sacrificing me."

Edith grabbed hold of Leah's hands. "I knew she was brave, but I had no idea."

"What she endured was supposed to be my fate, not hers. If it had been me, though, I wouldn't have survived."

"She saved your life, Leah."

"And then you saved hers, Edith. You saved mine, too. If Nellie had died for me, I could never have lived with myself. As it is, I don't think she ever told me the truth about what she went through."

"I'm certain she didn't." Edith shook her head slowly. "You couldn't have borne it if she had."

Leah searched Edith's face. "But you were there with her. It's because of you that she came back to me."

"Is she here now?" Edith glanced around as if expecting an apparition.

"No, not anymore. My grandparents sponsored her immigration—as far as the State Department was concerned, she was their granddaughter, after all. Once she got here, we swapped our documents. I became Leah Blom again, and she was Cornelia Vogel. She stayed with us for a little while, but she was never comfortable here. Even after everything she did for me, she couldn't forgive herself for not saving my parents."

"And what about the two of you?" Edith asked.

Leah shook her head sadly. "We made each other promises it turned out we couldn't keep. We were never able to revive the relationship we once had. What she sacrificed for me, what I owed her—it was all too much."

"But where did she go?" I asked, imagining Cornelia making a fresh start somewhere far away, like California.

"She's here, in the city. She lives in Yorkville. She's a translator for the United Nations. We stay in touch, of course, but since my grandfather died, my life revolves around taking care of Grandma." Leah put her hand on Edith's knee. I'd never seen two women become so intimate so quickly. "She told me all about you, Edith. She told me about Bad Arolsen. I'm sure she'll want to see you. Let me give you her address."

Edith looked shell-shocked as Leah got paper and a pen. Somewhere in the apartment, a clock chimed. Leah looked up. "Grandma always eats at six thirty." Indeed, at that moment a woman in a maid's uniform appeared. "Yes, Josephine, please tell Mrs. Gottlieb I'll be there as soon as I show my guests out."

At the door, Leah wished me good luck and offered her best to Jacob. To Edith, she said, "When you see Nellie, I think you should go alone."

There were a million questions I wanted to ask Edith on

our way out of the Dakota, but she seemed so lost in thought I doubted she'd even hear me. We mindlessly joined the crowd crossing Central Park West, but at Terrace Drive she stopped me from following her farther. "I need to take a walk. I'll talk to you soon, Rita."

I hoped she didn't plan on walking far; those Italian pumps were sure to blister her feet. "When will you get in touch with Cornelia Vogel?"

"Maybe tomorrow, maybe Friday, I don't know yet. I need a minute to think, okay?"

"Sure, fine." There was obviously more to this story than anyone was letting on. "But I haven't said anything to Jacob yet. I'm starting to feel like I'm lying to him."

"It looks like there's a lot of that going around."

I didn't have the chance to say anything else before Edith walked into the park. The subway entrance was right on the corner, but I figured the trains would be overcrowded what with the bus strike going on. Besides, Jacob wasn't expecting me until the fireworks started. I strolled toward downtown beneath branches overhanging the stone wall of Central Park. My mind was so occupied with Leah's story I barely saw where I was going. Cornelia had put herself in the most terrible danger imaginable to save her friend. Would I have had the courage to do the same? I wondered. I doubted it—until I thought of David. I knew instantly I'd throw myself in front of a train if it meant saving his life. Wouldn't any mother? Why was it, then, I'd lacked the courage to simply keep hold of his tiny hand?

"Hey, watch yourself, lady!" An outthrust arm stopped me from walking into traffic at Columbus Circle. My heart racing, I stepped back and turned down Fifty-Ninth Street past the horse carriages. The big beasts stomped and snorted, magnificent in their feathered headdresses. They wore blinders to keep the sights of the city from making them nervous, but their ears freely twitched and flicked. I worried they'd be frightened when the fireworks started going off.

I ended up walking all the way back to the Empire State Building. I'd been hoping Jacob would take me up to the 103rd floor, but after we found each other on the observation deck, he explained that the parapet was reserved for celebrities on a night like this. As the sky darkened, we found a spot with a view of the Hudson River. Jacob stood behind me, his arms around my waist.

I wanted so much to tell him about visiting Leah Blom, but I kept quiet. I still didn't have anything concrete to offer, and I didn't want to raise his hopes. One thing had become clearer to me, though, as I mulled over Leah's story: she and Cornelia had been more than friends. The way she'd talked to Edith about their relationship made me realize they must have been lovers. It was sad they hadn't stayed together after being reunited against all odds, but it didn't surprise me. I couldn't imagine feeling responsible for the horrors Jacob had suffered. I'd never be able to really understand what he endured, but maybe that was for the best. Maybe, with me, he'd be able to leave the past behind.

A collective gasp accompanied the first burst of fireworks. I rested the back of my head against Jacob's breastbone, feeling the vibration in his chest as he joined in the cheers that followed each explosion. A week ago, he'd been in the psychiatric ward at Bellevue. Now he was on top of the world. I'd tell him everything soon—but not yet. I wanted to keep his head near the clouds for as long as I could before bringing him back down to earth.

Chapter Twenty-Six

Cornelia Vogel

New York City
June 1960

Cornelia Vogel's dog starts barking at the first scrape of her key in the lock. The high-pitched yips inject urgency into the mundane routine of her mistress returning from work. As soon as Cornelia comes into the apartment, the toy poodle dances with excitement, pawing at her knees.

"Stop now, Meisje, you'll run my stockings." Cornelia puts down her pocketbook as the phone rings. Tucking the dog under her arm like a loaf of bread, she lifts the receiver. "Hello?"

"Nellie, hi, it's me."

"Leah." Cornelia sits down and eases off her shoes. It's been years since the sound of Leah's voice kicked off the cascade of symptoms Sappho so poetically described. Now a call from Leah is as comfortable as an old quilt. "How goes it?"

"Fine. Grandma says hello."

Cornelia settles the poodle on her lap. "What did the doctor say about her blood pressure?"

"The usual—eat less salt, drink more water. She hardly needs a specialist at Mount Sinai to tell her that, but she insists on seeing the best cardiologist in the city, even though she always ignores his advice. She wants to know when you're coming to visit."

"Soon. It's been busy at work lately. The Argentinians are demanding the United Nations force Israel to return Eichmann, but it's all bluster. Everyone knows Ben Gurion will never let that murderer go."

A long pause tells Cornelia this isn't one of Leah's typical check-ins. "Listen, Nellie, someone came to see me today, but she was really looking for you."

Cornelia's throat constricts as her heart speeds up. "What do you mean? Are we in trouble with the State Department?"

"No, nothing like that. It was Edith Silver, from the Jewish Aid Committee."

Edith Silver. Cornelia hasn't heard that name in over a decade. She feels the tug of the tunnel pulling her toward memories of Bergen-Belsen. "Hang on a second, will you?"

Cornelia goes into the kitchen for a glass of water, Meisje trotting at her heels. She focuses on the feel of the glass in her hand, the wetness of the water in her mouth, the solidity of the kitchen floor beneath her feet. With a deep breath, she manages to keep the tunnel at bay. Still, her hand is shaking as she picks up the phone again. "Edith Silver came to see you?"

"Well, she came to see you, but she got me instead. She was with another woman—not *with* with, just working with. A girl named Rita. Anyway, they were asking about those punch cards you saved from Bergen-Belsen. I told them I didn't know anything about that, but I gave Edith your address and phone number. I hope that was okay? I guess I should have asked you first, but, Nellie, she's so . . ."

"So what?"

"She's so beautiful, Nellie. I've been telling you for ages to get in touch with her, and then, there she was, looking for you. It seemed like fate."

Cornelia gulps down the rest of her water. "Is she coming over here?"

"I think so, yes."

"When?"

"Tomorrow, maybe, or the day after?"

"Well, which is it?" Cornelia's tone is sharper than she intended.

"I don't know. I wanted to tell you, is all. You don't have to see her if you don't want to. But, Nellie . . ."

"What?"

"I think you should. See her, I mean."

Cornelia is struggling to keep her mind from slipping into the past. "Thanks for calling, Leah. I'll think about it."

"Are you okay?"

"I guess I'm a little shaken up."

"Maybe a shake-up is what you need."

Cornelia sighs dramatically for Leah's benefit. "Goodbye, Leah."

"Good night, Nellie."

As Cornelia hangs up the phone, a memory flashes into her mind—not of Bergen-Belsen, thank God, or the basement, but of the moment when she came through customs at New York International Airport and saw Leah waiting for her with a bouquet of tulips. That moment was the North Star toward which all her steps had been turned since leaving Bad Arolsen. My ordeal is finally over, she thought, as she stepped into the circle of Leah's arms.

At first, the rekindled flame of their love shot up like sparks from a struck flint. But as the weeks went by, the tension between them grew. Like the tip of a tongue worrying a bad tooth, Leah couldn't stop herself from probing for details. Cornelia was forced to relive the worst moments of her life whenever Leah asked, What was it like? How did you suffer? What did my parents endure?

Their lovemaking changed, too. Lost was the playfulness and imagination of their nights in Leah's attic. Now Leah treated Cornelia like a precious relic, a fragile treasure, an object of devotion—

anything but a flesh-and-blood woman. When Cornelia confessed to her affair with Edith, she wanted Leah to be angry and jealous. Instead, Leah forgave her as easily as if she were a child admitting to taking one too many cookies from the jar. Cornelia accused Leah of no longer loving her, of staying with her out of guilt. That's not true, Leah would say. Let me prove it to you. Afterward they lay beside one another, their fingers intertwined but their minds elsewhere, the divide between them palpable.

It might have gone on like that for years, if not for the night Leah took Cornelia to the roof of the Dakota to walk the promenade. Looking east, Cornelia said, "Lillian told me once she had all of Central Park as her front yard. I didn't understand what that meant, until now." Leah sighed wistfully and said, "I'm jealous of those months you had with my mother. It should have been me who was with her at the end." Cornelia choked on the spiteful words that filled her throat. How can you covet the time I spent with Lillian at Bergen-Belsen? she thought. Your mother was so delirious from fever she stripped off her lice-ridden clothes. The last time I saw her alive, she was stumbling around in a snowstorm with only a blanket over her naked, emaciated body. My heart is the one that broke that day, not yours. My mind is the one that will carry that image to the grave, not yours, you spoiled, selfish bitch.

What Cornelia said out loud, on the rooftop promenade of the Dakota, was this: "I can't stay here anymore, Leah. I have to go live on my own." To which Leah replied, "I know, Nellie. I know."

The dog is whining at her feet, luring Cornelia back to the present. "Yes, all right, we're going." The leash she attaches to Meisje's collar is slender as a string, but the dog is so tiny a strand of pasta would be sufficient to tether it. Out on the sidewalk, Meisje sniffs and piddles at each of the locusts and ginkgoes they pass on Eighty-Second Street, enthusiastically engaging in the neighborhood's canine conversation. The trees are sparser on East

End Avenue and the dog trots steadily alongside her mistress. At the corner of Gracie Square, they cross into Carl Schurz Park. As they wander the park's pathways, the casual words Cornelia exchanges with neighborhood acquaintances calm her mind. No one here knows that the middle-aged woman who walks an adorable dog and can greet neighbors in half a dozen languages was once imprisoned in a Nazi concentration camp. Cornelia prefers it this way, but there are times, like tonight, as the East River sparkles in the long light of a summer evening, when her past is a lonely burden.

At the playground, a tolerant nanny allows her charges to play with the little black poodle. Meisje gleefully entertains the children with her tricks while Cornelia sits on a bench shaded by a sycamore. Hearing Edith Silver's name has stirred her memories like a gust of wind down a leaf-strewn street. She remembers sneaking out of that hotel room in Bad Arolsen, Edith still asleep in the bed they'd shared, determined not to let herself be sidetracked any longer. Those damn punch cards were a useless distraction, she told herself as she roused the concierge to take her to the station. During the months she'd worked for Gertrud Slottke at Bergen-Belsen, saving the cards had become a compulsion, as if salvaging pieces of paper were tantamount to saving lives. But as the train took her through the German countryside, Cornelia realized it was all a delusion. The cards were meaningless. The only life she'd managed to save was her own. Her night with Edith was an enchanted dream. Cornelia was awake now. All she wanted was to get home, to see her family, to find Leah, to keep her vow.

When she was finally back in The Hague, she stood on the stoop of the house their families had shared, strangely surprised that the nameplate over the neighbor's door wasn't BLOM anymore. She rang the bell labeled VOGEL. Her father opened it. His face was unshaven, his hair uncombed. A threadbare robe was tied around wrinkled trousers and an untucked shirt. She stared in disbelief at the diminished figure of the proud man she remembered.

Gerard Vogel stepped back, wordlessly inviting his daughter home. His leg dragged, as if the foot were a dead weight dangling from his ankle. His arm, too, hung useless on that side. Cornelia saw the scars of a burn on his neck, pink ropes reaching toward his ear like vines on a trellis. She'd been ready to vent her fury on him with the vengeance of a harpy, but all she felt as she followed him toward the kitchen was pity.

"What happened, Father?"

"What do you care?" The kettle was whistling. She expected to see her mother at the stove, making tea. Instead, her father poured water into the waiting pot. The kitchen was in worse disarray than Lillian Blom's ever had been. Through the window, Cornelia saw her mother's beautiful garden overgrown and gone to seed.

"Where is Mama?"

"On holiday in Vlissingen. At least that's what she calls it. The truth is, she's left me."

"Left you?" Cornelia looked around, as if her mother might have simply escaped her father's notice. "And Dirk?"

"He's with your mother. He dropped out of the Lyceum to work for a cousin of hers. He thinks catching fish is a more honest profession than anything a degree can qualify him for." Her father put the teapot and two cups on a tray. "The milk's spoiled, I'm afraid."

The philodendrons in the sunroom were dead in their pots, their brown tendrils denuded of leaves. Cornelia took the cup of tea her father handed her. "How long have you been here on your own?"

"Your mother stayed long enough to nurse me through my injuries. As soon as the doctor said I'd made as much progress as could be expected, she packed up and left. By then, Dirk couldn't stand to look at me."

Cornelia didn't think her father's scars were so unsightly they'd drive her brother away. "Not because of this," he said, touching his neck. "Because of the Jews. Everything we did at the Ministry of Information became public after the British bombed Huize Kleykamp."

"Huize Kleykamp was bombed? When?"

He looked at her in wonder. "What do you mean, when? Didn't your people direct that operation?"

"Father, I wasn't with the Resistance."

"Tell me, then, where have you been?"

Cornelia's memory retreats from the scene in the sunroom like a movie camera pulled backward on a dolly. The years go by in a dizzying montage until it's 1960 again. The children on the playground have had the dog dancing on her hind legs for so long her fluffy little knees are trembling.

"Come now, Meisje. Time to go home."

It's been years since Cornelia has thought about that conversation with her father. When she told him the truth about what she'd endured, she expected him to weep with shame, beg her forgiveness, cradle his lost child in his arms. But Gerard Vogel was no longer capable of emotion. The statistician had supplanted the man. His only response, on hearing his daughter's story, was to gruffly state that, given the odds, her survival was a mathematical anomaly.

Helena, on the other hand, ran up to her daughter on the train platform in Vlissingen, screaming her name and snatching her up like a lost treasure. Cornelia didn't understand, at first, why a strange young man was kissing her cheek until she recognized her brother's boyish eyes above a scraggly beard. The months she spent with her mother and brother in that lovely fishing village were as restorative as a spa, but Cornelia felt out of place, now, in the country that had been her homeland.

She emigrated to the United States as soon as her application was approved, which, thanks to Leah's grandparents, happened quickly. Cornelia and her mother resumed their epistolary relationship, blue airmail envelopes crossing monthly over the Atlantic, but they haven't seen each other since. Helena, a grandmother now, is too busy helping tend Dirk's ever-growing brood to visit her unmarried daughter in America, while Cornelia has never returned to Holland—not even for her father's funeral.

Meisje leads her mistress home, the low sun casting long shadows across East End Avenue. When Cornelia turns up Eighty-Second Street, there's a woman in a black dress standing in front of her apartment. She's barefoot, pointy shoes dangling from her hand. Cornelia's heart recognizes her before her brain puts a name to the face her eyes are seeing. If Leah hadn't called, she'd have sworn she was having one of her visions. But the woman standing shoeless on the sidewalk is no illusion.

"Edith? Is that really you?"

"Yes, it's me." Edith takes an unsteady step forward. "But I don't know what I'm supposed to call you."

"I'm not sure what my name is right now." Cornelia looks down at Meisje, who is licking Edith's bleeding feet. "What happened?"

Edith gestures with the pointy shoes. "Turns out these aren't meant for walking."

"Come on, let's get off the street."

Up in her apartment, Cornelia sets a basin of warm water with Epsom salts on the floor in front of an armchair. "Go ahead, soak your feet." Edith winces as she submerges her torn heels and swollen toes in the basin.

"Now, tea or wine?"

Edith twirls her ankles, swirling the water. "Wine. Have you got anything red?"

"I have a bottle from Bordeaux, how's that?"

Edith closes her eyes and rests her head back. "Perfect."

Meisje's nails click nervously on the kitchen floor; she's uncertain about this unexpected visitor. Cornelia opens a can of dog food and plops it into a dish. "Edith is a special friend of mine," she says, uncorking a bottle and pouring two glasses. "I need you to be nice to her, Meisje."

The poodle takes Cornelia's words to heart. Having finished her supper in swift little bites, she trots into the living room and jumps onto Edith's lap.

"Do you like the wine?" Cornelia pulls over another armchair and sits with her legs folded beneath her.

"Delicious." Edith looks at her with wide eyes. "I can't believe you're here."

"It's my apartment, where else would I be?" Cornelia teases.

Edith smiles. "I guess what I mean is, I can't believe I'm here, with you. I hope I didn't give you a fright."

"Leah called. I was expecting you. Not so soon, though, and not barefoot."

"Those damn shoes. I was dressing up to meet you when I picked them out. I ended up walking all the way over here."

"From the Dakota? You're lucky you're not crippled."

"Actually, I might be." Edith swirls her feet in the basin. "Listen, Leah—oh, I'm sorry, it's Cornelia, isn't it?"

"Call me Nellie, okay? I'm sorry I never told you my real name. By the time you found me, I'd been Leah Blom so long I honestly forgot who I was for a while."

"Nellie's a nice name." Edith takes another drink. Her face flushes as she nervously twirls the stem of the glass. "I hope it isn't too hard for you, seeing me."

"Why would it be hard?"

"I must remind you of all the things you want to forget."

Cornelia takes a long sip of wine, staining her lips purple. "Can I be honest with you, Edith?"

"Of course."

"I feel like you're the only person I can be totally honest with. You may not have known my real name, but in some ways, you know me better than anyone in the world. Leah used to beg me to tell her what I went through, but you can't explain that to someone, can you? You were there, though. You know. I don't have to say anything. It's such a relief, to be understood like that."

"I'll never forget the first moment I saw you for as long as I live."

"Or me, you. Sometimes I think I was born all over again when you found me, like Athena from the head of Zeus."

Edith pets the dog on her lap. Meisje stretches and sighs. "I never wanted to let you out of my sight."

Cornelia nods. "I shouldn't have left like that, Edith. I'm sorry."

"There's nothing to be sorry about. You wanted to go home."

"I did, yes, but I was also afraid if I stayed with you one more night, I might not go back to Leah."

Edith looks into her glass as if her fortune might be hidden there. "She told me it didn't work out with you two."

"Remember how so many survivors got married right there in the DP camps? They may have been strangers a few months before, but they bonded quickly. It's like they knew they could never be intimate with anyone who hadn't gone through what they went through."

The word "intimate" hangs in the air. Edith waves it away with her glass. "This is very good wine."

"The French delegation imports it by the case to give as gifts." Cornelia gets the bottle from the kitchen and tops them off. They touch glasses, the crystal chiming like a soft bell. "*L'chaim.*"

"To life, Nellie," Edith repeats. The toast has never been more appropriate.

After contemplating the rim of her glass in silence, Cornelia says, "I named you on my immigration documents so you'd know I was here."

"I used to stand outside the Dakota, hoping I'd see you."

"Really? Why didn't you ever come up?"

"I didn't know if you'd want to see me. I figured I'd leave that up to you."

"I don't suppose I was ready to see you, at first." Cornelia takes a sip. Her mouth is getting dry. "I went by your house once, too, a couple of years after I moved out on my own. I saw the woman you live with. She's very pretty."

"Carol." Edith nods. "She's gorgeous, isn't she?"

I don't know about gorgeous, Cornelia thinks. "She's very blond."

"She left me. I live by myself now."

"In that big town house? That must be lonely."

"It is. I am."

Meisje's paws start paddling as if she's dreaming of chasing a chipmunk. Edith and Cornelia both laugh.

"Here, let me take her." Cornelia leans over to scoop the dog up from Edith's lap. Touching her forehead to Edith's, she whispers, "I am, too. Lonely, I mean."

After placing Meisje on a blanket, Cornelia says, "Now, why don't you tell me who this girl Rita is and why she wanted to know about those punch cards?"

The fireworks display begins while they talk, explosions thudding in the distance like falling bombs. The basin at Edith's feet has gone cold by the time she finishes her story. Cornelia dumps it out while Edith dries her feet on a dish towel. She stands up gingerly and takes a few tentative steps.

"I'll lend you some slippers," Cornelia says. "And we're calling a cab."

"A cab?"

"We're certainly not walking to your house, not at this time of night, not with your feet like that."

"My house?"

Cornelia takes Edith's hands. "I want to see my punch cards."

Edith sways a little, but it isn't because her feet are hurting. "I kept them all these years. I never let them go."

"I know, Edith. I know."

At the town house, Cornelia follows Edith up to the attic, each step they ascend a new beginning. They kneel in front of the footlocker as if at an altar. Cornelia lifts the lid. She gasps at the sight and scent of the cards. Her vision narrows. Time begins to collapse. She sweats and sways as she feels the tug of the tunnel pulling her down into the dark. She catches a whiff of rotten potatoes, feels the grit of coal dust in her mouth.

Edith grabs her hand. "Nellie, what's the matter?"

Cornelia blinks and swallows. Her vision adjusts. She is in New York, in Edith's town house, on this summer night. Once again, Edith has saved her from the darkness.

"I'm all right." Cornelia shuts the lid of the footlocker. "Can you call Rita tomorrow?"

"Sure. What should I tell her, Nellie?"

"Tell her I have the codes."

Chapter Twenty-Seven

Rita Klein

New York City
July 1960

"You really ought to have a telephone, Jacob." I set down my suitcase Sunday morning and opened my arms for his hug.

"But I never needed a telephone," he said, squeezing me tight. "I never wanted anyone to call me, before you."

"I don't think you wanted anyone to visit you, either. Maybe instead of getting a telephone installed here, you could move to a nicer apartment?"

"Do you mean to tell me there are apartments in New York City nicer than this room?"

That lopsided smile of his really was adorable. I laughed, relieved to find him in such a good mood. "There are closets nicer than this room and you know it."

"But do these nice apartments have laundry service?" Jacob pulled back the curtain that hid his bed. "Look, Little Rita. Clean sheets." He scooped me up like a bride and carried me the three steps it took to reach the mattress.

"Wait a minute." I wriggled out of his arms. "We have a lot to talk about first."

"Talk about?" His smile disappeared as he sensed the nervousness in my tone. "What do you want to talk about?"

"Let's sit down, okay? I haven't even had a coffee yet."

Jacob put the percolator on the hot plate while I opened the bag of bagels I'd gotten from Katz's on my way to his boardinghouse that morning. The last time we'd been together was Wednesday night—well, Thursday morning, actually. We hadn't planned for me to stay at his place after the fireworks, but it was so romantic on the observation deck of the Empire State Building that after the last explosion I asked him to take me home with him. My period had finally stopped, and even though I knew sex would be reckless, I figured it was one last time before I saw the doctor on Friday. Instead of desperately clinging to each other with our eyes closed, Jacob and I took our time, that night, for wide-eyed exploration. I was afraid he'd notice the stretch marks on my tummy or ask why my pubic hair was so short, but neither of those concerned him as he walked his fingers over my skin.

When we were both settled with coffee and bagels, I launched into my story. "Remember after we read the Blom Report, how I asked if you wanted to see Edith Silver? You said I could if I wanted to, even though it wouldn't change anything. Well, I did go to see her, and a lot has changed."

I told him about Edith, and that she had the punch cards, and how we went to see Leah Blom and learned about Cornelia Vogel. "Edith called me Thursday night to tell me she was with Cornelia. Jacob, you're not going to believe this, but she has the codes. I wanted to tell you right away, but you don't have a phone, do you? Besides, you were working Friday night and I was helping my dad in the store yesterday. I wanted to wait until we were together to talk it over."

I was afraid he'd start pacing or tearing at his hair, but Jacob listened in wonder to everything I told him. "This is marvelous. You're saying those cards from Bergen-Belsen have been here in New York City all this time?"

"I'm sorry I didn't tell you all this sooner, but I didn't want you getting all worked up if it turned out to be a dead end."

"You've seen me at my worst, Rita. I understand why you'd worry about telling me things that might upset me." He reached across the table and took my hand. "I know the chances we'll find out anything about my mother are slim. I promise, I have no expectations. The fact that you're doing all this means the world to me." He brought my knuckles to his lips. "Thank you."

"*Graag gedaan.*" I couldn't pronounce it properly, but I really was glad to do it. Besides, I had a theory that the more I helped him, the less my lies mattered, as if there were a cosmic scale somewhere balancing out my good and bad deeds. "Edith invited us to her house today to meet Cornelia and see the punch cards. Once I learn the codes, I'll figure out how to process them."

Jacob did get up now, though he disguised his nervousness by clearing the table. "And the computing machine at your work can do that?"

"We'll find out soon enough. I asked Mr. McKay to lend me a key to the office in case I had time to work on the Olympia account over the holiday weekend." Antiquated would be closed until Tuesday, so we'd have the place to ourselves. Whatever information those cards held, the sooner Jacob knew it, the better.

"You're miraculous, Little Rita. I might have to start believing in God again."

"Believing in fate is enough, don't you think?"

"So you agree with me now that our meeting was *beshert*?" Jacob pulled me up from my chair and took a step back, then another, leading us toward the bed in an awkward waltz.

"Wait. There's something else." I summoned all my courage. It was now or never. "Remember I told you I had a doctor's appointment on Friday?"

"You said it was for a checkup." He held me at arm's length, alarmed. "Are you ill?"

"No. The doctor says I'm a perfectly healthy young woman, but that's the problem, isn't it?"

Jacob frowned. "I don't understand."

I'd gone into that fancy Park Avenue doctor's office expecting to be looked down on, but instead I'd walked out with my head held high. After he examined me, the doctor said, "You've learned the hard way a woman has to look out for herself, Miss Klein. From now on, I want you to promise me you'll determine your own destiny." He'd given me a package of condoms and a bottle of pills that would start working after I'd taken one every morning for twenty-one days. Apparently, enough money could buy a girl something besides a safe abortion. For fifty dollars, I'd been treated with respect.

"Healthy young women tend to be fertile, Jacob." I paused to give him time to catch on. He didn't. "I'm taking a new medicine. It's a pill that will prevent me from getting pregnant, but it won't start working right away. In the meantime, the doctor gave me these, for you." My cheeks were burning as I got the condoms out of my suitcase and handed them to him.

"You want me to use these when we're together?" Jacob sounded incredulous. "But I thought men only used condoms with prostitutes."

I grabbed my suitcase, furious and ashamed. I was halfway out the door when Jacob grabbed my arm. "Don't leave, Rita, please. Let me apologize." He pulled me back into the room and shut the door. "I only said that because I was taught to use condoms to prevent disease. I wasn't thinking about pregnancy."

"You weren't thinking about it because you don't have to." I dropped angrily into a chair, my arms and legs crossed. "Do you have any idea how much courage it took for me to give you those things?"

He knelt at my feet. "What I know about condoms is not from personal experience, believe me, it's just what men learn. You're the most wonderful thing that's ever happened to me, Rita. I'll do anything you want." I still refused to look at him, but I did let him uncross my arms. He kissed my fingertips, my palms, the insides of my wrists. "Do you forgive me?"

My anger was subsiding, but that flash of rage had warmed me up. "I'll let you know if I forgive you after you show me how sorry you are."

Pretty soon, our clothes were on the floor and his sheets weren't so clean anymore. I was afraid it would be terribly awkward making love with the condom, but Jacob was so cavalier about the whole thing it actually added a playful moment of anticipation. The second time around, I put it on him myself. It would be easier once I could rely on those pills, but for now I felt free to enjoy myself without dreading the consequences.

"Have you forgiven me yet, Little Rita, or should I apologize a third time?" Jacob was gazing at me the way you look at paintings in a museum, like I was rare and beautiful and precious. I felt the words "I love you" forming in my mouth. I swallowed them down. I wanted him to say it first.

"I'll forgive you, but only because there's no time for another apology." I leaned out of bed and picked up his wristwatch from the floor. "We should get going. Edith Silver is expecting us."

We walked up to Greenwich Village hand in hand. Washington Square Park was like a carnival on that summer Sunday. A watercolorist sat at her easel, painting portraits for tourists, while children splashed in the fountain and people gathered around an impromptu folk concert. When we reached Edith's town house, I asked Jacob, "Are you ready for this?"

"As long as we're together, I'm ready for anything." He squeezed my hand. I felt those words in my mouth again. Not yet, I told myself.

Edith was back to wearing slacks and a blouse, her hair unruly and loose again. "Come on in, you two." A black poodle came racing up, yipping and dancing. She scooped it off the floor. "This is Meisje." She took its paw and made it wave. "Say hello, Meisje."

Jacob scratched the dog behind its fluffy ears. "Hello, little girl."

"That's right, you're Dutch, too, aren't you? I had to ask Nellie what her name meant." She led us into the living room, calling out, "Nellie, they're here."

Edith's town house was a little shabby but spectacularly spacious. I wondered, though, why all those big windows were shut on such a warm day. Then I saw, through the open pocket doors between the living room and the dining room, a large table covered with piles of neatly stacked punch cards. A breeze would have sent them fluttering like confetti at a parade. I stepped closer to pick one up, careful to handle it by the edges. Holding it was like going back in time. Adolf Eichmann was now in an Israeli jail awaiting trial, but fifteen years ago, the card in my hand—and millions like it—had been used to help him orchestrate the Holocaust.

A spark shot through my fingertips. I dropped the card and jumped back. I felt a warm hand between my shoulders. "Don't be afraid of them, Rita. They can't hurt us anymore."

I almost expected to see the emaciated ghost Edith Silver had described in her report, but nothing about the woman's horrific past was evident on her face. Her brown hair was streaked with a bit of gray and her jawline was a little soft, but the eyes that rested on me were as green and lovely as moss in the forest. I almost didn't believe it was her until I saw the Star of David necklace. "Cornelia Vogel?"

"Please, call me Nellie." She picked up the card from the floor. "I spread them out like this so I could see what condition they were in after all these years. Those over there are the cards I kept from Westerbork. I've already checked the alphabetical

double-punching, and there's no card for Nassy. The cards from
Bergen-Belsen have no names, only numbers. The ones in that
pile, there, are obviously damaged. We'll have to punch new ones
to replace them. The rest might go through a Hollerith without
causing too many jams, don't you think?"

I picked up another card. It was flat enough, but the edges
were no longer crisp and the paper had lost the smooth finish that
was so crucial to the operation of the computer. Ever since Edith
had told me about the cards and the codes, I'd been planning
how to process them on the old Hollerith. I figured we'd run them
through in multiple sorts until we narrowed them down to the
one we were looking for. Now, seeing the condition of the cards,
I doubted they'd survive even a single trip through the sorter. We
could punch duplicates for every one of these thousands of cards,
but that would take days. Jacob needed answers now. The alternative was to sort for multiple data points in a single processing
operation, but the only computer I could program to do that was
Mr. McKay's precious IBM 602.

"They're not terrible, all things considered," I lied, "but I don't
think the old Hollerith is the best choice." I calmed my nerves and
explained my idea about using the 602. "I'll need the templates
at Antiquated to draw the wiring diagram. We can go up to the
Empire State Building tonight, once you've taught me the codes.
Edith said you still had them?"

"I do." A troubled look clouded her eyes. "At Bergen-Belsen,
Fräulein Slottke kept the codebooks locked up, but she had me
punching cards every day for months. The codes never changed
in all that time. I studied them every chance I got. After she
locked me in the cellar at night, I wrote them down before she
turned out the lights. Even after I left the punch cards behind, for
some reason I kept the codes all these years. Then Edith showed
up, because of you, and it turned out she had the cards after all."

She looked at me with wonder in her eyes. "It's like you stirred up the universe, Rita Klein, and now our stars are falling into place."

"I told her it was fate we met." Meisje was asleep in Jacob's arms, his fingers buried in her curly fur. "Thank you, Nellie, and you, too, Edith, for helping us."

"I'm glad you asked Rita to find my report," Edith said. "I might never have reached out to Nellie if she hadn't gotten in touch with me." She turned to give Cornelia a look I recognized. It was the same look Jacob had given me that morning. It made me smile. Edith had gone to see Cornelia on Wednesday night. It was only Sunday now, but the heart doesn't care about clocks and calendars. Four nights was plenty of time for two people to know they were in love.

"Shall we get started?" I asked.

Edith interrupted. "Before you get to work, I have lunch ready. Come on downstairs. We're eating outside."

An old locust tree shaded the patio, where a wrought-iron table was already set, a bouquet of flowers in the center. Edith brought out platters of antipasti she'd ordered from a nearby trattoria, along with a basket of crusty bread and a dish of olive oil. Cornelia set down a bottle of white wine in a bucket of ice. The whole thing was so charming, I felt like we were in a European courtyard. Before I knew it, we were eating and drinking and toasting each other as if we were old friends who'd gotten together for a garden party.

Cornelia broke the festive mood. "Jacob, may I speak frankly with you? Edith explained what you're looking for, and I'm glad to help, but during the months I worked in the Labor Office at Bergen-Belsen, I was only able to save punch cards that were thrown away. I'm very sad to say this, but I want to be sure you understand that most of my cards are for people who perished. If your mother survived, her punch card would probably have been

burned along with all the files the Nazis set aflame before they
fled the camp."

"I understand, Nellie. It's the uncertainty that torments me more
than anything. It would give me peace to know for sure, but I'll be
fine, whatever the outcome." Jacob's words sounded reasonable, but
I heard a worrisome warble of hope in his tone. He was still holding out for a miracle, I realized. I knew he believed in them. His
own survival, and Cornelia's, was evidence enough. That we had all
found each other, here in New York, was even more miraculous. He
seemed even-keeled now, but I remembered Bellevue. I was afraid
of what might happen if he ran out of miracles.

"Now, Jacob," Edith said, refreshing his wine, "we still don't know
all that much about you. Why don't you tell us about yourself?"

I sat back while Jacob narrated the story of his life as if he were
giving a tour. I listened for tidbits I hadn't heard before, but most
of it covered familiar ground. Cornelia interjected occasionally,
comparing her experience growing up in Holland to his.

"It's unbelievable, isn't it, how much you two have in common?"
Edith said, her hand resting momentarily on Cornelia's. I wished
I knew how to tell them it was okay with us if they were lovers.
Though I hadn't mentioned it to Jacob, I couldn't imagine his being
scandalized.

When Jacob said that he and his parents were born in Suriname,
Cornelia gasped. "But I knew some of the Surinamers in Westerbork. I was learning Sranan from one of them."

"Then you know more about the language than I do," Jacob said.
"My parents spoke it to each other when they didn't want me to
understand what they were saying. All I remember is the children's
songs my mother sang when we played together." To my surprise,
Jacob tipped his head back and started to sing. Soon, he had us
joining in, though I had no idea what the sounds we were making meant. After a few rounds, we all clapped, the festive mood

restored—until Cornelia asked Jacob how he and his mother had become separated. His face became somber as he told her what happened on the Boulevard des Misères that day.

"There were a number of mixed transports, but I only remember one like that," she said. "It was in the springtime, wasn't it?"

Jacob nodded. "Yes, in April 1944."

"Leah's parents and I were deported on September thirteenth. I learned later it was the last transport to leave Holland. A couple of days later, the Dutch railway workers finally went on strike." Cornelia shook her head. "By the time they stopped the trains, it was too late for us. There were only five hundred Jews left alive in Westerbork."

Suddenly the wind picked up, shaking the pods off the locust tree. I looked up to see anvil clouds forming in the blue sky. It seemed a summer storm was brewing. Edith started clearing the table, saying she and Jacob would take care of the dishes while we got to work.

In the dining room, I followed along on one of the punch cards as Cornelia taught me the Bergen-Belsen codes. "I wrote the categories in German," she said, "because that's how I learned them. The category for the first two columns was *Einlieferungslager*."

"Consignment warehouse?" I was surprised at the industrial terminology.

"It means which camp the prisoner came from. A concentration camp was a *Lager*, as if we were simply items in the warehouse of their war machine." Cornelia went down the list of codes. Dachau was 01, Auschwitz 02, Budapest 03, Drancy 04, and so on. Westerbork was 18. I was shocked at how many there were. The names of these places were the stuff of nightmares, but seeing them represented in sterile digits made them seem eerily banal.

I made a note on the pad I was writing on. "What are the next two columns?"

"Columns three and four are *Grund der Einlieferung*. That's the reason for someone's imprisonment."

I assumed *Jude* would be at the top of the list, but Jews were coded 05, behind 04, for military prisoner; 03, for political prisoner; and 02, for homosexual. Code 01 baffled me. "What did the Nazis have against Bible researchers?"

"*Bibelforscher* means 'Jehovah's Witness.'"

"Oh, yes, there were a few Jehovah's Witnesses in Westerbork," Jacob said. He had come upstairs carrying a tray of coffee and cake. "They lived with the baptized Jews, didn't they, Nellie?"

"Keep that away from the table!" I didn't mean to shout, but I was terrified of anything ruining the cards.

"We'll set it over there, how's that?" Edith pointed to the coffee table in front of the couch.

"Thanks, Edith. I'm sorry I yelled at you, Jacob."

He handed the tray to Edith before kissing the top of my head. *"De rien, ma petite."*

The next six columns were for birth date. "In the European style," Cornelia reminded me. "First day, then month, then the last two digits of the year. Do you know your mother's birthday, Jacob?"

"Of course." He told us, then asked, "Can't your machine find her that way?"

"We'll use birth date as one of the variables," I said, "but I don't want to rely on it completely." I wanted to include as many relevant data points as possible. Besides, a mistake could have been made at some point. Jacob needed certainty.

Column twelve was gender—1 for man, 2 for woman—so we'd sort for that. Next was nationality, which I assumed would be Dutch, but Cornelia wasn't sure a Jewish woman born in Suriname would be coded 201 for Hollander. "Suriname Jews were part of the Portuguese Israelite Community, so she might have been coded for Portugal. There's no code for Suriname, but they used 099 for anyone without a known nationality." She called over to Jacob. "Would the Nazis have considered your mother *schwarze?*"

"I don't think so. Most Surinamese Jews are Creole to some extent, but my mother's complexion was the same as mine."

"What's a Creole Jew?" I asked.

"Descendants of Jewish plantation owners and the Africans they held as slaves."

"Wait—what?"

We took a coffee break while Jacob enlightened me on this aspect of Suriname's Jewish history. I understood how enslaved people might take on the religion of their masters, but I couldn't square what I was learning with the Passover ritual. How could a people who commemorated our history in bondage celebrate a Seder served by slaves?

A flash of lightning lit up the windows, followed by a distant rumble of thunder. The tree in front of Edith's town house started to sway. It seemed the storm was getting closer. Cornelia finished her coffee and stood up. "Let's get back to work, Rita."

The next category was *Arbeitsfähigkeit*. Jacob said that in Westerbork, his mother assembled dolls in the toy factory, meaning she was fit to work, which was code 1. By the time she was registered at Bergen-Belsen, though, her condition might have deteriorated to the point where she was of limited use, 2, though hopefully not 3: *unverwendbar*, "unusable." The categories for original profession and learned profession wouldn't be useful, either, as we had no idea what kind of work she might have been assigned at the camp. As for column thirty-one, we didn't know if a woman whose husband had been sent to Sobibor would still be coded 1 for married. Columns thirty-two and thirty-three were for number of children, but Cornelia thought it best we skip those, too.

"Once she was separated from you, Jacob," she said, "your mother might have decided it was best not to mention that she had a son. She may have thought you escaped the train."

"Yes, I've considered that." He and Edith had set up a chess game, though their attention was more on our conversation about the cards than on the carved pieces on the board. "It torments me that she may have thought I abandoned her."

We had exhausted the categories that would help us narrow down the thousands of cards to the single one we were looking for: a Jewish woman transferred from Westerbork with Rebekah Nassy's birth date. In column thirty-four, we arrived at the category that would tell Jacob what he was desperate to know: *Grund des Abgangs,* "reason for departure."

Cornelia and I silently reviewed the list of codes. There were only six ways to leave Bergen-Belsen. If Jacob's mother had been transferred to another camp, her card would be coded 1. Code 2 was death by disease. Code 3 was *Hinrichtung,* "execution," while 4 was *Flucht,* "escape." "Fräulein Slottke hated to admit when a prisoner escaped," Cornelia recalled. "She made us punch duplicate cards coding them as dead for the reports to Berlin. Eichmann must have thought Bergen-Belsen was as secure as Alcatraz."

Discharge was 5, but I didn't understand code 6. "What's *Sonderbehandlung?*"

"Special treatment." Cornelia's face grew pale, her forehead suddenly slick with sweat. "The Nazis had a way of making the simplest words sinister. Special treatment is what they called extermination, like in the gas chambers."

Edith abandoned the chessboard and came over to put her arms around Cornelia. "Bergen-Belsen wasn't built as a site for mass exterminations, but when we were compiling the Harrison Report on displaced persons, we saw that word a lot on the documents we found at other camps."

"I'm all right, Edith," Cornelia said. "We're almost done here. The last five columns are the prisoner's inmate number, but we won't know what hers was unless we find her card."

We were gathered around that table like mourners at a graveside. Each one of those cards represented a human being, most likely dead of disease or executed or exterminated. The best we could hope for, if we found Rebekah Nassy's card among them, was for her son to finally give her the memorial she deserved.

A huge crack of thunder scared us out of our wits. Meisje howled as hail started crashing down. We scattered around the town house, checking all the windows and bolting the doors. We'd just gotten back together in the living room when the electricity went out. Edith lit some candles and put batteries in a transistor radio. The news on WNYC said power was out all over the city, leaving subways stalled on their tracks and cars navigating the streets without traffic lights.

"Well, no one is going up to the Empire State Building tonight," Edith announced. "I don't want you two trying to get home, either. Why don't you sleep over?" Jacob and I politely protested, though really, it was impossible to imagine going out in that storm. "It's no problem. I've got three bedrooms. Nellie and I will share, so you can each have your own. Unless you only need one?"

I don't think I ever blushed so deeply. Even by candlelight, they could see my cheeks turn red. We started laughing, then, a welcome release of emotion. I liked the idea of staying in this lovely town house instead of Jacob's dingy room. It would be like a vacation—or a honeymoon. I asked if I could use the telephone to call my parents so they wouldn't worry.

"Sure," Edith said, "it's out in the hall."

My mother was grateful to hear my voice. They'd been driving home from visiting Charlie and Debbie when the hail started beating down. Wherever I was, she said, I should stay put for the night.

Edith handed me a glass of wine when I came back to the living room. The radio was tuned to a station playing jazz. The leftover bread and cheese from lunch was on the coffee table. Meisje had settled down into a fluffy ball on Cornelia's lap. I sat on the floor at Jacob's feet so he could rub my neck. It really was the coziest gathering I'd ever been part of.

"Is this what you'd call *gezellig*?" I asked, remembering a word he'd taught me.

"*Gezellig* is exactly right." He and Cornelia raised their glasses. Edith and I joined in.

We were a bedraggled bunch the next morning, dry-mouthed and bleary-eyed. Edith insisted we eat a hearty breakfast before we set out. We left Meisje secure in the kitchen with a bowl of water and a blanket for her bed. "*Ik ben zo terug, mijn lief hondje*," Cornelia told her. Jacob whispered the translation in my ear: "'I'll be back soon, my sweet little dog.'"

There were some tree limbs down in Washington Square Park, but the roads were clear and our taxi made good time up Fifth Avenue. The Empire State Building itself never closed, even on the Fourth of July. We shared a sense of solemn anticipation as we lugged that old footlocker, packed once again with thousands of punch cards, into the elevator. On the way up, the operator told us in nerve-racking detail about a group of tourists who'd been trapped for hours last night because of the storm. When the doors opened on the fifty-seventh floor, we stepped out with a sigh of relief.

Antiquated Business Machines was deserted, as I expected. I was curious to see Cornelia's reaction to the Hollerith. She walked around the old machine as if in a trance, trailing her hand along the cover plates. "We had this exact model at Huize Kleykamp, but the machine at Bergen-Belsen was manufactured by Dehomag. The design was more"—she made a shape with her hands—"square. The tabulator in the Labor Office wasn't an alphabetizer. It could only process numbers. Fräulein Slottke was so proud that her office was the most efficient in the *Lager* system." Cornelia's lip curled. "I hope that woman goes on trial someday, the same as Eichmann."

"You don't have to be here, Nellie," Edith said. "Rita can do this."

"I know, but I want to." She rested her head on Edith's shoulder. "Promise you'll stay near me?"

Edith kissed her on the forehead. "As close as I can get."

"Shall we get to work?" I asked.

"How can I help?" Jacob's voice had that warble of hope in it again.

"Why don't you unpack the cards? Carefully, please. The ones that are damaged need to be duplicated. Maybe Nellie could show you and Edith how to use the punch machine?"

I gave them a box of Olympia's unused cards to work with. It took Jacob and Edith a while to get the hang of operating a punch machine, and at first, more cards ended up in the bit bin than back in our collection. Meanwhile, I stood in front of Mr. McKay's blackboard, drawing connections between circuits that would instruct the IBM 602 to sort, compare, and tabulate the cards we fed into the hopper. By the time Cornelia came over to help me, I was ready to wire the control panel.

"I used to think the punch cards were a kind of language the Hollerith could speak," she said, watching me plug wires into sockets, "but really the machine is just a parrot that says things without knowing what they mean."

"I guess you could think of it like that." It certainly made no difference to the computer if the data it searched for was a spoon on a shelf or someone's long-lost mother.

I was nervous as I slid the control panel into place, knowing

Mr. McKay would never put cards in this condition through the temperamental machine. I turned on the power, hoping for the best. It hummed quietly as I set the dials and placed the first batch of cards in the hopper.

"Will this really work, Rita?" Cornelia asked.

"I hope so, for his sake."

Jacob and Edith had finished punching replacements for those cards that were obviously damaged. I was sure more damaged cards would be spit out by the machine, but we were ready, now, to get started.

"Jacob, do you want to push the button?"

"I'm too nervous, Rita. I'll walk around while you do this." He took off, his strides at least a yard long. Let him wear himself out pacing, I thought. I'd rather have him tired than hysterical.

"I'll do it," Cornelia said.

It was as easy as that. The 602 jumped to life, a list scrolling up from the typebar while cards whizzed through the machine. Jacob came running over, unable to look away after all. He lifted me up and whirled me around until I was afraid we'd both be too dizzy to stand. "It's working!"

"Put me down." When he did, I saw he was crying. "You promised you wouldn't get too emotional, remember?"

"I can't help it." He kissed me so hard I tasted blood. "I love you, Rita Klein."

I brushed the tears off his cheeks. "I love you too, Jacob Nassy."

A buzzer sounded. A red light blinked. The machine stopped.

"What happening?" he asked.

"It's only a damaged card." I removed it from the pocket where it had been shunted and restarted the 602. "See? Nothing to worry about. Why don't you go punch a replacement?"

When the buzzer sounded again a few minutes later, we weren't as startled. "Here's another one for you," I said, handing a damaged card to Jacob. But this time, when I pushed the button to restart the machine, the buzzer kept sounding and the red light kept blinking. I switched it off, checked the hopper, and tried again. The buzzer and the red light came right back on. I got sick to my stomach thinking I'd broken the valuable machine.

A door slammed. The overhead lights flickered on. Mr. McKay's voice rang through the office. "What the hell is going on here?"

We froze in place like ogres turned to stone by the rising sun. Mr. McKay strode toward us, spine straight and shoulders back, his son, Max, jogging behind. He looked over the 602 and pressed some buttons, but the buzzing wouldn't stop. Finally, he unplugged the machine. The silence felt ominous.

"I asked a question, Miss Klein. Who are these people, and what are you doing?"

It took a lot of explaining before he calmed down. When Cornelia told him where the punch cards came from and how she'd saved them, I could read the sympathy on his face. He didn't have to imagine what she and Jacob had been through. He'd seen those camps firsthand.

"I came up with a program to identify any card that might have the information we're looking for," I said, "but something's gone wrong."

"You're lucky the security guard called me, Miss Klein. You could have done permanent damage to the machine." He took off his jacket and hung it over the back of his chair. "Now, let me check your wiring diagram."

Max pulled on his father's sleeve. "Aren't we going to see the ships?"

"*Ja, mein Sohn, bald.* I'm going to help these people first." To me, he said, "The Second Fleet is anchored in the Hudson. Max and I were leaving to go tour the aircraft carrier when the security guard called."

"But you promised, Papa."

Jacob stepped up. *"Hallo, Max. Ich verstehe dass du Deutsch sprichst, ist das richtig?"*

Max's face lit up. *"Ja, das ist richtig."*

I wanted to listen to what Jacob and Max were talking about in German, but I had to focus on explaining my wiring diagram to Mr. McKay. "Ah, see there?" he said. "There's your problem. Take the panel out, we need to switch this wire."

"Mr. McKay," Jacob asked, "is it all right with you if Max comes with Miss Silver and myself to the newsstand in the lobby? We find ourselves in need of a deck of cards."

"Bitte, Papa. I like talking to Jacob. He speaks German!"

"Yes, I heard." Mr. McKay nodded gratefully. "Be warned, though, Max always wins at *Quartett."*

Cornelia looked on as Mr. McKay and I rewired the control panel. Jacob, Edith, and Max returned with a deck of cards, as well as boxes of Cracker Jack and bottles of soda. They were deep into their game by the time we restarted the 602. It processed a few hundred cards this time before it stopped again, buzzing and blinking to reject another damaged card. Mr. McKay got it restarted while Cornelia punched a duplicate and dropped it into the hopper.

The processing proceeded in fits and starts. Most of the cards had gone through the machine when it stopped again, the silence of the typebar as sudden as a cease-fire. Instead of a flashing red light, a green light shone steadily. A single card had been shot into a pocket by itself. A card that met all of our criteria.

"Is this it?" Jacob ran over, practically panting.

"Take it out and we'll see."

He held the punch card up to the light. We gathered around him like astronomers scanning the night sky. Columns one and two were coded 18, meaning the person represented by this card had come to Bergen-Belsen from Westerbork. Columns three and four were coded 05 to indicate this person was a Jew. Column twelve told us she was a woman, columns thirteen through fifteen that she was a Dutch national, column sixteen that she was a good worker. According to column thirty-one, she was married, but columns thirty-two and thirty-three indicated no children.

"She must have lied to protect me." Jacob could barely control the tremor in his voice. "What about her birth date?"

"Here it is," I said. "Columns five through ten."

He touched the punched holes as if reading Braille. "It's my mother's birth date." He looked at us in wonder. "This is her card."

"I can't believe this, Edith." Cornelia's voice was thick with emotion. "I always hoped, when I was saving those cards, they would help someone, someday."

"And now that day has come." Edith put her arm around Cornelia's waist. "See what a mitzvah you've done?"

"Rita." Jacob looked up at me, his eyes pleading like a lost puppy. "Tell me, what happened to her?"

I took the card. Column thirty-four was *Grund des Abgangs*. Reason for departure. There was a hole punched clean through the digit 2.

"Death by disease," I whispered. "I'm so sorry, Jacob."

He took back the card, cradling it in his hands as if it were a paper infant. We stood around him silently as he grieved afresh the mother he'd lost so many years ago.

Mr. McKay put his hand on Jacob's shoulder. "I'm sorry for your loss, son. May I have a word, Miss Klein?" He pulled me aside. "I have to go now, but I want you to leave the 602 exactly as it is. Don't touch a thing. I'll finish processing the cards myself. You can box them up when you come to work tomorrow."

I'd assumed he was going to fire me. "Thank you, Mr. McKay, that's very generous of you."

"From each according to his ability, to each according to his need, wouldn't you agree, Miss Klein?" I was trying to remember where I'd heard that quote when he said, "Come on, son, let's go."

Max shook Jacob's hand goodbye. I hadn't realized how much he understood of what we were doing until he said, *"Ich vermisse meine Mutter auch."*

Jacob didn't even try to hide his tears. "I'm sure your mother misses you, too, Max."

After they left, I asked softly, "What happens now, Jacob?"

He inhaled deeply and blew out a long breath. "I know what I want to do." He tucked the card in the breast pocket of his shirt. "Please, would you all come with me?"

The four of us followed Jacob up to the parapet on the 103rd floor of the Empire State Building. The afternoon sun hovered over the Hudson River. Wispy clouds drifted by below us. There was no noise, no birdsong, only a holy silence. We were as close to heaven as a person could get on the island of Manhattan.

Jacob held out his mother's card like an offering. "You're supposed to have a quorum of ten men to say the Kaddish, but as far as I'm concerned, you three are all the minyan I need." He cleared his throat and began: "Blessed be God's great name to all eternity. Blessed, praised, honored, exalted, extolled, glorified, adored, and lauded be the name of the Holy Blessed One, beyond all earthly words and songs of blessing, praise, and comfort. Amen."

Together, Edith, Cornelia, and I said, "Amen."

Jacob asked me to hold the card while he took a book of matches from his pocket. Shielding them from the wind with his cupped hands, he got one lit and set a corner of his mother's card on fire. He dropped the match and took the card from me, turning it until the flame licked every side. Even though it burned his fingers, he held the card until it was reduced to ashes that were carried away by the wind.

I kissed his blistered fingertips. He bent his neck to kiss the top of my head. "She is free now, and so am I."

We were a solemn quartet, that evening, as we walked down Sixth Avenue toward Washington Place. The aroma of a Chinese restaurant we passed lured us in. We feasted in memory of Rebekah Nassy and in celebration of a new chapter in all our lives. Later, back at Edith's house, Jacob telephoned Rudy to tell him what had happened. When he joined us again, we raised a glass to his mother, to Cornelia, to Edith, and finally to me.

"My darling Little Rita," Jacob said. "Who makes miracles happen."

I knew my parents would want to hear about this. When my mother answered the phone, I launched into the story, talking so fast it was hard for her to get a word in. "I'm very glad for Jacob," she said, finally, "but aren't you coming home tonight?"

"I brought clothes with me for work tomorrow. Actually, Mom, I might stay in the city for the rest of the week."

"You can't do that, Rita. You have to be here on Wednesday. You'll need to take the day off. And don't bring Jacob with you, either."

"Why? What's happening Wednesday?"

"It's been six weeks, Rita. That social worker is coming to see you."

I hung up on her. My hand on the phone was all that kept me upright. As soon as I let go, I dropped to the floor like someone had taken a baseball bat to the back of my knees. For the past few days, I'd actually thought it was possible to forget I'd had a baby. Now everything came flooding back. My brain might one day be convinced of that lie, but my gut would always remember. I thought, again, of the closing scene from *The Wizard of Oz*. Dorothy hadn't wanted to stay in that magical place, but now that she was home, she needed the family and friends gathered at her bedside to know she was telling the truth about having been there. Even if I truly believed giving up David was the right thing to do, I'd never recover from the hurt of denying he existed.

I was vaguely aware of Jacob and Edith and Cornelia asking what was wrong as I huddled on the floor, keening like a banshee. Meisje wriggled in close, licking my face. I clutched the dog to my chest, soaking her fur with my tears. Jacob shook me by the shoulders. "Rita, you have to tell us what's happened."

The stone of shame and silence in the pit of my stomach turned out to be fragile as an egg. Its shell broke open. My secret spilled out.

"My baby," I wailed. "I want to see my baby."

Chapter Twenty-Eight
Cornelia Vogel

New York City
July 1960

Cornelia doesn't understand what Rita is so hysterical about. She turns to Edith. "Baby? What baby?"

"I don't know. Jacob, can you get her to the couch?"

Jacob hauls Rita up from the floor, her arms like shackles around his neck. He carries her to the couch and kneels beside her. Looking over his shoulder at the women, he asks, "What should I do?"

"Stay with her, we'll be right back." Edith takes Cornelia's hand. They race to the kitchen, where Edith grabs a bottle of brandy while Cornelia wrings out a wet towel. Back in the living room, Rita's sobs are so deep she's gasping for air.

"Here, drink this, Rita." Edith holds the bottle to her lips. Liquor dribbles into her mouth. She chokes, coughs, sips again. Her grip on Jacob's neck slackens. He ducks out of the circle of her arms and sits back on his heels, holding her hand. Cornelia leans over the couch, soothing Rita's face with the towel. Edith sits on the coffee table facing Rita. They are disciples gathered around their stricken saint.

Edith speaks slowly, as if she's talking someone down from a ledge. "Tell me, Rita, do you have a baby?"

Her head swings back and forth in manic arcs. "I don't have him, not anymore."

Edith has heard enough horror stories about babies abandoned in dumpsters to be terrified for Rita's sake. She edges Jacob aside, takes the girl's face in her hands, and looks into her eyes. "Where is your baby now?"

Rita's violent sobs are settling into pathetic whimpers. "I don't know. I left him there."

"Where, Rita, where did you leave your baby?"

"At the hospital." Rita yanks her hand from Jacob's grasp and covers her eyes with her bent arm.

"When was that?"

"Six weeks. It's been six weeks."

"You gave birth to a baby six weeks ago?" Rita's chin lifts and lowers. Edith turns to Jacob. "Do you know anything about this?"

"No, nothing. We met for the first time on June sixth. It was a Monday. She was crying."

"What happened just now, Rita," Edith asks, "when you were on the phone?"

"My mother reminded me Miss Murphy is coming on Wednesday to follow up. She said I'd forget, but I can't forget. I don't think I'll ever forget."

"Who's Miss Murphy?"

"The social worker from the adoption agency."

Edith heaves a sigh of relief. "So you had a baby and gave it up for adoption through an agency?"

Rita's face is still hidden. "Him. His name is David."

"How could you—" Jacob only gets those three words out before Edith stops him.

"Jacob, would you go make us all some coffee?" Edith puts her hand on his shoulder. "She'll be okay, I promise."

He stands up, then bends at the waist until his lips touch the top of Rita's head. "I'll be right back."

When his footfalls reach the bottom of the stairs, Edith asks, "Can you tell us about it?"

Rita blinks her wet eyes open. "Is he gone?"

Cornelia rubs the back of Rita's hand. "Yes. It's just us now."

The story spills out of Rita like a breaking wave. As angry as Edith is to hear of Leonard's lies, she's relieved to learn Rita wasn't raped. As for the girl's parents, she's disappointed but not surprised. She's heard about situations like this often enough from Carol. "Rita, tell me, did you want to surrender your baby?"

Rita looks baffled for a moment, as if she's translating Edith's words from a foreign language. "I don't know. No one ever asked me what I wanted. They all told me what to do."

Jacob comes in carrying a tray with four cups of coffee, along with a bowl of sugar and a pitcher of milk. Cornelia pours a shot of brandy into each of the cups. Jacob picks one up, stirs in some milk, and hands it to Rita. "Here you are, darling. Drink this."

She takes the warm cup from his hands. "Don't you hate me now?"

"No, of course not." He reaches out to tuck her hair behind her ear. "I could never hate you, Little Rita."

"But—" She looks at them each in turn, confused. "Miss Murphy said no man would ever want me if he knew."

"She sounds like an idiot." Edith is furious now. "Listen, Rita, something about your story isn't adding up. I have a friend who's a social worker. I'm going to call her and ask her a few questions, if that's all right with you?"

Rita shrugs. Edith signals Cornelia to follow her into the hallway. "Do you mind if I call Carol? I want her to come talk to Rita. It's not right, what happened to her. Don't get me wrong, it's a beautiful thing when a girl decides to give her baby up for adoption. If single women were allowed to adopt, I'd have filled this house with kids by now. But I don't think Rita made that decision for herself. It sounds like her parents and that social worker decided for her."

Cornelia lets a moment pass before she responds. "It's not my place to say whether or not you can call Carol. If it's really for Rita, of course I don't mind. But if you're still carrying that torch, Edith—" Cornelia puts her hand on her heart. "You wouldn't do that to me, would you?"

"Oh, Nellie." Edith peels Cornelia's hand from her chest and kisses her palm. "That flame went out a long time ago. I was carrying a torch, I won't lie to you, but the minute I saw you again I put it down for good."

Cornelia's face relaxes. "Don't ever pick it up, okay?"

Edith pulls her in for a kiss. "I promise, Nellie."

The woman really is gorgeous, Cornelia admits to herself, opening the door to Carol's blond hair and blue eyes. She comes into the living room while Edith goes outside to pay the cab fare. Rita is sitting up now, a blanket across her lap, Jacob on the couch beside her. Carol pushes aside the coffee table and pulls over a chair as if she owns the place. She used to, Cornelia thinks, but not anymore.

Carol introduces herself to Rita, then says, "Edith told me a little about your situation, but would you mind walking me through it again?"

It's the first time Jacob hears the whole story. Rita never thought she'd utter a single word about her baby to another living soul as long as she lived, but now that she's said David's name, there's no reason to hold back the rest of it.

"It sounds like your parents didn't give you any choice about going to the unwed mothers' home, did they?" Carol asks.

"I wasn't kidnapped or anything. There just wasn't anything else to do."

"Well, that's not true. It's your baby. You get to decide."

"But my parents would never have let me bring him home."

"Then you live somewhere else," Edith interrupts. "You could live here." She reaches for Cornelia's hand, the gesture a question. "With us."

Cornelia squeezes Edith's fingers. Her answer is yes.

"But Miss Murphy said I couldn't support a child on my own. I mean, how can I take care of a baby and have a job, or finish college?"

"You get help," Carol says. "If your parents won't do it, then you hire a babysitter or ask a friend. Lots of mothers work or go to school. It's not against the law."

"I'll help, Rita," Edith offers. "I only volunteer a couple of afternoons a week."

"And I'll be here after work," Cornelia adds, "if you wanted to take night classes."

"There's welfare benefits available, too. I can show you how to apply for them," Carol says.

Rita looks from one woman to the other with a puzzled frown, as if she's trying to read their lips. "But wouldn't it be selfish of me to keep him?"

"Let me guess," Carol says. "This Miss Murphy told you the other kids on the playground would tease your son for being a bastard?"

Rita looks at her in wonder. "How did you know that?"

"Because it's a script. Social workers are trained in how to convince girls to give up their babies. Psychologists do research on it. I've never thought it was ethical, but it is effective. The adoption agencies believe they're doing the right thing by placing children in households with a mother and a father, but they don't consider if the best place for a child is with its own mother, even if she is unmarried."

Rita drops her cup. The dregs of coffee spill onto her lap as she covers her face with her hands. "What does any of this matter anymore? It's too late now."

"Wait a minute." Carol pulls Rita's hands away from her face. "Edith said the social worker is coming for a six-week follow-up on Wednesday?" Rita nods. "So you haven't signed the final documents yet?"

"I did. I signed the papers she gave me in the hospital."

Carol shakes her head. "Those papers gave the adoption agency temporary custody to place the baby in foster care. A judge won't sign off on a relinquishment of parental rights until six weeks after the birth."

"Foster care?" Rita is confused. "But I thought his new mother was taking care of him all this time."

"A newborn isn't legally available for adoption until its mother signs the final papers. That's what the follow-up visit is for. In the meantime, the babies go to a foster home."

"You're saying she can still change her mind?" Edith asks.

"Legally, she can, yes. The social worker will give her hell for it, though. I've known girls who went into that follow-up determined to get their babies back only to be bullied into signing the papers after all."

"But won't I have to pay them back for everything if I change my mind?"

"Is that what they told you?" Carol sounds disgusted. "Sounds to me like that's another lie."

Rita wraps her arms around her belly. "I don't understand. You're saying David still belongs to me?"

"He does," Carol says, "if you want him. Do you?"

Rita looks at Jacob. "What do you think?"

Jacob opens his mouth, but Carol takes Rita by the chin and turns her head. "Don't ask him. Don't ask anyone else. This is your choice to make."

They stare at Rita as if she's a magician about to pull a rabbit out of a hat. "I want to see him. That's all I know for sure. I need to hold him again before I can decide."

"All right then." Carol stands up. "I suggest you don't wait for Miss Murphy to come see you. You should go up to the Hudson Home first thing in the morning. Catch her off guard. But don't go alone."

"I'll go with you, Little Rita." Jacob kisses her hand. "I'll never leave your side."

"Not you." Carol looks down at Jacob. "Don't get me wrong. It's great you want to stand by her, but she's going to be very vulnerable to outside influences. It'll be hard enough for her to sort through her own feelings, what with everything those social workers are going to throw at her. She really has to figure this out for herself. She needs support, not approval. There's a difference."

"I'll go," Edith says. "I'll call for one of my father's cars."

"You should have his lawyer on standby, too. They're going to try every trick in the book," Carol says. "Listen, Rita. You've got a legal right to see your baby, and the right to make your own decision about whether or not to give him up for adoption. Get some sleep, if you can. It's going to be a long day tomorrow. Speaking of which, I've got to get home."

Cornelia calls a cab while Edith goes outside to wait with Carol on the stoop. The gibbous moon is high and bright in the dark sky. "Thanks for coming over, Carol."

"That's what friends do." She puts her hand on Edith's arm. "We are still friends, aren't we?"

Edith manages a smile. "I guess we are."

Carol takes back her hand. "What's the story with this Nellie?"

"Her name's Cornelia Vogel." Edith feels herself blush. "When I knew her before, I thought her name was Leah Blom."

Carol's big blue eyes get even bigger. "That's Leah Blom, from

Bergen-Belsen?" A taxi coming up the street flashes its rooftop sign. "The two of you will have to come over and tell us that story one of these days."

"One of these days, sure." Not for a while, though, Edith thinks. Her bruised heart knows where it belongs now, but the muscle is still tender.

Rita is drowsing on the couch, emotionally spent. Jacob pulls two chairs together and says he'll stay by her for the night. "I'll have the coffee ready for you in the morning. And, Edith?"

"Yes, Jacob?"

"If she chooses to keep him, I'll love her son as if he were my own, I promise."

"I believe you will. Good night, now."

Before they get out of bed in the morning, Cornelia offers to go along, too, but Edith asks her to stay behind. "Maybe you and Jacob could get one of the attic rooms ready for Rita and the baby, in case she decides to bring him home with her?"

"That's so generous of you, Edith."

"No, it's selfish, really. I've always wanted to have a child in the house. This place is too big for only one person."

"Me and Meisje aren't enough?" Cornelia teases. "You need Rita and her baby, too?"

Edith kisses her. "You're more than enough for me, Nellie."

"Good, because I think I might live here for a long, long time." The poodle stretches, yawns, turns in a circle, and settles back down on the bed they share.

Downstairs, Edith calls her father's attorney at home, interrupting the senior partner of one of Manhattan's most revered law firms at his breakfast without a second thought. Once Edith has explained the situation, he asks to speak with Rita. She listens for a full five minutes, nodding silently. "Thank you, I will."

"What did he say?" Jacob asks.

Rita shakes her head. "I'll tell you later. It might not matter, anyway."

"I'll be here when you get back." He pulls her into a hug and whispers in her ear, "Remember, Rita, I love you."

"I've never asked you how to say that in Dutch."

"*Ik hou van jou.* It means I'll hold on to you, no matter what."

Half past seven finds Cornelia and Jacob waving goodbye as Edith steers her father's Bentley down Washington Place. Rita leans out the window to blow them each a kiss as the car turns up Sixth Avenue.

When they come inside, Jacob turns to Cornelia. "What do we do now?"

"Edith asked me to get a room ready for Rita and the baby, just in case. Will you help?"

"*Ja, natuurlijk.*" Now that it's the two of them, they find themselves slipping into their mother tongue.

"Oh, I almost forgot, I'm supposed to call the plumber about that bathroom upstairs."

"Shouldn't we call Antiquated as well, so Mr. McKay knows Rita won't be coming in today?"

"Yes, of course, I should've thought of that." Cornelia shakes her head. "I can't believe that all happened only yesterday."

The plumber says he'll come by that afternoon. Antiquated isn't open yet, so Jacob leaves his message with their answering service. After one more cup of coffee, Cornelia and Jacob go up to the attic of the town house. Choosing the room facing the garden as being quietest for the baby, they start by opening the windows wide. Dust motes fill the air as they move out boxes of books and old luggage and extra pieces of furniture until all that's left is a bed, a wardrobe, a chest of drawers, and a rocking chair.

"The room could use a coat of paint," Cornelia says, "but let's do what we can. *Zullen wij hem schoonmaken?*"

"*Goed idee,*" Jacob says, rolling up his sleeves.

Together they turn the mattress, then Cornelia takes the curtains off their rods while Jacob rolls up the rug. Downstairs, she soaks the curtains in the kitchen sink while he shakes the rug out on the patio. Cornelia fills two buckets with hot water—one soapy, the other clean. Jacob hauls them upstairs, leaving a trail of spills, while she carries a mop and some rags. They're both sweating by the time they've finished scrubbing every surface in the room, from the tops of the door frames to the floorboards under the bed. Back in the kitchen, Jacob dumps the dirty water while Cornelia wrings out the curtains. Outside, they hang them to dry, the white cotton waving gently from the clothesline.

"I'll make us some iced tea," Cornelia says, pulling a corner of fabric away from Meisje, who tugs it like a toy.

They sit on the patio, glasses of iced tea sweating in their hands, the locust tree speckling them with shade. "The world is a place of mystery and surprise, isn't it?" Jacob says. "Yesterday, I was a son without a mother. Today, I could become father to a son."

"Don't get ahead of yourself. Rita's got to make up her own mind. Anyway, it's not as if you've proposed to her, is it?"

"Proposed?" A lopsided grin spreads across his face. "Do you mind finishing without me, Nellie? I have an errand to run."

Chapter Twenty-Nine
Rita Klein

New York State
July 1960

I never thought I'd come back to the Hudson Home for Unwed Mothers. A knot formed in the pit of my stomach as Edith turned off the Beacon Highway and started down that long drive. When the old mansion came into view, I thought I was going to be sick. Coming here was a mistake. We should have telephoned the agency, made an appointment, arranged to meet Miss Murphy at her office. Not ambushed her in the midst of all these girls.

"Here we go, Rita." Edith parked the Bentley and turned off the engine. The sudden quiet seemed ominous. My hands were so cold, they started to shake.

"I can't do this."

"Yes, you can, like we practiced, and remember what Mr. Solomon said."

Even though Edith's lawyer had assured me that morning I had every right to see David, his support had not been the full-throated defense I was expecting. "Listen, Miss Klein," he told me on the telephone, his disembodied voice deep and persuasive. "I'm on the board of Louise Wise Services, and I can promise you adoption agencies like theirs have the best interests of the child at heart. If you do reclaim your baby, you'll be charting a difficult course for both his future and yours. Legally, though, you have the right to decide for yourself, and Miss Silver's retained me to represent you in this matter, so you can count on my advocacy."

A couple of girls strolled past, summer dresses stretched tight around their pregnant bellies. They glanced at us with shy curiosity before disappearing into the mansion.

Edith came around to open the car door for me. "Ready to go inside?"

Why was I doing this again? I'd been thinking through the problem ever since we left Manhattan. Allowing David to be adopted by his perfect parents still came out as the most logical conclusion. How was seeing him again going to help me know for sure if that really was the right answer? It would be easier for everyone if I decided right now. All we'd have to do is drive away.

I put my hand out for Edith to pull me to my feet. "I'm ready."

The place had seemed like a fortress while I lived there, but no one stopped us as we walked into the home. Edith and I planted ourselves under an elaborate chandelier in the entry hall, waiting to be noticed. I heard Miss Murphy's muffled voice coming from the library; she was conducting one of her group sessions, I supposed. Some of the girls I knew were probably in there, huddled on the old leather couches. I wondered what I'd say to them if we saw each other.

As it turned out, I wouldn't have the chance. The house matron spotted us and stopped in her tracks. She hustled us into the study and commanded us to wait there while she got the social worker. After she closed the door, Edith placed her hands on my shoulders. "Remember, Rita, it's your decision to make."

Miss Murphy must have dumped an entire bottle of Shalimar on herself that morning, I thought. Her voice started out as sickly sweet as her perfume.

"Rita, honey, what are you doing here? You knew I was planning to see you tomorrow. Why didn't you wait for me to come to you?"

My voice shook as I delivered the line I'd been practicing the whole drive up the Hudson. "I demand to see my baby."

"You *demand* to see *your* baby?" Her astonishment seemed utterly genuine. "That baby isn't yours anymore, Rita. You signed him away, remember? Besides, I can't see how someone who's made such poor decisions in the past is in any position to be making demands, do you?"

"I've got a legal right to see him." Inside, I was cringing like a schoolgirl caught shoplifting, but I lifted my chin and forged ahead. "I need to see him before I make up my mind about relinquishing my parental rights."

"Your *rights*? Tell me, Rita, what gives you the right to deprive this innocent baby of a decent future?"

Instead of letting her rope me into answering her question, I simply repeated my demand to see David. When Miss Murphy launched into her well-worn diatribe, I didn't attempt to counter her arguments with reasons. Knowing everything she said was scripted, I focused instead on appreciating her performance. She delivered her lines with conviction, but the longer I held out, the more her desperation showed. She was just a working girl, I realized, same as me, trying to succeed in one of the few jobs open to educated women. Allowing me to see David would be a blot on her record, I was sure. Failing to convince me to give up my baby might even get her fired. What would she do with that fancy degree from Smith College then? I wondered.

"Let's see what your mother has to say about all this, Rita. I've got her number right here." Miss Murphy waved a piece of paper and picked up the telephone on her desk. "I'm sure she'll be able to talk some sense into you."

"Okay, that's enough." Edith took the phone from Miss Murphy's hand. "Rita's not a wayward minor you can bully through her parents. You'll be talking to her lawyer, not her mother." Edith dialed the law firm. While she waited for her attorney to get on the line, she said to Miss Murphy, "Don't take it personally, it's just not going to work this time." A deep voice vibrated the receiver. Edith held it out to Miss Murphy. "Here you go."

After bombarding her with his credentials, the lawyer started shouting so loudly, Miss Murphy held the phone away from her ear. I caught a lot of what he said. "If you prevent Miss Klein from seeing her son, you'll be committing kidnapping. You remember the Lindbergh baby, don't you? Then you know what happened to Bruno Hauptmann."

It was gratifying to see the blood drain from Miss Murphy's face. His fury on my behalf was bought and paid for with Edith Silver's money, but the law he quoted was real enough to crumble her professional façade. "Yes, sir. No, no need to telephone my agency. I'll arrange it." She handed the phone back to Edith. "He wants to talk to you."

"I will, yes," Edith said after listening for a while. "Thank you, Mr. Solomon." The three of us stood silently facing each other after she hung up. "Ball's in your court, Miss Murphy."

"It seems I can't stop you if you insist on seeing your baby," she said, nervously buttoning up her cardigan. "The foster home is in Newburgh. I can take you there now, if you'll follow me."

My heart sped up, but this time instead of making me feel cold and sick it flooded my veins with warmth. I was halfway to the door when Edith raised a finger.

"Not so fast, Miss Murphy. Mr. Solomon wants you to get Rita's file first, including the original birth certificate, so there won't be any more delays."

"But the files are at my agency's office in Poughkeepsie. It's an hour away." She looked genuinely afraid. "Look, if it's not for sure she'll want him back, why bother with all that now?"

"Because she needs this to be over and done with today, one way or the other, isn't that right, Rita?"

Edith's confidence gave me courage. My insides felt like jelly, but I imitated her straight spine. "That's right, Miss Murphy. We don't mind driving up to Poughkeepsie."

"No, no, no." Miss Murphy shook her head so fast she sent a fresh waft of Shalimar across the room. "I'll take care of it. You wait here. But outside, please, and don't talk to any of the girls."

Cornelia had packed us a picnic that morning, so Edith and I got the basket out of the car and wandered across the lawn to the bluff overlooking the Hudson River. Down along the bank, a train chugged by, heading upstate. Its passing scared up a heron who'd been standing so still among the lily pads I hadn't spotted her. I watched her rise over the water, those elegant wings spread wide. Were her chicks still depending on her deliveries of minnows and crayfish, I wondered, or was she flying for herself again?

"Want to go for a walk?" Edith asked when we'd finished our sandwiches.

"No, I'll stay here awhile. I've got a lot to think about."

She ruffled my hair like I was her little sister. "Sure thing, kiddo."

After Edith wandered off, I contemplated the crenellated ramparts of West Point across the river. How many of those cadets had fathered a child out of wedlock over the years? Hundreds, I supposed, though their careers had probably progressed without so much as a demerit. And what about all the girls who'd carried those children, children they didn't—or couldn't—keep? The mansion behind me was full of such girls, and there were other homes like it all over the country. We were an invisible population within our own nation, yet it was thanks to our errant bodies that so many married couples were able to replicate the families they saw portrayed on television. Because of us, no one had any idea how many perfect parents were actually incapable of producing children. But what thanks did we get, except to be shamed for not conforming to an ideal we ourselves propped up?

I reeled my mind back from social commentary. The only thing I had to worry about right now was what I was going to do about my own baby. I thought it all through for the thousandth time. Most of Miss Murphy's reasons for giving up my son had already been proven wrong, or to be lies. I had friends to help me now, and a place to live, too. If I did reclaim David, my mother might never talk to me again, but that would be her choice, not mine. If people stopped coming into my father's store because they heard a rumor his daughter had a child out of wedlock, that was out of my control. Dad was a grown man, and a smart one, too. He'd figure something out. It wasn't fair to put the weight of my parents' fears on the tiny shoulders of an infant.

I hoped Mr. McKay would keep me on at Antiquated, but even if I lost my job, the pay I'd already earned would get me through the summer. I'd figure out what happened next when the time came. Whatever I did, at least I wouldn't have to face the future alone. Jacob had already promised to take us both under his wing. David Nassy, I thought. It had a nice ring to it.

I shook my head. I was getting ahead of myself. Jacob loved me, but for him to say he'd love a baby that wasn't his own was merely a rhetorical flourish at this point. He might balk once faced with the truth of some other man's flesh and features. However I solved this problem, it would have to be an answer I arrived at on my own.

Edith came back to tell me all about the history of the property, which she'd learned from a loquacious gardener. I wondered what the lumber baron who'd built the place would think of his family estate having been turned into an unwed mothers' home. Why even call it a home? I thought. It should have been called what it was: a warehouse where pregnant girls were shelved and fed and kept out of sight until the products of their bodies were ready to be brought to market.

The July day was warm and the breeze off the river light, but I felt a chill that made me shiver. "Can we go wait in the car, Edith?"

"Sure, whatever you want."

I must have dozed in the passenger seat. The next thing I knew, Miss Murphy was knocking on the car window. "I've got your file, Rita. You two can follow me."

Edith's Bentley trailed Miss Murphy's old Ford down to the Bear Mountain Bridge, across the river, then up the opposite bank. The sun was falling into the western sky by the time we pulled up to the farmhouse outside Newburgh where my son was being fostered.

For weeks, I'd been picturing him cradled in the arms of an adoring woman. The foster mother seemed nice enough, but she was taking care of three babies all at the same time. She kept them in a row of bassinets, swaddled as if in cocoons, only lifting them up to change their diapers or give them their bottles. Each bassinet was labeled, but none of them said Baby Klein.

"What have you done with him?" I curled my hands into fists. This time, I was ready to fight if I had to.

"Calm down, Rita. We've already given them the names of their real—" Miss Murphy took a breath. "The names of the parents waiting to adopt them." She opened the file folder and handed me a paper. "See? That one is yours."

Everyone crowded around me when I picked him up: Edith, Miss Murphy, even the foster mother. I couldn't breathe, let alone think. "I'm taking him outside."

Miss Murphy grabbed my arm. "You can't take him anywhere, Rita, not until—"

"Don't touch her," Edith said, peeling back Miss Murphy's fingers.

"I'll sit on the porch swing," I said. "You can watch me from the window."

I don't know how long I sat on that swing, kicking my feet out and back to keep us swaying. David fussed, his little body hot and heavy in my arms. I brought him up to my shoulder and steadied his neck with my hand. Nuzzling my nose into the fluff of dark hair on his crown, I inhaled.

The missing part of the equation, I realized, was me. It didn't matter, really, what the final calculation added up to. No bridge was going to collapse. There wasn't a right or wrong answer to the question of whether or not I should keep my baby. Whatever conclusion I came to would be correct as long as it was made in my heart of hearts.

David yawned and stretched. I lowered him to my lap, but I must have moved too fast. He threw his arms wide, startled, his hands opening and closing like sea anemones. I touched the center of his palm. His tiny fist closed around my fingertip, the strength of his grip as surprising as the first time he'd grabbed hold of me. He opened his brown eyes. They wandered a moment, then focused on mine.

I didn't arrive at the answer so much as I let it appear, the problem elegantly solved.

"I'm bringing you home, David."

It took another argument and a phone call to the lawyer before Miss Murphy surrendered the birth certificate naming me as David's mother. The sun was setting by the time we put that farmhouse in our rearview mirror. Crossing the George Washington Bridge an hour later, I looked up at the white circle of the moon waiting on the horizon to take over the night sky. I'll have to learn the names of all the constellations, I thought, so I can teach them to my son.

Driving back down the Henry Hudson Parkway, we passed

Riverside Park. Barnard College was at the top of that bluff, and the Watson Laboratory, too. All that was in my past. The loss still stung, but it was balanced, now, by what I'd gained. When we reached West Street, I looked out across the river. The ships docked along the Hudson piers were lit up like holiday decorations. Wherever those passengers were going, their journeys couldn't be more momentous than the one I was about to embark on.

I looked down at David. He'd woken up hungry and crying for a while, but after I fed him the bottle the foster mother had sent along with us, he'd snuggled up to me like I was his favorite blanket. He'd been fast asleep ever since. I could tell from my damp lap that he needed a fresh diaper. I'd give him a bath before bed tonight, I decided. I hadn't yet seen his whole little body. I assumed he'd been circumcised at the hospital, but he'd never had a bris. I couldn't stop myself from conjuring an image of Jacob holding David in his arms while the rabbi chanted his blessing.

Edith pulled into an open spot down the block from her town house and tooted the horn. Cornelia and Jacob came out on the stoop, backlit by the welcoming glow of the open door. Once we were all inside, they gathered round, cooing and gazing. Then David started to cry, and his diaper needed changing, and as soon as it was clean he messed it again, so then he really needed a bath, but when I was in the middle of washing him in the kitchen sink, he got hungry and started to wail. Cornelia sterilized the bottle while Jacob ran to the corner store for evaporated milk. Edith watered it down according to the formula the foster mother had given us while I paced the patio, patting David's back. He'd been howling for so long by the time the bottle was ready, it took him a while to settle down and eat. When he did, he burped most of it up, spewing sour milk all over me. Cornelia wiped his chest with a wet rag while I blotted my ruined blouse.

An hour after coming home, we were all sprawled in the living room. David was swaddled on the couch, finally happy and clean and fed. The rest of us were exhausted. One baby had worn out four adults in less than sixty minutes. I had no idea how any woman managed this on her own.

"Leave him with us awhile," Cornelia said. "Jacob's got something to show you upstairs."

The attic room was as inviting as a painting. White curtains hung in the sparkling windows. A bouquet of flowers stood on the chest of drawers. A crocheted blanket was spread across the clean linens of the bed. We'd go out tomorrow to look for a bassinet, I thought, adding it to the mental list I'd been making all day. Tonight, David could sleep between Jacob and me.

"Oh, it's perfect." I hugged Jacob tight. "I can't believe you and Nellie did all this for me."

"For you and the baby. And now, Little Rita, I have something to ask you."

When he dropped to one knee, I thought he was tying his shoe until I remembered the kiltie loafers didn't have laces. Even after he got the little velvet box from his pocket, I still wasn't sure what was happening. Then he held it up and lifted the lid. The diamond was tiny but bright. Its facets caught the lamplight, casting a rainbow across the ceiling.

"Where did that come from?"

"I have a friend who works in a jewelry shop on Forty-Seventh Street." He looked up at me, his eyes shining with hope. "You deserve so much more, but I didn't think you'd want me to overspend, now that there's a baby to care for."

"But—when did you do this?"

"This afternoon, while you were gone. I wanted you to know I would have proposed to you whether or not you decided to keep your baby. Now that you have, I'm asking to be more than your husband, Rita. I'm asking to be David's father, too."

In the back of my mind, I heard Miss Murphy's voice saying that no respectable man would take on someone else's bastard. She'd obviously never met Jacob Nassy. The man kneeling before me had been to hell and back again. He'd been tempted by death but chosen life. In laying to rest his long-lost mother, he'd returned my son to me. He knew everything I was ashamed of and still saw me as beautiful. Sure, he was burdened by a loss that would never go away, but its weight would be lighter once we carried it together.

I don't remember saying yes but I must have, because the next thing I knew, Jacob was putting the ring on my finger. I looked down at my left hand. There must be something magical about that circle of gold after all, I thought, for it to be strong enough to build a bridge from the past into the future.

Author's Note

I t is a historical fact that the vast scale and astonishing efficiency of the Holocaust was made possible by punch-card computer technology. This novel is deeply informed by Edwin Black's book *IBM and the Holocaust: The Strategic Alliance Between Nazi Germany and America's Most Powerful Corporation,* which documents how the Nazi regime's systematic identification, arrest, concentration, deportation, labor exploitation, and extermination of millions of people depended on the organizational power of punch-card computers. In Holland, where the Hollerith infrastructure was strong, the efficiency achieved was monstrous. According to the Anne Frank House, the Netherlands "had the highest number of Jewish victims in Western Europe." Edwin Black writes, "Of an estimated 140,000 Dutch Jews, more than 107,000 were deported, and of those 102,000 were murdered—a death ratio of approximately 73 percent."

The fictional character of Gerard Vogel was inspired by Jacob Lentz, the real Dutch civil servant who developed the identity card, or *persoonsbewijs,* that all Dutch people were required to carry during the German occupation. Lentz also used Hollerith computer technology to create the population lists that were so crucial in identifying Jewish people in the Netherlands. After the war, Lentz was sentenced to three years in prison. In the novel, I imagine how Gerard Vogel, a man dedicated to statistics, could be drawn into collaborating with the Nazis, while also imagining how his daughter, Cornelia, might find a way to resist.

The Ministry of Information is a fictional government agency inspired by Holland's Central Statistical Bureau. Huize Kleykamp was a real place that housed the Dutch Central Population Registry, but I invented Gerard Vogel's office, the room where the punch-card operators work, and the Hollerith bunker. The scenes showing the actual use of Hollerith machines throughout the novel are likewise fictional, but I did my best to ground my imagination in fact by learning as much as I could about early computer technology. I made up the computer codes that Cornelia uses at the Ministry of Information to suit the story, but the codes on the punch cards from Bergen-Belsen are real. They were documented by a Jewish Holocaust survivor named Rudolf Cheim, whose first-person account of being forced to work with Hollerith machines in the labor office at Bergen-Belsen is preserved in the YIVO archives at the Center for Jewish History in New York City.

I invented Cornelia's job as a punch-card operator in Westerbork, but otherwise I made every effort to depict the camp realistically. In describing the weekly transports to concentration camps such as Auschwitz, I endeavored to use accurate dates and numbers from Yad Vashem's Transports to Extinction: Holocaust (Shoah) Deportation Database. Etty Hillesum, who befriends Cornelia at Westerbork, was a real woman, whose diaries inform the character you meet in the novel. Another real character is Gertrud Slottke, the German secretary to Holland's "Jewish expert," who worked at Westerbork and at Bergen-Belsen. In 1967, Slottke was put on trial in Germany and convicted of the murder of 95,000 Dutch Jews, including Anne Frank. After serving less than two years in prison, she died in 1971.

The Jewish Aid Committee (JAC) is a fictional organization inspired by the many relief efforts made by American Jews on behalf of their European brethren, particularly those made by the Joint Distribution Committee. Today, the information on the victims of Nazi persecution initially collected by the International

Tracing Service is part of the Arolsen Archives. In the novel, the Blom Report is a fiction, but its depiction of the concentration camp at Bergen-Belsen is, sadly, accurate. While a person's prisoner number in the Nazi concentration camp system usually matched a Hollerith number, please note that the numbers tattooed in Auschwitz did not typically correspond directly to a computer code. In the novel, I was careful not to state this as a fact but as a supposition on the part of the characters.

While Rita Klein is an entirely fictional character, she was partly inspired by a story my mother shared with me of a high school friend who became pregnant and was sent to a home for unwed mothers, where she surrendered her baby. My depiction of Rita's experience as an unwed mother follows a well-established pattern described in Ann Fessler's book *The Girls Who Went Away: The Hidden History of Women Who Surrendered Children for Adoption in the Decades Before* Roe v. Wade. During the Baby Scoop Era in the United States, which is usually dated from 1945 to 1973, it's estimated that up to four million women surrendered babies for adoption. At the time this novel is set, unmarried women in the United States were generally denied contraception, and abortion was illegal except to save the life of the mother. However, a 1967 article in the *Columbia Daily Spectator* quoted a Barnard student saying, "My experience has been that if you have the money and the nerve, it's pretty easy to get an abortion, and a good one . . . not one of those baseball bat jobs." Dr. Marjory Nelson really was the college physician at Barnard, and her dialogue in the novel about menstrual health is paraphrased from her own writings. The summer computer course Rita completed before being dismissed from college really was offered at the Watson Laboratory on the campus of Columbia University starting in 1947. I was inspired by a photograph of Mr. Eric Hankam teaching control panel programming to a class of twelve men (all in suits and ties or military uniforms) and one woman.

My own family history also inspired me in writing this novel. My parents really did meet in the Empire State Building, where my father worked in an office where my mother was a secretary. Growing up, my mother's Jewish family were the relatives I knew best, but we frequently traveled to the Netherlands to visit my Dutch family. My father was born in Rotterdam in 1934 and lived through the Nazi bombardment, the German occupation, and the Hunger Winter of 1944 to 1945. After a troubled adolescence, he emigrated to the United States and was proud to become an American citizen. I'll never know the extent to which his childhood experiences during the war contributed to his depressive episodes; he died from suicide in 1987, at the age of fifty-three. Aspects of my father's character, including his handsome looks, generous personality, loving nature, and struggles with mental health, informed my depiction of Jacob Nassy in the novel.

As I got older, I came to feel the difference between myself and my Dutch family was not only that I was American, but that I was Jewish, too. I remember visiting the Anne Frank House as a young adult and wondering what would have happened to me had I lived in the Netherlands during World War II. My father's Calvinist family, who helplessly witnessed their Jewish neighbors being arrested and deported, suffered peril and privation, yet all survived. As a person with a Jewish mother and two Jewish grandparents, I would have been a *Mischling* under Nazi race laws, targeted for arrest, deportation, and extermination. That personal history informed my approach to the character of Cornelia Vogel, a young woman who experiences the German occupation of the Netherlands as my father's family did, but who becomes a victim of the Holocaust as did my Jewish ancestors in Eastern Europe— except that, in my novel, Cornelia survives.

Acknowledgments

I am ever grateful to my agent, Mitchell Waters, for guiding this novel through tempestuous squalls into a safe and welcome harbor. It's a dream come true to be working again with Tessa Woodward, the editor who changed my life at the New York Pitch Conference back in 2013. I'm indebted to Aja Pollock, copy editor extraordinaire, and to the entire team at William Morrow, especially Ellie Anderson, Amelia Wood, and Madelyn Blaney. I have yet to write a novel without a first read from my friend and colleague Neil Connelly; hopefully, I'll never have to. I'm so grateful for the family and friends who read and responded to drafts of the novel, including Petra Wirth, Rita van Alkemade, Alex Hovet, Glen Van Alkemade, Sara Van Alkemade, Anna Drallios, Nancy Middleton, and Harper Glenn. Heartfelt thanks to Jackie Cantor for her enthusiasm for this project. My thanks also to Armando Lucas Correa for his encouragement and generosity in reading a draft of the novel. I'm especially grateful for the time I spent with my aunt Petronel Hacquebord-van Alkemade, who helped me understand the experiences of my father's family during World War II. All my love and gratitude to my partner, Mariel Martin, who opens my heart, reads my drafts, and listens to my endless talk about the stories in my head.

I was supported in my research for this novel by Katharina Menschick, a member of the research and education department at the Arolsen Archives International Center on Nazi Persecution. Katharina not only gave me valuable insights into my topic but also generously translated portions of an important primary source. During the time I was writing this novel, I was inspired and stimulated by my participation in the 2019–2021 Scholars Working Group at the Center for Jewish History in New York City. I'm grateful to Amy E. Traver, professor of sociology at Queensborough Community College CUNY, and Susan Jacobowitz, associate professor of English, also at Queensborough Community College CUNY, for organizing the group. My thanks to Martha Tenney, director of the Barnard Archives & Special Collections. Thanks also to archivists Gunnar Berg and Stefanie Halpern at the YIVO Institute for Jewish Research. Many thanks to Elli Jansen for kindly helping me with research in the Netherlands. I'll always be grateful to the faculty, staff, and students at Shippensburg University for their many years of friendship, support, and inspiration. My appreciation to the Saratoga Book Festival for involving me in the local literary scene, and to Rachel Person, events manager at Northshire Bookstore, my hometown independent bookstore in Saratoga Springs, for inviting me to be part of an amazing community of writers.